Codename: FLAME

The untold saga of a young, defiant Freedom
Fighter in the Polish Underground.

Dr. Robert Niklewicz

To Al,
I hope you
enjoy the story.

Bob

D1738837

authorHOUSE®

AuthorHouse™
1663 Liberty Drive
Bloomington, IN 47403
www.authorhouse.com
Phone: 1-800-839-8640

Published by AuthorHouse   7/16/2012

ISBN: 978-1-4772-2053-5 (sc)
ISBN: 978-1-4772-2052-8 (dj)
ISBN: 978-1-4772-2051-1 (e)

Library of Congress Control Number: 2012910932

Acknowledgements

Deepest gratitude and special thanks goes to several people that helped make this book project possible. They include:

Jim & Ellie Hall, from the Creative Circle Inc. for their professionalism, expert support, and guidance that was a major key in the development of every aspect of this book.

Anne Giosso SLP for her exceptional skill and help in the editing and development of the manuscript.

Paul Niklewicz for his skill and passion for development of the cover artwork.

Emilia Larsen, Art and Design consultant for her work on the photographs, and cover materials that were used in the book.

My family and I greatly appreciate these wonderful people and their work, support and kindness in the course of this adventure. I am deeply indebted to them and sincerely give them my thanks.

Dr. Robert Niklewicz PT DHSc

Prologue

"The Oath of the Polish Boys Scouts and Girl Guides" taken at ages 11-15 years:

> "It is my sincere wish to serve God and Poland with the whole of my life. To give willing help to others, and to obey the Scout and Guide Law."

Motto:

> "Czuwaj"...Be Vigilant (Be Prepared)"

Compared to "The Oath of the Jungvolk" (Young People's Oath) taken by ten- year-old boys upon joining the Hitler Youth:

> "In the presence of this blood banner which represents our Führer, I swear to devote all my energies and my strength to the savior of our country, Adolf Hitler. I am willing and ready to give my life for him, so help me God."

Motto for boys:

> "Live faithfully, fight bravely, and die laughing. We were born to die for Germany."

Polish Scout Promise:

1. A Scout fulfills his duties as set out in the Scout Promise.
2. You can rely on the word of a Scout as much as on the word of Zawisza. *(Zawisza Czarny was a famous Polish Middle Ages knight and diplomat)*
3. A Scout is useful and carries help to others.
4. A Scout sees all people as close to him, and regards every Scout as a brother.
5. A Scout is chivalrous.
6. A Scout loves nature and tries to get to know it.
7. A Scout is obedient and listens to his parents and all his superiors.
8. A Scout is always cheerful.
9. A Scout is thrifty and generous.
10. A Scout is clean in his thoughts, words, and deeds.

Dedication

When countries are determined to go to war, the focus is on the perceived injustices and the insults that were made upon them to warrant their country's coming hostilities. Often there are hidden agendas based on economics, politics, geography and the always-present and deep-rooted hatreds that ignite the causes of war and then fuels man's inhumanity to mankind. No matter what the cause, the sheer magnitude of the conflict is destined to become world headlines and millions of columns of text to be read and debated far from the conflict itself.

Obscured in the shadows of the countless notable front line battles and the objectively reported facts, there are small and often singular moments of heroism by small groups or even by the single individual behind enemy lines. These isolated and stealthy Underground tasks are usually performed against great odds for survival and are made for the greater good. Underground warfare actions are desperate engagements done by Partisans who act with courage while experiencing fear, resolve, and the belief that failure is not an option. Most of these events never make the newspapers or historical chronicles. Nonetheless they are crucial for the cause of freeing their country from occupying forces. It is a sad fact that more civilians die during war than do soldiers.

These life and death actions in the Underground are not limited to adult combatants, but they also involve children that grow up in the midst of war and are compelled to experience the brutality themselves. More tragically these times of despair and terror are often spent alone and isolated as they try to survive to the next moment, fighting against enemies that are older, stronger and better equipped than these young defiant souls.

This book is based on the true story of one of those young freedom fighters, Stanislaw Niklewicz, a Polish Boy Scout in 1939. The names of the actual characters and events that were the basis of this book have been combined or changed. However, the history and conditions depicted here are true.

The Scouting movement was a strong one throughout Europe and produced adult leaders that served honorably during both peace and war. This book is dedicated to the millions of unheralded youth heroes who helped make a profound difference in the outcome of World War II. Many of them were Scouts and Guides of Poland (as well in other countries) who fought to free their country from the power and control of the German and Russian invaders. Thousands of them paid the ultimate price to do so.

There are no age limits on who should be called "Hero". This book is dedicated to the boys and girls who were not big enough or ranked high enough to be noticed by history, but grew up quickly and were as brave as any adult. To these young Hero's we owe great thanks, gratitude, and the promise of not forgetting them. To my father Stanislaw, I am keeping that vow.

Chapter 1
May 14th 1972: Mauthausen K.Z., Austria

THE MERCEDES BENZ sedan navigated the narrow country roads without difficulty at a steady 40 miles per hour. The sleek black car quietly made the last tight turn and crested the knoll that allowed the occupants of the car to see the gray stone fortress sitting patiently in the misty fog. The long high walls with guard towers at each corner still stood, doing their intimidating sentry duty as they had 27 years earlier.

Staszek, the passenger, gazed out the window without moving anything except his eyes as he scanned the walls and buildings that had harbored so much pain for tens of thousand of people, of which he had been one. His right elbow perched on the door's armrest while his fingers supported his chin. Their pressure against his lips added to his contemplation of the vision of which he did not wish to speak.

Kurt, the driver, brought the car to a stop, turned off the ignition, turned to his guest and asked, in German, "Staszek, do you really want to do this?"

There was a moment's hesitation as Staszek absorbed and translated the question, which produced a slow silent nod. Even if he had changed his mind, he still would have gone. He knew that he had to, but wasn't sure why.

Kurt nodded in supportive understanding, and opened his door. He needed to use his left hand to lift his left leg out of the car. The dampness made his always-stiff knee feel like cement. Once Kurt was out of the car, he walked around to its front with a slight limp. He leaned back against the grill just to the left of the famous emblem, pulled out a pack of cigarettes and lit one as his passenger exited the car and approached him.

"I can't believe you're still smoking those cursed things after all of these years," Staszek grumbled, first in Polish then in German with some indignation. He followed with, "Didn't you learn anything in that movie theater?" This taunt was delivered with a smirk and a slight smile from his eyes.

Kurt half grinned as he puffed, coughed slightly, and answered, "Sure, I learned that American cigarettes taste better than the crap we tried to smoke back then. This isn't a cigar, you know." He showed Staszek the smoldering butt held between his index and middle finger.

For the better part of five minutes the two old friends stared at the camp's back gate, which was closest to the parking lot. Mauthausen had been a class 3-death camp. People were sent there to die. More to the point, they were sent there to die a horrible, usually painful death at heavy labor. Kurt stared at Staszek. Kurt's gray, nearly white hair was cut short and stood up around the edges, giving the look of a flat tabletop, highlighting his dark blue steely eyes. Staszek was gray around his sideburns but otherwise had his dark brown hair intact. He was casually dressed, but stood in obvious discomfort.

Turning to Kurt, Staszek asked, "Do you want to come or not?" The question was delivered in a pointed way as he stepped away from the car and looked back.

"No," Kurt sighed, as he threw his cigarette to the ground, "I've already been here a second time. I do not need a third. I'll wait for you in the car." Blowing his last puff of smoke slowly out through his nose he headed for his door.

Without another word, Staszek headed for the entrance to this one-time prison and current museum. The walk to the gate was only slightly less stressful than the first time he walked this path. Then he was young and cocky, being nudged ahead by the barrel of a gun through deep snow, and wearing thin clothes. Today he was alive and moving forward of his own volition, but, as before, he was in no particular hurry. He scanned the walls as if it were 1945, and his senses became as heightened now as they were then.

When he reached the gate, there was a line with Australian tourists ahead of him. They were chatting and complaining about the cold and damp. Staszek rolled his eyes, and closed them as his memories and senses could see and feel the snow that buried the camp in 1945. In that moment he started to feel as though he really did not want to be there, and thought he should turn and leave.

His indecision was forced by the young male clerk at the counter, who said to Staszek in a fatigued but business-like manner, "3 Marks please."

That snapped Staszek back into the present and shot his blood pressure and heart rate up immediately. "I didn't pay the first time I was here, and I am damned if I will pay now." His look of resolve and intensity was not lost on the clerk. This response, though spontaneous from Staszek, had been the reaction from other former prisoners of the camp, and the policy of the museum was to acknowledge their statement and offer them a pass at "No Charge," which was usually taken by the former prisoner with defiance and a little disdain.

Staszek looked at the ticket, and said calmly, through tight teeth, "Thank you," as he took, then folded it between his fingers and flicked it into a trash can near the door. His remarks to the clerk were overheard by several of the Australian tourists one of whom understood the German and approached Staszek.

"Excuse me, but I could not help but overhear your comments. Were you really here during the war?" the middle aged man asked Staszek in school-learned German.

Staszek calmed quickly with the eager words and the effort being made by the man. He nodded gently and responded to the question in slightly accented English, "Yes. I was here from January 18th, 1945 to Liberation Day, May 5th, 1945."

The Australian, with some excitement and relief in his voice, said in English, "I am the chaperone for this group. Would you like to come with us? I would very much like to hear what your memories are about the camp."

Staszek paused while listening to the friendly accent that calmed him slightly. He weighed the offer and said, "This is a difficult time for me. I'll walk with you for a while but I'll see how it goes." The Aussie smiled appreciatively and the two joined the others in front of them who were getting an introductory tour by a young Austrian woman who would be that group's guide to the camp.

The guide began with a welcome to the museum, and explained that where they were standing was a "processing area." Staszek leaned over to the Australian and said, "This was more like a holding pen. They would jam 2,000–3,000 people in here for up to two days to '*process them.*' 10% would be dead before they made it out of the yard."

The group proceeded up some stone steps to the main entrance and reached a point where a sign indicated "*courtyard.*" Staszek looked at the sign and felt as if the walls on either side of the steps, as well as the walls of the towers, were closing in on him. The steps narrowed here, causing a compacting of the tour group on the steps that increased his sense of confinement. Staszek started to imagine guards with sticks and snarling barking dogs lining the stairs. Seeing the "*courtyard*" again took his breath away for a moment. It was clean, painted, and detailed, as a museum should be.

Thirty years ago, the reality of the camp was dirty, frightening, and oppressive. To Staszek the sign should have said, "The Foyer of Hell." What was missing was the sensation of death that always lingered in the air over this spot, which would be covered by the dust from the Krematorium chimneys above him and to the right. The stench of rotting flesh on those who were actually the walking dead but did not know it yet was also missing. A moment later when a strong breeze pushed against his face, Staszek closed his eyes and his brows furrowed as he could smell them again and his shoulders drooped. Too often the walking dead were resigned to their fate and waited for their turn in "The Oven" and to drift home. In a strange way they, of all the prisoners, were the most at ease.

Across the assembly area was an empty field that was the location of the infamous "Barracks K". The "K" comes from the German word "Kugel," meaning bullet. In this barracks, selected prisoners, mostly Russians, upon arrival to the camp were herded to this walled-off compound, and then marched through a maze of desks where they were identified, classified, and stripped of their uniforms and clothing. Once naked, they were marched to the outside wall and shot in the back of the head by the SS guards. The Kapos would direct other prisoners to pick up the bodies and load them onto a cart to be wheeled out to pits outside the fence and buried in mass graves. The prisoners, at the end of any given day on this duty, were also shot and placed in the graves that they had dug. Staszek stared at the field and the fence beyond, and could see death walking out the gate in the form of hundreds of men who never returned. To the far side was the "Hill of Ashes," where the ashen remains of hundreds of thousands were placed.

Staszek stared, focused on the open space, and said to the man next to him, "This was the assembly area. This wasn't a hotel. There wasn't a courtyard." After a pause, "Here is where they had us stand in the cold for hours starting at 5:00 AM, before we were allowed to go to work." He pointed with a waving finger as several of the Aussies turned to where Staszek pointed. "During the coldest days they would take a fire hose and soak us. Some more than others, but the plan was to hasten death from exposure."

A few of the members in the group mumbled and one giggled at something that struck her funny as she mimicked the shivering of a naked person who was trying to keep whatever dignity they had left by covering their genitals.

The guide took the group into the first barracks building and pointed to neat rows of bunk beds and stated in a glib manner, "Here were the sleeping quarters for the detainees." The two-high bunk beds were nicely stained in a walnut finish.

Staszek again started to feel his heart race and his blood pressure turn his face red. "Bunk beds?! We did not have bunk beds! We slept on the floor or on wooden shelves three high; four or five people in a space meant for one. We were packed so tightly that you could not turn unless everyone turned at the same time." His anger grew and he became overwhelmed with the sights and feelings that were pouring back into him. He turned and walked quickly back outside to get away and calm down, as well as to slow his breathing. He found himself facing a stone wall that towered seven meters above him, with rusted but still dangerous barbed wire strung across the top. He flashed back to this place of executions and could almost hear the bullets hit this wall, as they passed through another victim.

He started to walk slowly at first, then more quickly along the wall and turned his head side to side as if to see if anyone was following him, or worse, was chasing him. His instinct for survival began to return in waves as he headed to a corner of the camp. He reached a recessed doorway halfway down the wall, and slid automatically around its shallow corner and pressed his back against the door.

"This was the place where he died." Staszek could see the boy's face looking up to him, his sunken eyes looking into infinity, never closing, as death claimed him.

Staszek looked out into the assembly area of what was a moment before just a handful of people milling around looking at history and taking photographs of an open field area. Now, he saw 26 barracks and heard the sounds made by thousands of gaunt men shuffling aimlessly between the gray wooden buildings. Nearly 64,000 men in structures meant for 1/10th that number. Even in this day's cold damp weather, he started to sweat as he saw the walking dead from so long ago. He could smell the stench of death and felt the emptiness that surrounded it. His breath was becoming shallow and fast. This was a horrible place that he could still feel to this day.

He looked towards the expanse of trees just beyond the barbed wire parameter and he could almost feel the rubber tube hitting him when he had walked there with his wheelbarrow. His mind could see through the trees of 1972 that acted as a curtain to the ash hill 100 meters beyond the electrified barbed wire fence, that held the remains of hundreds of thousands of souls. He recalled the gray mist with the fine powder that floated continually above the area in 1945. The painful memories intensified as he felt in his increasing panic the need to run—but his feet wouldn't respond.

In this living nightmare, he thought of places to hide, but knew there wasn't anywhere safe. For support he pressed his back against the cold granite wall. There the sights and sounds that had been locked up in his soul for years pounded their way to the present. Until now, they had been suppressed by sheer will to not allow them to surface; to not remind him of what happened here, nor of the war that consumed his youth for six years before that and continued to consume him to this day.

Staszek sank deeper into the past as he had the sense of being chased. He could almost hear the dogs as he struggled with the urge to get away and not be caught. *I need to hide.* His visions became more intense and tunneled. He had the need to fight back, but couldn't see from where the blows were coming. The flashback of rifle butts, sticks, clubs, boots, and short hoses raining blows down on him came in a cyclone of images and pain as he covered his head with his arms. He had to run, but instead pressed hard against the damp stonewall where he was frozen in time trying to be invisible. The Flame was captured again in a hideous place that humans could have neither dreamt of nor could have been built if they had had souls. *"NO!"* his mind screamed, but its voice was stifled by the weight of 30 years as he slid down to the ground.

Chapter 2
March 5th, 1938: The Pilica River area, Poland

THE WHEEZING WAS becoming audible, and a dry burning sensation in his chest made breathing painful. The low moisture in the air was drying his mouth and nose to the point that his chapped lips were beginning to crack and bleed. Staszek pulled a small tin of greasy salve from his pocket and smeared a small dab onto his lips, moving his jaw forwards and back to rub in the soothing goo in between his rapid breaths. Running in snowshoes was difficult enough, but the hounds were catching up to him and he must not stop.

The sky was high, with a thick cloud layer that made this midday sunlight gray and hard to distinguish from a similar mid-morning fog. For the past two days the dark clouds had threatened more snow but never produced a single flake. *Just a fast dusting of snow would be great,* he wished, in order to help hide his trail, but it was not likely now, when he needed it. His body heat had melted the snow on his gloves, leaving his hands cold, wet, and crusted. He carried his fur cap to try to cool off his head despite the cold temperature that was more than compensated for by the heat his body was generating. His sweat had started to become damp under the several layers of clothes he wore. Though his jacket was unbuttoned, he was starting to feel uncomfortable between his hot body and the cold penetrating his clothes, but he had to keep going because he was the last one of his patrol on the trail and he wasn't going to be caught again. He was getting tired and he had to do something to get shelter and recover his strength.

His instinct was to run along the ridge between the open meadow and the tree-lined creek. His eyes darted side-to-side, up into the bare branches of the trees, and just as quickly down again looking for a place to hide before he was tracked down. As he came around a bend in the creek he spotted a place. *"There,"* he thought as he deliberately ran past the snow-free patch at the base of a fallen tree that was surrounded by ample piles of dry brush. The spot could easily hide a careful person. He stopped momentarily at the edge of the creek, and then walked backwards into his own footprints for several meters to disguise his tracks and to check out the spot where he could hunker. A tree with some of its roots exposed due to flooding a year or more before would work fine as a hiding place, but how to use it without being discovered? His snowshoes were leaving deep dents in the crusty snow and the prints would surely lead anyone right to him. There were other tracks in the snow, but his snowshoes were big, and were a beacon pointing to any direction he would take.

He continued forward, around the bend, and just 10 meters ahead was a horse nibbling at branches and bare brown grass around another bush and tree. Staszek saw an opportunity and slowly approached the small horse with her heavy, dirty, matted black coat. The horse turned to watch Staszek and did not seem frightened, but kept an eye on him. Staszek approached slowly and made a gentle clicking sound with his tongue to get the curiosity of the small beast. He tried to whistle softly but his sore lips could not hold a note. With open arms in a low position along with some soft words he was able to get up to the horse and caress her. Staszek had ridden horses since he was a young boy on his Uncle Jozef's farm in Babiak, and knew how to handle them. With a calm touch he walked and turned the mare around so that she faced the creek. With a sudden movement Staszek sprang up into the air, spread his arms and slapped down on the horse's rump and flank. The sting of his hand on the animal's coat startled the muscular beast causing her to bolt into the creek and up the other side, leaving deep hoof prints on the bank.

Upon seeing the animal disappear into the trees on the other side, Staszek removed his snowshoes and walked backwards, placing his foot into his previous footprints until he arrived at the tree stump. He was able to sidestep onto a spot without leaving a print, which allowed him to lie down under the base of the tree stump, hidden by the twisted roots. The placement could not be seen from the trail. His heart was pounding and the sound was so loud in his ears he had to strain to hear if the hounds were approaching. *This Fox is not going to be caught this time,* he promised himself.

Within minutes he could hear the quick steps of several people approaching and talking. Staszek held his breath as they approached his hiding place and continued to move around the bend without seeing him. His burning lungs felt like they were going to explode, but he did not move.

"Where did he go?" one of the boys asked the other two.

Looking into the near distance one answered, "Look! There's his trail, and it stops where a horse was standing. Look at the hoof prints, they go across the creek."

Another excited voice called out, "Quick, he can't be too far ahead unless he got on the horse." With that the three boys continued around the bend trying to run while inadvertently covering Staszek's tracks and his deception. They went passed the place where the horse had darted for the creek and they searched in vain around the area for a clue to Staszek's presence.

"He must be on the horse," one boy announced. "Quickly, to the creek." The three, hoping to close in on the remaining "Fox," followed the hoof prints beyond the water's edge.

As the boys began running towards the creek, the impatient 13-year old Staszek decided not to wait, and left the shelter of the tree stump. He was sure that it was best to get away rather than waiting to see if the boys would stop and retrace their own steps. He picked up his snowshoes and slowly worked his way around the tree on his stomach to the opposite side from where the boys who trailed him were searching. He crawled up to the edge of the trail and began to walk in the dents made by the other boys' snowshoe prints. Looking over his shoulder, he was certain that he was going to get away, reach the tree line of the meadow, and get back to the camp. Unable to keep his composure he began to run. The trees were getting closer and Staszek became excited about his clever ploy and let his guard down by running and looking behind him rather to the front. Then with the suddenness of a bear trap he stepped hard on the packed snow, and without his snowshoes on he fell into a swampy mud hole that resulted in him being covered with slimy ooze from his feet up to his waist and hands. He rolled sideways up onto the snow around the hole and tried to get back on his feet. Once up, he ran for the shelter of the tree line the whole time shaking the muddy paste off his hands.

At the edge of the trees his blood froze as he heard a voice yell, "HALT! We got you!" There on the edge of the trail sat the 4th and 5th members of the Beeches Patrol, who were too tired to keep up with the other boys. They had by chance caught the last "Fox" from the Birch Patrol after an hour of tracking.

Seeing that he was about to be caught, Staszek made a sideways dash away from the boys but without his snowshoes on he became trapped in the deeper drifts of snow away from the trail.

"Stop!" the boys called again, "We got you."

The two boys reached Staszek and were about to pull him up from the snow when he swung his elbows at them, which drove them back and allowed him to get up on his own. One of the boys made a special effort to pull on Staszek's jacket in order to hold him in place, and started laughing at Staszek's appearance and bad luck. This enraged Staszek, and he was about to throw a punch when the remaining members of the Beeches arrived and pounced on him. Staszek was able to fight back and push away his captors, but soon he was overwhelmed by the numbers and surrendered to the hounds. Though angry, he was helpless at this point. Resistance was futile.

Staszek's goal had been to get behind the tracking patrol and return to the camp to claim victory. Today Staszek was again the caught "Fox." Each time this skill training was done, he was always the last to be caught, but caught he was. He clenched his teeth in near rage. Not for being caught as much as being so stupid as to not watch what was ahead of him and literally fall into his captor's hands. *You didn't catch me, I made a mistake.* He mentally condemned the gleeful boys, who moments before were too tired to continue the hunt and now, thanks to his error, reaped the reward of Staszek's impatience.

By the time they returned to camp, the Beeches were almost skipping and laughing in the snow as they surrounded Staszek, their trapped "Fox."

Fox and Hounds was a Scouting game that tested skills and fitness levels. The Birch patrol members that were the Foxes were reunited and they slapped each other on the backs as Staszek glumly returned to his group. They had all been caught, "But the Beeches had to work to get us," was the consensus of the patrol.

Artur, the youngest in the Birch patrol, tried to cheer up his tent-mate Staszek with, "You did great! I was caught before I was able to get my snowshoes on." Which was the truth. Artur seemed to have a problem tying basic knots and buckling on snowshoes tight enough to be useful. The 15-minute head start the Birch Patrol got was not enough for Artur to get out of sight, and he was caught shortly thereafter. He tried to run awkwardly, with one of his snowshoes off his foot, which dragged sadly behind him. In frustration he sat down embarrassed, and helpless as he waited to be captured and brought back to camp. Staszek did not acknowledge Artur's comment; he just looked sideways at him with the corner of his eye then looked down again.

The camp was in a very small meadow that had belonged to the Scoutmaster's family for many generations. Along the creek sat a modest cabin that generally served as a hunting lodge when the Scoutmaster came out for solitude. He generally offered it to his troop for winter and summer campouts. It was small, solid, and tucked under a picturesque grove of trees, and it was just large enough for three or four adults to sleep snugly, with a small fireplace for heat and cooking. Outside was a large fire pit, with a large wooden lean-to that sheltered more than half the pit. The wall protected them from wind and snow where the troop activities took place, especially the evening campfire.

The patrols collectively sat under the leadership's lean-to to eat a snack, but no sooner did Staszek sit on a log near the fire pit than it began to snow. "NOW it snows," he mumbled in frustration, and he got mad at the clouds. It was not more than 10 minutes before the light flurry of snow began to come down harder and faster as the temperature quickly dropped several degrees. The light dusting of snow was intensifying with the addition of a progressively strengthening wind. The thick blanket of powdery snow would have been a perfect cover for his escape. Staszek continued to pout and lament over his capture. He bit down and tore off a chunk of beef jerky, and chewed it with indifference as he mulled over what he could have done differently. At least his body heat increased as he scraped the frozen mud from his jacket, pants, and shoes.

After the light meal, the boys began to run and play in the snow, engaging in snowball fights and tackling each other in a very aggressive game of tag. The contact and activity burned off some of the anger Staszek carried within him, and he calmed considerably. Before long, the leadership advised the Scouts to return to their tents and make sure that their tents were well anchored, as the increasing wind could easily blow the tents over if they were not securely tied down. Once secured, the boys would be allowed to stay in their tents to read a book or write in their journals. The morning had been full of skill events, and a rest was in order.

The day was busy, especially for the new boys who were tested in their skills on basic first aid, knot tying, and foraging skills. The higher-ranking Scouts did fire building, knife and hatchet use, and target practice with small caliber rifles for the senior boys, to improve upon these traditional skills. By late afternoon, the younger boys were exhausted and eager to get back to their tents. With the wind blowing ever colder, they were motivated to secure their tents and warm up.

Staszek's and Artur's tent was up, but the anchor lines put up two days ago had slackened, and in the short period of time that the wind had been blowing, several of the lines had become loose or untied altogether. The boys returned to their tent and began to work on it. Being already damp from his earlier run and recent snowball fight, Staszek was acutely aware of the cold and was having difficulty with the simple task of tying a knot.

His fingers stung from the cold as he clumsily tried to tie another knot that would secure his tent against the freezing wind and snow. Staszek looked up towards the opaque sky, hoping that his nose and ears would not snap off and fall from his head before he was finished with his task. His gloves had become useless some time ago, after being saturated from the crusted ice. His dark fur cap, now back on his head, protected him, but the snow that melted on top of his cap was slowly freezing over his earflaps. To finish the job faster, he was forced to work barehanded and needed to watch his fingers to make sure they were doing their task correctly. The tips of his fingers were nearly white when he tugged on the rope and found the taut-line hitch firm and stable. The sensation in his fingers was like dozens of needles sticking him, but he worked through the pain.

Looking over to the other side of the tent he saw Artur becoming frustrated and angry as he struggled to get his line tied. Staszek slid over next to his tent-mate to help him. Artur's fingers had refused to bend some time ago, and the impatience intensified as the cold became overwhelming to the point where he started to cry from his burning pain and anxiety. The tears had frozen to his cheeks, as did the drops from his nose onto his upper lip. He growled in frustration and hit the rope with his cold hands and then sat down in the snow with the untied rope in his hand. As Staszek reached Artur, he reached for the rope and said, "You are almost there. Here, let me show you."

Artur gratefully gave up the line and watched more experienced hands complete the knot and secure their shelter. He self-consciously looked around at Jakob, Karl, Marian, and other patrol members who were still setting up their tents and did not feel so bad at his own lack of skill.

Without taking a moment longer to admire his handiwork, Staszek slid under the flap of his tent at nearly the same time as his 11-year old tent-mate jumped in. Both of them shivered from the cold, but relished the protection of the canvas walls. In the dim confines of the tent, which was built around and over a large snow bowl they had dug, their teeth chattered. Uncontrollable shaking raked their young bodies as they rubbed their chests to increase circulation to their upper body. "Just rub your chest hard and fast," Staszek mumbled. "Your arms will get warm with the work." Slowly their efforts resulted in an easing of the shivering, but their noses started to drip. Swipes of their wet sleeves against their faces only replaced one type of moisture with another, but they were safe and protected in the tent, and that was great.

The pointed top of the tent was no more than 25 cm above their heads as they sat slouched forward on the blankets and bedrolls. In the green-tinted light coming through the canvas, they stripped off their wet hats and jackets and shirts and replaced them with a layer of dry clothes from their backpacks. Though made of snow and ice, the tent's deep floor was filled with evergreen branches that in turn were covered with an oiled canvas, and together they acted as a soft insulated mattress that slowly allowed the boys to warm their bodies. After a couple of minutes they were able to talk without their teeth making noise. The conversation was punctuated by mumbled words from their chapped lips that made Staszek and Artur laugh at each other's speech. Once their wet boots were off, they covered themselves with two of the blankets and slowly warmed each other while lying on their sides, knees and hips flexed against each other, front to back.

Artur, who was slightly larger, though younger than Staszek, tried to get a little more warmth for his hands by sliding them under Staszek's back which was only 30 cm in front of him. Unfortunately Staszek's sweater and two cotton shirts had pulled up out his trousers exposing a very small area of his skin, an area that just happened to be where Artur's hands searched for heat.

With a yelp Staszek twisted away as he swung his elbow backwards and up, catching Artur squarely on the forehead. Now it was Artur's turn to yelp.

"What's wrong with you?" Staszek exclaimed bluntly, as he questioned his whimpering friend. Noting the obvious pain on the younger boy's face as he twisted further to look behind him, Staszek added, "That was your fault, you only have yourself to blame." Though he said it with conviction, Staszek felt bad about hurting his clumsy friend. Then, reaching out to the side of the tent where the wall of ice met the canvassed floor, he took a small fist of snow and tried to press it against Artur's forehead. Initially Staszek had thought that it would sooth the pain, but at the last moment he just smeared the cold ball on Artur's face, causing another yelp followed by a flurry of punches. Each boy landed several blows–none were of enough rage or power to do any harm. The exchange increased their body heat, consequently warming both and letting them fall to asleep for an hour and a half after their tired laughs ended the short battle.

They were awakened by a bugle call that alerted them to assembly and dinner. A community meal was being prepared under a large lean-to made by the older Scouts and leaders. The area had enough room for the twenty-four boys and five leaders to cook under the shelter of a thick layer of evergreen branches. A large fire ring was made, and it produced enough heat to cook potatoes, carrots, and chicken, which were brought by different members of the troop for their dinner meal. Bread dough on sticks baked at the edge of the fire pit produced biscuits for the delight of everyone and to the amazement of the six newest Scouts, known as Tenderfeet. The fire felt wonderful and the food was good, all of which was not wasted by the end of the evening. Several of the boys took a stone from the fire ring and wrapped each one in a piece of cloth which they carried and placed under their sleep rolls, which provided extra warmth for several hours into the night. This special Scouting technique gave the boys great delight and warmth on a cold night like this.

Before entering his tent, Staszek stood outside of it and gazed for a moment or two into the black and clearing sky. He slowly began to absorb the light coming from billions of fireballs above him and tried to identify constellations. A shooting star darted by, leaving a momentary light streak that had him in awe of the beauty of the sky and weather. He, like the other boys, returned to their dens and quickly fell into a deep sleep. Each Scout savored the events and memories of this night, which would be with them for the rest of their lives. The heat from the stone was perfect.

The following morning, the bugle blared reveille before daybreak. That brought the boys out of their tents and to the lean-to cooking area. They stood at attention while the Polish Flag was hoisted on a fairly long mast. They saluted it while they sang the national anthem. This morning, unlike the previous day, was progressively becoming more brilliantly lit by the sunrise. The sunlight promised warmth and increased energy amongst the Scouts. After eating and doing basic hygiene, the boys gathered in their patrols of six in an open meadow beyond the pup tents, but just before the tree line that surrounded the campsite. Here they would compete in several more individual skills, as well as team events. Skill and events contests included Morse code, semaphore, fire building, map reading, compass, and orientation; ending with patrols building a rope bridge over the creek where the winning patrol was the first group to go over their own bridge without it collapsing.

This last event of building the rope bridge involved construction that took most of the afternoon. Using previously cut poles; the patrols organized and distributed duties to each boy. Each boy leader had a job to do, and each depended on the other to get the bridge built. This way, leadership and organizational skills were taught while hidden in a contest or game. The least-skilled young Scouts worked along side an older leader to watch and to do their share. Climbing trees and tossing ropes across the creek to anchor the three-meter bridge were activities that required serious skill, but were great fun. Snowball fights and games of tag in the snow easily distracted many boys, who had to be brought back in line by older Scouts who had themselves behaved much the same way only a year or two before.

One by one, the bridges began to be raised and be placed over the creek with one bridge desperately unstable and poorly built. Under the watchful eyes of the senior Scouts, the patrols would eventually cross over the creek on their projects with the winner getting a red ribbon for their patrol flag. The remainder of the patrols would win white ribbons that would motivate them to win the red next time.

At this point, the construction was moving quickly between the Oak and the Birch patrols, which were well ahead of the other two patrols. Pole by pole and knot-by-knot, the race was becoming a focal point for the entire troop. The slowest of the patrols that did not have a chance to win became cheerleaders for the two competing groups. Staszek looked to Karl, the senior boy, for encouragement and directions but only saw intensity on his face as he pulled one of the last lashings tight. Only an anchor rope would be needed by each of the crews to secure their bridges before they could cross the suspended ropes. Each patrol looked for one more place to securely anchor the last line and almost at once they identified large boulders near the bridges. However the assumption was proven wrong when it turned out that the boulder was actually fragmented and when the lines stressed the stone, they caused it to crumble, leaving no anchorage for the patrols to use.

Again at nearly the same instant, a boy from each patrol pointed to a series of nondescript bumps in the snow that hid old tree stumps several meters beyond the crumbled stone. They were equidistant between the two competing teams, and would easily hold the anchor for them once the rope was tied.

Karl and his counterpart on the patrol dashed up to the stump but to their surprise and horror, their lines were too short and could not reach around the last meter of the stump. Now they ran back through the snow and across a fallen branch to find more rope to secure their bridges so the team could pull it taut and then cross it. Karl got back first, but could not find any rope to finish the job. He was wide-eyed and nearly growling when his search failed to find a measly two meters of rope.

The Oak's leader, who also was short the same amount of rope, improvised and gathered all the belts from his patrol, and began to run towards the crossing point of the creek. Karl realized what the other leader had in mind and likewise collected the belts from his patrol but gave half to Staszek to link together as the two of them ran after the other leader. The time they saved by linking them together as they ran as a pair made up the head start of the first boy. Within moments Karl and Staszek had crossed the creek and were nearing the stump when the Oak's leader inadvertently lost some of his balance, which allowed Staszek to catch up with him. The loss of balance forced the other boy to bump into Staszek, and that in turn caused Staszek to fall into the snow. The bounce and support given him from the contact with Staszek gave the Oak's leader enough time for him to regain his footing and then loop the belts around the stump and lace the rope to the belts.

Meanwhile, Karl waved Marian, Jakob, and Artur across the bridge while at the same time he ran back across the creek to cross the bridge himself. Staszek was seconds behind him. They still had to loop and tie their belts and rope, and return to the other side to cross the bridge. Despite their best efforts, the time they had left was not enough. They were second by less than a minute after a full afternoon's work. Watching the Oaks celebrate returned the rage he had from the Fox and Hound competition back to his memory. *The bump from the leader made us lose the contest. We should have won.*

Staszek went over to the euphoric Oak leader with the intent of confronting him over the contact during the race. Karl, seeing Staszek heading towards the Oak patrol's celebration blocked his path and grabbed the slightly smaller boy and forced him back to his own patrol. "Stas, it is only a game. We will win next year. Don't ruin it for everyone by showing your temper again." Staszek squirmed within the grasp of his patrol leader and began to calm down. "It isn't fair," he mumbled into space, aimed at no one.

Staszek, as part of the Birch Patrol, received a white ribbon for second place. Staszek was not happy with the white, but this was only his third year, and his skills and speed needed more practice, as did the rest of his patrol. Karl vowed that next year they would win, because the biggest boys in the Oak Patrol would advance to the Rover level of Scouting and the age differences would be less. "A couple of tenderfoot Scouts in that group next year will surely slow that patrol down." Karl a strong, fit boy of 15 carried a slight grudge at losing by barely a minute, but understood the growth and skill-building purpose and ignored the individual attention that Staszek focused on. Karl watched with stiff lips as the Oaks waved their ribbon-decorated flag in large figure eight motions. He walked around to his patrol members who were glum, but happy not to be working, and put his hand on each of their shoulders and said, as he looked into their eyes, "Next year we will win the red ribbon, right?" Marian, Jakob, Artur, and Staszek nodded or shouted their agreement at the Oak's eventual demise. Staszek walked back to the winning bridge and examined it. He thought that his bridge was as good as the winner's, and vowed that the red ribbon would be his next year. *We were better and they were lucky*, he concluded. He walked back to his tent, and began to prepare for the last campfire of the trip.

The traditional last campfire started with the serious business of initiating the newest Scouts to the troop. This entailed them being smeared with mud on their faces. Small branches and dead grasses were stuck into their pockets and under their belts. The decorations gave the air of a somber ritual initiation that included becoming part of the earth and the trees. The more each Scout looked like a walking scarecrow, the quieter the inductees became, and the more glee the older Scouts experienced, though they sat stoned-faced to add to the intensity.

The string of six boys holding tightly to each others hands were led into the darkness blindfolded and dependent on the person in front of them to make a path that was safe for all of them to walk. After what seemed like hours to the young Scouts, but in reality was no more than 15 minutes, the group returned to the fireside and there their eyes were uncovered. A discussion of the importance of teamwork and loyalty to the troop and patrols was made, using the past three days' activities as the example. The hard work the new Scouts did in team building, as well as skill development, allowed them to be part of the troop.

To seal their commitment to the troop, they solemnly swore an oath to God, family and country. They, like all Scouts before them, promised loyalty, honor, trustworthiness, courage, and piety. The most senior Scout, who was flanked by his assistants, led this tradition. Each of them reflected on their own blindfolded trip through the woods, years before. At the end of the ceremony each inductee was greeted by the other boys with a "left-handed handshake," the symbol of the Scouting tradition and brotherhood around the world. After the ceremony, chocolate was provided to each Scout in celebration of the event. The distribution of the candy was another tradition that was well received by the boys, and was laid to waste in short order.

It was three years ago and shortly after his 11th birthday that Staszek took a similar walk through the woods. He boasted at that time that, "I was not frightened," to all of the others who played the same game of mock bravery. Each boy bragged that they, too, were unafraid, and that it was the boy next to him who was trembling, not them. Secretly, each knew that when they had their blindfolds taken off they each experienced a flood of enormous relief. As the boys passed one another, shaking hands, Staszek added a hard slap to each arm at the same time, telling many of the new Scouts, "Now that you're Scouts, we don't have to babysit you anymore." To which some laughed and others wondered if they would be able to manage in the woods without others to watch out for them.

The evening's weather calmed and the snow stopped fluttering to earth, as many songs and bad jokes brought gaiety around the campfire.

The camaraderie was strong and joyous, with the evening ending with a historical story of bravery and courage of days gone by. King Sobioeski and his knights against the Turks, and Koscieko in America painted a grand picture of what could be done by people in common cause. This was the sixth campout the troop had made in the past year, but only the second with new inductees. Many of the stories were being repeated, but were welcomed by the older boys and listened to intently by the new Scouts. The radiant heat on the faces of the young campers blunted the cold of the evening. However, the heat did not easily penetrate their layered clothing and the long night could be very cold. As was the case the night before, at the end of the evening each Scout took one of the stones from the fire ring, wrapped it in an extra shirt and carried it back to his tent. The hot stones, once placed under the bedding materials, gave enough heat to make the night a comfortable and restful one.

After breaking camp early the next morning, the Scout troop hiked six hours to get out of the forest under heavy packs but light spirits. When camping in the open fields, the Scouts would often ride their bicycles to the camp, but this densely forested area was best accessible by foot or horse. Poland was blessed with abundant forests and rivers that the Scouts appreciated and enjoyed. During the hike home, the Scoutmaster Pan (Mr.) Olechowski walked with Staszek for a while and talked about the campout, while the assistant Scoutmaster, Mr. Klys, talked with the other boys in the patrol.

Mr. Olechowski, who was also Staszek's English teacher for the past two years said, "Stas, you did very well during the Fox and Hounds, as well as in the bridge building competition." Mr. Olechowski also said, as he matched Staszek's walking stride and cadence, "But you seemed very angry and disrespectful of the boys in the patrol that caught you. Is there a problem?"

Staszek was tired but the thought of being caught welled up inside of him and he told his Scoutmaster, "I was mad that they caught me because I made a mistake. Then I was mad because the boys who caught me got lucky and it wasn't their skill that did it. Then they made fun of me when they brought me in," Staszek concluded, with obvious frustration.

Mr. Olechowski listened, and let the thoughts settle in as Staszek calmed down. He quoted Saint Francis De Sales, first in English then in Polish. "Have patience with all things, but chiefly have patience with yourself. Do not lose courage in considering your own imperfections, but instantly set about remedying them. Every day, begin the task anew." He continued, "Staszek, your passion is your strength and your weakness. If you can control it, you will do great things. If you don't, you'll always be frustrated. Time and growing up will help you deal with such things." Mr. Olechowski let his words sink in, and after a moment he then pointed down touched the small metal badge on Staszek's shirt. It was a small four-sided dark steel medallion with the scout "fleur-de-lis" surrounded by a wreath and the words "CZU WAJ" ("Be Vigilant") on it. As he touched it he asked, "What is the Scout's Motto?"

Staszek replied quickly, " 'Be Vigilant'."

"That's right," said Mr. Olechowski. "Be Vigilant in your deeds, but also in thought and purpose. Being impulsive can be a trap. Be mindful of your behavior, because someday you may be sorry for your actions."

Staszek continued to walk without saying anything. He pondered what was said. He had great respect for Mr. Olechowski and took his words to heart. He still struggled with his anger for letting his guard down, but began to realize that he was not the first to feel this way. He said very little the rest of the trip.

Though tired and slightly glum, Staszek thought it was a good hike and campout for all the boys. They walked to the train station in Piotrkow Trybunalski, and by the early evening were back in their hometown of Łódź. The hike to the train was an arduous one, but was not encumbered by falling snow or rain. The Scouts worked hard and played hard while they learned skills and built confidence that would protect them in ways that they would not appreciate for some time to come. However, as with most boys, manners and patience still needed to mature.

Upon returning to his home, an apartment above his father's shop not far from the train station, Staszek stripped off his pack and dragged it the last couple of meters into his room where he pushed it into a corner and immediately headed for the kitchen.

His mother called at the sound of the slamming door, "Stanislaw?" She used his formal name for emphasis, as she recognized his slam of the door as not that of his older brother, Zdzislaw, or his sisters, Fela and

Basia. Their oldest sibling, Danusia, had moved away a month before, and now lived in Poznan, a large city to the west.

"Staszek," Helena continued in the familiar less formal way, from her bedroom, where she was reading, "How was the campout?"

"Fine," was his answer, as he searched for the jar of dried plums.

"Where did you go?" She tried to engage the hungry youth while putting her book down on her lap in expectation of him coming to her room.

"The forest," was the bored answer from the kitchen.

"The forest near Radom?" Helena tried again.

"No, a different one," was the distracted answer.

"Did you learn anything?" Helena followed up her last question with some frustration in her voice.

"A little," Staszek answered as he headed back to his room and peeled off his soiled sweater after he pushed two plums into his mouth.

"Like what?" she pursued.

"Things." He called over his shoulder, as a clean sweater came on over his head. Without a wasted motion he headed to the pantry to look for some bread and jelly. Upon finding both he carried them to the table where he knelt on a chair and consumed a large chunk of jellied bread that was washed down by some milk before his mother arrived in the kitchen.

As Helena was about to sit down at the table, Staszek stood up and started to move towards the bedroom. Helena reached up and pulled him back for a moment, and asked again, "What kind of things did you learn?"

"Just things; camping things. I am very tired. Goodnight mama." He began to pull free from her grip but failed, so he came back and gave her a kiss on her cheek and sat down. Helena let go of his arm as she slid her hand down to his.

After a momentary pause Staszek volunteered, in a bland voice, "Oh we had campfires and worked on forest skills and hiked in the snow and built a rope bridge." His mother nodded and that encouraged him to continue. "Well, we almost won the bridge building contest but lost by seconds. Our bridge was the best one, but the other patrol was a little faster. We'll win the contest next year." Staszek proclaimed with confidence. He continued, "I almost won the Fox and Hounds contest. I would have gotten away but I did not see some of the boys who were resting under a tree, and they caught me." Staszek became angry, "They would never have caught me if I had not started to run and had not fallen into that mud hole. One of them laughed at me for being caught. I would have punched him, but the whole patrol pinned me down. I didn't like it when he laughed at me."

Looking up to the boy, she said, "You did not give up and did not surrender, and you'll do better next time. Your anger has to be used to your benefit, not just for satisfaction." Staszek did not say anything, so she finally said, "Goodnight," and released his hand, while she gently pushed him away.

Staszek turned back to his mother, kissed her on the forehead, and continued to the room he shared with his brother. His mother sat quietly at the table and slowly shook her head as she looked at the jam jar, still opened with the knife stuck into it. "Boys," she muttered, and opened her book to read some more. Then, in some irritation, she called, "Pick up your clothes; do not leave them on the floor." She hated to do laundry and Staszek's clothes always seemed to be the dirtiest.

Staszek lay in his bed for some time, still mad over his capture and his patrol's loss in the bridge building event. *I swear that if only I was bigger, I could have beat them and won. If I were a grown-up, this would not have happened. No one is going to push me and laugh about it for very long.* The talk with Pan Olechowski came back to him and he thought about it for several minutes before he turned over and pulled the covers over his head. His oath not to tolerate being scorned, seemed to do the job, and he calmed down. Within minutes, he dozed off, and his fatigue guaranteed that it would be a deep sleep.

Chapter 3
March 12ᵗʰ, 1938: The German-Austrian Border

MASTER SERGEANT REIZTMAN held a single piece of paper in his left hand, as he stood motionless in front of the border's inspection station that he had manned until 10 minutes ago. He looked down at his orders in disbelief, and read them once again, *All border crossings will be open, and Austrian border posts will not impede or delay the crossing by the members of the German military units into Austria. Any attempt to do so will result in the removal of personnel from their post and their immediate imprisonment. Signed, Dr. Seyss-Inquart, Minister of the Interior of the Republic of Austria.*

The light snowfall, together with the heavy quiet air, muffled the sounds of hobnailed boots marching and the wheels turning that produced an eerie echo through the valley. The sergeant gritted his teeth to the point of nearly cracking a molar, as his heart rate raced and anger raged inside of him. At his shoulder, his tight right fist, which held his weapon's strap, ached to pull it down and defend his country. It took all his strength to obey this miscarriage of national interests, but these were his and his company's orders, and they had to be obeyed. He watched in silence as the German Army, the Wehrmacht, took over power in Austria.

He looked to the thirty-six other Austrian soldiers standing on either side of the border crossing, each with their weapons on their shoulders, like his. All were looking side to side in naive bewilderment as they watched the gray uniforms march by. Each border guard at one moment or another looked to the master sergeant in confusion, hoping for directions. All they received was the somber stare from their leader. All any of them could do was to stand still and watch as they tried to comprehend what had happened. Their duties had been subordinated to the new guards, who wore the insignia of the mighty Waffen-SS, the combat arm of the Nazi Party. The Germans were the border guards between two countries that were now one, for all intents and purposes.

The Austrian guards looked northwest for kilometers, into the distant fog, and all that could be seen were the long orderly columns of soldiers on foot, on horseback, and on bicycles; all riding with perfect posture in different types of transports.

My God, even the horses march in straight tight lines, the sergeant thought with envy at the discipline he observed in these endless ranks. He slowly looked up at the two long red and white striped poles that were the border gates standing nearly vertical and no longer offering that token barrier between Germany and Austria. Now they looked like long arms being held up in what first appeared to be a Nazi salute, but it then became clear to him that they looked more like arms held high in surrender. Like a vast river overflowing it's banks, the German troops steadily poured over the border, smothering it by sheer volume of numbers.

By the hundreds, then thousands, they came, and the Austrians stood there, overwhelmed by the Wehrmacht that entered easily and unchallenged. Whether it was an invasion or an invitation, his country was now under a foreign nation's control, and he did not fire a shot. The sergeant turned his eyes towards the ground and closed them for a moment in embarrassment. He had always worn his uniform with pride, but today he felt like his impotence to act made him not worthy of the trust that he vowed to the country when he first put it on.

The politicians had convinced the people that promises of greater times were free for the taking if they followed the "Führer," (the "Leader)," to a better world. The veteran Master Sergeant was all too familiar with the recent elections, where over 90% of the Austrian population voted to unify with Germany for hope and change in their futures. The common foe was not the new government, but the Jews who handled the money and were rich. They were the problem because they had more and the poor had little, which was unfair. They needed to be dealt with, and the new government would see to it. The Anschluss, or "Connection," which was coming to fruition in the form of a silent invasion, was one of the changes that was not necessarily hoped for. The promises seemed to be just too good to be true but could all those voters be wrong? The sergeant had a bad feeling about this, and tried to see the benefits of this new world order, but could not do it. Taking that which belonged to one group to reward another for their support was part of politics, but was wrong nonetheless.

The gray sky could not darken his mood any further than it already was. He wanted to hide, but he was a soldier, and this was where he had to be.

How did this happen? was the question he asked himself but he could not answer. He stood there and did not run, he did not fight, and he did not protest the loss of his country. He felt like a helpless boy. His rifle stayed slung vertically on his shoulder and remained mute—at the time that his country needed it most.

Author's notes: Chapter 3

"When an opponent declares, 'I will not come over to your side,' I say calmly, 'Your child belongs to us already...What are you? You will pass on. Your descendants, however, now stand in the new camp. In a short time they will know nothing but this new community'."

Adolf Hitler

Chapter 4
October, 1938: Babiak, Poland, two hours from Łódź

ZDZISLAW STRAINED TO pull the 25 kg sack of flour from under the trough, and wrestled it to the scale to make sure it was filled properly. Uncle Mieczyslaw watched him closely, correcting any error in his handling of the flour, which was often. Mieczyslaw owned the mill with his brother, Jozef, and they needed a reliable boy to work in their mill. Their brother Feliks' son seemed to be that boy. The plusses were that he was family, they could work him hard, and their brother would have some extra income earned outside his business. Feliks would make sure Zdzislaw would be on time and work the long days needed to keep the mill profitable.

The gristmill was the only one in the little town of Babiak, where the family clan was centered. Babiak was a small town of about 200 people who made their living by farming. Fruit trees, all kinds of vegetables, and wheat were plentiful in this area. The gristmill was not only the only one in town, but also the only one in the surrounding area. This mill had recently been converted from wind power to electricity, thereby making it available all day, every day, to grind the local flour. This was a lucrative business, and Zdzislaw was perfect for the needs of the business.

The downside was that it was very hard work for the 15-year-old boy, where the sacks that were moved weight nearly as much as he did and hundreds needed to be moved daily. For the time being, while learning the job, Zdzislaw would work two days a week at the mill, and the rest of the time (when he was not in school), for his father. Zdzislaw did not know which situation he liked least. His father was not a kind man, and did little to encourage or support Zdzislaw. He was treated more like hired help than the oldest son. This relationship did little to foster respect, nor willingness to work for his father. Zdzislaw was an honorable young man, even at the age of 15, and he did as he was told and what was needed, all without complaint, because that was what was expected of him.

However, working at the gristmill had even less rewards, and was very physically strenuous. The work in those two days was so demanding that Zdzislaw often fell asleep as soon as he got on the train, and would have the conductor wake him when he got to Łódź. He grew a voracious appetite that could not be appeased, which left Zdzislaw always hungry and his mother befuddled by this aspect of being a boy, much to Zdzislaw's detriment and discomfort.

During the summers of the early 1930's, the whole family would meet in Babiak to swim in the lake or ride the horses that Jozef kept. These outings took place many times during the hot summer months, over several years. This was the one trip that Helena looked forward to. She, too, was born and raised in the Babiak area. She was a Wdowiak. Her family raised cattle, and were successful farmers. They were even more prosperous than the Niklewiczs in this town, thus giving her more status than Feliks.

The marriage between Feliks and Helena was for the most part a forgone conclusion by the patriarchs of the families, though the principals never seemed to be as amorous as a couple would be expected to be. They were two people who wanted to leave the small town for bigger and better things, and marriage seemed to be the way to do that.

Their marriage produced five children. At this time Fela Niklewicz was 19, and the second oldest behind 22-year-old Danuta, who lived in Poznan. Fela worked in Feliks's store nearly every day, often alone while he went to his sources for items and merchandise. She was an efficient and hardworking woman, who had a good customer relations sense that was the driving force behind whatever success the business did have.

Barbara, the next daughter, had just turned 17 and also worked in the family store but her interests did not include only the store. She was able to find a job in a small restaurant run by Jan Szymański. Jan was a policeman during the day, but was part owner of the restaurant and managed it during the evenings. Jan was in his early 20's, and was a very good businessman who helped the restaurant grow steadily in popularity. An important part of his success was the charming and extroverted Barbara, who had a very easygoing rapport with the patrons of the business. Many came in regularly because of her. Barbara was able to slowly decrease her hours in the store and increase her time at Jan's as that business grew. Staszek, as the youngest, seemed to get a pass for most anything he did, which often involved mischief and risks. He had a broad wonderful smile that disarmed people easily. Early on, he spent an inordinate amount of time figuring out ways to snare or trap the chickens at Jozef's. Their seemingly aimless pecking and walking patterns fascinated Staszek so much so that it became a point of irritation for family and chickens alike. More than once, he would place his hands in his armpits and wave his elbows like wings while chasing the hapless birds around the yard. His clucking sounds and running irritated Jozef's wife, Melia, the most because she knew that the chickens would not lay eggs for several days after Staszek went home because of the stress he put them under. He made a slingshot once but Melia promptly took that away from him after he learned to pelt the birds from a distance. "Torture the crows if you need to but leave the chickens alone or I'll have you collecting their fertilizer with your fingers." She threatened, successfully.

When not teasing the chickens or goats, Staszek loved to run and would race anyone, anytime, just to see who was the best. Though not a sprinter, he was able to run for long distances at a steady pace. If he challenged an opponent to the distance he liked, he was hard to beat.

Where both Staszek and Zdzislaw had the most interest in was shooting the destructive crows that ravaged the farms in the area, of which Jozef's was one. The destruction to the fruit trees, as well as to baby chickens, was appalling. Both boys became accomplished marksman with their uncle's small-caliber varmint rifle and to a lesser extent with the slingshot. They would return home after presenting their uncle with a dozen or more trophies to show for their efforts at the end of a weekend hunt.

The trip back to the much higher energy levels found in the big city were a marked contrast to the quiet and much slower paced life in the countryside, a trip that always produced mixed feelings in Staszek and relief for the chickens and Aunt Melia.

Chapter 5
May 23rd, 1939: Adolf Hitler's Personal Residency, Berlin

THE ROOM WAS quiet for the moment, with only the scratching sound of fountain pens marking on paper the key points from the Führer's lengthy introduction to his most ambitious plan to date, Project "Fall Weiss" (Case White). Adolf Hitler stood looking down over the collection of fourteen commanding officers seated around the deeply polished black walnut table. His cold and focused eyes scanned the room to make sure that the plan and details were being accepted, as he was sure that they would.

General Von Rundstedt leaned over the table and looked down at his own notes regarding Project "Fall Weiss." He rolled his pen back and forth slowly between his fingers and thumb as he reread the historic plan for the invasion of Poland. The plan was one that he and General Von Manstein had formulated and fine-tuned during the past 4 months, under orders from Hitler.

His brown leather upholstered chair squeaked a little as he leaned back, satisfied that the plan was nearly perfect. Too many things would have to go wrong for it to fail, and he had accounted for every possible one of them to ensure that the invasion would be successful. He knew that the invasion would not be like Czechoslovakia's simple walk-through occupation, but without question it would be successful. It would be too much to expect that the Allies would give away any more land to pacify the English and French fear of war, so he did not make that expectation, and the Fall Weiss plan was created.

Did I miss anything? He pondered, but could not find a single phase that did not have a backup contingency.

He was so sure that the plan would be successful that he had also drawn up the plans for the invasion of Russia. *Once we take Poland back, Russia will be ours as well.* His heart raced a little faster at the thrill of what was before him as his eyes savored it's brilliance.

To calm himself, he turned and stared out the bulletproof window into the courtyard area at the leaves on the trees that were moving ever so subtly in the spring breeze. A moving form in the near distance caught his eye. He carefully and thoroughly watched one of the female secretaries walking slowly and gracefully across the compound. He appreciated what he saw, as an experienced man would. She was young, and nearly perfect in posture and appearance.

I'll have to see if I can get her on my personal staff. He mused, knowing full well that a position on his staff was highly sought after, and the power and authority that a commanding general held quickly swayed young malleable staffers to his wishes. He jotted down a note to himself. A new hunt and chase had started, as he smiled inwardly and he tuned out the rambling of his Führer in favor of lust.

His attention was brought back into the room as the Führer slammed his fist on the table and began to speak once more. "The shedding of blood is inevitable. We must attack Poland, and then, if necessary, Britain and France. Our expansion of German Lebensraum (living space), across Europe is the only action that will solve our economic problems. The peasants living in our past and now future territories will be a great source of cheap labor that will allow our brave young men to fight for what was and will be again ours. Poland is the first military target, and then Germany will meet and defeat all others that will follow from this action, as they defy us. Secrecy is the operative word for this plan, and the time for it is soon. This will not be like Czechoslovakia, but the results will be the same."

Von Rundstedt's ears caught Hitler echoing his own thoughts, and nodded slowly.

"Yesterday, we signed the 'Pact of Steel' with Italy. Now Germany's invasion of Poland is destined. The recent conflict over Danzig and the Polish Corridor was a pretext to our need to conquer the eastern territories that are rightly Germany's. Our only concern at this time is whether or not Russia joins the Allies or stands separately. We will know the answer in two months.

"Therefore, there is no longer a question if there is a need to spare Poland, so we are left with only one decision still open, and that is when." This pause brought everyone's eyes to his. "To attack Poland at the first suitable opportunity is the plan. We cannot expect a repetition of the Czech affair, so there will be war. Heroes of Germany," Hitler stopped once more for a dramatic pause, "the hostilities will begin on August 25th." With that statement his fist is brought down and it struck the tabletop firmly, with a finality that punctuated the date.

Hitler looked towards his elite leaders and made eye contact with his cold penetrating gaze onto the faces of his commanding staff. No one said a word. No one moved; no one was that foolish or that brave.

Von Rundstedt allowed himself a tiny outward smile. What he had been training for since 1904 was now at hand. He had the power and influence to make this happen, and he experienced the thrill of anticipation. There wasn't an army mighty enough to stop the Armies of Germany from ultimate success. Any that tried would be buried in their own dust, under the boots of his unstoppable war machine, the magnificent armed forces of Germany, the Wehrmacht. His elitist plan would make history that will be remembered for a thousand years. Of that he was sure.

An 8th grade classroom; ŁÓDŹ, Poland

The classroom of 40 students in this two-story brick building was silent except for the sound of pencils scratching on paper. Staszek leaned slightly forward as he looked down indifferently at his blank page. *Why does he want a paper on King Sobieski? We've been talking about history all day,* the bored boy thought glumly, as he flicked his pencil back and forth between his fingers. Lost in scattered thoughts, his mind drifted left towards the window and the trees outside.

Why do we need to remember all this stuff? He lamented through his frustration and restlessness. He started to bounce his leg up and down quickly on his toes, shaking the wooden floor with a perceivable vibration. After a minute his gaze was diverted back to his paper and was about to start to write down the things he heard regarding the King during the Scout campfire.

As he looked up again to gather his thoughts, he was captured by the sight of the back of Heidi's head, several centimeters in front of him. He stared at the light brown braids as only a 14-year-old boy could. He was mesmerized by the silky strands that were tightly woven and hung down over either side of her neck, easily in reach from his desk and his suddenly still hands. Her white skin glowed like a beacon between her braids.

A slightly less than innocent thought came to him. *I wonder what they feel like?* This infatuation for the braids floated through his mind for a second before the ruler snapped down on the junction of his neck and shoulder, bringing him a sharp sting ten centimeters below his right ear. His hand automatically reached for the impact point as a muffled howl came from the startled boy. With a grimace, he turned with a jerk to look at his assailant.

Professor Werner, the history and German language teacher, who was standing to Staszek's right and slightly behind him, asked, "Are you looking for the answers on Miss Bieloski's neck?"

Feeling embarrassed in addition to the ruler's sting, Staszek turned back to his desk with his head down and said, "No Professor."

Heidi had turned at the commotion, but returned to her work after seeing Staszek's squinting red face and pained look.

Kurt, sitting across the aisle, smirked at the sound of the impact of the ruler finding a spot above Staszek's collar, and took some satisfaction in seeing someone else feeling the ruler's imprint for a change. Staszek, with his head still down turned his eyes to the right and glared at his friend and classmate.

The professor took a step forward, and with a turn looked back at the flexed form and asked, "What is significant about the date September 11th, 1683?" He paused staring intently at the bowed head. The professor's long wooden ruler was held with both hands against his vested stomach. He expected no reply.

In the silence Staszek slowly looked up at the professor and for a brief moment made eye contact then looked down again. The professor lowered the long ruler and tapped it against the floor in a disparaging way. As he moved back to the front of the classroom, the floor squeaked in the otherwise quiet room. He heard from a bold definitive voice, "September 11th, 1683 was the date when the final battle started for

Vienna. King Sobieski and the Holy League, along with the Holy Roman Empire Army's 80,000 men, saved the Habsburg Empire and Europe from the invasion by the 150,000 Muslim Ottoman Turks, thereby keeping Europe Christian." The professor looked back and squinted slightly as he continued to the front of the class but did not say anything.

Jakob, one of Staszek's friends and fellow Scouts, wanted to add that Jews lived here, too, but knew that would be a futile gesture and kept his thought silent.

Heidi looked back towards Staszek with her eyebrows raised.

Staszek looked towards her sheepishly, and said quietly, "It didn't hurt." He leaned back into his seat with his jaw relaxing slightly. *History is so boring, why do I have to know it? To save my neck, I guess."* he concluded. He turned again to the right briefly and shot a scowl at his friend. Kurt, who also had slouched back into his seat, smirked and shook his head slowly, savoring the incident.

During the last period of the school day, there was usually soccer practice for students taking sport class. Three days a week, Staszek had 60 minutes to play ball before he had to go to work. On one of the other days, he attended Scout meetings during the last period, or was tutored in 3rd year English. Today, Staszek had picked up his soccer ball and started to trot towards the school's playing field. It was a very warm day and his team was to be "skins," so he did not have his shirt on. The heat of the afternoon sun felt good on his pale white back. He bounced, then kicked his ball several meters in front of him. He ran up to the rolling ball as he dribbled it with skill that came with practice and focus. As he approached the field he saw Kurt Zajfert, his teammate with his shirt off tying his shoe as he sat on a small green area of the otherwise well-worn soccer field.

When Staszek was within 15 meters of the unsuspecting boy, he placed a well-aimed shot that ricocheted off of his friend's naked back. The ball was not kicked with a lot force, but it had enough to sting and knock the hunched figure off balance. Kurt rolled with the impact and sprang onto his feet as he let out a string of profanity in German (his native language) in the direction from which the ball came. Staszek returned the insult quickly in German, then called him a "butt" in

Polish (Staszek's language). Łódź had more foreign people than natives, and being multilingual was more the norm than the exception. There were Jews, Germans, Russians, and others. Staszek, like most of the people in Łódź, spoke three languages and was learning English as the fourth.

Kurt calmed down on seeing that it was Staszek and asked, "What was that for?" He squirmed and twisted his arms behind him to rub the sore spot on his back.

"That's what you get for laughing at me today in class. Did you think it was funny?" Staszek answered, for lack of a better reason, his face taut in a confrontational manner.

"Naturally, when you get hit, it's less likely that I will be," Kurt said, in a matter of fact way, still rubbing the growing red spot on his back.

The reality was that Staszek just wanted to get Kurt mad. The school soccer games were generally 11 on 11 and lasted 45 minutes. Kurt had a tendency to start slow and walk a lot rather than running for a play. He played midfielder and was very fast, slightly faster than Staszek who played fullback. Staszek did not like it when the midfielders did not go after the ball and the opponents had only the fullback and goalie to contend with. When Kurt was mad, he played better, which made Staszek happy. Today, Kurt was not mad enough.

On one play, the opponent's goalie sent a long arching kick well into mid-field, not far from Kurt, who did not make the effort to challenge for the ball. The opposing shirted forward, Nikoli, a Russian boy, caught up to the ball at full stride and dribbled past the left fullback and was streaking down the left wing towards the goal. From his right wing position, Staszek had the angle on the forward and caught up with him just before the penalty box. Nikoli was just about to strike the ball towards the goal when Staszek made a slide tackle and touched the ball a fraction of a second before the forward kicked it. The tackle deflected the ball and also tripped the forward sending him tumbling onto the grass and dirt field where he rolled twice and returned to his feet in one motion, wearing red abrasions for his effort.

Looking up, Staszek saw Nikoli recovering, so he sprang up quickly to play the ball back to the goalie before the forward could get to him. The forward recovered, and in three long strides was next to Staszek, posturing his rage for being tackled. Nikoli was nearly a head taller than Staszek, who had started to turn away from where the ball was passed. With a quick snap of his wrist, Nikoli landed a low energy slap to the back of Staszek head. The slap/punch slowed Staszek for a moment, but he continued jogging to the midfield, smiling, because from Nikoli that type of slap was a compliment.

Misinterpreting the blow against his teammate's head, Kurt yelled, "What's wrong with you? Are you stupid? That was a clean tackle." Kurt ran towards the Russian player, challenging him. Nikoli turned slightly and made a rude hand gesture as he jogged back to his position. That made Kurt pick up his speed and head for the Russian.

"Leave it," Staszek called to Kurt, "the game is not over yet. Don't make him madder."

"Why not?" Kurt asked, "Do you think he'll play better?"

"Of course. You do." The boys laughed at the well-known truths and returned to the game. Kurt did not laugh as sincerely as Staszek.

After school, Staszek hurried to his father's newspaper and novelty shop. The small shop was located on a busy street in Łódź, not far from the railroad station. There was a street stop half a block away, with good foot traffic every day. The shop sold newspapers, magazines, film, candy, perfume, lighters, cigarettes, cigars and many other small items that business people might need during the day. The shop was lined with shelves with jars, boxes, and individual items stacked so high that they required a small ladder to reach items on the top shelf.

Staszek's job was to go to the local newspaper publisher and get between 50 and 100 newspapers, depending on the headline news. He did this task every day, before and after school. If he came straight over after school, he would often have to wait for the papers to come off the three ancient presses. The machines that produced the piles of newsprint impressed him, but after learning much about their simple and straightforward operations, he would watch them for only brief periods before becoming impatient or bored. During this time he would wander about the shop and occasionally help the typesetter frame a page, or get extra paper and feed the noisy presses. He became familiar with the operation of the press and some of its idiosyncrasies.

Occasionally, the machines would jam, and wrinkle and blotch the newspapers. The sudden chaos always made Jerzy, the pressman, swear and kick at the machine as he desperately tried to the stop the cascade of wrinkled pages before too many of the papers were damaged. Seeing the pressman swing into action while saying "dog's blood" (a mild but common Polish profanity) made Staszek grin. *Adults have problems too,* he observed.

Jerzy would address the machine on a personal level. "Why do you taunt me? Is it because you know that we will be moving you into a dark basement once the new press arrives? You are old and it is time to retire. Go peacefully and let me do my job!" Jerzy never expected an answer, knowing that the press must be too ashamed of its behavior to make a case for itself.

The wrinkled newsprint just added to the work the pressman had to do, and extended the time he would swear. The spontaneous fouling of the machine amused Staszek, but delayed his departure with fresh papers. To kill the added time he watched the resetting of the press or read the paper while he waited. He often sat at a small table in the workers lunch area unconsciously bouncing his knee up and down with nervous energy. The wait was often boring, but it was a time when he caught up on local news. It was hard to be a boy who did not sit still easily, or for very long.

When the newspapers were ready, Staszek walked them back to the shop and, if possible, tried to sell a couple before he got there. If he failed to sell any, his father would declare, "Are you stupid? All those people hungry for news and you couldn't get them to give you 2 Groze (pennies)?" Though he often heard his father use the phrase "Are you stupid?" as a response to any action Staszek or his siblings did, or for oversights that displeased their father, the words came out far too easily and always hurt. The pain was not as strong as the crack of the belt that his father would use on him when he was enraged or drunk, but the words were worse, because they were always with him like a bad smell he would ignore, but could never forget.

Feliks Niklewicz, Staszek's father, was a rotund man, but very conscious of the way he dressed. The family was not wealthy, and often would go without basic needs until Feliks sold something special, and suddenly they would have an influx of cash. The cash never lasted long, since Feliks usually thought that this new deal was the start of a richer future, which it never was. The nature of the business was one of selling high volumes of inexpensive items, but when there was money in his pocket he became complacent. Soon the money would be gone, and he would be frustrated.

The shop was in a good location, and most of the people coming in or leaving from the train station would come into the shop for something, at one time or another. Feliks liked meeting and talking to people, and knew almost everyone in the district. He engaged people in conversation easily, and always had a story or joke to tell them. Often the jokes were not very funny or were in poor taste, adding to the awkwardness of his conversations. Everyone knew this, but after many years most expected it, and looked forward to the "peculiar humor" from this likeable man.

Feliks's store was making a profit, but not enough for him to be well off; just enough to keep him interested. He was a big fish in a small pond, and as such swam around in circles thinking he was going somewhere. He had an eye for the ladies, which was known by the people in the neighborhood. He was not necessarily any more interested than other men, but perhaps a little more blatant about it; a behavior that Staszek, as well as his brother and sisters, were aware of when they helped at the store. This angered them because of the disrespect it showed their mother.

Feliks had visions of large stores all over Poland, but did not like to do the work to accomplish his dream. He was more likely to talk to people who came into the store and tell them about the plans, but over the years he never took action on any of them. Except for one.

When Staszek became 13, Feliks thought that was old enough for Staszek to work in the shop in addition to selling the newspapers on the street. Staszek's older brother Zdzislaw, now 15, had been helping at the shop for two years with occasional relief from their sisters, Basia 17, and Fela, who was 19 and spent the majority of time in the shop. With Zdislaw coming to work in the store two years ago, Basia moved into other jobs, independent of her father. She was pleased with her work in Jan Szymański's restaurant, and now only helped in the store under special circumstances. Fela remained in the shop any time her father needed to go on a trip or be away from the shop. Basica's wages were low, but they came from a source other than her father, adding a new income source to the family, and freedom for her. Fela took her salary from the shop when there was money to be had.

The new arrangement, with Staszek coming in and helping Fela and Zdzislaw, gave Feliks time to tend to another shop he had in a small vacationers village on the Baltic coast, some 190 kilometers away. The shop was located in a village called "Hel," founded some 400 years before by the Nordsmen. It sat at the end of a long peninsula that was the furthest point north in Poland. The sandbar sat on a projection into the Baltic opposite the final destination of the Wisla River at Gdansk. A large army garrison of about 3,000 men was located on the Hel peninsula. They were the last outpost before invaders could enter the mouth of the Wisla, which would take them all the way to Warszawa. Feliks felt that this location had potential for good profits, because of the troops and vacationers that were there every summer.

Hel had a spectacular waterfront location that during the summer months was known for breathtaking beauty, yet in the winter it could be so cold that a person could think they were within the Arctic Circle when the wind blew off the Baltic. The establishment of a business this far away from his home puzzled many people, but it made great sense to Feliks because he saw the opportunity for better times there. He, like his father before him, liked to travel. His father went to the United States during the 1880's, but returned to Poland to marry and raise a family. Three of his father's brothers stayed in the United States, settling in New York and Texas, so traveling was a common trait for the Niklewicz men.

The tourist business in Hel was only active from the beginning of June until the end of September, when the weather was as good as it gets that far north. The time was coming soon when Feliks would leave for the summer to work at his vacation shop. During the rest of the year, he would travel there for a week or two in order to provide services for the soldiers who were at the garrison. He hired a local young man to manage the store while he was gone, but the business never grew and often lost money during the winter while Feliks was gone. His ability to make conversation with the tourists often increased the number and kinds of sales he generated.

With school ending in June 1939, Feliks would spend more time up north, and Staszek started helping his brother and sister run the shop. The work was fine with him because he liked the energy in found in the contact with shoppers. On the other hand, Zdzislaw was a hard-working boy, but hated doing shop work. He liked building, and jobs where he could use his hands. Working in the flourmill satisfied some of his interests, in spite of the heavy lifting. Though not tall, he was very broad across the shoulders and had powerful hands. He could easily lift his own body weight, now that he had started at the mill. Staszek being younger and smaller had experienced that strength when he'd gotten too close to his slow-to-anger but quick-to-react brother. These confrontations often had Staszek tossed onto the ground like a sack of flour, wondering how he got there so fast.

Staszek had a good head for business and numbers, so he was not intimidated by the prospect of occasionally being in the shop alone. Being alone gave him an opportunity to work and be independent. He was good at finding interesting items to sell, and liked to display merchandise. He had a talent for trading. When money was not available, he would network between people and broker trades for merchandise in exchange for either a small portion of the product or a comparable-value item.

There were a couple of other benefits to being in the shop. One was that his father was not there to order him around, which always caused friction between the two like-minded males. Fela was usually happy that Staszek kept busy and out of her way, while appreciating his work around the store. This worked well, as long as Staszek did as he was told, which was not often, and that proved to be an unsafe behavior around the powerful Zdzislaw and his older sister. Even an irritated shove by the larger boy would send Staszek flying. It was dependent on the place where he came to rest that would determine the amount of pain he would pay for his error in judgment. Fela usually settled for an ear to twist in an effort to "help his hearing" when she talked to him.

Second, Staszek could usually set his own hours, so he would come and go as needed. Fela would come at pre-determined times to watch the store while Staszek or Zdzislaw went to get the newspapers or other cash and carry items that were sold in the store.

The problem in this relationship was that when she and Staszek were together, he did not have a good sense of, or interest in, watching the time. Minutes and hours were roughly the same to him. This drove Fela nearly insane when she would have Staszek promise to be back a specific time, and he would drift back to the store 30-120 minutes late, on a good day. "Something came up," would be his normal answer to her barrage of questions. "I am here now, so what's the problem?" would be his defense.

"May a duck kick you!" (Another mild piece of Polish profanity) would be Fela's response to her little brother's timing issues. Staszek was always surprised that she made a big deal out of his tardiness. For emphasis he would often be rewarded with a cold stare or punch on the arm.

One of the things that Staszek did well was to write and paint posters or sale signs. He had exceptional handwriting style and technique. One of his previous teachers felt that he should be an architect because of his precision in writing. His father had him make all the signs for the store, to put his flair for drawing and writing to good use. These regular drawing assignments were especially gratifying to Staszek, because it was one of the few times his father would praise his work.

On this weekend, Feliks announced that he was leaving for Hel and would be gone for several weeks, if not longer. Though not a surprise to his wife, Helena never liked it when he traveled for such a long period of time. She was a very reserved person who was not easily motivated, and preferred to stay home and read or do housework. She knew that Feliks's leaving would make the house short of money, since the shop did not generate as much business as Feliks could when he was at the top of his game. Nonetheless, she would do her best to keep the household together and in order, while depending on the children to take care of themselves. More to the point, she needed the children to take care of her. With her husband away the boys would have to provide for the household. To her way of thinking it was up to the men to provide for the women of the house. Without a husband or grown boys, her life the way she saw it would not be possible. That is how it was for her mother and that would be the case for her as well.

Feliks made a point of saying goodbye to each of the children while giving them instructions and orders to follow during his absence. Most of the instructions would fall into the category of threats of punishment if something went wrong or missing. Feliks was impatient when it was time for him to leave. His mind was already on the road and making plans for his destination. This made his goodbyes more of a relief for the family than a sad time. It was common that if he was ready to leave and a problem or other situation came up, his temper would cause him to lash out and punish the person who had the problem or who had delayed his departure.

Each of the children had felt the sting of his leather belt on their legs or buttocks at one time or another when he was angry. The girls were at an age that he would use his open hand on them rather than the belt. That, combined with a shrill voice as his temper reached its zenith, had the children cowering when he was leaving, or upon his return home. Helena would keep a card of bad behavior or misdeeds of each child for their father to deal with once he returned home.

On one memorable evening, after a "difficult day," Staszek attempted to slide thin magazines into his pants in anticipation of being punished. The paper was to ward off the intensity of his father's belt. Staszek was not a stranger to the belt, and their acquaintance was a far too frequent occurrence. Staszek was particularly obstinate when he did not feel he desired the belt, and was coming to an age where he was willing to endure the belt just to show his father defiance.

On this day, Feliks was unbuckling his belt as he entered the room, and pulled the belt from his pants with one smooth motion. Feliks leaned over the boy who sat rigid on the bed and he pushed the folded-over leather belt under the boy's nose saying, "Smell this, it is your punishment for disobeying me." He then hoisted Staszek up off the edge of the bed by his arm and spun him around to expose his backside. With the timing and coordination of a lion tamer, Feliks snapped the belt and continued the motion of the belt down into an arch that landed it against the back of Staszek's buttocks.

The impact was different in two distinct ways. First, the smack of the belt lacked the crisp report of leather on cloth and on skin but rather the dull thud of newsprint being struck. The second was the normally expected yelp by Staszek was also absent and was replaced with quick breath in and held. Only a moment or two after the strike did Staszek know that the magazines had functioned as intended, and that, in a strange way, gave him satisfaction. Unfortunately for Staszek, the realization was short lived, since Feliks also heard the uncharacteristic sound and stopped in mid-stroke before the next strike was delivered so he could retrieve the paper from Staszek's pants. Staszek's momentary reprieve turned to terror as Feliks became more enraged over the deception and continued the spanking with more intensity and frequency of strikes. The result of the encounter was Staszek having welts raised on his legs and backside that interfered with normal walking for several days. When Zdzislaw saw his brother after his father had left the room, Staszek looked back at him while standing against a wall. Zdzislaw asked, "Are you all right?"

Through his clenched teeth Staszek responded. "It didn't hurt." But his red eyes gave him away.

On this current departure, Feliks would only gave a stern and loud lecture to Staszek about being on time, and to listen to his brother and sisters, or he would smell the belt upon his return. (Staszek was not likely to adhere to either of these commands, now that he was angry and hurt by the uncalled-for lecture from his departing father.) The attitude was part of the belligerence from Staszek's Aries personality at its pinnacle. His father's departure was a relief as well as an opportunity for Staszek, and it also solidified his tenacity under stress; an unappreciated gift that he did not recognize at the time.

For the first several weeks that Feliks was gone, Staszek had all his energy directed to working in the shop and making changes to displays and signs in order to promote sales. Fela and Zdzislaw found the change in Staszek behavior welcome and positive. Business actually improved with the things that were done which made everyone happy. This was especially true of Staszek, who almost flew with energy and motivation from the success he was finding.

With all the time he was spending in the shop, Staszek was not able to spend time with his friends as he had before the summer started. He was still in school until June, so he saw his friends in class, but late afternoons were absorbed with work. He continued his Scout meetings and English lessons, but soccer time was greatly cut back. His favorite activity at this time was going to the movies. He enjoyed the Westerns that were coming from the United States, but he loved the comedy team of Laurel and Hardy. In Polish Laurel and Hardy was difficult to pronounce so they were called "Flip and Flap" on the movie posters. Staszek understood most of the dialog and often laughed before the others in the theater who had to read the subtitles to get the subtle parts of the spoken humor.

One such week after Feliks left for Hel, Staszek met his friend Kurt, and together they planned to see a movie. Staszek had told Fela he would be back in a couple of hours. Fela immediately warned Staszek that he had to be back in an hour, the maximum time he could be away. Staszek waved to her as he trotted towards the theater. His plans for the movie superseded the need to return to work in a timely manner and as such he would worry about Fela's order upon his return.

To add adventure to their day on the town, Kurt brought a large sack of gumdrops and candied walnuts, while Staszek had brought a pack of cigarettes and a couple of cigars to smoke...large cigars from the shop. With excitement, they purchased tickets to see a western, plus "Way Out West," featuring Staszek's favorite comedy actors. As they entered the Theater, Nikoli and three of his friends also arrived for a showing of the film and preceded Staszek and Kurt into the darkened auditorium. Nikoli and his friends eventually found themselves in front of the two other boys as Staszek and Kurt flopped into their seats behind them.

There wasn't much of a friendship between Nikoli and Kurt, who at the deepest levels really hated each other, but comedy was a binding agent in the movie house; laughter being universal. The movie was extremely funny and had all the boys laughing to the point of tears. Midway through the movie, after the sack of gumdrops and nuts were consumed, Staszek and Kurt thought it was time to enjoy a smoke. They took two cigarettes each and passed them to Nikoli, who accepted them, but his two friends turned them down. Kurt brought out a very ornate lighter that belonged to his father and lit his cigarette, and then gave the lighter to Staszek to light his and Nikoli's. Smoking was a popular activity for adults, but was something that none of the boys had done before. Nikoli's friends were teased by Staszek and Kurt for turning down the cigarettes, and by doing so made Nikoli angry once again.

During the second half of the movie, all the cigarettes and cigars were smoked down completely and taken deep in the young lungs. The effect of the nicotine and the copious amount of sugar that was consumed started to show their ugly sides as they stressed the boys' insides. Staszek began feeling a cramping sensation in his gut, while starting to sweat. Kurt, who was quiet, was feeling much the same way as Staszek. They tried changing positions in an effort to relieve pressure in their stomachs, but to no avail. The jovial atmosphere of the Flip and Flap movie was completely dampened by the pain and discomfort that was being experienced by the end of the second feature. The boys who did not smoke were a little ill from the air they were breathing, and were sending verbal jabs at the smokers. When the dim house lights came on at the finale of the show, Staszek and Kurt were very slow in getting up from their seats. Nikoli turned and looked at Kurt who was directly behind him and laughed out loud when he saw his and Staszek's pale faces. "You German sissy, you are green. Get outside before you puke." His finger pointed at the hapless couple behind him and his laughter punctuated their plight.

Nikoli's warning and prophecy came only a couple of seconds before reality struck. The words alone were enough to stimulate Staszek to heave the contents of his stomach onto his own chest then over the fortunately empty seat in front of him. The vile stench had two of the boys in that front row lunge to the side to avoid being splashed by the grotesquely colored and chunky spray. Nikoli turned towards the retching sound coming from Staszek who was bending in half over the seatback, two positions away. That moment of horror observed by Nikoli was enough to distract him from teasing Kurt, as he turned his head to look at Staszek. It was then that the sight and smell of Staszek's cascade made Kurt unceremoniously hurl his stomach's contents onto the back and neck of Nikoli, spilling over his collar and down inside his shirt. That warm, nasty, fluid had the young Russian explode in rage as he twisted in a vain effort to get away from the foul-smelling wretchedness. He began to curse at Kurt and lunged over the seat between them in a violent effort to choke him. He was unable to catch the now emptied and nimble German who vaulted over the seat behind him and headed for the exit with Staszek in close pursuit.

Kurt and Staszek ran unsteadily out of the theater as fast as their rubbery legs and fear could carry them, waves of nausea slowing them slightly. For several blocks they ran down alleys and between buildings dodging cars, buses, horses, and people, hoping that they would not be seen or smelled, but, more important not caught by Nikoli and his cronies. Finally running through the cathedral and exiting a side door beyond the rectory, the boys found a place behind a butcher shop where the smell from the work being done there hid the tired putrid runners. They were able to get a pail of water to rinse off the leftovers of their afternoon treats from their shirts. Staszek was wearing a dark plaid shirt that hid the stains fairly well. Rinsing their mouths and sitting in the sunlight to dry they recounted the awful events while their stomachs returned to their starting positions.

From his squatted position against the wall Staszek asked, "Why did you puke on Nikoli? You know he is going to kill you if he catches up with you."

Kurt looked at the pale face of his so-called friend and said, "Kill me? You brought the cigars, and bathed the floor first. You're the one that will be murdered. Those Russians will hunt you down if it takes a lifetime." Staszek weighed the possibility that Kurt could be right. To die because of vomit troubled the boy for a moment, after which he shrugged it off.

Looking down the alley left and then right, Staszek determined, "We'd better get going before they find us. If we can keep out of sight for a couple of days, maybe it will calm their anger. Otherwise they *will* kill us." He looked at his friend and said, "Of course, that's if your mother doesn't kill you first. You stink!"

Kurt looked up from his squatted position and called Staszek a pig's ass in German while slowly getting up while he looked down at his stained shirt and muttering, "Mama *will* kill me." Looking at the wide eyed boy next to him he added, "You don't look like some one who will be alive tomorrow either." He pointed to the large stain on Staszek's plaid shirt. He turned and said, "Come." The boys started to jog towards their neighborhood, not knowing who to fear the most, their angry mothers or the crazed Russian; the truth being that they might have to face both.

Two blocks from Staszek's home and one from Kurt's, the pace the boys were running slowed considerably. They had detoured to the soccer field to think through what had happened at the theater. Sitting on the ground near one of the goalposts, their earlier fears had once again turned to laughter as their stomachs settled down and the chaos of the event turned to caricatures of truth. "We're lucky Father Sebastian at the cathedral did not see us run through his church".

"Then God would be mad at us too," Staszek muttered, mostly to himself. Fr. Sebastian had known him since he was baptized in the church, and often called upon him to behave and act in a holy way, usually to no avail.

"It felt like a freight train coming up, and I couldn't stop it," Staszek said. "When it came up, I must have sprayed two, no, three rows." He mimicked his posture and exaggerated his agony of that moment with his left hand on his stomach and the other waved up and forward to simulate the vomit.

Kurt gave his version of the event by adding, "When you got Nikoli to turn his head, I had only a split second to fill his collar and shirt and I took it! It was a PERFECT shot!"

They laughed about the faces the Russians made, and how mad they must have gotten when they could not catch Stas and Kurt. "Nikoli has been after me for a long time." Kurt said with a little stress in his voice. "He has a bad temper and a long memory." After a time, Staszek remembered that he was supposed to be at the shop two hours ago. *Fela is going to be a little mad,* he thought, and corrected himself, *She is going to be really mad.*

The boys headed for Kurt's home, and when they got to the building

Staszek waved goodbye and continued on as Kurt headed up the stairs to his third story apartment. As Staszek turned the corner he put his hand in his pocket and found that he still had Kurt's father's lighter. Knowing that Kurt would get in trouble if it were missing, he turned around and jogged back to Kurt's building.

As he went up the first flight of stairs he heard a commotion on the second floor landing. When he got to it he saw Nikoli and his two friends beating and kicking Kurt, who was curled up on the ground trying to protect himself from the blows, but was overwhelmed by the three and was failing to move fast enough for his safety. The force and the intensity of the punches by Nikoli were more than frustration and revenge for the theater incident; they were the total hate and rage that Nikoli had stored up for an unknown time. For whatever reason, this was the moment he chose to vent it, and Kurt was a defenseless target. Without thinking, Staszek jumped the boy closest to him, and caught him by the collar and hurled him backwards off of Kurt and down a couple of steps stopping half way down against the wall. A moment later he took a swing at Nikoli and landed a punch on the back of his head, causing Nikoli to stand up and punch Staszek in the chest. That blow knocked Staszek on his back causing a high-pitched groan when he landed onto the stairs going up to the third floor, cutting a gash on the back of his head. Nikoli started to jump on Staszek, who reflexively got his left foot up and kicked Nikoli squarely in the stomach, then quickly swung his right foot up catching the boy directly on the left ear as he bent forward from the blow to his gut. By this time, the first boy had gotten back up and jumped onto Staszek and landed several blows to his head and face as he pinned Staszek down. Nikoli added punches to Staszek's nose and chin, both of which began to bleed.

With the diversion made by Staszek Kurt was able to get away from the boy on top of him and tried to roll away but Nikoli had turned his attention back to Kurt and landed two more sweeping kicks to his ribs and head. Staszek was able to push off his opponent and tackled Nikoli, pushing him into the wall. Nikoli reached back and grabbed Staszek in a head lock and punched him several times on the top of the head and only released him when Staszek swung his arm up between Nikoli's legs and made direct contact in the groin that had him release Staszek as he dropped to one knee. From there Nikoli was kicked again by Staszek, sending him onto the landing grimacing in a heap. The two other boys, sensing that the tide had turned made a retreat for the stairwell just as

Kurt's father started up the steps after his day at work. His appearance stopped another kick from Staszek but not the last punch from Kurt that missed badly spinning him back to the floor. Slowly coming to near full standing Nikoli glared at Staszek and Kurt before he slowly pushed pass Kurt's father, limping and bleeding as he left the building.

Kurt's father knelt down and examined the cuts on his son's face. Finding several that needed attention; he pulled Kurt up off the floor and headed for his apartment. Once at the door Kurt and his father stopped and turned to Staszek. Staszek had sat down on the stairs to rest and to wipe the blood from his face with his arm, and after a moment of staring at the bloody boy Kurt's father said, "Are you all right?" His question was stated with only the slightest amount of interest.

"Yes, Mr. Zajfert," Staszek responded as he tried to sit up straight on the steps while avoiding tender spots on his legs and back. Staszek wondered what Mr. Zajfert would do or say since he was sure that somehow the elder Zajfert would know of the movie misadventure and be mad. Staszek tilted his head back when he sensed some blood coming from his nose and lip; reflexively he stuck out his tongue and licked it.

Looking at Staszek and nodding, Mr. Zajfert ordered, "You better go home." Kurt turned and went over to and locked wrists with Staszek pulling him up off the stairs. In the moment before he let go, Kurt looked at Staszek and said, "It didn't hurt." Which made Staszek start to smile but his facial pain partially stopped him. Without saying a word, they followed the instructions of Kurt's father.

Staszek walked slowly back the last block to the shop and his home because of the pain all over his body. The taste of stale vomit and blood started to make him feel ill again. When he got to the door he decided that, *Momma AND Fela were going to be really, really mad this time, but maybe they won't kill me.*

He entered the shop and paused as Fela came over, took one look at him and said, "What did you do to deserve this?" She reached out and turned his head side to side to examine the bumps and cuts, her face showing some agitation and frustration. Not having a good answer, Staszek started to moan slightly. Fela turned with some acceptance of the situation and went to the back room to get a towel and water to wash his wounds. Staszek was delighted and very surprised that Fela was so sympathetic to his condition. He thought it would be best to spare his poor worried sister the terrible details, and only told her about the fight the Russians started when they ambushed Kurt. Staszek determined that more details about the event in the theater were certainly not necessary at this time. The taste in his mouth was awful so he reached over the counter and took a licorice gumdrop hoping to cover the offensive smell and taste. Chewing it quickly, Staszek was sure that the odor on his breath and shirt would have gotten in the way of the sympathy that was being offered by Fela, and thought it would be unkind of him to deprive his sister of her concerns. So he sat down on a high stool with a slightly smug plan and waited for the attention to his wounds by his loving sister.

Maybe a moan would help keep Fela from being angry at me. Staszek calculated during her absence. So as he was about to deliver a mournful sound, his eyes widen and he did moan- but for real as the latest gumdrop reached his stomach and did not like it there. This sensation was all too familiar to him and he started to sweat again.

Returning with a dish of water and a cloth, Fela leaned forward to clean his face and the back of his head. While leaning completely over him she noticed the smell of cigarettes and odor of vomit on him. Standing back and directly in front of him she stopped and put her hands on her hips, as she looked intently at her little brother. She had become suspicious of her brothers story. Her lips pursed and her eyes squinted slightly as she then asked, "What did you do to have Nikoli beat on you like this? And why do you smell of cigarettes?"

While trying to come up with a plausible answer Staszek's stomach began to knot up again as the thoughts and smells of his shirt came back to haunt him to the point where he felt like he was going to throw up again. *Don't throw up now or you will be dead,* he ordered himself. Alas, the sensations came rumbling back to his mind and stomach as he began to quickly sweat and turn green again. With desperate shallow breaths, all he could sense was the gumdrop, the smell from the smoke, and impending puke. His eyes opened wide as the feeling of a freight train pressure came again and the dry heaving started. Fela leaned back reflexively but stood in stunned disgust as Staszek gave her a reason to kill him.

Chapter 6
August 30th, 1939: Hel, Poland

FELIKS TURNED THE large iron key in the lock of the shop, and shook the handle to make sure that the door was secure before leaving. He pulled out his small gold watch from a threadbare vest pocket and looked at the time. 10:05 PM, it read under the yellow glow from the street lamp above and behind his right shoulder. *14 hours with only 31 Zloty to show for working all day. Half of what I would get in Łódź, and barely enough to replace what I sold,* he muttered, as he snapped the watch closed and walked away from the souvenir and candy store that also served as his home this summer. He was bored, and did not want to stay in the small room at the back of the shop. Business had suffered from a marked decrease in foot traffic this month. The normal flow of tourists had slowed dramatically, with all the talk of war and conflict over the free town of Gdansk, just south and across the bay from the Hel Peninsula. Very few people wanted to venture past Gdansk, even for the beautiful weather that was the main attraction for this small community. This time of year the sun stayed up well past 9:00PM, and provided beautiful colors for the tourists who strolled the beach and boardwalk in this tiny hamlet.

"If it weren't for some soldiers on a 24-hour pass, it would have been even more miserable business than this." Feliks looked at his money purse that fit too easily in his hand as he bounced it up and down in his palm. He shook his head with more than a little annoyance at its lightweight. The military garrison of 3,000 men was less than a half-kilometer east from the shop, and there was little in the way of entertainment for the soldiers who came out on leave. Beyond his shop was the Fisherman's Restaurant and Bar, while on the other side there was a pastry shop, a sausage stand, a bike and sail boat rental, and a small clothing store near the end of the waterfront. A drug store, laundry, and several more eating establishments mixed between the homes in the blocks beyond the beach made up most of the town. Beyond that, there was a forest area for a kilometer before reaching the northern beaches on the Baltic Sea. The long beautiful narrow strip of sand on the southern shore stretched out in a curve, and widened like a feathered quill in front of a couple of small hotels where the tourists stayed. A cement barrier interrupted the curved line by jutting out into the bay and surrounded a safe harbor for small boats. There were several piers with ramps for people to reach the boats and to allow easy access to go ashore. The soldiers would come into the tourist area for the food and liquor that was of better quality than on the base. Cigarettes and Spiritus (Polish Vodka) were a mainstay for men out on pass.

Sitting and drinking on the beach, or sitting on benches along the boardwalk was boring, but better than sitting on a bunk bed on the base. The soldiers' enjoyment was improved only with the presence of the adventurous women who came to town for their own kind of adventure. The women were as acutely aware of the garrison's soldiers as the solders were of them. The thick wooded area north of the town provided romantic seclusion for those seeking excitement and privacy. Sadly, tonight there was a shortage of both women and soldiers; hence the lackluster business.

Frustrated by poor sales, Feliks walked next door and pushed on the heavy wood door of the brightly painted Bar and Restaurant. The massive door was carved with great detail in the style that was very much part of the folk art in the area, and was admired by all who entered through it. The heavy door was wonderfully balanced and opened with little effort. Berta, the hostess of the bar lounge called to Feliks as he entered. A smile came across Feliks's face, causing the corners of his short mustache to rise up.

Berta was a widowed woman in her late forties, and was pleased to see Feliks because her business was struggling too and Feliks was good for a meal. If she kept him talking, he would also buy her drinks.

The bonus for each of them was mutual companionship during a quiet evening. They sat at a table near the south-facing window that looked over the long sandy beach that formed the north border of the Bay of Gdansk. The light from the moon rising overhead gave a silvery reflection off the modest waves breaking on the mostly abandoned shore. There was a chill in the air, and those who were out for a stroll were making their way back to their homes or the hotels, leaving a deserted harbor and the ebb tide.

Berta sat with Feliks and only had to get up a couple of times to seat three soldiers that came in 20 minutes after Feliks. The bar stayed open until after midnight, but with no women in the bar the soldiers drank by themselves listening to the piano player who was happy to play his cherished instrument to one, or a hundred, people.

Berta went over to check on the soldiers and tease them a little with innocent innuendos. The flirting was good for their spirits and good for the business.

In the darker corner of the room, two tourists had been sitting quietly for over two hours. These men with casual clothes nursed their beers and cigarettes in idle conversation. One checked his watch regularly. Neither man looked at the other while they talked. Their eyes scanned the beach beyond the windows to the south as well as towards the soldiers and at Feliks and Berta. Berta would occasionally get up and make her rounds, ending with the two men who were not interested in any conversation beyond their own. They drank slowly but consistently, and that was fine with her.

Berta returned to the chair across from Feliks and said, "Those two," swinging her head slightly across the room towards the tourists, "they're Germans on vacation. They have come in at different times over the last couple of days, and have usually sat talking with the soldiers. They laughed and drank a lot too. They are much quieter today."

Feliks had two beers and a couple of shots of vodka during his meal. He talked and laughed with Berta nearly the whole time, and listened with curiosity to her comments, but soon the vodka and his fatigue took over. By 11:30 he was singing along with the piano player and complained that the piano was out of tune, otherwise his singing would have been better. The soldiers and then the two tourists must have agreed, because they left right after Feliks began to sing.

Sitting back down and recovering from his musical efforts, Feliks and Berta talked and drank for a while after midnight, at which time he gave Berta a long kiss on the back of her hand, whispered something to her, and left through the door he came in. The piano player had finished for the evening and the dishwasher came to wipe down the tables and stack the chairs on top of them to sweep the floors. Berta emptied the cash drawer and told the cleaning boys to lock up when they were done.

Berta pulled a finely crocheted red shawl over her shoulders as she left through the side door of the lounge. She walked about two meters, and stopped to raise the shawl over her head. She took another couple of steps and looked around the corner of the bar and smiled into the shadow. There stood Feliks. He took a step forward as Berta reached out for his hand. Arm in arm they walked towards her apartment, a block into the village. Upon reaching her home, they entered and a single candle was lit and burned discretely on a corner table near the front window.

Two hours later, Feliks left Berta's apartment and walked in a slow deliberate way a man does as he works off the effects of too many drinks and the late night companionship of a lonely woman.

His path back to his own bed brought him to the boardwalk and eventually to the side door of the shop. As he fumbled for his keys, he looked out towards the beach and harbor along the seawall. In the dim light of the moon he thought that he saw two figures leaning against the seawall below the boardwalk. He tried to focus his tired eyes past the glow of the street lamp at the front of the shop but could barely make out a slight difference in the shadows that could have been people down below. One was holding something and Feliks thought he saw several quick flashes of a green light, but in his foggy state of mind he shrugged and turned back to the door. As he reached for the lock with the key, the clumsy control of his hand allowed the key to fall and hit the stone threshold and the clang echoed between the buildings. The distinct sound of the key was almost lost in the cool air and rising fog. He picked up the key and successfully opened and closed the stiff door behind him. He made his way in the dark to the near corner of the room, all the while dropping some of his clothes on the floor and next to the bed. He was half dressed and heavily asleep moments later.

The two figures on the beach heard the sound of the key but could not see where it came from. It seemed to be from the candy shop, but they were not sure. They looked and wondered if it was important to know. They stared towards the street lamp and shop. When it was determined that no other activity or strollers were in the area they turned back towards the bay. In the distance, a series of red flashes lasting only three seconds returned in response to the green.

###

The following morning, Feliks was awakened, as he was nearly every day, by the activities of the bakery near the store. If the noise of creaking doors opening and closing did not announce the beginning of a new day, the smell of the bread and pastry certainly did. Rolling over and pushing himself up to a sitting position Feliks gathered his senses and wondered why he did not feel well. He did not drink that much at the restaurant. Then he remembered that the late night rendezvous included several more drinks. Even with heavy eyelids, the memory brought a small smile to his moustache that was displaced by the urge to use the chamber pot stored under the bed. Evaluating his chances of successfully making it to the outhouse versus using the large ceramic pot, he chose the latter. It was a wise decision.

Later, after washing his face and hair, Feliks began the business day. He went to his desk where he unlocked the top drawer and pulled it open to retrieve the cash box that was stored there for the night. Behind the box was a revolver that he kept for protection. During the unrest of the past several months, many people were moving away from the peninsula, which would be vulnerable and isolated if a war were to break out. There had been break-ins at some shops, by those who needed items and money for their journeys to move inland to a more protected cities. Feliks had not fired the old weapon in years. He remembered showing Staszek the gun and allowing him to shoot it while visiting Uncle Jozef's family farm in Babiak. It was a relic of the Great War, when he was a soldier of the Prussian Army, doing quartermaster work. For some reason Feliks picked up the gun and spun the chamber noting that the five 9mm bullets were at the ready. He waved it slowly at imaginary targets across the small room when there was a knock at the door of the shop.

Starting to stand, Feliks replaced the gun and closed the drawer. *A customer already,* he thought, *maybe today's business will be better,* he hoped with some enthusiasm. He left the desk in the back room and went into the shop as he tugged on his vest to pull out some of the wrinkles. He looked towards the door. Through the window, he could see Fredo the baker, dressed in his white smock, looking into the shop as he tapped on the glass in a rapid sequence, his eyes and head darting towards the bay and then back to the glass.

As Feliks opened the door, Fredo called to him as he pointed south. "Feliks, look there!"

Confused Feliks first looked towards Fredo's intense eyes and face then looked out towards Gdansk on the other side of the bay. There, anchored no more than 500 meters offshore, was a German battleship, its colorful flags flying and looking like a small gray steel island in the green-blue water of the bay.

"Are we being invaded?" the portly baker asked in an anxious tone.

Feliks shook his head and said, "If they were going to invade us they would have blown us to pieces at dawn while we were asleep. The Germans get down to business in a very straight line." Feliks remembered the organization and detailed systems and logistics that he managed when he was in the service. "They have signal flags all over the ship. There must be something else going on." Feliks concluded, with great suspicion in his voice. All the mast lines had multitudes of colored flags waving in the moderate breeze. Men were moving all over the decks of the ship and some were moving down a ladder to smaller boats alongside the German dreadnaught, with its implied and real authority so close to the shore of a peaceful Poland.

For the rest of the morning, every shopkeeper and citizen of Hel went about their work and daily activities with one eye on the bay waiting for but praying against hostile actions from the German ship. By midday a large company of sailors arrived in the harbor and came ashore in their shore leave uniforms. Their hats had black ribbons around them boasting the name "SMS Schleswig-Holstein" in white letters, the name of the German battleship that saw much action in the Great War and now was only a half-kilometer off shore. Approximately 100 men came to town, and before too long they were walking across all the streets and into many of the shops. Feliks thought about what Fredo had said, and vaguely remembered the flashing lights the night before and what Berta said about the German tourists, and decided to call the constable of Hel.

As Feliks was finishing the call from the phone that hung on the front wall of his shop, two sailors came in. Feliks gently but quickly replaced the receiver and went to assist his new customers. They milled around and eventually picked up several packs of cigarettes, chocolates, a couple of rolls of film, and vodka. As the men shopped, Feliks struck up a simple conversation with them and asked, "What brings you to our small village? Such a large and impressive battleship will not find much here except trees and sand."

In what seemed to be a well-practiced answer one of the sailors replied, in broken Polish, "We are here for a good-will visit and have some shore leave. We have been to several ports from Germany to Russia putting out the hand of friendship. " Proud of himself, the sailor turned to his friend, smiling and nodding quickly in an attempt to secure his approval.

Trying to establish a rapport with the sailors, and perhaps sell them some more trinkets, Feliks replied in German, "I have not heard about your visit, but if you want to buy some wonderful cigars or Schnapps' to make your day better, I have that too." The Germans seemed pleased by the offer made in German, and were complimentary of Feliks's effort.

The first sailor continued to chat, "We would like to go to the lighthouse. How do we get there from here? Show us on this map."

Feliks looked down at the crude map and saw that there was an "X" on a place that corresponded to his shop, and only the main streets marked on the piece of paper. "If you go out this door and go up to the next block and turn left, and stay on that street until you get to the railroad tracks, there is a road that you can use to get there. The road and tracks will get you to the eastern tip of the peninsula in about 30 minutes." Feliks offered these directions as he often did for tourists who wanted to climb the spiral stairs to the top of the lighthouse where a person could see for dozens of kilometers out to sea or to Gdansk and watch the water and waves. Then the thought struck Feliks, *That is an odd place for sailors on shore leave to go and see more waves. They usually stay in town and look for other types of entertainment.*

The second man, who had been looking at different items of clothing, small cameras, and candy, turned and pointed to the telephone on the wall as he asked, "Can I call my mother in Germany on that?"

The telephone in the shop was one of about only a dozen in the town, and was a draw for the curious or the traveler who was rich enough to have someone far away who had a phone to be called. Feliks thinking that this was a sincere question answered, "If your mother has a phone, then the switchboard operator could connect you to her. Of course it is expensive and you pay by the minute."

The sailor with a light tone in his voice but heavy stare from his eyes asked, "Even Frankfurt?"

"Yes, that is possible. It would take a little time to patch it through, but it could be done," Feliks replied, in a helpful way.

"How about if I wanted to call Warszawa? Could you connect me there too?" This question was more deliberate and to the point by the sailor who looked right at Feliks over the small counter that separated them. In stiff silence they waited for an answer.

Why Warszawa? Feliks thought, but the tone of the question put Feliks on guard and he began to have doubts about the purpose of the inquiry. Not wanting to be rude or continue the line of questions he responded, "Well in theory you could call anywhere there is a phone, but that phone has never been reliable and is often broken. I can't remember when it was used last. You could try to call your mother and tell her you are bringing home some wonderful Italian wine." Feliks kept a big smile on his face and pulled out wine and several small souvenir-type items for the sailors to see. Neither man gave the items any serious thought; their minds appeared to be elsewhere.

After looking at everything in the shop the sailors purchased the cigarettes, Schnapps, and some Spiritus and biscuits, leaving with some purpose in their steps. Feliks called out to them as the reached the door, "auf Wiedershen."

The first sailor waved while the other looked back with a smirk under a cold focused stare. Feliks looked down to the 20 Zloty that he was given for his items. Feliks, like most Poles, had never been fond of the Germans, who had been desirous of the land that was Poland. This exchange, though profitable, did not change his feelings on the subject, nor about Germans in general. Feliks was having a feeling he could not explain, but felt throughout his body, to the point of feeling a chill. He looked at the phone and wondered blankly what to do and whom to call. He decided to wait to see what would happen next.

The rest of the morning, many sailors walked past the shop, but surprisingly, none came in. Except for the two who came in first thing in the morning, the other sailors walked by Feliks as if oblivious to his presence. He stood outside for long periods of time, trying to coax the sailors to come in by addressing them in German, but after a brief gaze they continued on their way. Some stopped at other shops, but none in any number, or into those that were already visited. In the early afternoon Fredo the baker came over to Feliks and asked, "Did those sailors buy much from you? After some initial sales in the morning, they spread like locusts throughout the town and into the woods. The first ones this morning asked where the police station was and if very many soldiers from the garrison bought bread in my shop." Fredo bit his lower lip and said, "They told me that 'we are here for a good will visit and have some shore leave.' They said that they have been to several ports from Germany to Russia putting out the hand of friendship. They seemed to have been practicing the sentences," Fredo concluded.

Feliks was stunned, and felt even worse with what he was told. "That is EXACTLY what they said to me. Word for word." He looked at the baker and asked, "Maybe we should talk to the constable or contact the garrison and tell them what they said."

Fredo said, "The constable must surely know, and would have passed this to the commander of the garrison. That ship is directly in front of the base."

"That's true, but I don't like all these Germans in town," Feliks said, with finality. "I think we should all meet with the constable and find out what he knows about this friendship visit. I think they're up to something."

Fredo, a timid man, said, "Let's not do anything that might upset them or be disrespectful. After all, they said it was a friendship visit, and they haven't fired upon us. They came and bought things. We should leave them alone and let the politicians figure things out and talk to them."

Feliks said, "Do as you wish, but I'm going to see Berta and see what she thinks and then go to the constable."

Fredo shrugged his shoulders, "I don't know what to do. Maybe tomorrow they'll be gone."

"Let's hope so," Feliks added, as he left the shop and walked to the boardwalk. In the distance the SMS Schleswig-Holstein was making steam, with grey plumes of smoke coming out of her stacks. "Look, there you see she is leaving." With some relief Feliks watched as the ship weighed anchor and slowly began to move towards Gdansk. *Thank God they are leaving so quickly,* he thought, with the sense of a large weight coming off of his shoulders.

Fredo smiled and said, "See I told you that they were nothing to worry about. See you in the morning." He waved with a nervous shake of his wrist as he turned back to his store.

Feliks sat down on the bench in front of his store and gazed into the distance. He tried to make sense of the bizarre and completely out of character appearance of the sailors that morning. After not finding any plausible explanation, he stopped his staring at the bay and returned to his tasks.

Once inside, Feliks began climbing up and down a ladder to the loft where he pulled down extra merchandise to be displayed. Going several times to a storage area outside for brooms and rags, he completed his cleaning and resupplying of the shelves. He made some signs to bring attention to the items he was overstocked with, and ended in the backroom to count what little money came in, and decided to prepare to go for dinner at Berta's. No one had come to the shop the rest of the day, and that also worried him.

It was after 10:00 when Feliks sat down with a thump in the hard wooden desk chair and leaned back to stretch. He was both mentally and physically exhausted from the day. Another day of poor profit lowered his mood even further. He opened the drawer to put away the cash box for the night. As he was about to close the box and drawer he heard a sharp tapping on the glass from the front of the store. Standing with some curiosity, but much more annoyance, he took an oil lamp with him and approached the door as he stared through his reflection on the glass to see who was on the outside. As he drew near his heart leapt into his throat and his face first flushed red and warm then dra just as quickly.

One of the sailors from the morning stood before him, beckoning him to the door. Feliks paused several steps short of the door with his lamp held high and announced in a strong voice although slightly higher pitched than normal, "I am closed. Come back tomorrow."

The German tapped again, with persistence, smiling and waving him to come to the door, and said in German, "Come here, I need to tell you something very important." He waved a "come here" motion again.

"I said, come back tomorrow. I am closed." Feliks repeated the sentence this time with more strength and firmness.

"Just for a moment." The sailor continued to insist and tap on the glass.

"I am going to call the constable immediately," Feliks said, and walked to the phone and picked up the receiver. He brought it to his ear and was about to dial for the operator when he realized that there was no dial tone. He looked back at the sailor who was shaking the door. He held up the phone to look at it once again then dropped it knowing that the dead phone was a sign of danger and that he needed his pistol.

With several quick steps he was into his back room and lunged for the open drawer of his desk drawer where his gun was stored, but it was gone. He quickly pulled the drawer completely out of the desk and there was no sign of the box or the gun. Then, to his horror, the front door tapping suddenly stopped, which made him stop to listen intensely. It was then that he heard or felt the presence of another person in the room. He turned to look into the dim light that penetrated to the side door and froze in his place as he saw the second sailor from the morning standing near the door pointing a Luger pistol at him, while he held Feliks's gun in his other hand.

The sailor took a step forward and motioned with his pistol for Feliks to sit at the desk against the far wall, thus having his back towards his intruders. "Did you call anyone this morning?" the German asked of Feliks as he pressed the muzzle of the barrel into the shopkeeper's neck.

"I called everyone I could think of to tell them you were here to invade us. So you better get out of here!" Feliks bluffed poorly, in German.

"Did you call anyone last night?" The German continued to probe.

That comment stopped Feliks to wonder what he meant by that remark. Feliks did not remember much about last night, except for the random pieces coming together for him now. At that moment the first sailor came in through the side door half pushing and half carrying Berta in front of him. His hand clamped on her mouth only allowed her terrified eyes to express her fear that was muted when he closed the door with his foot and pushed Berta onto the bed.

"I found her coming over here, maybe to investigate the tapping I had been doing at the window," the German told his partner as Berta recovered from the push and came back to sitting on the edge of the bed. Feliks stood to go to her side, but was hit on the head with the gun, which dropped him to the floor, stunned for the moment. Berta slid off the bed onto the floor next to Feliks and stared back at the two men standing over her. It was at that moment she recognized the two. "You were the two men in the bar the last couple of nights. You were watching everything that was going on in the bar and outside." She said with an accusing tone. "What do you want from us?"

"Did you contact anyone about seeing us last night in the bar or outside at the harbor?" The German with the gun asked bluntly.

Berta stood up with a puzzled look, and shook her head in an honest response to the pointed question. "You bastards you were spying on us!" She spit on the one closest to her, and for her efforts she was slapped across the face and knocked down to the bed again.

Feliks looked up and got up on one knee with his hand still on the floor. "The flashing light last night; that was you?" He said as the pieces came together. "You were signaling someone."

The sailors looked at each other then back to the two on the floor. "Too bad," the one with the gun said, and shot Berta in the chest as she struggled to get back up.

The gunshot flashed and the sound of the shot made Feliks fall backwards to the floor where his hand hit the chamber pot under the bed. With all of his remaining effort he grabbed the handle of the porcelain container and with one large swing of his arm he pulled it out from under the bed and flung it against the second sailor, hitting his gun hand and splashing both men with the foul smelling contents. As he hurled the pot, the lid fell off in front of Feliks, and he immediately grabbed it to be thrown next, but when he brought his arm back to launch the weapon he was kicked back to the floor and stomped on by both men, who were outraged at the attack on them. The first sailor grabbed Feliks and pushed him back onto the desk chair and held him by the throat and asked once more. "We saw you on the phone, who did you call?"

"Go to hell!" he said, through the chokehold.

With a thrust the sailor released his grip and pushed him down onto the desk chair. Before Feliks could sit up the second sailor raised the old revolver and placed the barrel against the right side of Feliks's head.

Feliks felt the pressure of the gun against his head, heard the click of the hammer coming back, and then nothing more.

Two hours later, the SMS Schleswig-Holstein opened fire on the garrison of Westerplatte in Gdansk, and at that moment the so-called "war to end all wars," also known as "The Great War" would now and forever be simply called "World War I."

The garrison at Hel was the last Polish garrison to surrender to the

Germans. The 3,000 men held out for 27 days after the first shot on September 1ˢᵗ. It was thought that they had been warned of the invasion in time to avoid the surprise attack.

Among the first victims of the morning ground invasion, in the town of Bydgoszcz to the west of Gdansk, was a group of Boy Scouts, aged 12 to 16 who by chance were in uniform heading for a campout. They were lined up against a wall in their Market Square and shot. When a priest rushed forward to give them last rites, he was shot too. Another hundred boys were rounded up on the streets of Bydgoszcz and massacred in front of the town's Catholic Church. Community leaders, doctors, teachers, lawyers, priests, and Scouts were on a short list of citizens who needed to be removed from positions of leadership and resistance as soon as possible. Without a head, the body will die. Without leaders, Poland would be lost.

Chapter 7
September 3rd, 1939: Łódź, Poland

THE NAME "POLAND" translates basically to "Land of Fields." The central portion of Poland is a bountiful plain, where for centuries invaders who coveted the food that was grown there murdered, raped, and pillaged to control it. Once past the mountains to the far south, which separates Poland from the Czech and Slovakia lands, the countryside becomes a series of rolling hills and flat farmland, clear to the Baltic Sea. To the east the Holy Cross Forest, one of oldest and largest forests in Europe, covers the high mountains near Russia. The land in the middle is divided by thousands of large groves of thick pine, birch, and oak trees that look like quilt patches from the air. On the 1st of September, these quiet fields were turned into racetracks by the German armored divisions; some 2,600 tanks and mechanized troop carriers charged for Warszawa, the capitol of the country. The city of Łódź was of specific strategic importance because of its large industrial and manufacturing capacity. Initially, a large portion of the 1.5 million men of the Wehrmacht (German Army) rolled past it to reach Warszawa, their prize to the north. However, the town was not totally forgotten.

The citizens of Łódź had read and listened to news in newspapers and from their radios about the Germans' attack on Warszawa. Polish troops from the Łódź Army raced in many directions hoping to fortify the city before the Germans arrived. Their goal was to secure the city and not surrender, though they would face overwhelming numbers of men and machines. Every day since the invasion started was a day to prepare and pray. It was also time to curse the lack of everything a modern army would want. Many brave men, women, and children using whatever hunting rifles or ancient pistols they had, waited to fight and repel the invaders from the west and north and south and east. Their city was vulnerable from roads in every direction. Their dismay and terror would also be laced with terror from above.

At 5:15 AM on the 3rd of September, two windows of the Niklewicz home exploded inward, showering the area where Helena often sat with shards of glass. The concussion of the blast shook his bed so hard that Staszek found himself trying to determine what had taken him from a deep sleep to the floor, and then to standing, in a matter of seconds. His reflexes had him thrust himself against the wall that separated his bedroom from the great room of his home for protection. He clung to the wall briefly before the hulk of his brother's frame crashed against his, to shield the smaller boy. Ten seconds later, a second blast, slightly farther away, shook the building. This time it brought screams from his mother and sisters, who were fully awake, but lay pressed against the floor among the splinters of window glass, wooden frames, and dusty debris.

The second blast was smaller, but was followed by a string of eight more murderous explosions that progressed eastwardly across the center of town. The impacts vibrated into a person's core as if they were standing next to giant kettledrums. Within twenty seconds, all that could be felt or heard were the distant thuds of many more bombs falling on the distant army barracks, railroad yard, and radio station. Only a single steady popping sound came from a solitary anti-aircraft gun a kilometer away, valiantly trying to protect the town. In the glow of the flames of multiple fires reaching and seemingly leaping skyward, the street came to instant life with firefighters and panicking people, some screaming as they ran. As the bombing caused life to instantly accelerate to full motion and total fear for some, it simultaneously produced the stillness from instant death for others. Cars and trucks sped in different directions. Horns blared to reach those who were in the wrong place at the wrong time this dreadful morn. The wailing emergency sirens were accompanied by isolated cries and moaning of the wounded scattered on the streets and in crumbled buildings. The noise was terrifying and unbelievable. This surely must be a bad dream, if it were not so real.

In the glow from the fires nearby, Staszek pulled on his shoes and worked his way towards the front of the apartment to see how his mother and sisters were. The light coming through the windows was accompanied by warmth generated by the fires down the street, with the smell of burning wood, paint, oil products, and flesh. "Mamusia, are you all right?" he called, as he spotted her slowly pushing herself up off the floor. Her normally tightly pulled back dark hair fell like a curtain over her face.

She was carefully trying to brush off the glass and debris that she had fallen on, and eventually muttered, "I don't know, I think so." She looked at her hands in her dazed state, and in the partial darkness it was hard to see them, but while she wiggled and touched her fingers, the warm sticking liquid she felt made it clear that she was bleeding.

Basia and Fela sobbed in the dim light of the morning sun. In the 10 seconds between explosions, they had run into the large room just in time to be sprayed by glass from the remaining two windows. Now they were trying to pull glass and some long wooden splinters from their hands and forearms that had impaled them as they tried to cover their faces and heads from the second blast. Their long-sleeved nightgowns had given only the slightest protection from the glass and wood. In the glow of the fires they slowly shook their arms in pain and disbelief. Helena came over and sat on a chair near the girls and looked at the damage with a glazed, numb look. She was stunned and robotically reached out to the shambles of the room in a sweeping motion, her arms waving back and forth like an orchestra conductor, but not knowing what to do other than moan slowly. She brought her hands to her cheeks in horror, still oblivious to the blood on them. Blood on the girls' sleeves was now matched by the blotches on their gowns that covered their legs, as those cuts started to soak through, as well.

Zdzislaw, having gotten his shoes on, went down the steps to the shop to see the damage there. Staszek was close behind, running down the stairs to see what had happened. Zdzislaw scanned the room in the dim light and he saw that the damage was much like the situation upstairs where the windows were blown in and items were scattered around the floor, but minimal other damage was noted. Small cans of lighter fluid and coal oil had been knocked off the shelves. If they had been bottles, and if blast had generated much heat, the shop and apartment would have been up in flames within seconds. Zdzislaw, angered by the explosion, took some solace in not having a fire.

Staszek went outside, and saw, to his amazement, that the train station, a mere two blocks away, was engulfed in flames, as were many of the buildings between his house and the station. In the distance, dull thuds and flashes of explosions were occurring in the direction of the western railway station and army barracks. Panicked people were all over the streets. Some ran, while others just stood and made small pirouettes while they cried at the destruction. Other people walked aimlessly down the street in complete horror from the overwhelming events of the early morning twilight. Staszek stood frozen in fear of what was happening, overpowered by the sights and sounds around him. Like a bad dream that would not go away, he needed a safe haven, and returned to the shop. His mind raced, filled with dread of what would happen to him and his family, but he did not know what to do. He had to do something, but all he did was walk randomly among the broken and scattered items on the floor. In shock, he would start to pick up items and try to put them on a shelf, though where and how they were placed exposed his disorganized emotions. His brain was no longer able to cope with the feelings and endless questions that placed him in a trance-like state.

By full daylight, the normally busy street filled with people on their way to work was filled with speeding trucks carrying men and supplies to the outskirts of town. The radio in the front room survived the blast and gave information about German troop movements and pleaded for reinforcements of key positions in the town to assist the Łódź Home Army.

Though the radio station was bombed and the antenna severely damaged, the fast work of courageous men had a makeshift antenna strung between two buildings that allowed transmission of the signals. The news had radios blasting information to those still in their homes. People with bundles on their backs or pushing handcarts were already leaving the downtown area in hope of finding safety in the countryside. The migration of people out of the city in anticipation of the Germans marching into town and the slaughter that would surely follow presented a chaotic scene on the streets of Łódź.

Feliks's younger brothers, Jozef and Mieczyslaw, lived in Babiak, 50 kilometers to the northwest of Łódź, but to get to them would mean cutting across the German lines, something that was not likely to happen. Helena sat with the family in the apartment and talked with the girls about packing and leaving for the country. However, the radio reported that the greatest amount of fighting was happening to the northwest of town, so the route to Babiak would be extremely dangerous.

This news prevented them from leaving, so there was no choice but to stay and wait—but for what? There were news broadcasts that called for the help of the French and British, who had assistance treaties with Poland in case of war breaking out. Though the radios broadcast the pleas for help, no news about a response was heard. The best thing at this time was to plan for a siege and gather as much food, water, and money as could be acquired. Even after six days of planning and preparing, whatever was gathered was surely not going to be enough.

"I wish your father was here." Helena lamented to the girls as she wandered from room to room trying to decide what to take if they had to leave. She turned to the girls and said, "When he called last week he said that war would be starting soon and to get to Babiak, but I did not think it would be this soon. I should have listened to him. Why didn't I believe him?" Her deep fear of being alone without a man in the house to take care of her was terrifying.

After several hours the boys had finished in the shop, and had gathered what items of food that they would need in the house in reasonable quantities while they separated other items to be used for sale or trade. Moving as much merchandise into the back storage room was of paramount concern, because no sooner had there been light that illuminated the broken windows of shops, the looting started. People leaving town would snatch from any store whatever they saw in the window displays that they would need or could carry. Items that were in the window were long gone before the boys were able to clear all the items near the front of the store out of reach of the frightened hoards of people.

By early morning, the looting and the thief problem had become so great that Zdzislaw took a long pipe and a butcher's knife and carried them in front of the store to discourage those that were looking for a vulnerable store. His size, and yelling while wielding his weapons, was enough to drive away the majority of single or small groups of people. His efforts finally failed when several men who wanted cigarettes and food overpowered and beat him. His attempt to protect Staszek and the shop, though a noble, effort cost him many bruises and cuts. The thieves were desperate men, not murderers, so Zdzislaw and Staszek were able to retreat into the back of the store to hide in safety while the thieves took what they wanted.

Staszek's emotions had tempered, and he helped Zdzislaw secure the shop with boards from the storage area. Handling the hammer and saw in a quiet and effective way, the windows were boarded up in short order. By midmorning, both he and Zdzislaw were exhausted from their labors and fears of what might happen next. The radio gave spotty information, and repeated pleas for men and equipment to the outskirts of town. The messages on the radio seemed to give hope and purpose to Staszek who was mesmerized as well as energized by news. He decided to run to the print shop to see if they knew any more than what was being broadcast.

He went to the bottom of the stairs and called to his mother, "I'm going to the *Gazette*. I'll be back later," then dashed out the door.

Helena, in a sudden new panic, ran to the window and yelled to Staszek as he burst through the door and ran down the street, "Staszek, come back here right now!" Her demand was either not heard or ignored, with the latter being the more likely scenario as he sped away without looking back.

At the shop, where the new printing press was into its second month of work, the volume and speed of the machine produced ample amounts of newsprint for sale, but with very few boys to sell them. Staszek's arrival had the dispatcher quick to give him a bundle of papers for sale. He ordered the boy while he pushed on his back towards the door, "Stas, be quick and get these out as fast as you can; then come back for more."

The headline read "WAR AT OUR DOOR!" with stories about the direction and locations of ongoing battles and damages to the city plastered over the purposefully thin gazette. Staszek sold his first bundle and returned for a second, then a third. People would run out of their homes or hiding areas to purchase the paper, and try to read it while looking skyward between paragraphs. On his fourth trip he sat down on the floor and watched the papers coming off the press. The typesetter made changes as the radio and reporters provided new information.

Jerzy, the pressman, said, upon seeing Staszek sitting and resting from the intensity of the day, "It's a good thing we moved that old piece of junk into the warehouse across town and we can use this beauty, or we would never have gotten this much done in such a short time!" The old man was almost gleeful in his ability to print so much bad news so fast. He fondly caressed a gear housing on the machine near him. Staszek remembered the effort to move the old press into the storage area in the back of the *Gazette's* warehouse. He was happy about the reduced blotching of the papers, because it had produced the cash that he now held after paying the printer for his share of the papers. This cash would be something that was immediately useful for the family, so he counted it twice, and placed it securely in his pocket.

Though tired, he went out once more, to a different block farther from the office and his home. The late afternoon had been quiet except for people who continued to run from one place to another. Bombers were flying high overhead, but for some reason were ignoring Łódź for the time being. They had bombed only selected parts of town and for the most part the city was intact. It was an eerie sort of quiet in that things were moving and people hurrying, but not talking; only the drone of distant engines raised the senses of people in town. Each person had a goal, and they did not wish to be interrupted. Small groups of people would ask each other if they had heard anything new. Those numbers had greatly diminished as the afternoon wore on. The sense of panic seemed to dissipate to a much smaller degree as it was now clear that there was no place to run–so people huddled in their homes. The sale of the papers slowed and became more routine, to the point where Staszek had papers left over at 6:30, and was returning to the office to pay the gazette's manager. The tragic events of this day were pushed aside as the excitement of selling the papers was a familiar and calming routine that gave Staszek a distraction and shrouded him in a momentary false feeling of victory and helped focus him.

That was when he heard the sound of an engine high overhead. The canyon of buildings made it hard to pinpoint from which direction it was coming. Staszek, and a dozen other people around him, stopped to find the source of the noise. It was not the drone of the large bombers that had made several runs over the city today, but a small single engine plane that sounded like it was gaining speed. Within a heartbeat of him looking up someone near Staszek cried, "Dive bomber!" as they pointed up at a 70-degree angle behind Staszek. Instinctively he began to run for the shelter of the office and the basement door around the corner in the alleyway. As he rounded the corner the engine became shriller and now were accompanied by a new whistling sound. Bombs were released and were a moment from impact as Staszek jumped down the steps into the stairwell and covered his head while crouched in the corner.

Across the street, a modest hospital that had been receiving the wounded all day long was blown apart as it was lifted from its foundation. Two bombs penetrated through the 2nd story roof and exploded halfway to the basement. Bricks, dust, and debris were accompanied by a deafening concussion of the blasts, followed immediately by the strange muffled sound of dust and chunks of brick raining on the ground.

After three or four minutes, Staszek was able to climb out of the hole, coughing up dust as he went and looked at the damage before him. To his horror, smoke and flames started by the bombs had taken over the destruction of the hospital and produced a surrealistic vision of orange light, diffused through the dust and smoke of the collapsed building. The colors and indistinguishable pile of carnage mesmerized him. The heat and rubble projectiles made people on the street scream, cry, and moan from injuries suffered from the flames and flying debris that was once part of the hospital. Eerily, there was no sound from inside. The two-story brick building was flattened to a single floor; entombing hundreds of people who just moments before were seeking help and shelter there. The bottom floor walls were blow outward, and the second floor collapsed on the first. It was clear that no one inside would need or receive help or shelter, ever again.

Trying to clear his nose and throat by spitting out the dirt, Staszek walked towards the pile of bricks, as did people from the neighborhood that came out to help with any rescue efforts they could provide. Like Staszek, they stood and did not know where to start, because the damage was so profound that all they could do was rub their eyes slowly to clear the particles trapped by their tears. Staszek saw what was an arm severed just above the elbow lying at his feet. He stared at it, but it did not look real, despite the blood that still oozed from it. One old woman rescuer studied Staszek as he stood in stunned silence and said, "Boy, go home. This is not a place you should be."

Staszek looked at the arm and then to her, wanting to nod, but his body just quivered. Her voice was difficult to hear through the ringing in his ears. He finally turned and walked home unsteadily. He was strangely alone in the street, though many people were around him. He started to cry, not from fear or pain but anger. He wanted to do something, but did not know what. He spotted and picked up a long stick that was from a splintered tree branch that just a short time ago shaded the street but was now held like a spear. He gripped the wood firmly, feeling as if he now had a weapon. He wanted to stab the bomber pilot in his eyes, stomach, and heart, but the monster wasn't on the ground. He had flown away safely.

Staszek walked with the stick in a ready position, regularly lunging forwards at imaginary targets with the shaft. He never found anything to stab, just holes between piles of bricks. Holding the spear calmed him down but he really wanted to hurt the one that had done these terrible things to his town. As he got home his emotions boiled over and he swung the stick as hard as he could against the building in an outpouring of frustration and rage. Then he dropped the stick from the stinging pain in his hands. He shook and then rubbed his hands together to relieve the feeling. He looked at his hands and blew on them in an effort to make them feel better as he entered the shop, and in a strange way he was now focusing more clearly. He wiped his palms on the sides of his pants and went upstairs, mad, yet he still did not comprehend the magnitude of what had happened today. Behind him sirens and fast moving trucks and cars rushed by, but he heard only his footsteps and the torrent of thoughts racing through his head; thousands of sounds and images quickly flipping through his mind like the pages in a book; too numerous and too fast to absorb all at once. Each registered a significant event, but together they melded into an exhausting collage that fatigued him and drove him to his bed where he slept restlessly, fully clothed and dirty, for two hours. The rest of the evening and the whole night he did not sleep, but he was not awake; he was between two worlds at once. He longed for the old world, but was living in a new one. The new one was a place where he could be killed, and everyone he knew could be killed, in an instant. He did not like this new world. He was scared, helpless, and vulnerable. He was fourteen.

###

By the seventh and eighth days of the war, it was clear that Łódź was not going to be taken by assault by the Germans, but rather by isolation and time. The invaders had surrounded the city and stopped all travel into or out of the town. There was rumor that there was a slaughter of soldiers and civilians on the road north to Brzeziny. Today, the horror was found to be true when hundreds of corpses that were strewn about at the road's intersection were carried to a nearby cemetery. Thousands of severely wounded and soon to die citizens and soldiers who had survived the first days of the assault were slowly and hopelessly starting to rot in the fields, with no hope for help. They waited in agony for the pain free peace that would only come from the eternal rest for their lives that were ended too soon.

In the days that followed, Staszek connected with a couple of his Scout patrol members, Karl and Artur, who with Staszek traveled to the train station but found no trains moving. They wanted to help, but felt that they needed to find their Scoutmaster to see what he thought was needed. Unable to find him, they connected with other boys and the police, to help cordon off places where unexploded bombs had been found. They helped people into ambulances, attended to minor injuries from flying glass or impact gashes, and carried food and water to parts of the city where barricades had been set up, to provide relief to the men guarding their homes. These men were civilian soldiers manning barricades with ancient weapons and gasoline bombs.

On one of these trips they found Mr. Olechowski, their Scoutmaster, among the men up against one of the barricades. Upon seeing him, the boys ran across the debris littered street to his side. He was at first surprised to see them and smiled, but the smile quickly vanished when he told the boys, "You should not be here. It is too dangerous right now, and you need to go home."

This was the second time someone had told Staszek that he had to go home to avoid the visions of war and death. This annoyed him and made him want to stay even more. Staszek could see German troops in the distance but they were not approaching the city. The boys were caught up in the energy and emotion of the time and would scan the sky for any sign that the Polish Air Force was fighting back.

"We want to fight, too," said Staszek, whose words were echoed by the other two boys, but not with as much conviction as his voice.

Mr. Olechowski smiled, and said, "I'm sure you do, and you would be good fighters, but this is not the place and not the time. Go back into the city. When the time is right, you'll know, and we will fight together then." He touched each of the boys on the tops of their heads, giving each a gentle shake as a sign of affection. "Go now. If the Germans overrun the city try to get away and head for my cabin for safety. Remember your training, and do not make it easy for the Germans to harm you. We will need you alive and strong to fight at a later time. GO! That is an order."

The boys looked at their Scoutmaster and then at each other. A moment later they broke into a dash to an area a block away from the barricade that bridged an avenue between the rubble of three destroyed brick buildings and one untouched structure that stood naked and alone.

The boys heard engines overhead and stopped to watch the planes. They could see, sadly, only German bombers, flying unmolested in the airspace over Łódź. Remembering his anger at the bomber pilot, Staszek grew angrier while he and the other two boys watched and yelled towards the sky with every curse word they knew, in a vain attempt to somehow fight back now. As their voices strained and they shook their fists at the planes far overhead they saw what looked like pepper below one of the planes. It was not until they heard the shrill whistling sound that was now becoming familiar to anyone in town that the boys realized that the Germans had a response to their obscenities.

They had but a couple of seconds to launch themselves to the ground before powerful deafening blasts buried them in dirt and debris. This was the third time in three days for Staszek, but the first for Artur, (who needed his sleeve yanked by Karl, the senior patrol leader, to get down), where diving for cover was vital. As the raining rocks and dust cloud diminished, the boys looked towards the barricade, 175 meters away and saw that it was gone, as were most of the men and the buildings on either side of the street. Those still moving there were stunned and tried to retreat over the bodies of those less fortunate than they. The moaning and cries of the wounded increased as the well-meaning survivors pulled on injured body parts and called for cars, trucks, and carts to carry the wounded to aid stations. For the most part, the calls were in vain.

Staszek and his friends, covered with dirt and mud, stood and looked at the massive amount of bodies and blood that seared the horror of war into their minds. Staszek relived his own experience from several days ago, while Artur lived through the blur of his first. The overpowering ability to kill from a distance continued to haunt Staszek. Unlike the earlier artillery and bombings, where he visually dealt only with the destruction of buildings and the surrealistic dismembered arm, this time the mayhem was all around him. In the days since the onset of the invasion, Staszek became more indifferent to the danger to himself and more accustomed to the vivid colors and the subtle sweet smell of blood that now attacked his senses at a deeper level. The verbosity that he showed earlier had left, but was replaced with more resolve to fight back. If he could hit a German right now, he knew he would feel better but there were none close by at the moment. The shock of seeing in the near distance a place where he had just been standing turned into a large hole finally overwhelmed him and he cried out in rage at the loss of his leader and role model. There were men moving around the area, but he was too far to see if any of them were Mr. Olechowski. Staszek turned to the boys and said in anguish "We have to go back to help."

Karl said, "No, Mr. Olechowski told us to get away."

Staszek became more incensed. He pleaded with his patrol leader to go and help the fighters. His passion started to turn Karl, but then an artillery shell explosion detonated between them and the barricade as the offensive thrust from the Germans had begun.

Karl said, "We have to get out of here right now!"

Staszek picked up a rock in sheer frustration and growled as he hurled it as hard as he could in the direction of the Germans in another hollow gesture of defiance. Seeing the rock stop rolling harmlessly, only meters in front of him, he finally turned and began to climb up a pile of rocks in order to run back into the city. As he did so he stumbled from his perch because of a small mound of dirt, and added another gash to his leg. As he regained his footing, he passed a part of a wall that was standing two meters high among the fallen bricks. Staszek saw, then picked up a piece of burnt wood, and in an action of spite scratched on the bricks, "Germans are made of shit." His brazen message gave him a sudden rush of success as he read the message twice.

Artur, stunned at first by the profanity, grinned and with a sudden impulse, spat on the word "Germans." He watched the small glob of dirty mucous stick and slowly blur some of the charcoal letter. He patted Staszek on the shoulder as he turned to leave. Both boys felt that they had done something positive for the war effort. Looking over his shoulder towards the barricade once more, he could see men moving and shooting irregularly. He prayed that Mr. Olechowski was still alive, and hoped to be able to fight with him, someday soon.

As they headed back into town and to their homes, the boys saw blocks and blocks of undamaged buildings, and then would come upon an area that was indistinguishable as any place they knew. Only the street signs gave them a clue as to where they were. Homes, stores, and large buildings were all ruined in what seemed to be isolated areas. The roofs that were normally three to five stories high were now at ground level. The living space below the tarred tops were gone, and transformed to graves. Across the street, the buildings still stood, with only broken windows as the damage they bore. No obvious reason for the areas of destruction; they were just there.

The Scouts walked in silence and just looked at the piles of ruins and the ever-present fires and rushing cars and trucks. Corpses that were beginning to be piled on corners or along the streets by rescue and recovery teams meant more to Staszek now. The bodies were of the old and the young, men and women, boys and girls. They were a message that patience and inaction would not be a safe haven for anyone, no matter where they were from or who they were.

In addition to the humans, there were animals, primarily horses, which had been killed. Those corpses did not last long though. Within hours, the horsemeat was sectioned and carried off by those closest to the carcass, as it was a prize to covet. Even before the horse had a chance to reach the total calm of death, hungry souls would be coming towards it with long knives and made short work of the 500 kg animal as others joined the butchering. Oddly, the work was done while others were walking and some were running away, all in different directions. Each person determined to protect him or herself by running or deciding to stop to see if they could claim a slab of meat where they found it.

The Germans had accomplished their goal. The chaos was nearing completion. The society was breaking down and the Germans were there to restore order and hope for the fearful forlorn citizens.

By the eighth day food, water, power, and fuel were in short supply, and the streets, for the most part, were eerily quiet while people waited for the Germans next move, which seemed to be one of waiting. People met in groups and in pairs talking about the "what ifs" that faced them. Many went to their churches or synagogues to pray. They knelt and hoped for a miracle, but were expecting more inevitable tragedy. The waiting was becoming worse than the fighting.

Many of the boys of the neighborhood roamed the streets, scavenging for items they thought were important to have. Staszek found that he could still earn money by selling his papers, while the presses were able to print information, and did so until they were stopped.

Schools remained empty as teachers and students alike had their own life-prolonging needs to attend to. People were moving around town with less panic, but even less purpose. There was more anxiety from not knowing what to prepare for than the reality that was before them. They were waiting for something, but were afraid of what would happen next.

On the morning of the eighth day, their fears were realized–the Germans came into town.

During the Invasion of Poland, the Łódź Army defended its home against German attacks. However, the Wehrmacht captured and overpowered the defenders by sheer numbers at the edges of the town, and on September 8th, without causing significant damage to its utilities or infrastructure, they marched into a silent city. Though strategic buildings and structures were bombed, the targeted buildings were planned weeks in advance by German spies, who had mapped and identified places that needed to be destroyed and those that would be needed later. Hence the selective bombing on the first day and selected targets thereafter. The Germans had also gathered names and addresses of people who needed to be controlled or eliminated. That work would soon begin.

The day had come when the large boulevards were still closed and blocked for defensive positions, yet were no longer effectively manned. Once into town, the Germans quickly overwhelmed the obstacles and pushed them out of the way in the matter of hours. All the people could do was to watch from their windows and see history repeat itself as German soldiers marched into their hometown.

Citizens watched as block after block the troops, in their squeaky-wheeled transports, rolled steadily into different districts of Łódź. Squads of marching men, all with their weapons in ready positions, scanned the buildings and windows above and around them. Anything or anyone who was threatening, or may have looked suspicious, was shot. Many stone-faced residents, most with tears in their eyes and hate in their hearts gazed from the deep shadows in their homes or from corners of buildings.

Surprisingly, there were also cheers and Nazi salutes from many other citizens of Łódź; most from the ethnic Germans who had lived here since before the Great War. Behind the first wave of stern-looking soldiers came a complete change in presentation. There was the sound of loud music, drums, and trumpets. The Niklewiczs watched from their second floor window, though Staszek ran down the steps to see what was going on. Helena told him not to go beyond the door. He called back, "Yes, Mamusia," but ran outside onto the sidewalk and looked towards a spectacle of flags fluttering in the wind. Soldiers in yellow uniforms and shiny black boots were stomping on the ground, making a crunching sound as their hobnailed boots hit the paving stones. Leading the band were several rows of soldiers carrying bold red flags with the black broken cross inside a white circle. The symbol of all the evil that Germany represented loomed over the heads of everyone on the street. The swastika representing the "1,000 Year Reich" flew against a gentle breeze. The drums pounded out a brisk beat that shook all the non-German citizens of Łódź to their core, while hundreds of ethnic Germans started to fill the streets and cheer for the invaders, Helena stood at the window and slowly rocked forwards and back as she cried. She had seen a parade like this one 25 years ago. It took her breath away to see it again, and she was not sure if she could live through the pain and agony of another German occupation.

What was even more upsetting were the cheers and shouts of "Heil Hitler," as arms rose in salute to the soldiers. Girls threw flowers at the soldiers who marched with smiles on their faces, smug in this victory. Down below her, on the very street that was bombed just days before were hundreds of men, women and children lining the streets welcoming the invading army as if they were liberators. These people were the ethnic Germans that lived in Łódź along with the Russians, Jews, and Poles, but today was a day of celebration for them. Among them were Kurt and his family, delighted at the grandeur of the Third Reich fulfilling its promise for change to what had been. The hope for a new order had arrived in the form of flags, music and force over a helpless city. It was now the national socialists that controlled the government rather than free citizens. Flags with slogans flanked the Swastika flags in a dazzling display of victory for those who wanted to rule the world, starting with Poland.

The Niklewicz family glared out the window at the battle flags and columns of men. They stood broken and quiet as Hitler's vision of Germany's future was coming to fruition at the common person's expense. There was no place to go or hide that would not be found by the invaders. Towards that point came the German police, the Gestapo, who started to arrest people as they went block by block, district by district, with hundreds of men to find and to record who they captured. The methodical search and seizure was performed with the precision of a dance company. First isolating an area and then sweeping through buildings, alleys and basements, systematically rounding up each person by overwhelming numbers of soldiers. Even if a person thought to run, they had no place to go, each path was guarded. There were a few, for whatever reason, who bolted when caught. Their charge to freedom never lasted more than one to two seconds before a bullet stopped them. Their lifeless bodies dragged back to the street or to a corner were left as an example of what not to do.

After the first sweep of the districts, the Germans broke into squadrons and canvassed neighborhoods for men and boys to start to clear away the rubble and debris from the streets. Staszek and Zdzislaw were given identity cards to carry and present any time a German ordered them to do so. Simple papers, with a picture, printed name, birth date, hometown, and under "occupation," the word "boy."

Almost immediately, they were placed in clean-up details. Using shovels, hammers, brooms, and wheeled barrels they worked to make the town useable once again. The ruins would stand as monuments to the dead, while those still living had to wait in fear of their own fate. The city was dirty, but busy with the cleaning. Red banners with the broken cross on it hung from buildings all over the city and covered City Hall. The Germans seemed as if on vacation, as they smoked and ate their fill in restaurants that were authorized to be open and receive food for sale. German soldiers were walking around taking pictures of themselves in front of bombed out buildings and historic sites. For laughs they would order a Jew to stand still while they pulled on his hat or his beard posing while he accepted the humiliation. Those with no souls took pictures of themselves standing next to the dead, as if they were trophies.

On September 17th when the people of Poland felt it could not get worse, the news came from radio broadcasts and newspapers, "The Soviets have invaded from the east and have stopped at the Wisla River's east shore." The newspaper's reports were odd and matter of fact for a news source controlled by the Germans. More peculiar was the fact that the Germans did not seem bothered by the news. Apparently the "Non-Aggression Pact" they signed in August has been put to use and was serving their purposes.

The invasion by the Soviet Army was massive, and overwhelmed the Polish Army that was regrouping after the German invasion. The Soviets captured 230,000 Polish prisoners of war, and shipped them deep into the Russia and her Gulags.

The rumors were that the Soviets had come to stabilize the eastern part of Poland in order to fight the Nazis and stop their advance, while other reports said that they had invaded Poland on their own to seize land for themselves. The Soviets immediately started to install Soviet governments in the areas they now occupied. It appeared that they were well prepared for the event, as they immediately sought out and arrested hundreds of people from different professions in each city and shipped them to the Gulags as well. Those who remembered the war between Poland and Russia in 1918, and the Polish Victory in 1920, knew with certainty that this was the Russians taking by treachery what they had failed to win in battle. The Soviets, with their invasion, were Allies in name only, occupiers in reality. The country of Poland was now torn in two and swallowed up to sit in the bellies of her two long-standing enemies. Once again, Poland as a sovereign state had disappeared, while the ill prepared western powers and commentators protested but did nothing except wait to see what would happen. The wait was not a long one for Poland.

Chapter 8
November 15th, 1939: Łódź Poland

THE MOOD OF the people was as gray as the skies that were leading Europe into winter. New rules and new mandatory jobs were ordered and changed regularly, putting everyone on edge. Each succession of rules became harsher than the ones before. Staszek and Zdzislaw worked for several weeks, along with hundreds of others, to make streets passable and safe. Staszek would shovel and constantly keep moving to do his job. He often would look over his shoulder to see his oppressors watching him and giving orders, along with the occasional snap of a wooden switch or leather rope against a person who was moving too slowly. After ten-hour shifts, he and Zdzislaw would return to their apartment to work on repairing the shop and their home.

Staszek would lie in bed and call to Zdzislaw to complain about the pain and blisters on his palms and fingers. Zdzislaw would calm the exhausted and miserable Staszek until he would fall asleep. Zdzislaw, being bigger, had his own pains and blisters because of the larger hammer he was given to break apart bricks and cement that could be hauled away. His inherited strength was substantial, but it was tested to the maximum by the number of times he had to swing the sledgehammer and impact the cement. Cement fragments that shot off from the impact sites pierced him, peppering him with dozens of small wounds on his legs. His feet were bloodied by chunks of rock that rolled onto or over his thin shoes. He never said anything about himself, but he would be there to listen and give comfort to his younger brother.

What began during the previous months, and continued without pause, was the Germans establishing a government in the town, as well as systematically carrying out 2nd, 3rd, and 4th sweeps of the town for specific people they were interested in. The targeted individuals were primarily the leaders of the community, and those who had the respect of their neighbors. City officials, teachers, doctors, lawyers, Scout leaders, and priests all made the list. A ring of soldiers surrounded and isolated the town under a tight curfew, a tactic that was meant to increase the power of the invaders while also increasing the helpless feeling of their captives.

The original plans were for the city to become a Polish city that was part of the General Government, as Warszawa had become. However, because of the intervention of a new local governor, and groups of ethnic Germans who were already living in the city, Łódź was annexed to the Reich and was no longer part of Poland. The city received the new name of "Litzmannstadt" after Karl Litzmann, the German general who captured Łódź during the Great War. Despite this name change and occupation, many Łódź citizens of German ancestry refused to sign the Volksliste (People's List) that offered them a chance to become Volksdeutsche (People of Germany). Kurt and his family did sign up. The change gave Kurt's father, Henric, a better job as a manager of several construction crews, entrance to the Nazi party, and possible higher-level opportunities in the government later. The signing also allowed Kurt to continue to go to school, as well as to join the Hitler–Jugend (Hitler Youth) movement. The Youths were set up in age groups, as the Polish Scouts had been. The Hitler-Jugend was for ages 14-18, Deutsches Jungvolk was for children 10-14 years old, and for girls, it was the Bund Deutscher Madel.

The Hitler Youth was a parallel organization to the Boy Scouts. However, where the Scouts swore allegiance to God, Country, and family, the Hitler Youth swore total loyalty and their lives to Hitler. This drove a wedge between Staszek and his long-time friend. When his mother asked what Kurt's family decided to do, Staszek answered, "He is a German, and being German is what they have to do. He doesn't know better." More than once Kurt tried to talk to Staszek about the Hitler Youth in order to get him to join, but was snubbed and rebuked by Staszek and the other Scouts. In return, Staszek tried to sway Kurt away from the Hitler Youth, with the same results as when Kurt had asked him to switch. Those gestures and differences hardened the boys against one another. Soon all the German boys started to wear their uniforms, and that made the alienation between the children greater. Poles would not say anything around them for safety's sake, knowing that they were traitors and could not be trusted. Kurt and Staszek would usually acknowledge each other when they met by chance, but it usually ended awkwardly with one calling the other a "pig's butt," though neither boy meant the words in malice.

In Łódź, unlike most other cities, there were no specific areas for Polish-speaking ethnic Germans to live. They were part of the whole fabric of the town. This quickly strained the relations between the Germans and Poles in town, since the Germans were generally hostile to the local Poles. When the war broke out, the two groups gravitated to polar opposite political positions, while still sharing the original community and district. The local Germans were eager to turn in any suspicious actions of their Polish neighbors, no matter whether they were Lutheran, Catholic or Jew. While some Poles did the same to get even with a Jew or a neighbor for personal gain, the isolation of the city was not as great as the isolation of the people among themselves.

Suspicion by everyone about everyone paralyzed the community. The motto during this time was, "The enemy and the traitors are listening." Societal distress and distrust produced a high level of tension in all areas of life. You could actually walk down the street and see friends who would give their lives for their friends and family; then in the next step see someone who would take those lives without a second thought.

On November 16th, all the Jews in the city had to wear armbands on their right arms to distinguish them as Jews. By December 12th, the bands had to have a Yellow Star of David badge on it. Even Staszek's friends Jakob, who was Jewish but did not go to synagogue, and Artur, whose father was Jewish but mother was Catholic, still had to wear a band on their arms. Staszek was puzzled by the need for the bands. He knew who the Jews were, as he knew who were Catholics or Lutherans. He knew that Nikoli was Eastern Orthodox. None of that seemed particularly significant to him. Germans were Germans as Jews were Jews, and they had their own customs.

Some businesses were allowed to open only as neighborhood district authorities permitted it, but none of the Jewish ones received these permits. One day some Jewish neighbors who had hid merchandise and now wanted to sell it for money approached Helena. Helena was not interested in business and was horrified by the prospect of making a deal for things that might get her into trouble. However, Fela was sympathetic to the needs of the neighbors as well as to the opportunity that was being offered. A fair price was set for fabric and sewing notions, but there wasn't enough cash for the whole lot, so they agreed that some merchandise was given on consignment. Fela knew that she could use the fabric to make clothes for sale, or to sell the items outright for enough money to make a profit and pay off the Jews. Most of the shops had little to sell, and remained closed. The Niklewicz's shop was one of these shops. Without Feliks and his connections outside of town for more merchandise, the store needed to save everything for eventual use by the family. The women of the Niklewicz household were busy during long fatiguing hours, making clothes to sell, while Zdzislaw and Staszek hustled odd jobs wherever they could find them, after working for the government.

On the other hand, by taking some merchandise that they still had in the shop, Staszek found that there was a great deal more value to be created by trading rather than selling. He had cigarettes from the shop, and with those he could get fuel for the stove. Several packs of cigarettes could get him enough coal for a week. What coal he did not need, he could trade for butter or meat. This trading was commonly known as "Black Marketeering" and was punishable by death if caught by the government spies or police.

Every time he left the store with candy, chocolate, coffee, cigarettes, lighters, liquor, lamp oil, or candles, he would not come back empty-handed. He knew that fabric, spools of thread, hats, gloves, blankets, liters of fuel oil or other items would soon be needed for the winter. It was November, and the weather would soon be turning cold. The prices for these items would be greater in the future, as would the penalties for black marketeering. The risk was something that worried his mother, but not Staszek, who was very well aware of the dangers that he was putting himself in as he went out to do his trading, though the actual gravity of punishment eluded the boy. Death was becoming a common sight, but it did not weigh heavily on him. At fourteen, his demise was not dwelled upon. When he left the house, his mother would ask, "Where are you going?" to which he would answer, "You should not know." A comment they both knew was true, but nonetheless desperately frightened Helena. As the youngest child, he had a special place in his mother's heart, and at any age she would worry about him the most.

Zdzislaw, who was good with his hands, traded carpentry work for items to use, eat, or trade to someone else. One job he and Staszek worked on was to repair stairs and a door that were damaged by the Germans who broke into a house looking for someone who was not there. Their labor was traded for two bicycles. One bike was used to trade for the wood and the other Staszek used to deliver papers, and give him a greater range to trade.

On one of these trips, Staszek encountered one of his Scout friends, Marian. Marian had interesting news. "Stas, the Germans have made belonging to the ZHP (Association of Scouts in Poland) a criminal act. Scouts are being arrested if they are caught."

This stunned Staszek, and made him feel confused and instantly apprehensive. "Are they tracking us down? And what are they doing to us if we are arrested?" he asked with trepidation.

Marian responded, "I've been told that some Scouts and the leaders have been shot on the spot, or sent to prison."

"That's unbelievable and horrible! The bastards!" was all that Staszek could say, while despair could be heard in his voice, anger and rage were building in his heart.

"Wait—there is good news to hear," Marian interrupted his friend's glowering thoughts. "The new Scoutmaster is Mr. Pawliczak, and Mr. Klys, our old assistant Scoutmaster, is the new master instructor. We've been having secret meetings. Come to the next meeting tonight. It is at his home. Make sure no one is following you."

"I'll be there," Staszek promised, and for the first time in weeks he had hope and a sense that he might be able to fight back against the Germans.

Later that evening in the home of Mr. Pawliczak, Staszek found that he was not alone in his frustration and desire to fight. A dozen boys and two Girl Guides (Girl Scouts), ages from twelve to fourteen met at the Scoutmaster's home to find out that there was hope, and there were things for them to do. There were a couple of boys older than fourteen, but most of the older boys had been taken to the German youth camps, had protected jobs, or had run away. The remaining boys and girls had to organize and plan their missions with their leaders, and they learned to be good at that.

For the next several weeks, the group met secretly and developed their strategy, with the help of Mr. Pawliczak, Mr. Klys, and those who were in contact with other groups who were all trying to organize an underground entity. In peacetime, the Scouts served the community and their God for the good of all. In war, the goals were the same, but the price of failure was much more lethal. With leadership and the natural desire to repel the invaders, the Scouts could accomplish and contribute to the war effort, which Staszek and the others were willing to do at any cost. The cost to many was the maximum price of their lives.

The letter addressed to Helena came more than two months after the beginning of the war. It was from the police station in Hel, signed by the magistrate. The letter simply said, "I deeply regret to inform you that Feliks Niklewicz was found shot in his shop on September 3rd. He was shot with own pistol, with his own hand."

Helena started sobbing and wringing her hands at the news. When the girls returned home in the early evening they found their mother sitting at the window where she had read the letter some four hours earlier. She had not moved during that time. She sat silently looking to the street then to them and eventually looked at the letter. The girls picked up the letter from the small table and read it. In their despair they embraced each other and cried. They slowly knelt on the floor on either side of their mother with their heads on her lap, Helena softly stroking their heads. All three began to cry in small whimpering waves that would escalate into sobs as they dealt with the sudden reality of their plight—their hoped-for survival was not going to be accomplished by anyone but themselves.

It had been dark for some time when Helena began to stir and turned on the small table lamp. She was cried out and had no more tears. At first she appeared to be gaining resolve and acceptance but it quickly turned out to be anger and rage as she verbally scolded Feliks for doing this to the family. She stood up and walked back and forth yelling her disdain and disbelief at how Feliks could be so selfish as to do such a thing when she needed him.

Zdzislaw came home sometime later to find his sisters sitting on the sofa, red-eyed and silent. Basia was biting her nails, as was her habit when nervous or frightened. On this occasion it was both. Zdzislaw read the letter, and was angry that they were just finding out about the death, as well as being angry that the increased burden of responsibility would be on him. He went to comfort his mother, and then his sisters, tears welling in his eyes, but his mind racing with the problems that had been ignored about the business, hoping that Father would be back and fix them.

Staszek's response was outrage. He was immediately furious at his father for leaving him and the family this selfish way. He was angry at the letter, at the war, at being hungry, and at being bombed, and everything else that had been turned upside down in the past months. He was totally without control in his life and lashed out at everyone. "This is not fair!" he yelled. "Why did he do this?" Deep inside, Staszek searched his heart and mind for any reason that may have been caused by him that drove his father to his end. Guilt for being happy when his father left, and that he thought he could do everything without him, swept over him.

The letter neglected to mention that he was found three days after the invasion. It also failed to mention that Bertha was also dead in his apartment. The magistrate did not want to burden Feliks's family with what he thought was a murder-suicide. After all, the times they were in would be difficult enough for everyone, and the details would not do anyone any good. The magistrate had other things to do rather than investigate a tragedy of two people he knew, but were of lesser importance in light of the war. His thoughts were to let them rest in peace and spare the families.

The letter deeply troubled Helena, who now had to deal with the war alone. This was devastating to a woman who was passive and subservient to her father, and then to her husband, who seldom asked her to be responsible for making important decisions. Her anxiety was profound, and left her in a deep depression. Her mood would not change for a long time to come. The one thing she did feel confident about was that whatever had happened in Hel, Feliks would not have shot himself. He had told her on the phone what to do when the Germans came and that he was coming home to be in Łódź. His instructions to her were clear and definitive. He was planning on coming home, she was sure of it. She was just as sure that she could not forgive him for not being home when she needed him. How could he do such a thing to her? She did not have time to mourn, and she did not have a body to bury. She was alone with children, during a war. She was overwhelmed both physically and mentally, and that made her a broken person and a heavy load for the children, who were powerless to help their mother.

Chapter 9
March 10ᵗʰ, 1940: Litzmannstadt, Poland

For five months, the deep gloom of the occupation had hung heavily over all parts of life in the town once named Łódź. The Germans had burned all the synagogues in the city and deported many of the Jews that made their list of undesirables. This process had been ongoing for five months, and showed no signs of slowing. For most non-Jews, reestablishing a life under occupation was a priority, even if it was only to a small degree of success. For the Jews survival at its most primitive level was the goal but the odds were greatly against them. In December, the new governor of the region declared that Polish was not to be spoken in any shops or markets, theaters, cinemas, or restaurants. Some shops opened and businesses continued, if they could manage in the German language. Other shops were boarded up and left empty. Jewish citizens once owned the vast majority of the shops that were forbidden to re-open. On any given day, the Jewish stores could be opened (or closed) for no particular reason. It appeared to be on the whim of the district director, or on a bribe. In any event, it was impossible for the Jews to function with any freedom at all in the city.

The oppression was not limited to Jews or ethnic Poles at this terrible time. During the last week of February, an act of sabotage by the resistance group the ZWZ, destroyed a train transporting gasoline. As it burned, it collided with a passing military transport, killing German soldiers. The German workers responsible for traffic safety and control were arrested and publicly shot.

In February, the forced concentration of the Jewish population into the Baluty Quarter and a portion of the Old Town began. It was only 3.5 kilometers square and suddenly held nearly 200,000 people where ordinarily 100,000 lived, but now another 100,000 were being forced in from surrounding communities. Three to four people lived in every room of every house in this section of town. A wooden fence and barbed wire barrier surrounded the area that was called the Jewish Ghetto. On Thursday March 16th, the remaining Jews were ordered to leave their homes within 15 minutes of being notified, and marched to a fenced area in the poorest part of town that for all intents and purposes would be a prison within an occupied city. If they did not move fast enough, or resisted in the slightest way, they were shot. Thousands of citizens of Łódź were marched to the Łódź Ghetto. More than a hundred were shot on the 16th, which would be known from that time on as Bloody Thursday.

Inside the Ghetto, the citizen prisoners were forced to work in exchange for a currency that was printed for them inside the Ghetto. This effectively stopped them from purchasing any goods or items from people outside the barrier. Those who tried and were caught were beaten and/or arrested and/or killed. Thousands of people were kept inside a barbed wired fenced compound like penned animals, while only meters on the other side of the cage, life continued in Litzmannstadt as if there was nothing unusual occurring within a million kilometers.

Staszek watched on the day that Jakob, his classmate and a fellow Scout, was marched into an evil looking camp along with a dozen of his other friends. A camp that was made from a several square blocks of his city and now was surrounded by soldiers, barricades and wire. Flanked by soldiers with rifles, Jakob was carrying his bundle of possessions when he saw Staszek standing on the corner he was passing. Their eyes met for a moment, and nothing could or needed to be said. Staszek took his right hand out of his jacket pocket and held two fingers in the Scout salute position at waist level and slowly waved it inconspicuously towards his friend. Jakob nodded and waved the salute back as he moved from sight. The gesture gave both boys a sense of courage and of not being alone.

Staszek watched the column march behind the high fence, crowned with coils of deadly barbed wire; not understanding why he felt guilty that he was still able to stand outside the fence while his friend could not. He grew angry when many of the people on the street jeered and taunted the Jews that walked by. Asking, *Why are they doing that?* produced no answers he could understand. Many of the Jews were neighbors and shopkeepers who everyone knew and were a valued part of the community, until this moment.

It isn't right, Staszek thought.

As the crowd started to disperse and the gate of the fence closed behind the prisoners of the ghetto, Staszek walked to the gate and looked in, then moved around to the guards who looked at him. For the most part, they ignored the boy. As he left the gate, Staszek looked up at the six strands of barbed wire that ran the length of the fence and were anchored into a corner of one of the buildings. Those strands were inside a long coil of more barbed wire that produced a formidable barrier between those imprisoned and those who were relatively free on the outside. Thousands of sharp points were aimed in different directions, each one capable of snagging and holding the clothes or flesh of whoever was foolish or desperate enough to try and cross it. He was fixated on the wire as he walked carelessly into a guard, who shoved him hard enough for Staszek to lose his balance and fall to the ground. As Staszek stood up, the guard laughed slightly to his partner and kicked Staszek in the buttocks which made him stumble, but he quickly managed to regain his balance. Startled, Staszek turned and walked, then started to trot, towards the Gazette building. He was embarrassed for not paying attention to where he was walking and getting unceremoniously booted. He could hear the laughter from the soldiers fade behind him. He hated that sound and those who made it.

As Staszek walked, deep in thought, the leaden gray sky only added to the darkness of his thoughts and fear for friends. Artur and Jakob as well as Zofia, David, Moshi, Ben, and Sarah, who were in the barbed wired cage. He had seen Artur and Jakob two nights before, at the Scout meeting. It was there that the Scoutmaster had given them more bad news, and then the new organizational structure and purpose of the Scouts into the future. The Scoutmaster reminded them of why they were Scouts, and how Scouting was in the blood of all Poles who wanted to be free.

He said, "We have come through a harsh winter, both of weather as well as politically. The snow that fell on us did not compare with the tragedy that is upon us now in the form of the murderous Nazi criminals. I have found out that our Master Instructor, Mr. Klys, who had been captured and imprisoned at Radogoszcz Prison, has been executed. " The solemn Scoutmaster paused and looked at each face, locking in eye-to-eye contact with each boy and girl there. The eyes looking back at him were filling with tears at the news. Staszek could not hold back his sobs. Since the invasion he had suffered one loss after another. From his father to his Scoutmasters, his role models and friends were being taken from him. This was another unbearable event that he would have to endure. He suddenly felt afraid and powerless.

The Scoutmaster continued, "We have been invaded, time and time again. We have thrown off the yoke of the Prussians in 1918, and the Soviet invaders in 1920. Poles must always be combat-ready. Our neighbors covet our land and resources, and despise us as a people. We will always be in danger. Therefore, we must always be ready to fight."

Staszek had a chill go up his back and grip him to his core at these words. He looked at the other members, and they, too, were frozen in reality.

"If we let evil run over us without an effort to stop it, we will always be under its heel. Our freedom depends on each one of us to say NO to the atrocities that face us now, and do whatever is necessary to throw off the oppression and clear our country of the soulless Nazis and Soviets once more." The Scoutmaster again looked at the faces of these *"children,"* who should be playing with their toys and friends, going to school, and laughing on the knees of their parents and grandparents. The faces looking back were innocent and worried, but sitting up straight and listening. Many of them had already seen more death than most adults would in a lifetime. There were few options for them or for their futures.

One small voice asked, "How do we do this? How do we fight? The soldiers are big and strong and have weapons. They won't hesitate to kill us if they wish. If our army could not stop them, how can we?"

The Scoutmaster listened and said, "Strength and courage does not come with age and size alone. Being part of a unit such as you have here gives strength in numbers. There are ways to fight back that do not involve guns, though you will learn to use them. Let us start tonight in learning what to do. The future of Poland and your families will start with you and thousands like you. We will not stop until we are ALL free. Are you ready to do that? Are you ready to fight back?" He looked around the room, saw most of the heads nodding and heard many voices saying, "Yes, yes, I want to learn to fight back."

It was a momentous night for Scouts, in that they were told that the Scouting program as they knew it was going underground and would continue their mission with a new identity. They would now be known as the Grey Ranks (Szare Szeregi abbreviated "SS"). They would no longer be called Scouts in public or in conversation, but rather "Bees," because though bees are small, they have a stinger, and when they swarm they could be a powerful force to be reckoned with. The whole country was divided into 20 regions called "Beehives," each of which was further subdivided into "Swarms," representing the pre-war Scout troops. Within the Swarms were the "Families," which were the smallest units, or the previous Scout squads. The Łódź region was called the "Chimney."

Their new job would be to cause mischief against the Germans and start doing "minor sabotage." This would involve propaganda actions, like distributing underground leaflets, disrupting German propaganda events, and destroying German flags and symbols and signage. They also carried out intense surveillance of German troop movements, which in turn would be eventually passed onto the Polish command and Allied armies outside Poland. At the end of the explanation, all the members, nearly 50 boys and girls, gave an additional oath to the one they gave when they became Scouts and guides. The new oath was,

"I pledge to you that I shall serve with the Szare Szeregi, safeguard the secrets of the organization, obey orders, and not hesitate to sacrifice my life."

In addition to the Scouting Code, the Grey Ranks followed a basic three-step path of actions. The program was nicknamed "Dziś - jutro - pojutrze" (*Today - tomorrow - the day after*):

- *Today* - struggle for the independence of Poland
- *Tomorrow* - preparations for the all-national uprising and liberation of Poland
- *The Day After* - preparations for the reconstruction of Poland after the war.

Staszek felt empowered by the new direction and opportunities. He wasn't alone, and the bonding of the group comforted his fear. The actions they would participate in were not in place yet, but for now they were to help identify Scouts and let them know what was happening so they could join the new movement. The other instructions were to start to live and be the Scout's motto, "Vigilant" ("Be Prepared" in other translations) and watch what the Germans were doing, where they were going, and how many were involved, information that was needed now.

Being a paperboy gave Staszek a closer contact to new information, and a cover for being on the streets, something that could be useful to the organization. He did not need to be a paperboy to see what the Germans were planning and capable of doing, it was there, in front of him. People, his friends were being treated like little animals herded into a stockyard and the Germans did not show the slightest sign that this was wrong.

After watching his friend disappear into the Ghetto, Staszek found the meeting the night before gave him new hope, but his desire to do something was now profound. Staszek continued towards the newspaper's office, where the gazette was printed only a couple of times a week rather than the usual several times a day. German agents approved every article and story, closely monitoring the papers as they came off the presses. All of contents had to be favorable about German victories and German social commentary. Staszek would often see an article before it went to the censor and would find out facts that the public did not hear, like the greater number of Germans that were being killed, or how many prisoners had escaped or were freed by the Polish "Bandits." He started to pass this information to his "Chimney" leader.

The newspapers also posted new rules, laws, and restrictions on activities, and grimly named the executed "traitors of the Reich." Proclamations, like curfew was started at 9:00 for the Jews, but 10:00 for others in town, and ending at 5:30AM, in time for people to go to their jobs. Not knowing the new changes could get a person arrested or killed, which improved the demand for the newspapers and forced people to spend the small amounts of money they did have on an item that the government controlled and profited from. In response, some people did not share their newspapers when they were done with them if they could sell them for half of what they paid in the first place. Others rotated paying for a paper among a family or group, and shared it with them all.

Though the papers were thin, the sales and the pay for selling them were even thinner, especially during these winter months. Staszek received only a fraction of what he sold, as did the printer. The rest went to the German overseer. Much of the day-to-day necessities, like fuel oil for lamps, wood for the stove, medicine, and food rations were consuming any money that was earned. Long lines formed everywhere, based on rumors or posted announcements about availability. Black marketeering was becoming an important part of life in town, just as bartering for services, bread, butter, or even meat became common. No matter how hard Staszek scrambled to find jobs or deals to broker, and even though, as a non-Jew, he was allowed to work, the times were hard for the Niklewicz family.

The government controlled everything "for the good of the citizens," but only those loyal to the Nazi party got what they needed because they were the *"good* citizens." The government controlled the banks, energy, newspapers, transportation, and communications. They had Nazi party members on the board of directors of all the functioning companies. They had their own special police, the SS, which did the bidding of the Nazi party. If you weren't in the party, you had nothing.

Helena, in her efforts to sustain herself and her home, discovered that she could take the large cans of pipe tobacco left in the store and roll hundreds of cigarettes, by hand, to sell. She had never been an aggressive person, and the problems that were befalling the town and her family made her depressed and anxious. Her fears of what might happen next constantly tormented her. She was exceptionally good at worrying, and seemed to get better at it as the days went by.

Zdzislaw had gone to Babiak to work for Uncle Jozef in his flourmill. Since Zdzislaw was 17, he would soon be eligible for military service in the German Army. Boys of 15 were being sent to indoctrination camps to prepare them for military service in the future. Fortunately, the job of a miller was a priority job for the Germans, thereby earning Zdzislaw a deferment as long as he worked at that job. It was backbreaking work that lasted from 6:00 in the morning to 6:00 in the evening, or longer in the summer. He was a hard worker, and sent every Grocz (cent) he earned home.

Fela and Basia both worked locally, in the manufacturing of German uniforms and coats. Evenings, for them, involved more sewing of the fabric that they had bought earlier, and whatever remnants they could find. Their eyes, necks and fingers performed the tedious tasks for 14-16 hours per day, often to the point of their fingertips bleeding from the swollen bruises they grew from the repetitive work.

Everyone needed to work, and had to contribute to the day-to-day work of staying alive and preparing for the next day. Staszek was always looking for ways to make money or acquire goods and items to trade. He was not the only one in this situation, so opportunities were few and far between.

One day, Marian found out about jobs chopping wood in the local forest and told Staszek about them. "Stas, we can make some money for at least a couple of months if we're lucky. Sign up like I did, and we can go together," Marian pleaded with his friend.

Staszek knew that it was getting harder and harder to find work and thought this would be a good plan. He asked "Wouldn't be great if we could get Karl, Jakob and Artur to come along too?"

"Haven't you heard? Karl ran away back in January. He turned 15 last year, and the Germans were looking to send him to Germany, but he did not want to go, so he ran away," Marian reported, with some surprise and glee.

"I hadn't heard that he ran away. I thought he got a job somewhere out of town. What about Artur or Jakob? Have you heard from them?" Staszek asked with some hesitation.

"Artur and Jakob are still in the Ghetto, and I don't know anyone who is getting out of there. I saw Jakob through the wire and we found a small cellar window of the house my aunt lives in so we could talk. The window has a broken lock on it, so if we're careful I can get things for them to eat. Artur has been making caps at the factory, and he smuggles a couple out to me for the food," Marian said, with satisfaction.

"Can you take me there and show me?" Staszek asked.

"Sure, but why?" Marian added.

"We have to get Artur and Jakob out of there or they'll die," Staszek said with conviction, remembering how oppressive the fence and wire looked. We will all die if we don't do something to get away. Karl had the right idea."

"So what do you think we should do?" Marian asked with some anxiety.

"I will have to run away soon, too, or be sent to Germany. I'll never go, so I have to do something." Staszek saw quite clearly that his freedom was coming into an uncertain time, and disappearing made perfect sense to him, now that his 15th birthday was a month away.

Marian was also conscious of the significance of that age, since his was coming in July.

Marian said, "Yes, absolutely. If we can get Jakob and Artur, we can go into the woods together, maybe to Kielce or Radom. We can live off the land. We could even stay at Mr. Olechowski's cabin," he said, without thinking through the magnitude of what he was proposing. They had to have a plan, but what could they do?

"We have to think of something," was all the boys could come up with that even resembled a real plan, and that was mostly wishful thinking.

For the following several weeks Marian, Staszek, and the 18 other boys worked at the firewood-gathering job. Like most boys of their age who had been thrown into manual labor tasks, they were thin but strong. Their experience with cutting wood in the Scouts gave them the confidence to use an axe or two-man saws, which made Mr. Jan, the supervisor of the group, happy and so he kept away from the two boys to watch for those who had problems with axes. During the course of the job the boys were sent to different parts of the forest to the southeast of their town, most of which they had hiked and camped in as Scouts.

They were transported to the woods on the back of a truck or wagon. These served as carriers to bring the wood back to town each day. On several occasions, the work group would spend several days in a row in the woods, and had to bring their own extra blankets and necessities because of the distance they were traveling. After a hard day of chopping wood, finding a place to sit on top of the wood or at times standing on the running boards of the trucks were the only ways to get home. Standing on the running board was fun initially for Staszek, but the cold wind and the fatigue from the hours of swinging an axe made the return trips terrible. More than once, a boy riding on the running boards lost his grip and fall off the truck. The fall usually resulted in at least a fractured arm or leg, if they were lucky. Those who weren't went under a wheel or died from the fall.

While working in the woods, Marian and Staszek talked amongst themselves, but never when there were others around who might overhear them. The less others knew of them, the better, was common sense during the occupation and true in any situation or location. It was a lesson everyone was learning, and that was you could not trust anyone because there were spies in all parts of the town and businesses. The Germans were not below paying traitors to eavesdrop on neighbors and strangers alike. These arrests often lead to the public execution of teachers, doctors, anti-German journalists, and others, who were accused just because the traitors needed to name someone for a few pieces of silver or for a favor from a person with authority.

While dragging a log that they had cut down towards the truck, Marian brought up the subject once more. "What are you going to do next month?" Staszek's pending birthday, which should be a joyous time for a child, as he started coming to manhood was very possibly the prelude to his road to incarceration as a Hitler Youth.

Staszek, pulling the rope with both hands behind his back, stared at the ground and snow in front of him, thinking with great anxiety and deep thought for an answer. "I don't know," was his first response then he followed with, "but I won't be here." He turned his head towards his friend who was also breathing hard as he pulled in tandem with Staszek. Marian could see that he was stressed and frightened, a revelation that made him feel the same way.

Staszek was about to turn 15, and he knew he would be sought and taken away from his home and job to be sent to camps in Germany for the purposes of being indoctrinated in the German way of doing things. He was very aware of this, and was becoming anxious about his pending birthday, on April 12th. After that date, his identity card would be checked, and when the date of birth was seen, he would be quickly moved away to a camp. To Staszek that was not an option or occurrence he would accept. He could not and would not go to be turned into a German; not after having seen the things the Germans were capable of doing in his home town. He had to leave, but to where, when, and how? He had more questions than he could answer. He had to have a plan, but Staszek did not like to make plans. He had to figure out something, or he knew he would die as a German soldier, a fate unthinkable to him. *There has to be something I can do to get away.* Each time he went through the situations, the answer was the same, *But what?*

Chapter 10
March 30th, 1940: Tuszyn, Poland

THE FLUCTUATING LOW, then high-pitched audible strain on the engine along with the grinding of gears gave background noise to the bouncing and swaying of the large truck carrying twelve sleepy boys to work. The snows of winter had slowly tapered off during the last weeks in March. Today, a thick foggy mist hung in the air, sealing in whatever heat the earth still held, thus making the trip less miserable from the cold. Snow was still falling and sticking to the ground, but it was more mud than snow as the tree buds were appearing on the once dormant branches for the first time in five months.

"Look, the trees must think the Germans have left. They're coming out of hiding," Marian quipped to Staszek, as he pointed to the changes in the branches of the trees they drove by. The boys were on their way to a new area to be cleared of fallen and dead trees near Tuszyn, east of Litzmannstadt, (the name change for Łódź that Hitler ordered on the 13th of March). Marian's comment did not get a response from his daydreaming friend.

For many days, Staszek had tried to decide what to do about the pending change in his work status due to his age, spurring him to create and problem-solve the few scenarios he had. Did he have the courage to stay and try to avoid being spotted in the known environment of his city? Or did he have the different courage that would take him into an unknown and potentially more dangerous place to fight back against his conscription. Until this day, he had talked very little about his dilemma, and even less about his fear of being caught in town. Just ten days ago, the Germans executed Scouts from K. Pulaski Troop 16, from the town of Zgierz, just five kilometers outside of Łódź. Both Staszek and Marian had the sense of being slowly trapped in town and of not being able to get away. The thought of being arrested and shot terrified the boys as much as being shipped to Germany to be fed into the German Führer's war machine like an animal to slaughter.

They rode to the forest on the east side of town, with ten other boys, while three men were in the cab. Marian, still waiting for a response at his attempt at political humor, finally reached out sideways and punched Staszek on the arm. "Hey, are you listening or are you deaf?"

Staszek turned his head slightly and looked at him with a blank stare, then looked back at the other boys, who were at the back of the truck, grouped tightly to stay warm. After sitting deep in thought for most of the bouncy trip, Staszek turned and punched Marian on his arm and flicked his gloved hand against Marian face, knocking the boy's hat back on his head. Only the string under his chin kept it from falling off. Marian was becoming tired of repeating his own fear and frustration to his silent friend, who was apparently indifferent to his plight. Marion did not like being hit so he pushed Staszek away with a sharp thrust. That action got him hit again by Staszek, and Marion sulked as he rubbed his upper arm.

Marian knew that the decision of what to do had been consuming Staszek, so finally in frustration he blurted out above the noise of the truck and said, "So don't come back home from the forest. Just jump off the truck once we get to where we are going and disappear; see if I care." After that Marian slid back down against the wall of the truck and crossed his arms in defiance and pouted. The push and the outburst got Staszek's attention.

The idea was brilliant in its simplicity, but short on the "what ifs" of potential risks. Staszek sat up sharply to mull the idea over some more. His energy instantly heightened with this unexpected scenario.

Marian looked puzzled at his suddenly interested friend and said "What? What are you thinking?"

After a long period Staszek said, "I won't jump today, but I can pedal away tomorrow." That statement caught Marian by surprise and now it was his turn to sit and think more of the idea.

Finally Marian asked, "So what are you going to do?"

I'm not sure, but you'll see. Tomorrow will be a three-day trip, right? I think I heard them say the town of Piotrokow Trybunalski," Staszek said, trying to recall what the men were talking about earlier. He then warned at the end, "Just forget I said anything." Marian nodded and leaned back on the wall of the truck while his mine raced through his own possible options as he rubbed his sore arm.

The truck stopped at the forest clearing, and Staszek and Marian jumped down from the open bed, as did the others. Staszek paused for a moment, and then on a hunch went back to the old man who had driven the truck for the ninety minutes from the city. "Mr. Jan, it was very cold in the back during the trip, would you give me a cigarette to warm up?"

The old man, who looked to be sixty, stared at the skinny boy and said, "I wish I had one for myself. I haven't had one in so long that I'm on the verge of rolling my nose hairs and smoking them!" He laughed, coughed, and laughed again at his joke. "Sorry boy," he continued, "I have none to give. Besides, it would make you sick."

Though the driver was saying that as an excuse as to why he would not give him a smoke, Staszek knew this was true, and if he'd gotten it, he wouldn't have lit it for fear of throwing up, as he had done last summer. "Thank you anyway. Oh, one more thing, are we going to Piotrkow Trybunalski tomorrow?"

The man paused, looking slightly puzzled, and nodded as he walked away. Staszek tilted his head slightly in thought for a moment, and slowly nodded as he and Mr. Jan headed for the trees.

Marian looked at Staszek dumbfounded, and stood in one place for a moment before getting his feet moving through the melting snow and mud to catch up with his friend and Mr. Jan. When he caught up with Staszek he asked, "What was that all about? Did you feel like puking again?" He knew the story of Staszek's infamous smoking misadventure.

Staszek, replied, "Not sure yet, but I'll know this afternoon."

The rest of the day, the boys worked with little or no conversation other than work-related. Staszek was deep in thought, and had Marian dying of curiosity. The day passed with the sun coming out from behind the clouds several times and warming the work area to the point where some of the boys took off their jackets to cool their overheating bodies. The hard work and warmth had Staszek working out some of the details he needed to deal with. He felt that the time was right for him to make his decision to leave, but how would he get through the many checkpoints? Not having a pass or good reason to be on the roads could be troublesome if stopped and questioned by soldiers or the Gestapo.

At the end of the day, they mounted the truck on top of the cut wood and rode home silently. Marian dozed off quickly. Staszek sat with his eyes closed, but his mind was doing mental gymnastics and finally came up with the details for his action plan. Still a lot of "what ifs," but he did not dwell on them because he had a general plan.

Late that evening Staszek packed his backpack with the supplies he felt he would need and raided the shop, where took half the remaining supply of cigarettes. They were packed in random types of tin boxes that were primarily made by his mother. He took six tins of twenty and put them in his jacket pockets.

He went to his mother to say good night. As he did so, he said, "Mumusia, tomorrow I will be going away for a while. I don't know when I'll be back."

Helena was startled by the announcement, but had expected it to happen, though she'd prayed that it would not be this soon. Looking up from her reading chair she asked, "Where are you going?" She anxiously put her book down and squeezed her hands together tightly, not wanting to hear what was sure to come.

"I don't know, and it would be best if you did not know. Just tell whoever asks that I've been bad a boy and have run away," Staszek said, as his foot started to shake a little. Helena, as she had in the past, was resolved to the statement, yet worried about the decision. Staszek went over to her and gave her a kiss on her cheek. She did not look up at him. Helena had lost her husband six months ago, and her oldest son was working many kilometers away. Now her youngest son was leaving her, and that put her into a deeper depression and sense of helplessness. She put her hands over her face and sobbed, certain that she would never see him again. Staszek, not knowing what else to say, said, "It will be fine, I will be back as soon as I can." He awkwardly touched his mother's head, more like a pat for a puppy than a caress for a despondent mother. Helena burst into deeper sobbing as she buried her face in her hands and then into her ever-present apron. Staszek watched the bun of black hair at the back of her head bobbing forwards and back in her sorrow.

Unable to watch, he turned, because he knew he had to go before something would change his mind. He felt guilt about leaving his mother, and briefly thought of staying, but postponing his departure would complicate his plans and might tempt him to stay permanently. He walked towards his room and said, "I'll be leaving for work early in the morning." His mother looked up and watched his back disappear into his bedroom. She turned to stare out the window, but the curtains were drawn for the curfew, leaving her to look at brown water stains on the fabric that blocked her view. She looked at the pattern of the stain and saw the shoreline image of a lake. *It would nice to be at a lake right now,* she wished. She sat without moving or feeling for some time.

The next morning Staszek took his things and his bicycle, and went to his normal pickup place for the trip to the distant forests in the east. After a brief wait, Mr. Jan arrived at the pickup point for Staszek. However this time not only was Staszek carrying his backpack but he also had his bicycle next to him. Mr. Jan asked, "And where do you think you are going?" looking at the bike then at Staszek.

"Mr. Jan," Staszek said, with his most sincere and thoughtful voice, "I have to go to visit my Aunt in Opoczno tomorrow. Could I take my bike with us on the trip to the woods? I would like to pedal there after work."

"You know that I can't take your bike on the truck. The inspectors won't let you take it." The old man said, in a matter of fact way.

"If you could, tell them it is yours, and you need it to check on the boys in the work area which you do now on foot but the bike would help in the job. That should not be a problem should it?" Staszek asked, and waited for the answer he needed.

Mr. Jan thought about it for a long time and finally shook his head once and said, "No, that would be too risky. He thought once more, "No, no, no, the guards, if they were in a bad mood, might lock me up and throw away the key."

"Well that might be the case, but what if they were made happier, let's say because they were given some cigarettes like these." From a small tin box Staszek shows Mr. Jan ten cigarettes. The old man's eyes widened to the point where his irises were clearly isolated by the yellow-white portion of his eyes. "Where did you get those?" As he reached for the entire lot, Staszek pulled out one and handed it to him and said, "Do you think this would help them ignore the bike?"

"I don't know if that would work." Mr. Jan lit and inhaled the greatly anticipated smoke, deeply.

"I really need to see my aunt, who is ill, and I have to help her as soon as I can." Staszek pulled out ten more cigarettes from a box and handed them to Mr. Jan.

"I'll see what I can do," the satisfied man said to the boy.

"One more thing. Could you give me a note for me to pedal to Opoczno? A note would help me get there, and afterwards get back for work." Staszek handed Mr. Jan nine more cigarettes. The old man took the smokes and rolled them into his handkerchief, which he tucked into his coat pocket.

Without looking at the boy, he moved his eyes to the side and grinned as he nodded. He carefully scanned for anyone who was within hearing range and said, "You are a bold boy. You'd better be careful on the roads. My note will not get you far." Mr. Jan continued, "Get your things into the truck. We have to get going."

"Yes, sir," Staszek said, as he swung his backpack and pulled his bike into the truck. Once the truck started moving he leaned against his backpack and let out a long sigh. Momentarily, he was satisfied, but then came the *Now what?* thought which was not to be answered, yet.

When Marian climbed up into the truck with his pack, he froze in mid swing of his pack being deposited into the vehicle. In the dim light he gazed at the bicycle, and slowly settled into the truck in order not to draw the attention of his look of surprise from the two other boys or Mr. Jan, who was nearby, finishing a cigarette. He just stared at Staszek, who for a minute gazed towards the back of the truck without acknowledging Marian at all. After the truck started rolling and going through the gears, he turned to Marian and with little expression said, "I am going to peddle to see my sick aunt in Opoczno.

Marian looked even more surprised, knowing that Staszek did not have an aunt there. He knew that Staszek was born in Zurawieniec, but did not think he had any relatives in Opoczno. The only thing special about Opoczno was that it was the first large city east of Łódź in the General Government zone.

The two boys sat in silence for most of the trip, with one common thought between them *Can this really be done?*

For the remainder of the day, they performed their work as usual and sat together several times. When they were totally alone, they talked about Staszek's plan.

"I'll leave tomorrow for Opoczno, but I'll actually try to make it to Mr. Oleckowski's cabin in the forest. After a day there, I'll head for Romania."

"ROMANIA! Are you crazy? Why Romania?" Marian asked in total disbelief.

"Why not? They are still free there, and I can get a job there with their newspaper," Staszek snapped back, with only the slightest bit of confidence but the maximum amount of hand gestures as he swung his arm in large south easterly direction.

"You *are* crazy, you just proved it," Marian declared.

"Well, I can't go to Russia, They attacked us too. Czechoslovakia? No. Germany? I'm trying to get away from them in the first place. I can't peddle to America. There isn't any real choice. It *has* to be Romania," Staszek ended, with more conviction.

"You're still crazy," Marian said, and then stood up shaking his head as he waved his hand in a dismissive manner at Staszek who was left sitting there alone.

"At least I'm going to do something," Staszek hurled the verbal taunt at his friend's back.

Marian stopped in his tracks and realized that Staszek had a point. He returned to sit down next to him again and said, "Okay, why not something closer? Or just stay in the forest? The Resistance ZWZ is probably out there, and you can go with them."

Staszek was getting irritated at questioning that felt more like badgering. "I'll figure it out when I get there. I can make it alone for as long as I need. With or without your advice, it will be easy." He proclaimed as he pointed his finger at his concerned friend.

"You may be right" Marian finally admitted, "But you're still an idiot."

"I'll be a free idiot," Staszek darted back, as he stood up to return to his job.

On the way to the clearing Mr. Jan called to Staszek and beckoned for him to come over to him. "Here is your note telling whoever reads it that you are being sent as a courier to the Opoczno office of fuel resources for an estimate of the fuel that would be available for us to harvest next month. I don't know if it will work, but it's your skin," Mr. Jan concluded. He handed half the cigarettes he had gotten back to Staszek. "You'll need these later. Besides, they make me cough more." He slowly turned his head to see if they were alone, and said, "Be Vigilant."

Hearing the Scout motto stunned Staszek.

Mr. Jan continued, "I felt the same way you do now, twenty-five years ago. Freedom is our only hope. Different war; same problem."

The comment made a lump come to Staszek's throat along with a rush of adrenaline.

After a pause, Mr. Jan looked around to make sure they were still unheard, "One more thing; when you can work your way to Kielce, go to the church on the north end of town. See the priest there, and say that you need to confess to Father Bird. He will tell you where to nest, so follow his instructions and tell no one that I have sent you." He reached out to Staszek with his left hand and gave him a left handshake that was the custom among Scouts. He said, "Mr. Oleckowski was a friend of mine, and he said to watch out for his boys." He slapped lightly on Staszek's cheek, and said, "Be Vigilant and cautious. Death is out there waiting for someone to be careless."

Staszek looked at Mr. Jan and thanked him. He said, "So does that mean I can go tomorrow morning?"

"You should be out of the camp before daylight and the other boys are up. There will be less commotion that way. Only your group will know you're missing. I'll tell them I sent you on a courier errand."

Staszek nodded, and headed back to his area much more focused, and with new energy. Both things he would need in the morning.

That night Staszek went into the group-sleeping tent where all the boys were tightly packed for warmth. After awhile he stood and said, "This place stinks and I can't stand it in here." With a show of disgust he took his things and went to sleep under the truck for shelter and for ease of his departure before daylight. He tried to sleep, but his mind was too stimulated to allow rest to overcome him. He turned side to side throughout the night, but never truly found comfort. As 4:30 displayed from the luminescent dial on his watch, he decided he should get up about two hours before dawn, but found getting up meant getting out from under his blankets, and lay back down to think about whether now was a good time or not. It only took a moment before he knew that he had to go now. He climbed out from under the truck, took one of the threadbare blankets that were given him by Mr. Jan, and cut a slit in the middle of it with his knife that he wore around his neck on a string. He draped it over his head and used a piece of rope as a belt to tie his new wind/snow shield in place. Within minutes he had pulled on his long gloves, thick fur hat, and loaded his backpack onto his bicycle before he began to walk quietly away in the morning twilight. Staszek walked cautiously down the road, away from his friends, and for all intents and purposes, away from his family and life, as he known it to be.

The hard, cold air began to penetrate his skin, but the effort to push the bike warmed him over time. The deep blue and purple sky promised a clear day to ride, but also a clear day to be observed by Germans. His fate, at this time, was not a concern. All he focused on was to get away. After thirty minutes there was enough light to safely ride his bike on the dirt road that led to the route through the river's forest. Riding on the slippery mud and snow took his complete and undivided attention in order not to fall off the bike. Except for two notable exceptions that left him bruised and muddy, he was successful. Through the wooded areas and small hamlets there was a road which found him wanting to ride faster in order to get where he had to go, the only problem being that as he went faster he would fall, and have to walk for a while. Second, he did not know exactly where he was going, but in any event he was on his way and that was good enough for him. Today he had made a momentous decision to leave the safety and comfort of the known and travel to live his life as a free Pole, not as a conscript of the Germans. This was a good day to leave, because today he turned fifteen.

###

As Staszek pedaled, he could see German troops along the road in the valleys, and in the small villages along the way. Staszek stopped and watched them from a place where he was concealed from view while he ate a hard-boiled egg. When he rode his bike away, he tried to pedal steadily so as not to attract attention to himself. On several occasions he stopped and hid in the bushes when he heard trucks coming, fearing being discovered as a runaway.

The ride was slightly difficult, due to the cold and hilly road. His egg and a piece of bread he washed down with some juice he brought from home calmed his hunger. After drinking about half the liquid, he packed the bottle with clean snow and put it in his coat pocket to help melt the snow slowly into water. He stopped three times in the afternoon, to listen for trucks or people on the winding road, but found only a few. At this time of the day, there were hay and milk wagons moving on the roads returning to their small farms deep in the woods after selling their products in the towns and villages. One time a German staff car that was moving at a great rate of speed, missed him and his bike by centimeters as it raced passed him. This unnerved him, but it also had him feel that he did not have a big glowing sign on his back that said, *I'm a stupid runaway boy; please investigate.*

By the following afternoon he was near Mr. Oleckowski's cabin, and managed to get to it for the evening. He set four snares for rabbits on trails that he had found. He also gathered some wood for a fire that he could use in the cabin after dark.

By morning he had warmed and dried the clothes that had soaked through during his travels and also had caught a rabbit in one of the snares. He cooked the meaty portions for a meal and overcooked several more until they were almost dry for later. Before leaving he cleaned up the evidence of his presence and headed back on the rode heading east.

For the next two days, he rode his bike early in the early mornings and late evenings, and camped well off the roads during the day. He slept in hollows of trees or under bushes covered with leaves and mulch for shelter along the way. He often had to push his bike, because the cold made the tires flat and possibly brittle. Both of those conditions made it dangerous to be on two wheels, but he rode the bike to make it easier to stay away from the Germans.

On the fifth day he was coasting downhill on a road that would take him to Opoczno when he came around a curve in the road that was hidden by large trees unevenly spaced on either side of the road. In the silence of the morning he could hear a motorcycle in the distance, driving in a middle gear up the hill. In a moment, he could see the shielded headlight of the motorcycle with a sidecar coming towards him. What he did not know was that it was ahead by a half kilometer of a line of six trucks and a troop transport at the front of the column. All were moving slowly but steadily up the moderate grade.

Staszek tried to get off his bicycle quickly, before the motorcycle soldiers could see him. However in the sudden motion from his effort to apply the brake and swing his leg off the bike, he lost control and fell sideways, skidding through the snow and slush several meters more downhill towards the oncoming motorcycle. Recovering quickly he was able to scramble up onto his feet and retrieve his bike but not before the motorcycle caught up to him. The sidecar soldier holding a rifle, sprang out of his seat and ran towards Staszek, catching and grabbing him by the back of his arm and then he shook Staszek firmly as he squirmed to free himself. While Staszek tried to pull away from the first soldier the driver had stopped the motorcycle and went to move the bicycle off the road in preparation for the slow-moving convoy down below.

When the soldier holding him turned to watch the driver remount the motorcycle, Staszek made a quick swing of his leg, and caught the soldier holding him squarely on the side of his left knee. The kick produced a sharp pain in the knee and a string of obscenities aimed at the boy. The blow made him loosen his grip on Staszek's arm and with a jerk he pulled free but fell backwards on to the ground towards the outside ledge of the road. The fall exposed him to the butt of the soldier's rifle that was about to come down on him. Seeing the butt of the Mauser rifle being lifted and aimed at him Staszek rolled right towards the side of the soldier's injured knee causing him to miss him with the rifle. This made the soldier angrier, and he turned the rifle around and he aimed it at the boy to end this defiance. Staszek who was on the ground resting on his elbows could see that he was going to be shot as he looked up from the ground into the barrel of the rifle then into the squinting eyes of the soldier before he reflexively closed his own eyes and held his breath, helpless before the German as a shot rang out.

He heard the shot and flinched, as something warm and wet covered his face, but did not feel the pain he expected. At almost the same time, something heavy fell on him. He opened his eyes as a second muffled shot came from the embankment in front of him, followed by a moan and a thud. He was stunned to find the one soldier lying on him and the other on the ground near the motorcycle. Neither was moving. He pushed the body off of him and sat up in shock but quickly scrambled to his feet holding a slightly crouched position while he looked at the men on the ground, the snow around them were splattered with their bright red blood, as was Staszek. The man that aimed the rifle at him was now on his side with his face spilling blood from a large gaping hole in his left cheekbone. The driver straddled the motorcycle seat, partially standing but bent face down over his handlebars. He had a large wet red spot on the right side of his back between his shoulder blades. As he stared at the second soldier, Staszek was grabbed again, but this time the profanity was in Polish, ordering him to get moving up the embankment. A strong grip partially dragged and pushed him as he clumsily scrambled to gain a foothold in the snow covering the small ditch. Staszek regained his balance and made it up the snow-covered bank then into the trees. He looked back at the road and saw three men with rifles pushing the motorcycle down into the ravine on the opposite side of the road; the bodies of the soldiers were flung in the same direction. A fourth man, with a machine gun hanging over his shoulder, had tossed Staszek's bicycle up the hill over and behind a bush, and quickly crawled up next to it while getting his gun ready to fire.

Thirty seconds later, the slow-moving trucks came around the corner, and as they passed the place on the road where the snow was disrupted and stained with blood the lead truck slowed down to figure out what had happened there. The soldiers in the lead truck turned and leaned to look on either side of the road for clues. Then a shout came from one of them, "There, in the ravine!" The truck stopped, and the soldiers' curiosity cost them their lives as they stood to see over the side of the truck. In an instant dozens of rifles and machine guns let loose a deafening roar of gunfire showering the trucks with bullets. The German soldiers had only moments to turn and fire their weapons spraying the hillside wildly with bullets in a frantic effort to defend themselves. They never had a chance to aim their weapons before they were mowed down, falling dead where they stood a moment before.

The drivers of the other trucks had only microseconds longer to live before they were shot at their wheels. The firefight lasted no more than forty seconds before all the Germans were dead or mortally wounded. Twenty-five men came sliding out of the woods to check on the Germans, taking all the weapons and ammunition before driving the troop carriers over the edge, into the deep ravine where one rolled over several times while the other rolled once and rested against a large tree. The transport trucks were driven away with the attackers jumping into the backs of the canvas-covered vehicles to inspect what they had captured.

In two more minutes the road was silent. Except for the blood stained snow and road, a dozen or more bodies, shattered glass, hundreds of bullet holes in the trees lining the road, and the wrecked trucks in the creek far below there was little sign of what had occurred there.

Staszek sat in disbelief, shivering not from the cold but from the adrenaline pouring through his body from the intense battle that had turned a quiet road into a slaughterhouse. The narrow escape from being killed by the soldier, the pieces of the German's face and blood splattered on his, then the noise and sights of the results of the ambush made Staszek soil his pants and left him pale.

A hand came down on his back and said, "Are you all right?"

Staszek nodded but was truly unsure if that was the right answer. "Come along," came the definitive message from the broad shouldered, squat-framed man wearing a Polish army cap, but a German long coat. He held a machine gun that swung from a strap around his neck that partially covered two very old bloodstained bullet holes in the left chest panel of the coat. He pointed towards the bicycle and said, "Get your pack."

Staszek did as he was told and took the pack off his bike. The pack had a bullet hole in it and when he pulled the pack off the bike he saw that a bullet had not only cut through the pack but through a spoke and punctured the rim and tire as well. He momentarily mourned his bike as if it was a favorite pet. His grieving lasted less than a couple of seconds before he hoisted the pack and walked after the man with the machine gun.

Staszek carried the pack deeper into the woods for the next two hours. Not a word was said nor asked during the trek on a circuitous path through the heavy canopy of trees. The light from above would make contact with the ground occasionally, but for the most part they walked amongst the shadows. Staszek was very uncomfortable and self-conscious about the sensation and smell coming from him and his pants. He looked shyly at the dozen men walking with him, wondering if they noticed.

They reached an area where there was a well-trampled clearing that had what appeared to be cooking area along with several log and branch shelters around the perimeter. The man with the machine gun pointed to a log and said, "Put your pack over there. Do you have another pair of pants in that pack?" Staszek nodded again. "Good. Go down to the creek and wash the shit out of those you're wearing and come back clean. Make sure you're washing yourself DOWN stream from the camp."

Mortified by the order and comment, Staszek retrieved his extra pair of pants and headed to the creek. The water was melted snow, and very cold. It motivated him to get the job done quickly. His embarrassment made him do it well.

Upon his return, he stood near a small fire. He self-consciously ran his finger down his thighs and slid his finger into four holes that marked where the bullets passed through his pack, puncturing his folded second pair of pants. As he examined the vents in his trousers, some men were cleaning their weapons after the assault on the convoy while others seemed to be breaking down the camp. The man with the machine gun came over to Staszek, sat him down on the log, and said, "Tell me what in the hell you're doing out here alone in the middle of a forest? You know that you nearly ruined the attack and got yourself killed."

Staszek flushed at the thought of ruining the ambush, but settled down and for the next several minutes gave a brief history about himself leaving Łódź, (he refused to call it Litzmannstadt), and his need to get away from the Germans and how he wanted to get to Romania.

That made the man laugh. "You're a determined little boy. You're wrong about Romania. They've fallen to the Germans, so that will not be a good solution for you now." The man stopped and watched the expression on Staszek face turn red, stiff, and stern.

"I'm not a little boy," he protested. "I'm fifteen, and if the Germans want me for their army, I must be big enough for someone else's instead." Staszek still wasn't sure if these men were soldiers or bandits making a business from the war, but his anger started to boil over. "If I can't fight with an army, then I'll set up camp out here and take care of myself. I'll get a gun, and I'll take care of the Germans too. They don't frighten me. I'm a Scout, and I can take care of myself," Staszek said boldly, without enough determination to make the statement very believable, but enough to make himself feel as if he had *some* control over his life.

The man smiled and gently slapped Staszek's cheek twice slowly. "Well, if you can take care of yourself you can do it here for now, but when we get close to a village tomorrow we'll leave you there." Staszek clenched his teeth at the comment. The man continued, "And if you want to take care of yourself, you should be careful about telling people that you are a Scout. You know that the Germans are shooting Scouts whenever they find them. So be sure of who you tell."

The comments made Staszek angrier but he also felt a little foolish about his boast. *Leave me in a village? I don't want to be in a village. I want to fight*, he thought, as he looked at the men working at different tasks in the camp, and continued aloud, almost losing control, "I want to fight with you!" He was so angry that he was about to stomp his foot like a little boy but stopped in time as the thought came to him about the message that would send.

The man was becoming a little impatient with the protests by the boy. He turned and glared at Staszek and said, "Understand that we have much to do and you would be in the way. There is nothing that you can do that we need, and we don't have time to watch over you." His squinted eyes penetrated deep into Staszek's to make his point and to get his message through to him he added, "Understand this boy; even though you are a brave Pole, you are too young to fight."

Staszek was not deterred by the statements and answered, "But to free Poland, I am old enough to die." He stared at the officer for a moment then continued emphatically, "I can do a lot of things: I can cut and gather wood, I can build things, I can cook, I can speak and read in German and English, I can read a compass and map, I…"

With his outstretched hand, the man stopped Staszek in mid-sentence and asked, "How well do you speak and read German?"

"I've taken three years of it in school, and know a lot of the swear words, too," Staszek responded eagerly. "I also speak English, but the reading and writing is more difficult. -I can swear in Russian." The last part was thrown in to impress the man.

Pointing to a spot on a map the man said, "If I gave you a map and a compass, could you find your way through the woods to that place and not get caught by the Germans?" The question came more specifically and deliberately.

"Yes, of course, easily," Staszek said with naive assurance.

"Stay here." The man ordered Staszek, who nodded rapidly, and let out a long breath as his shoulders relaxed slightly.

Time passed slowly as Staszek started to feel the cold penetrate to his skin. Sitting on the log and looking at the snow-laden trees and the various paths into the woods had him wanting to get up and wander around, but he knew he had to sit and wait. Ten minutes later, which felt like an hour, the man returned with a second man who was wearing a Polish officer's overcoat and Polish Army fur cap. He had a scraggly beard covering an angulated nose. The man looked at the boy and said, in German, "I am Hubal. I am in charge here. Do you understand me?"

Staszek looked up from his perch on the end of a log. He nodded in a short quick arc and responded correctly in German, "Yes, I do."

The officer continued in German, "Tell me about how you got here."

Staszek became uneasy at the question. Because of German being spoken, he began to think that maybe these were bandits after all, and were stealing and killing from the Germans and the Poles. "Are you bandits or soldiers?" he asked first.

The officer smiled and asked in return, "Why, is that important?" "I don't want to fight for crooks," Staszek replied, with suspicion.

Hubal laughed, "Crooks? No, we're not crooks. We are part of the ZWZ. Do you know what that is?" The officer sat down next to Staszek.

"Yes sir. I heard about the ZWZ and the SZP. I want to be here," Staszek began to get excited at the interest the officer showed.

"Good. Now tell me how you got here, what you remember about the road, and anything else you remember seeing of the Germans in the area." He added, as he swung his head toward the man with the machine gun, "Tell me in Polish so the sergeant can understand."

Staszek gave whatever details he could remember, and drew a small map of the areas and what he'd seen. He gave estimates of the number of men and trucks, tanks, and staff cars that he observed from his bike. He told them he thought they were resting or not preparing to leave their camp.

The officer looked towards the sergeant and said, "That was what we saw, too. The boy has a good eye for details." Hubal paused for a moment, the whole time looking at Staszek with deep piercing eyes that gave no sign of emotion or decision. Slowly he leaned back slightly and reached into his coat's inside pocket and pulled out a folded map and handed it to Staszek. Accepting the map but not opening it as he brought it down to his lap, he looked back at Hubal.

Hubal looked at him as he leaned forward, knelt next to Staszek, and said, "Find where we are on the map." With that said he rocked back on and sat on a tree stump. As Staszek looked at the map, Hubal lit a cigarette and blew smoke out his nose.

Staszek opened the map and orientated himself to the compass points, searched for several key mountain peaks and the flow of the creek that was near the ambush site. After a couple of minutes, he put his finger on a spot and while holding it there he looked to Hubal and said, "Here."

Hubal looked down with a glance, moved his eyes to the sergeant, and smirked, "That's good." He said, "The sergeant gave you the code name of 'Pants' but what's your real name, boy?"

"Stanislaw Niklewicz, but I like Staszek or Stas. -My codename is Pants?" The last part was asked in a deflated and rather bewildered voice.

"Stas, I was a Scout, and you are a Scout, and obviously a good one. I might have a job for you. Are you interested?" the officer asked.

"Absolutely! Anything!" Staszek almost blurted.

"I need someone to go to Opoczno with one of the other men, where we can use some of your talents. There is danger to the job, and I can't guarantee that you'll come back, but it's an important job. Are you willing to go?" The officer proposed something that, no matter how dangerous it was, Staszek was ready to do it. For the first time since the war started, he felt like he could fight back.

His heart almost leaped from his chest. "I'm ready. When do I leave?" Staszek answered, with excitement.

"Very well Pants, I will get things set up, and tell you what you need to know in a little while. If you are going to be part of us, you should take an oath to God and country. Will you do that?" Hubal asked.

Staszek, a.k.a. "Pants," stood up, snapped a salute, and said, "Yes sir!"

In a brief minute, Hubal produced a small Polish flag, placed it on his palm and told Pants, "Put your left hand on top of the flag, raise his right hand in a Scout salute and swear this oath after me, 'I swear that I will fight for the freedom of Poland and her people with all my strength, blood and life. As God is my witness, I swear my loyalty'." Hubal put his hand down and said, "welcome to the Zwiazek Walki Zbrojnej" (ZWZ, Union for Armed Combat).

They shook hands. Hubal said, "You are now part of the resistance against the Germans and Soviets." Pants grinned as his chest inflated with the honor and oath.

"In the meantime get some bread and soup from the sergeant." With that, the officer nodded once, turned, and walked away with deliberate strides. The sergeant also walked away and was about to disappear into a small log and branch hut when he stopped and turned back to look at the boy.

Staszek turned to watch the sergeant and wondered what to do next. The sergeant waved to him and said, "Come this way, Pants." Staszek followed the man to get his hot meal and hoped that his code name would be only a temporary one.

By midday, all the camp equipment was loaded onto a couple of horses and into the packs of the men. Staszek was introduced to a slender man, code named Needle, and he was told that he was to leave immediately down the hill with Needle, who would tell him what he was going to do. As the two started on the journey it was amazing to Staszek that this morning he was going to go to Romania, and this afternoon he had a job with the resistance. He was excited to be doing something so risky. The downside was that he had a code name he hated, but he could see why the sergeant thought it up. It was certainly better than a codename like, *"Shit".*

The trip on foot lasted the rest of the afternoon. Needle was careful about not being seen, while at the same time he listened and watched for activities that the Germans could be doing. At every opportunity, Needle gave Pants instructions and taught him about reconnaissance and stealth behavior in the woods. By the end of the day, Needle and Pants had arrived at a farm and spent the last 45 minutes waiting for total darkness to fall. Quietly, they sat at the edge of a tree-lined field watching the small farm settling down for the night. Needle told Pants, "This is one of the safe houses. That means that these people are sympathetic to our fight, and will help us in whatever way they can. We have to wait until dark, in case the enemy is watching them. We must not put them at risk or danger by showing ourselves."

Pants studied the area, and had a general idea where the farm was in the forest in relationship to the roads he'd been on before, and the maps he'd seen in the past. Staszek was told that the plan was to use him as a courier between the underground campsites and contacts in the villages between Opoczno, Kielce, or Łódź. This was roughly a wedged-shaped area, with Łódź at the northwest tip covering a maximum distance of about a 110 km. He would be given a good set of forged papers, stating he was newly fourteen. He would use youth as a tool to get around the areas that he knew, without too much suspicion being drawn to him. The farm they were observing was near Konskie, and was one in a chain of farms that he would have to visit or use as the situations warranted. First, he had to prove that he could do the job, and the farmers had to know him. After dark, Needle introduced Pants to the farmer and his wife. The farmer, Samuel, was in his late 30's but his wife, Gertrude, was only in her early 20's. Samuel had a stiff leg from a farm accident years before that badly damaged his knee, leaving him with a definite limp.

Needles told them that Pants would be passing through, and to help him as they could. They showed him a drop spot for messages he had to leave. The hiding place was a hollowed out post in the barn, where a wooden peg covered it, and was used to hold a broken bridle.

Gertrude would place two-colored aprons on the clothesline when a message was left by one of the other couriers. If there were none, they were to stay away.

The farmer invited them to stay for dinner before they left for the next farm, an invitation that both Needle and Pants were delighted and thankful to accept. It was a chicken dinner, with potatoes and milk. Pants was encouraged to eat his fill, which was surprisingly more than the farmer expected, but graciously did not comment on. After dinner they packed up and thanked their host and his wife for the "Best meal that I ever had! I love chicken!" said the well-fed Pants.

Two hours later, they arrived at the next farmhouse. This time, after knocking on the doorframe in three sets of two knocks they were let in and given a place to sleep in the loft of the barn. The loft was directly above the three cows and two horses that the farmer owned. The heat generated by the warm bodies below made sleeping in the hayloft comfortable. Pants slept soundly, after a very long day.

Over the course of the next two weeks, Needle and Pants covered nearly two hundred kilometers on foot or by hitching rides through some of the most beautiful but isolated areas of Poland. Needles, who was an officer in the Polish Army, and now an intricate part of the underground resistance, taught Pants about path-finding, survival skills, and ways to determine and observe the vehicle markings, uniforms, ranks, and organizational activities of the enemy in their camps or transition points. These new skills placed Pants far beyond his experiences in the Scouts. The art of camouflage, using shadows and lighting as natural advantage points greatly improved Pants' skills, and enhanced his chances to be successful as a courier for the underground by not being caught or observed during the reconnaissance done during a mission. His job would be assisting the resistance in any way that was necessary and ordered by his superiors. He would do this by carrying information via letter, film, or parcel to the places designated, or leading personnel to specific areas where others would take over as guides in their own operational areas. This was a responsibility that would challenge any soldier, especially if they were only fifteen years old.

Crisscrossing meadows and high hills with Needles, Pants met a dozen farmers or shopkeepers who would be his contacts and safe havens in the near future. Pants met many brave people who would help him as needed. He learned how to go from town to town and from point to point on a map. All the contacts he met were regular people who no more wanted a war than he did, but, as Pants discovered, he was not alone in his determination to keep the German occupiers from staying in his country. He now knew that he was not going to fight this battle alone. His hatred of the occupiers was shared by the hard-working people of the fields, who were willing to fight and, if necessary, die for their country.

Just because the Germans were there in power and presence, their tyranny would not last if they could not keep the people suppressed. The people of the fields needed time and a lot of luck to win their country back. It was at one of these farms that he found out that the officer Hubal, who Pants met on his first day with the resistance, had run out of luck and time when he was ambushed and killed by the Germans several weeks before. If that wasn't enough, the talk was spreading through the countryside that the Russians had killed ten thousand Polish officers in the Katyn Forest, near the Russian border. Some said that the total dead were double that amount, but even the most suspicious Pole could not believe they would kill that many people in cold blood. The Russians, on the other hand, were blaming the Germans for the massacre. To those who were familiar with the area, they knew that the Russians controlled that forest area, and this was the kind of work their secret police, the People's Commissariat of Internal Affairs (NKVD) was known for.

The news of these killings sent a chill up Staszek's spine and left him feeling scared and vulnerable again. Could he do his job and not get killed? If the commander could not survive, what were his chances? Staszek tried not to think about it, but the thought was seemingly always there, that he would die doing his job but no one would know where he died. That reality made him think deeply about what he needed to learn to stay alive, and that was a good thing. After much thought and soul-searching, this 15-year-old boy made up his mind. Being here in the woods was where he felt he should be, and he made the moral and conscious decision to stay with the resistance.

The decision was profound, because between the 14th and 16th of May, 1940, three hundred boys from his home Scout district were arrested and sent to the local prison of Radogoszcz. Nearly all of them were classmates or friends from Scouts. All but nineteen were from his church parish. The nineteen were Jewish boys that were in the Scouts with him. How the Germans found all of them was a mystery to Pants and the Underground.

In June of 1940, he was sent back to Łódź for a new assignment, which required him to get in touch with Jerzy the pressman. The *ZWZ* and it's Bureau of Information and Propaganda (BIP) had been publishing *Wiadomosci Polskie* (Poland's News; a propaganda publication) but had been discovered by the Gestapo, and most of the operators and couriers were arrested during a sweep of their facilities. The Grey Ranks had decided to set up the old printing press to produce flyers and bulletins themselves, to fill the void made by the arrests. The counter-propaganda that was being produced by the Grey Ranks was slow and cumbersome to do on small hand printers. Acquiring larger equipment would greatly expand the small sabotage's effectiveness. Pants knew the Łódź area, and knew the pressman and how to distribute newsletters. To put all the pieces together he was sent with another underground officer, "Hammer," to make contact with the pressman who was known to be anti-Nazi. Jerzy was pleased to see Staszek (Pants), and felt that he had a reliable contact to work with. Trust was a crucial part of this operation. Everyone's life depended on a tightly held, skillful, and secret organization. Jerzy would have his life in Staszek's hands, as Staszek's was in his.

Jerzy had already set up a small printing unit in June, where he published the *Pochodnia* (The Torch) in the basement of a brothel. Pants traveled between designated apartments and places to put the plans to work and then to deliver messages and materials as needed. Pant's knowledge of the town and where to locate key individuals and supplies accelerated the development of the Information Bulletin. Jerzy's resources for supplies, and his skill, got the program up and running in less than a day. They needed more support, and turned to the Scouts for help. The help came in the appointment of Mr. Letowski (who was one of the Scouting instructors in Łódź) to be the head of the BIP. His code name was "Maly Janek" ("Little John"). Maly Janek was able to recruit a large number of Scouts from all over Łódź to help in the publishing and distribution of "Pochodnia."

Though he could travel through most of the city, Pants was ordered not to return to the district where he'd lived, nor go to his home. It was feared that individuals sympathetic to the German government could identify him in his home district, thereby putting the operation at risk. German agents and informers were everywhere in this "German" town now called Litzmannstadt. Though the Germans had changed many of the streets to German names, his hometown would forever be

"Łódź". He did not stay with his family, but rather in a shelter that was in one of many safe houses in town. On occasion, Pants would walk by his family's store that was battered and boarded up. He would look for his mother in her window seat but seldom did he get a glimpse of anyone, which left him sad and on the verge of tears. Resistance fighters and Scouts do not cry, so the tears stayed in while his heart sank with heaviness. *It isn't fair that you're fighting in a war and you can't even go home, even when you are next door,* Pants bemoaned his orders.

Pants, along with another Scout, distributed newspapers and bulletins through their assigned districts in Łódź. They ignored the danger of what they were doing, and were exhilarated by their daily tasks. They carried out their duty in all weather, and walked many kilometers through rubble-covered streets or busy normal-appearing communities. As part of their mission, they climbed endless stairs, often carrying heavy packages to the distribution points where other Scouts broke them down into smaller parcels, and eventually those were distributed to still other individuals. This next level of messengers carried them to destinations outside of town, via train, wagon, and car, or even the innocent school backpacks that the youngest of the group would carry.

Punctuality was not one of Pants' strong points, but on this job it was vital, because the parcels of illegal newspapers and counter-propaganda could not be allowed to be stored in any one spot; whether in a shop, apartment, office, or basement, for more than a few hours for fear of them being discovered. Those who were in possession of these newspapers would surely be killed after being tortured, if caught with even one page of propaganda. Many of the messengers were captured and tortured to get information about the others in the organization who were distributing the anti-Nazi material. Some were even in Pant's group, and it was difficult for a trained soldier to resist the "interrogations" that were mounted by the SS or Gestapo. A young fighter of 12 or 13 did not have a chance of avoiding the eventual disclosure of the names of those in his group. Every Scout in the Grey Ranks assumed that somewhere on a piece of paper their names were very possibly already written, therefore making the need not to know too much of your cohorts a vital one.

Pants and others in the Grey Ranks had to deliver each paper or bulletin to their contacts at a particular hour, to make certain that there would be someone there to take in the papers. This had to work smoothly in order to cover not only the city, but also other parts of the country. The newspapers Pants and the others worked on were carried by truck or train and dropped off to other groups of Scouts to cover the widest possible distribution area. Eventually, tens of thousands of papers were regularly produced and distributed every day from different clandestine printing presses. They were so bold that they even sent a copy to the Gestapo headquarters on a regular basis, just to irritate the invaders.

The Gestapo commander's satisfaction came from knowing that the cards he collected, that had dozens of names on them, would someday produce the information that would help him break the back of the resistance in Litzmannstadt. He was a patient man, and he would be victorious. In the meantime young boys ran through Łódź, doing what they could to make sure that this victory would never happen.

Chapter 11
August 17th, 1940: Opoczno, Poland

By the end of May, Staszek was placed under the supervision of a fifty year-old carpenter, Mr. Wach, in Opoczno. Mr. Wach was a Scoutmaster, and kept a safe house for boys who were traveling to distant locations. He also taught an underground school for the boys and girls in the area, teaching Polish history and mathematics. His classroom rotated on an irregular basis through several other homes, apartments, and even a barn in the community to avoid being discovered.

While Staszek was staying with him, his cover was that he was an apprentice to Mr. Wach, and would help him with projects, as needed, when he wasn't away. Staszek was learning his way around the villages via train, truck, on foot, and on horseback, as well as learning some carpenter's duties. Despite the danger of his travels, the adventure was exciting for a fifteen year-old boy. Needle spent several days a week coming into town to meet with Staszek, to give him progressively more involved assignments.

Needle had been traveling between operation centers all over the Łódź- Kielce district and up to the Warszawa region. He was a courier, which had him transporting maps, communications, microfilm that was sent to England, and sending other vital organizational information to where it was needed. He was training several boys to act as messengers, and eventually couriers, to take his place. Pants was one of them.

Whenever possible, Needle would take Pants to improve his skills at stalking, approaching, and observing the Germans in the field without being seen. He instructed Pants in ways to avoid capture and camouflage himself, whether in the forest or in the fields. Knowing how to hide among rocks or in the open was needed to give Pants the best chance of not being shot, or worse, being caught, tortured, and then shot. It was vital that German encampments were found, quantified, and reported to commanders in order to plan actions or to know when it was safe to move through an occupied area.

Needles also took Pants on trains, buses, and on foot, in order for him to be able to blend into a crowd, anticipate danger, plan ahead regarding escape routes, and use evasive tactics. All were crucial skills that could extend his life and those that he may know. Being able to approach, collect information without being seen, and return to command centers in a timely manner with the findings, were literally a matter of life and death for many including Pants who was placing his life at risk to do the job. There was no room for errors.

One week, Needle took Pants to an area some fifteen kilometers into the rolling hills towards Warszawa. They left in the middle of the night, to get there before dawn. Never talking but always listening, they walked at a brisk pace on a wide path for five hours. Once in the area, they carefully worked their way through the trees until they came to a clearing where the ground fell away sharply. There, on a small outcropping Needle and Pants crawled on their stomachs to reach the edge of the cliff. They were moving very slowly to avoid moving bushes, grasses, or small trees that would give away their location to any German patrols that were in the area. Using hand signals, Needle directed Pants to follow him around a far edge of a rock. From high above, they could see an intersection of several roads where there was a German camp and supply station. They used a small pair of binoculars to gather information.

"Start with the big picture, and estimate how many men are there," Needle ordered. Pants looked around and started to look anxious as he tried to count men who were moving around in some cases, while in other areas they were working on equipment or marching. "Pick an area where they are not moving, and hold your thumb out to a place where it covers those men. Count the men under your thumb, then figure out how many thumbs it would take to cover the area where the men are."

Pants did as he was told. "About three hundred," said Pants.

"Very good. As you get better, you'll get to know how many can be covered by two or three fingers, or from the circle in the binoculars, from this distance, and that will make the counting faster." Needles watched as Pants worked the numbers through his head. "Now, what kind of vehicles are they? Are they mostly troop transports, armored trucks, tanks?"

Pants scanned the field and jotted down numbers.

Needle continued, "Is there a hospital or ammo dump? Where is the communication center and headquarters?"

"There" gesturing with his finger held close to his face, "where the large antenna is sticking out of that tent and the staff cars are under cover. The hospital is where the ambulances are parked and the men are coming out with bandages." Pants pointed with his finger only millimeters above the ground. "The ammo dump is under that netting where there are extra guards and anti-aircraft guns on the trucks."

"Which way are the troops moving? Are they coming or going, and in which primary direction?" Needle continued to quiz Pants.

Pants bobbed his head slowly, looking through a small bush as he took his notes. He had the urge to lean further over the edge to see what was below the cliff. As he automatically started to move forward, Needle grabbed and held his leg, squeezing it hard.

"Think what you are about to do!" Needle said firmly. "You are nearly invisible to those on the ground. If you move or break the line of the rocks you can be spotted. If you can be spotted, you can be shot or captured. *Never* expose yourself to the enemy. They have guards, and, believe me, they are looking for us, just as we are looking at them." Needle made sure that Pants was looking right at him when he said that. He finished the lesson with, "They also have planes high above that look for anything out of the ordinary around their camps. If a guard on the ground doesn't see you, it doesn't mean that a spotter in a plane can't. In a couple of seconds, a sniper could put an end to your life."

Pants absorbed the lesson, and quickly saw how easy it would be for him to be seen since he could see the camp so well. A high-powered scope on a rifle could kill him before he heard the sound of the shot. The thought sent a chill through him.

Needle patted him on the back and indicated that they should slide backwards, into the tree line, and get out of view as soon as possible. Once in the woods, Needle sat down with Pants and pulled out a map.

"Look at this map and find where we are." Pants turned and twisted the map a couple of times, focused on a couple of landmarks, and pointed to spot on the map.

"Right. Now use these coordinates to find where you have to go, and what are the problems about getting there." Needle watched as he gave Pants the coordinates and studied him as he figured out where he had to go.

Pants again pointed to a spot and said, "There are no direct roads, but there are open fields to travel without cover." Pants looked at Needle for a reaction that did not come. "There is also one spot that seems to have some deep water to cross that also might leave me in the open. Then I have to go about one kilometer more to the town."

Needle nodded and asked, "What are your options?"

Pants paused and moved his head side to side as he thought of his answer, "I could keep low and move slowly, or travel at night and use my compass and flashlight." Needle nodded and said, "Fine. Get to this point by tomorrow morning at 6:00 AM. There is a bakery that will be working when you get there. Go through the back door and tell the baker that you want some two-day-old bread, and could you have it for one Groz?" Pants was surprised but not too concerned, because he had walked that far in the dark before. If there was any moon at all, he would be fine. There would be a half moon after midnight. Needles patted Pants on the head, and pointed in the direction that needed to be traveled.

For the next couple of hours, Pants worked his way through the forest until he was sure he was alone. He found a good spot to bed down, and quickly fell asleep.

The evening was quiet and warm when he woke, and he was on his way in short order. In the morning, he made contact with the baker and gave the prearranged phrase. The baker, with only a slight hesitation, went over to a shelf, pulled down three loaves of bread, and placed them in a cloth-handled sack. One loaf was extremely hard and must have been a week old, while the others were softer and still smelled fresh. The baker did not miss what the smell did to Staszek. The look, and Staszek's lips moving, brought a small smile to his face. He said, "The stale loaf is a decoy. It has several small but obvious holes in it that could hide messages, or just be holes." The baker placed the loaves into a sack and handed the load to Pants. "If soldiers stop you and take the bread, protest a little but do not fight for the bread. The message is in the handle of the sack; that you have to keep. Carry the loaves and you can eat part of the fresh loaf, but not all of it. That's part of the decoy, too. Do you understand?" The baker watched as Pants looked back at him and nodded. "Good. Now return to your base and try not to get caught. You have until tomorrow night to get back to your contact." The baker paused a moment and said, "Wait." He pulled one more loaf of bread off the shelf, went into the back room, and brought out a ceramic cup of butter and gave them to Pants. "Here. This should help you for today and the next."

After giving a sincere thanks to the baker, Pants picked up the sack with the bread and swung it over his shoulder. As he started onto the road to Opoczno he stopped for a moment and put his flask of water and his cap in the sack. He studied, and then burned, the map he had. He knew the direction that he needed to go, and he did not want to be caught with it from this point onward. He had his compass around his neck, tucked inside his shirt for safety. Pants walked for several hours until the sun was becoming warm and the road well lit. He decided to leave the country road and cut into the woods to where there were a couple of farm houses he had seen on a previous trip in the area, hoping to rest there for the remainder of the day.

As he cleared the woods near the farms he could smell the odor of burned wet wood on the breeze. As the smell registered he saw the source of the smell. The farm was burned to the ground, with only the chimney and foundation where they should be; the rest of the house was collapsed into itself. The Germans had left a sign on the gate, which now guarded only charred rocks that read, "Traitors of the Third Reich." The sign seemed out of place, Pants thought, since the Germans always seemed to make their message clear. He could see the burned corpses of three people huddled near the door of the farmhouse. The family died together, trying to protect themselves from the flames that engulfed their home. The smell of burnt flesh in the air was distinctive to Pants, after having experienced it in Łódź. It was a smell of death that could not be forgotten, and it reinforced the memory that strengthened his resolve to be in the woods.

Pants walked back into the forest, unable to stay at this place of pain. He slipped into the woods, far off the trail, to get some sleep. He was exhausted and fell asleep quickly, but did not rest well, as visions of the burning hospital and the smell from it returned to him in his vivid dreams.

In late afternoon, he woke and made his way to the road while being careful not to be obvious in his walk cadence that was trying to break into a run. He wanted to get back to Opoczno quickly, but running would bring attention to him if spotted. He had about four hours of light left, and maybe another hour of twilight where he could move faster. He would move through patches of trees to cut down his time on the road, and in most cases allow for faster moving. That was true until just before dusk when he crested the last hill that went down the valley to Opoczno.

As he got to the edge of the tree line he came upon a large hay wagon that was apparently heading to Opoczno. It was empty after making a delivery somewhere in the area. Pants caught up with it, and walked down the gentle rolling slope alongside of the wagon, making small talk with the driver, who was a man of few words but lots of suspicion. After a half hour with the wagon the sound of the horse's hooves, the wheels, and chains of the wagon distracted Pants for a few moments as he looked down and away from the road towards the town in the distance. What he could not see was that around the bend of the road that traveled parallel to the trees and partially blocked by the wagon was a check point manned by several soldiers. At the last moment Pants looked back toward the curve, but it was too late.

"Halt!" came the lackluster order that was obviously one that had been repeated many times from the bored soldier who had his rifle slung over his back. The horse was pulled to a stop, and Pants froze at the front wheel on the side away from the soldier. Behind the first soldier walked a second who moved to the rear of the wagon on the opposite side, away from Pants, his rifle in a loosely ready position as he examined the empty wagon. Further down the road were two more soldiers searching a truck and its contents, while on the embankment of the hill a sergeant stood, overseeing the roadblock and looking at a notebook.

Pants felt his face turn red, and he clenched his teeth. *You idiot*, he thought, *the hounds caught you because you were not paying attention!* He scolded himself, and felt the rage building like it had two years ago at the Scout camp.

The soldier came to the man in the wagon and asked for his papers and where he was going. As the man answered to the satisfaction of the soldier, the attention went to Pants. "Where are your papers?" came the question from the bored private.

Pants pulled out his false ID folder that had a false name and age on it. A very good forgery, more than a boy would need, even if he were under suspicion for some reason.

"Where have you been and what were you doing there?" The soldier asked as he handed the ID card back to him.

Pants still fuming from the situation and angry over the murder of the farm family snapped, "Not from the farm where you murdered those people!"

His words startled the soldier as well as the driver of the wagon who tried to defuse the confrontation by saying "The boy is very tired and doesn't know what he's talking about." Turning to Pants he continued "Apologize to the private for saying those things that can't be true."

Pants stood without saying a word, just staring at the soldier, who could not have been older than twenty. He added, "Why don't you go back to Germany and leave us alone?" The defiance by Pants must have reminded the soldier of a younger brother who was getting on the older one's nerves. The private smirked at the comments then grew stern at the statement that earned Pants a slap to the head and had him grabbed by the collar followed by another slap across the head. Pants backed against the wagon's side pressing his sack against it while he covered his head. The commotion brought the sergeant to the wagon to see what the problem was. The soldier told him what Pants had said and at the end slapped Pants once more across the head for good measure.

The sergeant stood in front of the boy and crossed his arms on his chest and asked "So you don't want us here? Don't you know that we could punish you severely for saying that?"

He quickly regained his composure and answered, "You make it hard to find food and I had to walk all the way to the village up the road to buy bread for my boss. It's not right for you to just take over Poland. You should go back to your own country and leave us alone." Staszek's temper, sharp tongue and tendency for lashing out when angry, was certainly not doing him any favors at this risky moment.

The sergeant pulled Pants away from the wagon and looked into the sack to see the bread. He examined the loaves and squeezed each until he found the stale loaf. He put down the sack and broke open the hard crust to examine something that looked suspicious but found nothing, then dropped it into the sack while retrieving the other fresh loaf and handed it to the first soldier. The soldier had expected the sergeant to also slap the boy or at least give him a kick for his insolence, but he did not. After a minute of walking around the wagon and coming back to

Pants, the sergeant told him, "Get going, and you'd better think twice before showing disrespect to German soldiers in the future. The ending may be very different for you." Pants picked up the sack and started to walk beyond the horse and then he broke into a light trot down the road, knowing full well that he was lucky today, but still wanting to hit someone or something to release his rage.

As the boy walked away, Sergeant Rietmann, from Austria, wondered what would have happened if he had told the Germans who marched into his home back in Austria, to go back to their own country. He knew the answer to that question; it was simple. He would have been shot. As Rietmann watched the boy trotting away, he tried to figure out whether it was the boy's courage or stupidity to challenge a soldier, which saved his life just now. What if everyone in Austria had said that to the Germans? Would things be different now? He turned and walked away to light a cigarette. He would never know that answer.

Over the next several months, Pants, along with some "new" recruits, all Boy Scouts, learned the skills needed to help the Resistance Fighters. Among the tasks they participated in were searching areas where the Home Army had fought, and eventually surrendered. The goal was to find any weapons and munitions that were buried to hide them from the Germans during the collapse of the Polish Army. They would climb to the tops of trees, or local hills and cliffs, to observe German Army movements, reporting back numbers, types of troops and directions of travel. They would travel to specific locations to report their findings. Just as important were the distribution of flyers and bulletins that gave a truer scenario of what was happening in the war.

However, the Nazis banned the Polish Scout Association, and being a Scout was punishable by death. Yet boys and girls continued to find ways to fight back against the Germans and sought out the Scout organization to join. Of the new recruits in the camp where Pants fought were six more boy Scouts who were about the same age as Pants, and who, like him, had run away to avoid going to the German indoctrination camps.

Their positive experience with their home Scout troops lead them to accept their organization's name being changed from the Scouts to the "Szare Szeregi (Grey Ranks a.k.a. S.S). The Szare Szeregi initials had other significance to countering the propaganda by the Germans in that the German Nazi Party's political armed police was called the "Saal-Schutz" or "Assembly Hall-Protection" or "S.S.", later changed to Schutzstaffel (protection squadron) in the early 1930's. The Nazi S.S. was separate from the German Army, in that S.S. members swore their allegiance solely to Hitler and not to Germany itself.

The Grey Ranks deliberately used the German group's initials to confuse readers of newsletters that were sent out by the Grey Ranks. Propaganda that looked very much like a German newsletter or bulletins was labeled with the lightning bolt-type symbol of the Nazi S.S.. These publications were distributed to the public and were never questioned by the readers, for fear of being arrested or worse. The printing of misleading news bulletins by the Grey Ranks was a simple but effective way to interfere with the German operations; something the Grey Ranks would exploit throughout the war.

Over the weeks and months, teenage children gravitated to groups of their peers who felt the obligation to not passively let the invaders take over their lives and country. Even in a small town like Opoczno, boys of all ages were forming "Bee-hives" (to replace the old Scout troop), to resist tyranny, as well as to provide support and comfort to each other. They formed cells of five to seven boys, and met periodically as a "Swarm," the equivalent to the old Patrols, but were anonymous by name to the other cells and hives, because the leaders wanted to avoid the chance of compromising the others if one cell member was captured. Though in a war situation, they were still children, growing through puberty under the most challenging of circumstances. Strength from unity with their peers helped carry the burden of being away from their families and doing the jobs they were assigned for the good of all. At the same time, if they knew each other's true name, it could be deadly to all of them if one was caught and interrogated.

The Grey Ranks organization was simple; boys twelve to fourteen were code-named after "Zawisza Czarny" (Black Knight, Z.C.), a famous Polish medieval knight and statesman. This group did not take part in active resistance. Instead, they were prepared in secret schools for an eventual national uprising in the future. They took Polish history classes and language, in addition to basic organizational and leadership courses. To learn Scouting skills and Polish culture were the primary missions for these boys and girls.

"The Bojowe Szkoły" (The Battle Schools, B.S.), were troops

formed by youngsters of fifteen to seventeen years of age. This group not only worked on military and resistance activities, but normal education classes like literature, writing, and mathematics. Their classrooms were apartments, houses, or warehouses that were rotated frequently to avoid detection. When in the field, they took part in various actions of the so-called small sabotage and propaganda; tearing down Nazi flags, distributing underground newspapers and anti-German leaflets, painting graffiti, putting up anti-German placards on fences or walls, and turning signs around to confuse Germans traveling through an area. The Scouts often changed German signs with directions to Group Headquarters or field hospitals, or for the roads to adjacent towns, all to delay or frustrate the occupiers. They placed nails under the tires of staff cars and trucks, trying not to be caught while the vehicles were being guarded. Often their game was deadly. Things that in peacetime would have been called malicious mischief or vandalism, when focused against the occupiers, were acts of resistance against the National Socialist state that was being imposed upon them. The main difference between the activities then and now was that when caught, the boy would not be sent home to his parents for discipline, but the German who caught the Scout would shoot him on the spot.

The boys who were seventeen years old and up were called the "Grupy Szturmowe" (Assault Groups, G.S.) and were trained in secret Underground Schools. These graduates became officers in the Underground Army. Most G.S. members were also studying at the secret universities, to gain experience necessary to reconstruct Poland after the war. The G.S. groups took part in major sabotage, which included armed struggle against the occupiers and assassination of traitors. The group where a boy or girl was placed did not always care about the age of the child/young adult. If a job needed to be done and that young person had the best chance of succeeding, they would be chosen.

Pants and his young Battle School "Bees" had the assignment to be on the lookout for buried stashes of weapons and explosives that were still hidden in fields and farms around Opoczno. Unfortunately, many of the weapons had been buried quickly in retreat or before capture to keep it from being used by the Germans. The guns were usually placed in the soft damp soil with little protection against rust or rot. After eleven months, many of the weapons and much ammunition was not useable from the negative effects of the moisture. These weapons were taken apart and their components were used to repair other rifles as much as they could. The boys became very good at field-stripping and reassembling many types of arms. The boys on this detail had the added advantage of handling and shooting the weapons they recovered and repaired. They became efficient marksman with a wide variety of rifles and pistols. Several were severely injured when a damaged weapon exploded in their hands

Collecting arms for battle was very provocative, as the more aggressive Scouts also sought out German weapons that were found, and "liberated," when possible, from the Germans. Parked trucks, cars, and even poorly guarded barracks or armories found their weapons liberated by the Scouts.

Staszek was given the assignment to listen to the BBC radio's English broadcasts to find out what was happening on the Allies' side of events. Under German martial law in the occupied territories, radios that carried AM bands were allowed. However, if a person was found to have short wave or radio broadcast equipment, possession of any firearm, or clandestine newspapers, it meant an automatic death penalty. Sudden death was something that was understood and accepted by everyone as a risk in order to get from or to the Allies.

Staszek also listened to the fifteen-minute Polish language broadcast by the Germans and compared the two broadcasts. Night after night, Staszek would sit at a small table in the loft of Mr. Wach's shop and listen. Sadly, the news was not good, like when he heard and reported to Mr. Wach the calamity on the beaches of Dunkirk, and that France had surrendered to Germany. The meaning of those disasters was that the Germans were no longer distracted by threats from any continental armies. They had swept the Allies into the sea, and increased their efforts and control over Poland and countries to the north and south.

Only the islands of Britain stood alone against the Germans and total conquest of Europe, and as the British were fighting for their own lives, so the fighting was left to people like the ZWZ, Mr. Wach, boy Scouts and Girl Guides to turn the tide that was pouring over Europe towards the Russian border. Mr. Wach, on hearing the bad news, grimly nodded and said, "There will be more Germans to bother us now." After a pause, he shrugged and sighed, "As they and the Russians have done so many times in the past." He reached for the top of the ladder and slowly descended the old wooden rungs to the shop below. Once there he picked up a leg of an unfinished chair and rubbed it automatically but gently, deep in his own thoughts and fears. Staszek sat and looked down at the radio, hearing but not grasping the years it would take to reclaim his country from the invaders from the east and from the west. Until Poland could be liberated, Staszek, and those like him, had to contend with fighting back in any way they could each day. The only options were that the Germans had leave Polish soil or be buried in it. No other solution was acceptable.

Until either of those things happened, those who had the courage to fight back did what they could, distributing underground newspapers, changing signs, slashing tires, pouring water into fuel valves, or stuffing up chimneys to show those with power that what they had was in no way total. Like flies around a powerful bull, the Grey Rank saboteurs were things too small to see or fight, but their presence was distracting and frustrating. During the summer and fall of 1940, Pants and other Scouts were flies around the German bull, and became good at being annoying. With every sign change or flag torn down, they felt that they were fighting back, even if it meant that many of them would pay with their lives.

Staszek and the other boys in his hive, and those in hives all over the country, worked with intensity and passion in counter-propaganda by writing slogans on the walls to manifest the resistance against the Nazis. Their acts of courage built up hope in Polish people during these difficult times.

German signs were being changed back into Polish; while a new symbol began to appear. It was the sign of "POLAND FIGHTS" formed by the two letters P and W stacked on top of each other forming what looked like an anchor (a Kotwica) that became the symbol of hope and the sign of the underground resistance.

Writing on the walls was a very quick and direct way of communication and defiance. It caught a person by surprise, whether they wanted to see it or not. Everybody was a potential receiver of the counter-propaganda. People who may have been despondent over the war situation would find a spark in the sudden appearance of someone fighting back, even if it were words on a wall. Changing the letters in the name Hitler to "Hycler," which sounded like the Polish word for "dogcatcher," had Germans, and very often prisoners, cleaning the signs throughout the cities and towns. One of the most satisfying stunts for Staszek was taking down the signs at the doors of theaters or stores that read, "For Germans ONLY," and placing them at the top of lamp poles where the Germans had previously murdered civilians by hanging them over the city streets.

Many days at a time, Staszek would cross the countryside to fulfill an assignment that required getting to different headquarters or rendezvous points in a timely manner. His travel soon became as automatic as Mr. Wach sanding a chair leg. Being a messenger was his job to do for the cause and he did it well.

Staszek often would awake on the forest's floor and find himself in a different world. His blanket could mute the cool of the night and morning dew, and the hard ground could be smoothed out with vegetation, but it was the loneliness that he could not completely eliminate from his being. He enjoyed the smell of the woods, and the peace and quiet there, but there was no one to share it with. He was motivated to get to his next contact quickly just to see and to talk to someone. The many trips were often boring, but being alone helped heightened awareness of the danger in the area and kept him focused, whereas the presence of another person would have been distracting. He did not wish to be careless again and get caught by the German "hounds." And so he travelled alone, taking the safe routes on foot, bike, or horseback, or hitching a ride with trucks or wagons. More commonly, he ran for periods of time between the tall Pole Pines, and then paused briefly to look and listen for anything out of the ordinary. When approaching a German camp or a town, he was always on the lookout for soldiers, and especially the dogs, when they started to bark to warn their handlers. Climbing to the top of a tree to see what was in front or behind him was part of his routine.

The views of the rolling hills and fields were unbelievably beautiful, while at the same time dangerous. The area was so much different than the speed and intensity of a city like Łódź. He was amidst an old forest, with tall trees of pines, spruce, birch, oaks, and silver firs. Clean, intoxicating air, lush green foliage, blue skies and the silence only broken by the song or caw of a bird during the day while a star-lit canopy of the sky filtered through the trees at night that could easily lull him into a false sense of safety. He walked on a carpet woven of mosses, grasses, herbs, and wildflowers, all for his exclusive enjoyment. Snacking on fresh berries, mushrooms, wild potatoes, dill, greens, and apples were the bonuses he got during this time of year. He did carry a slingshot and became good with it. On these trips that skill was very useful. Whether with the slingshot or using a snare for birds or rabbits he added to his diet and continued his work. He did try eating bugs and grubs as part of Scouting once, but so far he had never been that hungry.

Then there were the times when things literally just did not smell right. Reaching a village deep in the forest, Pants would find mass destruction where bombings from planes or artillery shells had wiped out large sections of the forest or a village. The ground and any type of buildings would be scorched and pockmarked. The smell, or rather the stench, of burned buildings, and sadly many people, lingered for many days or weeks; a smell that had fogged the air of Poland since the start of the war. Coming upon them riding his horse through these islands of carnage nestled in the forest was surrealistic in the eerily quiet way. They existed in the center of the otherwise beautiful countryside, and then were left behind. The automatic need and ability to forget these places of sadness once Pants reentered the woods on the other side became a defense mechanism for his emotions. The village was nearly forgotten at that moment he reached the undamaged woods. The only memory that lasted was the smell; the God-awful smell that would live forever in his nostrils rode on with him as a weight he could not avoid.

Upon reaching a sleeping village before dawn, Staszek, would often silently draw water from a well in order not to wake the owners. At times, instead of water he would make friends with a cow and draw a bottle or flask of milk. It was very tasty, and when straight from the cow in the mornings, gave him some warmth as well. The villagers or farmers would give him the milk and bread, with lard or bacon when they knew he was there. They were generous to him, because they knew what his purpose was in visiting. More often than not, Pants would walk many kilometers, and sometimes days, on an empty stomach, where the noise from the cavern of his gut easily got his attention, but he learned to ignore those nagging sensation. On occasion, he would have to liberate food from a storage shed or barn, but he usually asked for items, knowing that he did not wish to alienate any of the people of the fields or the high valleys.

Pants was like a ghost going from place to place, leaving little sign of his presence that would bring attention to him. He would successfully delivery crucial materials to those who were bigger, stronger, and had weapons to fight the Germans. His skill and importance grew, and the resistance groups he traveled for recognized him as being trustworthy and skilled.

Pants would leave on assignments that took him fifteen to twenty kilometers or more, and then, after its completion, make a quick trip back with a new order or response. All together, he'd travel thirty to forty kilometers on foot, or one hundred and more if on horse, with his backpack and blanket. The places where he had to go on foot, he would often run for kilometers at a time when the terrain and cover allowed. At times during these assignments, he would literally run into farmers with their wagons, or a German car or motorcycle. On a rare occasion, a girl would be walking on the forest road. On those unique meetings, he wanted so much to chat, to flirt, but knew that any lapse in caution could be his last mistake, so he would get off the road and away from its occupants as quickly as possible.

When he encountered German cars or young women on the road, he would duck into the brush and watch them go by. In each situation his heart rate would go up, but for different reasons. After all, he was becoming a young man. His life for the next several months centered on getting from one place to another without being detected. These potentially deadly games of hide and seek honed his skills and abilities while doing a strategically important job for the resistance, which he did for the remainder of the fall and into the winter. It was only then that he was allowed to go home while carrying out one of his assignments.

Late one afternoon, three days before Christmas, Pants was in Łódź and carried a heavy package wrapped in white paper, with a big green ribbon around it. It was decorated with a sprig of holly with its traditional red berries sitting proudly on top. In the parcel were the master copies of the news information bulletin and copies for distribution. He, with a partner, got on a streetcar and headed for a drop point for his "Christmas gift." Pants sat across from a middle-aged woman, while his partner stood near the door at the back of the coach blending in with the adults around him.

The woman opposite him stared at Pants for a minute, then said, with a smile, "Aren't you Staszek, the boy from the shop near the train station?" She looked at him closely and smiled. "Yes, I used to buy candy and a newspaper from you and your father when I worked in that part of town." Her smiled softened as she remembered those days. Pants instantly went on alert; he was to blend in with other people who were also carrying gifts and who were hurrying home during the light snowfall. He should not have been identified nor had any attention brought to him; this was not good. He stared with an awkward smile and answered, "No, I didn't work over there," trying to keep any emotion out of his voice.

The woman was about to insist that she was sure about him, but stopped in mid-thought, realizing that this was no longer the happier days, and she should not be bringing attention to the boy, nor especially attention to herself. "Forgive me, I see that I am wrong," was all she said, and looked blankly to the floor, and then out the window behind Pants.

Pants tried to look indifferent to the woman by also glancing out the windows, trying to be calm by watching the snow that fell gently to the street. He noticed that there were a few other people who looked at him for a moment, and was sure that all of them were able to recognize him as someone who did not belong there. As the car began to slow for the next stop a man in a long black coat who had been standing several seats away, fixed his eyes on Pants and his gift and started to move towards him. Pants picked up his package and stepped into the stair well at the back door. This was not where he wanted to be, but he knew he must get off the streetcar now.

The doors began to open as the man caught up to Pants and touched his shoulder saying, "Halt. Gestapo." The words froze Pants for the moment as they did to everyone around him. The other people instinctively leaned or stepped back from the stair well to not get involved with the arrest that was surely about to happen.

Not looking back at the man, Pants stopped as ordered. As he did so, he felt the hand on his shoulder loosen slightly and that was all Pants needed. Like the soccer player that he was, Pants twisted to his left breaking contact with the man and leaped from the step of the car with the man jumping off right behind him. Unnoticed by the man was another boy pushing through the arms of the passengers, and he too jumped from the car step. Pants ran around the back of the streetcar in a tight right circle, his package under his right arm. As he was about to turn, he passed the car and crossed to the sidewalk. He dropped his package and accelerated away, with the man still in pursuit. Without the package he was able to nimbly maneuver through and around the crowd and obstacles that he used to deter his pursuer. The Gestapo agent, being bigger and stronger shortened the distance by physically pushing people aside or knocking them over.

Around one corner, Pants darted down an alleyway just three meters ahead of the man who slipped on the slick snow and ice on the corner. At the far end of the high-walled alley were two horses tied to a rail fence; their delivery wagon blocked the exit to the busy main street beyond. Pants heard the breathing of the man behind him becoming labored with the cold air and long run. As Pants saw the alley blocked, the Gestapo also spotted what looked like a cork in the bottle and slowed ever so slightly, thinking he had the boy trapped. Without breaking his stride, Pants ran headlong towards the wagon and with perfect timing dropped down on his side and slid under the wagon, scattering snow and slush everywhere. With his momentum carrying him beyond the wagon he popped out to the other side where he was able to quickly get onto his feet. As he looked over his shoulder he could see the Gestapo bending down to look under the wagon. In that brief moment Pants was around the corner and had hopped on to the running board of a truck moving down the street. Pants looked back towards the alley, and the Gestapo was not to be seen. He looked at the driver who had opened his window with suspicion. Pants looked at him and said, "Sorry, I won't be here long." The driver smirked and reached down on the seat next to him and picked up an apple then handed it to Pants through the window. Pants smiled and put it into his mouth where he held it with his teeth. One block later he nodded thanks and jumped off the running board, hitting the ground running, and in ten steps disappeared into a long alley between two buildings.

Leaning back against the wall, he rested while his breathing slowed. He looked cautiously up and down the street and was thankful to find nothing that alarmed him. He bit the apple again and savored the flavor and the success of getting away from the Gestapo. He did not feel frightened, but rather exhilarated by the "game." *"The Fox won this one"* he whispered under his breath still scanning the street for trouble.

Earlier, as Pants had headed for the alleyway, his partner picked up the package and ran in the opposite direction. He too disappeared into a crowd at the corner and quickly slipped into another alley where he watched to see if he was followed. Finding nothing threatening, he continued on to the drop point, hoping that Pants was safe. Together they had delivered their assignment as planned. The teams had again proven their worth and skill, as well as their luck, this time.

One day later, Staszek went by the restaurant where Basia worked, and when the time was right he slipped in the back door to talk to her and hopefully get some food. Basia quickly found leftovers for Staszek that were a wonderful feast. Basia introduced him to Jan Szymański, her boss who provided a place to eat the meal. Staszek did not realize how much he missed seeing his family, and Basia. The visit made him want to come home, even if it was for only a short while.

So, on Christmas Eve he took a chance and defied his orders and went to the family apartment. At the bottom of the stairs he stared at the door at the top and wondered if he should go up. The feeling of his home began to overwhelm him to the point he could not help himself, and he slowly ascended the stairs, pausing for a moment before knocking on the inside door.

Fela cautiously opened the door in the dim light to see who would be there at this time of night. When she recognized the face outside the door, she could not help but let out a scream to the rest of the family, "Stasiu is here!" His mother, who was not normally an animated or affectionate person, hurried to the door with her arms open to embrace her youngest son. She touched his arms and then his face. Her hands, still soft and warm, made Staszek's eyes well up with tears of joy and sadness. Helena stepped back, looking her son up and down, and said, "You have grown taller and thinner." Both were true.

Zdzislaw and Basia soon joined the welcome and brought their prodigal brother into the warmth of the room that was missing many pieces of furniture that had been sold for money or food. The windows were boarded up, except for the one where Helena liked to sit, a remnant of the beginning of the war. There was bread, soup, and some fish for the Christmas Eve meal. The three large candles on the table near the fireplace lit the simple barren room, yet it could not have been a better Christmas for the Niklewiczs.

Staszek could not tell the family where he had been or what he had done, but in an effort to please and satisfy their curiosity he left many false hints, like getting as far away from the Germans by going south and that he hiked a lot near Katowice.

He said Katowice since it was south of where he knew he would be, and therefore he assumed that saying it, was not harmful to anyone.

The family talked about the problems in Łódź since the Germans had taken over. He heard about the terrible things that were happening in the Ghetto, and how the Germans had taken control of all the facilities in the town. The factories were all busy, many twenty-four hours a day, making uniforms and other war materials for the Germans.

The news was less than hopeful, and no one could see an end of the occupation coming soon. The rules of living were getting harder each week, and round-ups were almost a daily occurrence.

They talked late into the night, and Staszek said that he would like to sleep in his bed before he left in the morning at the end of curfew. He was in his own bed for the first time in over nine months, and dreamed stressfully for the hours that he slept. Dreams of his family being arrested and interrogated, and being burned to death in the apartment, like the farmers. The visions awoke Staszek early in the morning, in a sweat; something that being in the forests did not produce. He felt it was a sign that he had to get away before something bad would happen to the family. He slowly got up and slipped out of the apartment to head back to the safe house across town. He reached it about the same time as old Mrs. Von Rupp, who lived across the street from the Niklewiczs, opened her blinds slightly to watch the morning go by.

In the morning Helena looked into Staszek's room hoping to find him still asleep but found that he had left. Looking at the empty bed made her sad that she did not say goodbye one more time before he left. She pulled on the bedspread to make it taut and felt lonely even as Zdzislaw snored a few feet away. She tried to think a little more positively on this Holy Day because she did see him briefly, and it was Christmas, which made the visit more like a gift to her. She dressed herself, and when curfew was lifted she went to the cathedral in the center of Łódź for Christmas Mass. She arrived early in order to light candles for Staszek and say a prayer for him. She was not alone on this holy day with many families in the same situation and as stressed as she. Helena went to confession to clear her conscience and soul of her offenses against God, and to ask the priest to say a prayer for her son, who went far away from the Germans and Łódź and was living in the woods. Though she was in the home of God, God was not the only one there today who was able to hear her sins and requests for prayers. Closer than Helena could imagine, a name and small details were being scratched onto a small piece of paper and carefully folded and placed in a small pocket.

By the following day, in a window across from the Niklewicz apartment, an elderly ethnic German woman now had developed more interest in the activities that happened on the street in front of her home. A Gestapo agent, in exchange for her noticing and then reporting, unusual occurrences at the Niklewicz apartment had given Mrs. Von

Rupp 10 Reichmarks and extra food coupons. She would be paid more if it involved the coming or going of the youngest son, Stanislaw. She said that she had not seen him in some time but did know him and would report his presence immediately to the agent. A description given by another agent from across town seemed to match demographics of this boy who had disappeared earlier this year and the agent was following all leads he had. Mrs. Von Rupp would be pleased to help the Fatherland, and would appreciate the coupons. She told the agent that she would be pleased to help the cause of reclaiming the land that was taken from Germany 25 years ago back to those who rightfully should have it. She did not say that the 10 Reichmarks were important too, but the agent already knew that.

Author's Notes: Chapter 11

During the years 1939-1941, the main efforts of the ZWZ were directed towards organizational work, preparing for later military action. During this period a large number of the independent military groups, which had sprung up after September 1939, were incorporated into ZWZ. At the same time, ZWZ was fighting the occupiers on three fronts: propaganda, reconnaissance, and sabotage.

Informational and propaganda activity consisted of printing secret bulletins, periodicals and news-sheets which were widely distributed among the population. In addition to the publications of ZWZ and the Delegatura, political parties and various ad-hoc groups were also distributing secret literature.

Chapter 12
April 15th, 1941: Konskie, Poland

ON THIS DAY, sixteen year old Pants was assigned to go twenty kilometers to a ridge near Konskie, where German troops were reportedly camped and rearming. He was to collect information about the numbers and types of troops and vehicles located there, and whether more troops were coming in by railroad. In addition, he was to take and show the area and the field procedures to a new member from the cell. The new member had been a Scout and needed to become familiar with the observation and reporting techniques that Needle had taught Pants.

This assignment gave Pants mixed feelings, because he wasn't sure he wanted to have anyone with him, while at the same time knowing that this was a sign that the commander trusted him, and was giving him a chance to be responsible for training and leadership.

He agreed to take the assignment, knowing that if he had turned it down, the decision would have been looked upon poorly. He was to leave in the late afternoon, travel through the night, and be at the ridge before dawn. A hard walk when alone, and taking a new person with him would slow him down, but there was no other way to get there quickly. There was going to be a half moon that would make travel easier, as there would be enough reflection from the snow to see his path, but also more risky because he could be seen, just as easily as were the paths. Traveling on the better roads was an option but they were partially covered by trees, while in other areas he would be exposed. He had traveled this route before, and was sure he could make it this time. He even found a couple of dens under some fallen logs where he was able to sleep when tired. To help camouflage him, he would tie a small white sheet to his backpack that could be used to help hide him among the large rocks on the ridge above the junction.

The jumping off point for the assignment was Mr. Wach's house, and Pants arrived with his pack and put some supplies into it that were in the back room. In a short time, Mr. Wach would introduce Pants to "Mouse." Mr. Wach told Pants, "Mouse has gone through much the same training as you did with Needle. He's young, but has not been on a reconnaissance trip before. He's worked only in the graffiti and pamphlet duties until now, but has done well on the long hikes, using map and compass. Pants, you are to teach him how to get close, observe, and return with the information tomorrow evening. Do you understand the assignment?" Pants nodded.

Several minutes later Pants had began to feel nervous and slightly anxious, wanting to get going. The doorknob slowly opened, and Needle came in and introduced Mouse to Pants. Pants was stunned, then delighted, then quickly composed, as he looked into the face of Artur, the young Scout from two years ago. Artur had grown taller and was not as round as Pants remembered, but they grinned to see each other. The obvious recognition did not please Needle or Mr. Wach, but the assignment needed to be done and they could not change it at this late time. They sat down at the table and reviewed the plan for the assignment once more. After acknowledging the details, the boys went for their coats and packs, and with some trepidation the two Scouts were sent out to do their jobs.

"Do you think they will have any problems out there?" Mr. Wach asked Needle.

"I don't think so," Needle answered, after a moment. "I think they will be all right." When he stood up, he did not have all the confidence he should have had. *Damn,* went through his mind, briefly. If the boys were too familiar with each other, that might take the edge off of their caution and vigilance, which could be dangerous for everyone. Needle weighed the options and let the decision stand.

For most of the night, the two Scouts walked quietly and carefully through the forest or on the roads, as they felt they could. They were making good time, with no traffic on the roads. When a vehicle was coming, the night allowed enough warning for them to get off the road and avoid any contact.

The couple of times they stopped to rest and snack, Mouse wanted to talk about when they were on campouts before the war started, but became sullen when he talked about the invasion. Mouse told Pants, "My parents are gone and my grandmother is the only family I have left. I don't know how long she'll last in the Ghetto. My mother was killed during the bombing of Łódź, and the Germans took father away during a sweep through the Ghetto. He was arrested as a political prisoner and shipped to Russia." He paused and tears welled up in his eyes as he continued, "Dozens of friends and neighbors of mine are dead. All the people I knew since I was a baby are gone. I will not forget them."

Mouse was as angry and frustrated as Pants, and looked forward to helping the cause fight against the occupiers, but a little more so. The difference was that Mouse was emotionally wrapped up in his anger much like Pants had been for such a long time. At this moment, it was the business of war, and there was a time to seek and take your revenge, but this was not the time for either of them.

"I can't wait to be able to shoot 100 of those Hitlerites for every one of my family and friends that are now dead," Mouse stated, with obvious malice in his voice.

"I know the feeling, and I want to do the same, but the mission is the most important thing right now. If we can help track the German movements, the ZWZ will take care of them for us. Stay focused on the mission," Pants demanded of Mouse.

"I will, but when I have the chance, I'm going to get even." Mouse said resolutely.

The answer did not ease Pants' concerns very much. He did not want Mouse to be foolish at the cost of their lives. He needed to be focused on the job at hand. Killing Germans beyond the mission is always on a soldier's, or even a courier's, mind. Being impatient had caused Pants problems before, and he was adamant about preventing a disaster in the future.

Before dawn, they reached the lookout point. Wearing the white sheets as covers over them, they crawled slowly to their vantage point. This place was only seven meters above the road. It was on the inside of a curve that naturally had drivers and walkers watching the outside edge that fell away even further to the meadow, thereby helping to keep the observers hidden, yet giving them a panoramic view of the activity below. The boys worked as a good team for the entire day collecting vital pieces of information for the report to Needle.

The most striking of all was that since Pants's last trip to this point, there had been a dramatic increase in the supplies in the ammo dump as well as the number of trucks and tanks at the camp. There was also a lot of new construction that seemed to be enlarging the grounds and increasing quarters for the soldiers. To Pants, these changes to the grounds meant that they were expecting more soldiers, and something big was going to happen. This was unusual, and needed to be reported to Needle. After collecting the information and writing it on a small piece of paper the details were rolled into a tight tube and slid into the brim of Pants's hat. They retreated into the woods, and moved several kilometers from the observation point to wait out the afternoon before beginning the long hike back to Opoczno. They needed to get some sleep, but they did not want to be near patrols that protected the camp, so moving a safe distance was prudent.

They decided that Pants would take a couple of hours of sleep while Mouse acted as guard, and then they would trade positions, assuring each other of safety and rest prior to their trip that night. They agreed to get two hours each before being awakened. Pants made a small nest under a bush and quickly fell asleep; a sleep that was very welcomed and badly needed.

Mouse sat and poked around the trees and rocks in the area to keep himself entertained. Though far from where they observed the camp, they were not far from a road that they would travel later that evening. During his exploring, Mouse came across a strange looking mound that looked very out of place in the debris of the forest floor. Pulling on a medium sized branch from the pile he felt and heard a metal sound beneath the ground made by the motion of the tree limb. He dug into the cold loose soil and found a metal box painted dark green, and an oilcloth wrapped around what looked like a cylinder. Upon opening it, he found several rifles rolled tightly together, and in the metal box he found two pistols. One was a Swiss 1882 Schmidt revolver with four loaded chambers and the other was a Czech CZ-38 semiautomatic pistol with one magazine of ammunition.

The rifles were badly rusted, with the bolts almost impossible to move. The pistols, though also slightly rusty, had their mechanisms workable. Mouse had not worked a semiautomatic pistol, but was familiar with a revolver. He opened the revolver and removed the bullets, which had some moisture marks on them, but were easy to remove and replace. The empty cylinder spun stiffly, but it appeared to work adequately after he pulled the trigger several time. He handled it with curiosity moving it from hand to hand checking it for balance and aiming it at objects to see how it handled. Dry firing the gun without the bullets and discovering that it still worked well made Mouse almost giddy about his find. He wanted to awaken Pants, but thought there would be time when his time sleeping ended. For the next half hour Mouse cocked and aimed the revolver many times until he could almost do it with one hand. He wiped the gun down with his handkerchief several times, and practiced drawing it out of his belt and aiming it. With each effort, he became more confident that he could use the weapon as intended. Now he had a way to kill Germans, and passionate revenge started to brew in his gut.

At the designated time, Mouse awoke Pants with a mild shake. Pants responded and turned over opening his eyes without making any sudden moves. In a few moments he was awake and looked at his watch and then the surrounding area. As he scanned the area his eyes came back to Mouse, who had a look on his face like that of someone who had eaten the last piece of candy in the store and wanted to brag about it. "What?" Pants queried. "What did you do that makes you smile like that?"

Mouse opened his coat to reveal the revolver in his belt then pointed to the cloth with the rifles and pistol on it. Pants quickly got up and knelt down next to the weapons and asked, "Where did you get these?" He touched each rifle to determine their condition.

"Buried over there," Mouse pointed, as he answered. "I found them when I turned over a pile of sticks." He moved over several meters and pointed to the area with a piece of stick. "They look old and don't seem to work very well, except for the pistols."

Pants looked at the rifles and quickly determined that if they were lucky they might get enough parts from all of them to get one that might work correctly. He picked up the semiautomatic, ejected the magazine, then pulled back the slide and looked into the chamber. Examining the bullets and magazine he pushed them into the handle and released the slide. "This works pretty good, for being in the ground so long." He looked at Mouse and then the rifles. "We have to bury the rifles. They won't do us any good, especially if we tried to carry them back to Opoczno." Pants did not want to leave the rifles just on principle, but had no choice. "The pistols are a problem," he told Mouse. If the Germans catch us, they will torture and then kill us to find out why we have them and where we got them.

"We just tell them the truth; we found them," Mouse rationalized.

"Great. They will torture and then kill us, but they'll appreciate that we are honest." Pants answered sarcastically. "We should leave them here and come back for them at a different time. The mission is the most important thing and we should not risk us not getting through with the information."

Mouse argued, "With the guns, if we were discovered, we may be able to get away so we can bring in the information." He watched Pants mull over the logic. "Without them, if we're captured, we have no options at all. I think we keep the guns."

Pants agreed with Mouse after a minute of weighing the options. "Okay, let's travel the rest of the night, like we planned, and we should not be in a position to get caught. We'll be back by early morning."

Mouse nodded.

They rolled up the rifles and replaced them as they were before. Quickly, they headed for the tree line at the edge of the road, where they walked until it was dark enough to walk on the road.

Throughout the night, Mouse would reach into his coat and grasp the handle of his revolver every time he thought he heard something. Pants had his deep in his jacket pocket. The feel of the metal weighing down his coat gave him confidence, yet here was a greater fear knowing that he would not be able to talk himself out of trouble if it was found in his coat. On the other hand, the thought of getting rid of a weapon that you have in your possession was unthinkable to him, so in his pocket it stayed.

Just before dawn, Pants told Mouse that there was a farm that was friendly to him, and they could get some milk from the farmer. The promise of warm fresh milk made both of the boys walk a little faster. The sun was just starting to shine through the trees at the far edge of the pasture when the boys arrived at the farm. As they approached the house they could see that the door was open and an unusually bright light was coming from the inside along with unusually large amounts of smoke up the chimney. Mouse looked at Pants, puzzled, but Pants felt that he had seen this before as he made out the shape of a person half sitting in a twisted manner at the doorway. *They killed him and the house is burning,* ran through his mind, reminiscent of the way the Germans tried those who stood up against them. In the distance, Pants heard voices talking in German coming from the barn near the house. "This is a fat one; it will make a good breakfast." A laugh followed from a second voice further back in the barn.

Pants pointed to the door and whispered to Mouse, "There are Germans in the barn. They killed the farmer."

Mouse's eyes grew big as he clenched his teeth looking at the man slumped on the porch, and he could imagine his father in the slumped shape. His brow furrowed, as the rage boiled inside of him, all his attention focused on the voices coming from the barn. His course of action instantly became clear to him as he pivoted and reached into his coat and pulled out the pistol, cocking the hammer with his opposite hand. Simultaneously, he quickly strode heavily and deliberately towards the barn with his arm extending to full length in the direction of the voices.

Pants, seeing what Mouse was doing, jumped up and grabbed his arm, pulling him in the direction of safety of the smoke house near the side of the barn. There was no time to wait, they had to get behind the protection and cover before the soldiers came out. Mouse stubbornly resisted being pulled, jerking his arm back which broke away from Pants grip. Still staring at the barn doors, Mouse moved forward without any effort to conceal himself, his weapon in front of him. He was possessed by what was boiling inside of him, determined to get his revenge now.

The first German came out of the barn with a big grin on his face as he held two chickens in his hands plus a block of cheese cradled in the bend of his left elbow. Upon seeing the boy and the pistol aimed at him, he dropped the chickens and cheese as he tried to swing his rifle strap off of his back. The effort was futile as Mouse moved even closer and fired his pistol twice at almost point blank range. He jerked the first shot, hitting the soldier's leg, which fractured the bone and produced a scream. The cry lasted only a brief moment as the second was fired straight into the chest of the German from only a meter away. The impact drove him back towards the barn where he fell dead.

As Mouse reached the body of the first soldier the second came out with his rifle drawn looking to see where the shots had come from. As he came out the door Mouse turned the pistol at him and pulled the trigger. The expected explosion did not happen, the gun misfired, with both Mouse and the soldier stopped for a split second in surprise. The surprised did not last as long for the soldier as it did for Mouse. As Mouse attempted to pull back the hammer to fire again the German quickly raised his rifle and aimed it demanding that Mouse "Halt!" to no avail. Mouse was determined to follow through with his goal. He stared intensely defiant at the man with the rifle and clearly reached across his body with his opposite hand to help cock the hammer in order to fire it again. In that instant Pants knew that the soldier would not wait for Mouse to finish the motion. Pants leapt forward from his hiding place aiming his pistol and squeezing the trigger as he bounded forward, aiming small at the center of the side of the soldier's chest. He fired his gun nearly at the same moment the German fired his. Both bullets found their mark. The man and boy both fell to the ground, neither moving.

Pants ran to Mouse's side and lifted his head to hold him. The hole in his chest was flowing with blood soaking completely through his clothes and coat. As Pants looked down at his friend, Mouse opened his eyes briefly, smiled at Pants, and tried to say something but choked and coughed. He paused and tried again, "Don't leave me." He whispered as he struggled for his breath.

In the distance Pants could hear a vehicle coming and he would soon be discovered. "Please stay." Mouse added, but the choice was not a choice for Pants who had to leave now, he could see Mouse would not survive much longer but he did not want to abandon him. Pants leaned over him trying to comfort Mouse but could not think of anything to say.

Pants then made his decision and said, "I am sorry, but I have to go now." As he lowered the head of his friend gently to the ground, guilt gripped his heart. Pants looked up and the light of the sunshine now overpowered the firelight coming from the house. The sun's life-giving rays shone on the death that littered the ground.

Pants gathered his senses while he looked at his friend for the last time. He knew that he had to get away quickly, for the soldiers did not work alone, and once found; the others would search for those who had killed their comrades. Pants leaned back onto his heels as he looked at his friend who still labored to breath.

From the corner of his eye he saw movement and turned to see the soldier that he had shot start to roll onto his right side as he tried to reach for his rifle. In an instant, Pants reached for his pistol and aimed it at the man. Pants did not pull the trigger he just held his aim. He did not shake at this moment, but held his composure. His aim would be true if he pulled the trigger but he waited for the soldier to grasp his weapon. Unable to reach it, the man dropped back to the ground producing his last breath that was long and moist. Pants lowered his gun and placed it on the ground next to Mouse hoping whoever found the death scene would assume that all the players were still there.

Briefly, in guilt, Pants thought that he should stay and wait to bury his friend, but there was no time as the truck was coming closer and he had to finish his mission. With all his senses on alert and his heart sunk low, he got up and retraced his steps back to the shelter of the trees. Once there he began to trot through the woods while holding back his tears for the tragedy that had just been played out. He had to get as much distance between himself and the farm as quickly as possible. Beyond this patch of trees was the road that would eventually take him to safety, but a road he would be going on alone while Artur joined his family and friends in a better place.

When Pants returned to Mr. Wach's shop, he climbed into the loft where his bed was placed. He dropped his pack and coat before climbing back down and sitting at the table in the adjacent room. He put his head down onto his crossed arms in fatigue. The events of the last two days seemed unreal to Pants, as the facts flipped through his memory. Several minutes later, Mr. Wach walked in and sat down at the end of the table and looked at the very tired boy. Touching him on the arm he asked, "Where's Mouse?"

After a long pause Pants lifted his head to reveal tear tracks streaming down his face, leaving clean streaks through the dirt on his face. Mr. Wach immediately knew that there was a problem and waited for Pants to debrief him.

At the end of the detailed message and synopsis of the farm battle, Mr. Wach stood and headed out of the house to pass on the information supplied by Pants and Mouse. As he passed Pants, he gently squeezed his shoulder and slowly stroked his head before leaving the house. Pants wished he were home with his family.

Later in the morning, Needle came to continue the debriefing about the intelligence that was collected. He saw Pants in the workshop and called him into the house, where they sat at the table. Needle placed a bundle of clothing on the floor then sat down. He interlocked his fingers on the table and stared at them for a while, his face reflected the man's effort to gets his thoughts together before he spoke, lifting his eyes up as he leaned back into the chair he asked, "What was the mission?"

Pants looked slightly confused, but answered the question, "Reconnaissance of the German camp for changes in troop numbers, activity, reinforcement preparation, and increased equipment concentration and types. Then report to you as soon as possible."

Needle nodded to all the parameters stated, and continued, "Were you successful in accomplishing your mission?"

Pants nodded, then interjected, "But I got Artur, I mean Mouse, killed." His voice was low and demoralized.

"No, Mouse was killed in the line of duty. He made a decision to act based on emotions that he had not dealt with from his internment in the Ghetto. That cost him his life. He could have cost you your life, too." Needle looked at Pants to see if that made an impression on the boy. He continued, "Whether or not having guns made a difference, we will never know. From your report, they very well could have saved you from being captured. As for Mouse's death, that's as much my fault as anyone else's. I should not have let him go with you if he wasn't totally ready, but to the bigger point, you did your mission successfully and the information was very valuable to us. You'll see, someday soon, how it made a difference."

Needle's analysis got through to Pants, and he saw the difference in perspective. He said, "Thanks, it happened so fast! What could I have done to save Mouse?"

"Only God knows that answer. If you want, I can get you to Father Bird and you can talk to him," Needles offered, as a closing.

Pants said, "I'll think about it. Thanks again."

Needle changed subject and asked, "Are you ready for a bigger assignment?"

The question surprised Pants. He nodded, automatically hoping anything would help to get his mind off of Artur.

"Good," Needle agreed. "With your report and those of other couriers, it's clear that the Germans are ready to start something big. They seem to be moving their troops further east. We need more information, and on a regular basis, throughout the region, channeled to us." Needle watched Pants begin to focus on the new task and lean forward. "We want you to be part of the circuit riders that will gather information from other reconnaissance teams and get them to us frequently. You will primarily go through the valleys and villages by horseback, avoiding contact with the Germans whenever possible while you transport communiqués. You will go to drop-off points, where the loyal farmers and shopkeepers will hand off their information to you, and you'll carry them to your assigned contact or drop-off place. Can you do that?"

The news that he had helped find something big that was going to happen piqued his interest, and he answered with an enthusiastic, "Yes I can!" to the assignment.

"All right then; here's what you'll be doing." Needle pulled out a hand-drawn map with coordinates labeled on key places. "Each of these coordinates indicates a contact place, and the location of the actual drop are on the line below the numbers. An earlier team has gone out and identified and confirmed that the numbers and information is correct." He gave the map to Pants to examine and become familiar with the directions. Needle continued, "You will carry this for your first trip, but if you suspect you are being followed or may be captured, you must destroy this, even if you have to eat it. Is that clear?"

Pants nodded briskly.

"If this map is found, dozens if not hundreds, of peoples lives will be at risk, and probably lost. After the first trip you will burn the map. It must be destroyed, and you must know exactly where and what you are to go and do."

That added the gravity and importance to the mission, and brought Pants back to his full attention and passionate commitment.

"You'll be at the far end of a long corridor, following train tracks and roads in a predetermined area. You will scout your area, and return, gathering your information to be brought here. Then you'll repeat the route towards Radom. You will be briefed once more before you leave."

Needle ended with, "You will begin on the 1st of May. Mr. Wach will help you get your supplies and kit together, as well as you getting to know your horse. He will give you your new identity papers and cover story. You will be transferred to another operations center closer to Radom. Get cleaned up and rested. You will have very little chance of either in the coming months."

Pants was stunned to find that he was being moved, and digested the instructions. Needle reached down and picked up the bundle he was carrying and placed it on the table. "Here's some clothing for you that will help you with the cold, as well as riding."

Pants opened the rope that tied the bundle together; to find a heavier sweater and wool riding britches that had a cavalry type flare and leather insert that protected skin from chaffing on the saddle. Pants examined the clothes and smiled at the wonderful items that were much better than the two or three pairs of pants he had to wear at one time now, He looked back at Needle for more information. Needle finished, "I know you will do this very important mission well, and be a service to your country. Needle reached across the table and patted Pants's cheek with an affirming touch, stood, and left the room.

Author notes: Chapter 12

"...You, my youth, are our nation's most precious guarantee for a great future, and you are destined to be the leaders of a glorious new order under the supremacy of National Socialism. Never forget that one day you will rule the world..." - *Adolf Hitler, 1938.*

On December 1, 1936, Hitler mandated "The Law concerning the Hitler Youth" that stated that all young Germans 10 years of age and older (excluding Jews) would be educated physically, intellectually, and morally in the spirit of National Socialism though the Hitler Youth. This law effectively ended all non-Nazi youth organizations such as: the Catholic Youth Organization, Boy Scouts and Girl Guides.

Hitler Youth watched over Polish families as they were evicted from their homes, making sure they took only a few basic possessions while leaving everything else of value behind for the new Germans residents. Hitler considered the war in the East to be a war of annihilation against the unwanted Poles, Jews, and Slavs. These peoples were forced into the southeastern portion of Poland, where ghettos, slave labor camps, and eventually extermination camps were built.

The "Związek Walki Zbrojnej - (ZWZ)" (Union for Armed Struggle) was one of the first organizations formed to fight back in guerilla warfare against the Germans. Its goals were: "to create centers of national resistance," and "rebuild the Polish nation through armed struggle."

Decrees of the Polish Government stipulated that ZWZ is "universal, national, non-party and non-class," and that it would include all Poles wishing to fight against the occupiers.

Other groups of partisans formed, holding their own ideas of what would be best for the new Poland. The People's Army, "A.L.," had a strong communist undertone, while the National Armed Forces, the "NSZ" had a strong leaning to anti-Semitism and Fascism.

In 1940 and during the first half of 1941, the Soviets deported more than 1,200,000 Poles, mostly in four mass deportations. They were sent to: northern European Russia, central and eastern Russia and to Kazakhstan. In 1941, it was determined, based on Soviet information, that more than 760,000 of the deportees had died—a large part of the dead being children, who had compromised about a third of deportees.

Chapter 13
June 1st, 1941: Zamek Checiny in the Holy Cross Hills

PANTS KICKED THE flanks of the mare a little harder, to encourage her to climb one more moderate grade. The moisture in the leaves made the footing a little slick and risky for the horse. The stocky, curly-haired horse was perfect for power activities, but her hesitation and poor effort needed a little extra rein work by Pants to clear a log that blocked the last easy step to the top. With one more lunge she made it over the decaying tree, much to the relief of horse and rider alike.

Once up to the crest, the effort was worth it. Pants was pleased with what he could see. It was 07:00, he had been riding for four hours, and the timing could not be better. The rains from the day before had moved out of the area late last evening, and the remnants had dried except for the morning dew. The ride was made possible by the bright moon that came out in the early hours, allowing him to make good time to this hill and identifying where he needed to be to watch what the Germans were doing. He was still in shadows and had time to find a perch for most of the day's observation, as well as a place to get some sleep.

Sliding off the sweaty dark brown horse, he placed his hands high up on the saddle as he stretched his shoulders by bending forward for ten seconds then backwards. Wiggling his hips gave him relief from the prolonged sitting, and slightly refreshed him. Turning, he scanned the nearby trees as he looked for a place to put his backpack and lie down for a couple of minutes. As the morning dew started to clear and the mist receded up the surrounding hills, Pants spotted an area that looked like it had potential for his purposes. His hips and crotch had become very sore from the long hours in the saddle over the past two weeks, and his back ached when leaning forward during the climbs up hills and through the trees. Pants walked slowly and slightly bowlegged to an acceptable spot and stretched out on the leaves and pine needles at the base of a group of trees. The moment was appreciated, as he could smell the clean air with a hint of mushroom odors. The soft surface beneath him was utterly relaxing. He felt very happy to be down.

After ten minutes or so of rest, Pants collected his flask and some bread and lard to eat from his pack. Putting them in his pockets, he slowly worked his way through the trees until he came to a narrow clearing that allowed him to get a full view of a gulley between the foot of the hill and a small village just beyond it. The location he had chosen was an excellent place to observe the German road and rail traffic below. He was on the lower of two hills that towered over a small village surrounded by its vast green and some golden-colored wheat fields. Pants had been riding the horse for nearly a month, and the lack of walking and running had made him very tired, hungry, and uncomfortable. Except for sleeping in a frequently-used sleeping hut that had certainly been shared by dozens of men who were traveling through to one of the many partisan camps, he hadn't slept in a bed since he left Opoczno.

To add to his misery, he was chaffed in the crotch despite the leather insert. He seemed to have some kind of rash on his head and legs, and the itching had become progressively worse over the last couple of days. "I need a bath," he muttered to himself. Ignoring the itch, he opened his backpack, retrieved his binoculars, and put away his heavy coat.

Using his binoculars he could see for about 12 km in a 270-degree arc. The weather was clear, crisp, and promised to stay that way for most of the day. Thunderstorms routinely rolled through this area, dumping brief but intense rain before moving on. Until they returned, he was well placed and ready to do his work. To the east, about ½ km further, was the best vantage point of all. That was the high peak of this row of hills, crowned by the ruins of Zamek Checiny (Castle Checiny) that had a 360-degree view of the hills and valley, a panorama that allowed the control and observance of everything around it. Unfortunately for Pants, it was occupied by German observers who were watching for intruders and problems, as he would be, but for different reasons. Luckily, they seemed to be guarding their sphere of influence against numbers greater than the one soul he represented. That was in Pants' favor, but did not guarantee he would not be noticed.

Pants was sent on this mission with the cover of being a trader of salt, cigarettes, lighters, and hats. Samples of those items were in a separate bag on the horse's saddle. Needle had provided him with false papers to keep him a year and half younger than he really was. He was also given the name and address of a boy whose family was killed during the bombing in Łódź, if he was questioned and investigated. That way, he had a plausible knowledge of his supposed history and could improvise accurately, as needed, in a worst-case scenario.

Pants tied the horse thirty meters away, in a grassy area where she could relax after her long night's work. The distance away from him was needed so that if the horse whinnied and was discovered, he would have space and time to get away and hide. He had been following the rail lines and observing junction areas for two weeks. Watching and noting the types of trains, their locomotives, and what they carried, Pants had stopped to pass along his information in three different places during this time. At each of those stops he was able to replenish his food supplies, and talk to farmers or shopkeepers for an hour or two while he ate and tended the horse.

His observations had found consistent increases of equipment, supplies, and troops movements towards the east at several of the main transit and marshalling centers. He'd noted and reported three separate areas where there were concentrated German activities. Today, he was about 40 km west of the Wistula River, and another 40 km from the border between the German and Russian territories. Needle had said, "There's something big going on" and Pants sensed that to be very true.

Pants was excited about finding the information, but could not make sense of it. The one thing he noted that had interested him was the amount of civilians coming from the east. Day and night, they moved painfully to the west. There was obvious misery in their souls that made them retreat from the direction of the Russians. Men, women, and children, farmers, or other types of civilians, marched as if to a slow dirge, tired and expressionless. Those who seemed mostly healthy were helping others who looked ill or wounded. They were fleeing by horse-drawn wagon, motorcar, on horseback, bicycle, or on foot, carrying all they owned on their backs or carts, trying to get away from something and hoping for safety in the west.

This was hard for Pants to understand, because he knew what was in the west—*Germans*. He didn't understand why people would be coming to them on purpose. Pants mused; *The Russians have to be as bad as everyone says for people to deliberately want to come to the Germans*. In the distance, flying in a wide, loose formation, two German fighters and two observation planes were patrolling the distant roads and nearby forests.

I wonder what's going on over there? Pants continued to ponder and observe the exodus, and questioned the need for planes. He crept farther out onto his point, and climbed a tree to get a better view. From an additional five meters above the ground, he hugged the trunk as he sat on a branch. With his binoculars, he was almost able to see as much as the soldier at the castle could, which was plenty.

In addition to the small camp where the soldiers were staying, at the far edge of the ridge, partially camouflaged by netting, were hundreds of troop transports parked in the dried creek runoff between him and the village. There were dozens of motorcycles with sidecars, and hundreds of bicycles. There were not enough soldiers to warrant this many vehicles, so he guessed that they would be coming soon. He could see that there were tracks cut into the ground beyond the vehicles that disappeared into the trees to his left. Those tracks were more like tank tracks than tires, and that many vehicles had been driven across the gulley into the trees and were blocked from his direct view. To add more mystery to the tracks, there were several guards on patrol, while others entered and exited a large metal-walled box that had been pulled from the back of a halftrack truck. It looked like a mobile command post of some kind, near several large company tents. The box had a narrow door with several very small windows, and could be entered via three steps to the door. The steps had two armed guards on either side of the trailer, walking the length of the truck with their rifles on their shoulders. A second trailer was parked not too far away from the first, where several horses were tied to it.

Pants watched for about 40 minutes, and sensed that there were no more guards other than those he had seen on patrol. They moved in and out of the trees with German regularity. When his curiosity got the better of him he decided, *I'd better go see what treasures are inside that forested area.* Rather than staying in the safety of his perch, he worked his way down the side of the hill, around and through the trees and rocks. Being very mindful of being not exposed, Pants did his job and reached the rim of trees, where he stepped slowly and quietly into the center of the tree patch. Within 20 meters, he found a winding path of wide tracks under the canopy of trees. Waiting again for any sign of patrols, he walked a careful path parallel to the tracks, until he found what he was looking for. Under extensive netting, laced between trees to give the appearance of a contiguous tree line, were 30 medium tanks and additional support vehicles. Their black paint crosses stood boldly against the gray/green painted metal. The tanks had a very angular shape, with stubby cannons mounted on the turrets, and a machine gun on the bottom right of the turret, while on top a distinctive circular hatch was guarded by another machine gun mount. He had seen this type of tank before, as they rolled through Łódź in '39. This time the tanks had bundles of rolled canvas attached that looked like tents and shovels. Strapped to the sides were extra replacement tracks, with extra cans of gasoline mounted on the back. To Pants, it looked like the tanks were outfitted for a long trip rather than being ready for immediate battle.

For the next 15 minutes he carefully studied what was to be seen under the netting. When he was sure that he had seen all there was, he made his way back to the slope he came down and began a quiet slow climb up the hill. He ran the details of what he saw through his head several times while trying to stay alert to danger.

The methodical ascension back to his perch took nearly 60 minutes longer than the climb down. Stopping and listening every couple of steps for noises that might be a German patrol or plane had Pants moving at a rate that fatigued him greatly. The information that he had gathered already this morning was of a greater magnitude than anything he had seen so far and had to be reported quickly, but without at the risk of being caught.

When he reached the place where he had tied the horse, he again checked for any patrol activities and planes. On finding none, he retrieved his backpack and put on his jacket, buttoning it half way up, and slid his binoculars behind his coat. He led the small horse down the slippery path, and crossed over a low ridge on the opposite side of the hill away from the gulley, where he mounted the horse on a level area. Once mounted, he picked up the pace to exit the hills and proceed to the closest drop point, some 20 km away. Carefully, he found his way through the thick grove of trees, using his compass for a steady direction setting.

His withdrawal progressed well until he kicked his horse a little to clear an open space among the trees. As he did so he became aware of an engine sound becoming louder than the breathing of the horse and the impact of the hooves on the firm ground. He looked up over his left shoulder and searched the sky for something he did not want to see. The sound became clear enough that he had to kick the horse harder to have her run for the edge of the distant trees. Again he turned his head this time to the right and was about to look left when the plane flying at treetop level soared over his head and immediately climbed steeply in order to reposition itself for another look at him and to give his location and direction to those following him. As the spotter plane went into its turn, Pants reined the mare still harder, and the short powerful legs of the horse began to run at her top speed. Leaning far over her neck, he held her mane with one hand and reins in the other while nearly standing in the stirrups.

The plane swooped over his head when he reached the tree line and he darted between the tall pole pines for the promise of safety. Pants reined in the horse as the plane continued overhead and away for another turn that gave him enough time to maneuver the horse into a space between several trees growing very close together. He waited for the noise to disappear, but it did not.

The pilot of the plane made several passes, each time at progressively slower speeds than the time before. Slowing the engine speed to improve his ability to see through the canopy of trees, the pilot looked for someone on a horse to the point of almost stalling his plane. Eventually the engine sound did not return, but Pants continued to be patient and made sure the plane would not see him when he moved. He shook the reins on the horse and began to work his way west, and with luck he would soon be to the edge of the woods.

Using the same trail he rode just this morning he settled into a comfortable pace for the horse, as well as for himself. As in the past, he would stop and listen for unusual sounds, and scan the sky through the thick cover for the spotter plane. The canopy that hid him also blinded him, a problem he had to deal with carefully. After nearly an hour without detecting any warning sounds, Pants was confident that he had gotten away, and began to think about getting something to eat in his pack. He stopped to pull the pack around and fish out some bread, and that was when he thought he heard something. A whinny, he thought, from the right side, but he wasn't sure he heard it. He sat dead still, but did not hear it again.

He put his pack back on and continued slowly, his ears straining to hear and his heart praying that they would not. There was a slight irregular pounding sound, like that of a horse possibly stumbling slightly, possibly on his left. Pants froze in place and listened, deep into the thick woods. They were so thick that within 25 meters a person could not see between trees without seeing another tree blocking the view deeper in. His heart rate started to climb, and instinctively he kicked the mare to pick up the pace, fearing that he was being surrounded.

No sooner than he picked up speed did he hear a horse, no two, then three coming from either side. He could not see anything, but his senses were on full alert as he maneuvered through the forest. Pulling the reins first to the right then to the left he weaved between trees and ducked under branches as he made his dash for safety. Gradually the trees began to thin out and he again accelerated his small mount to a full gallop, her powerful muscles working nearly without effort in her efficient truncated stride.

Suddenly, on his right, a horse and soldier appeared on a tangent heading for him. Pants pulled the reins and leaned left away from the rider. Breaking clear of the trees he saw that he is now being chased on the left side as well. Two riders on large heavy mounts quickly gained on him, their rifles on their backs and long coats fluttering behind them. The third rider that came at him from the right was also on a bigger and much faster horse than his. Pants wanted to get away, but he was surrounded and resistance would only get him shot; he would never outrun his pursuers and knew it. With this reality and no good option for him, he increased his pressure on the reins and brought his flight to an end. Leaning back into the saddle he raised his hands high over his head and looked to the left and to the right where he saw three rifles aimed at him.

"Aussteigen (Get off)!" the soldier on the right said, as he waved his rifle at Pants and then in the direction of the ground. As Pants started to lower his hands, the other two soldiers dismounted and ran over to Pants and pulled him the rest of the way out of his saddle. Pants had one leg coming over the back of the saddle when they grabbed him, which made him fall backwards onto the ground with a thud. A moment after he hit the ground the soldiers each delivered two to three kicks at the boy, as he rolled on the ground trying to protect his head from the blows that were directed at his sides as his backpack protected most of his rib cage. Each impact knocked his breath out of him and produced a quick sharp pain and a muffled groan. No sooner did the kicks stop than he was hoisted up by his arms to a standing position. The kicks left him out of breath and doubled up, so when he was pulled up he failed to hold the position as they let go of him. Pants, holding his stomach and side, fell to his knees because of the pain. The second time he was pulled up, he was able to hold himself in a bent position and stayed on his feet.

"Papers!" They demanded next, as they quickly searched his body for any weapons. Pants reached into his trousers and pulled out his identity papers, handing them to the soldier closest to him who in turned handed them to the corporal in the group. The corporal examined the pages and slid them into his pocket and asked in broken Polish, "What are you doing here?"

"Heading west, like everyone else." He answered in German. The tart answer earned him a slap to his head.

The German repeated, in German this time, "What are you doing here and where were you going?"

Pants looked at the corporal and let his shoulder relax a little as he was now able to stand straighter and continued in German, "I was sleeping in the woods for the night, and I want to go to Łódź." He looked at the corporal, then to the other two to see their reaction to his statement. They were thinking about it.

One of the soldiers squeezed, and then removed the bag tied to the saddle and opened it. He was a little surprised to find 20 packs of cigarettes in it as well as the lighters, tins of salt and hats. He pulled out a handful of items and held them up to show the corporal who took them and examined them. "What is all of this?" he asked as he pushed them partly towards Pants.

"I have been trading things for food and other items to sell." Pants unbuttoned his coat and showed them his binoculars. Knowing that they would find them soon, he thought he could use them as a bargaining item.

"See what I got yesterday from a man on the road?" He handed the binoculars to the corporal. "I gave him a pack of cigarettes and he gave me those. I'm sure I can trade them for a couple of blankets or a sweater or two, somewhere."

The corporal thought about the response and weighed the plausibility of the answers. He was on the verge of letting Pants go, but his instinct and training stopped him. He finally ordered the soldiers and Pants to get back on their horses. They would return to the camp to let an officer decide what to do with the boy.

Pants declared passionately, "I haven't done anything; I was just sleeping in the forest. I haven't bothered anyone," he insisted in German, and tried to pull away in an effort to be a nuisance and not worth the work to take him in. The real possibility that he could be shot for being a spy raced through his mind.

He protested as he squirmed in the grasp of the two other soldiers, which caused the corporal to lose patience. He leveled his rifle, and froze Pants in his place. "Get on your horse. NOW!" The tone was unmistakable as to the alternate choice.

The soldiers flanked Pants as they rode slowly around the hill to where the command vehicles were parked. Pants became more scared as they approached the trailers. He tried not to look conspicuous, but his eyes darted to every possible escape route he could identify. His stress increased, as his options were becoming less than zero. When they arrived at the camp, one of the soldiers dismounted and tied his horse to a rail next to the trailer Pants had determined was the headquarters. This second trailer was where the soldiers reported to their commanders and got their duty assignments. The first soldier went to Pants and gestured for him to dismount and go up the metal steps of the trailer.

Pants climbed the stairs in a slow and labored manner, as if his feet were in cement. On the final step, the corporal, who wanted to deliver his catch quickly, pushed him from behind causing Pants to stumble into the door jam with a thump. The inside of the trailer was busy with several soldiers working at tiny desks, while others moved in and out of the command center with orders. Pants understood that the orders were for platoons checking in and out of the field. He was shuffled to a far corner of the structure and was placed on a chair; his hat was knocked off by one of the other soldiers who had captured him. The soldier took off his long coat in the trailer that was warmed by the many bodies. Afterwards, he stood next to Pants to guard him. After 15 to 20 minutes, a lieutenant came over to Pants and asked the soldier what the problem was. The soldier explained the chase and capture, and produced the bag that had the items Pants was purportedly trading, and everything he had in his pockets.

The lieutenant took the bag and sat down on the corner of the desk next to where Pants was sitting. He pulled out the items dropping them on the desk and with a finger spread them out to see them individually. He picked up and examined the binoculars and the compass that had Russian markings. He opened and looked into the backpack but just squeezed it from the outside, then passed it to the soldier and told him to examine the pack closely. Finding dirty clothes, twine, matches, stale food, and a pocketknife, he closed the pack and placed it on the floor.

"What were you doing here?" he asked, in good Polish, and stared at the boy waiting for an answer.

Pants, already sweating from the chase and still wearing his heavy clothes in the warm trailer, paused with his heart pounding in his throat. After a moment he started to speak but nothing came out his mouth. It was coated with a thick mucous stuck on his vocal cords from the stress he was feeling. He cleared his throat several times before he could say anything. "I was trying to get back to Łódź, and I spent the night in the woods." He choked out.

"Litzmannstadt." The lieutenant corrected Pants. "The name is Litzmannstadt." His eyebrows furrowed and his lips became tight as he focused intently on the boy.

Pants instantly knew that calling it Łódź was a mistake, one that he did not want to make. Quickly he sat stiffly in the chair and responded in German, "Of course, Lieutenant, it is Litzmannstadt, I'm a little nervous right now. I've never spoken to a German officer before, and I had forgotten the new better name."

The lieutenant softened a little upon hearing the answer in passable German and then stood up and walked around the desk looking at the items on it then picked up the binoculars and compass and asked, "Why do you have these?" He dangled them from their straps hung over his fingers.

Pants swallowed deeply and pointed to the compass, "I know I have to go west, and that helps me in the woods. I've been using the binoculars to spot rabbits and birds to eat. I have set out snares." He looked down in embarrassment, then added, "but I haven't had much luck in catching anything. I was hoping to trade them for food when I got to Litzmannstadt."

The lieutenant moved back to the front of the desk and crossed his arms and stated, "You know that you can be shot for black marketeering these things. Why should I not shoot you for that?" He waited with a smirk, anticipating the answer.

"I am not black marketeering!" Pants protested, "I was trading these things, for other things that I could use to get money or food while I was trying to get home."

"Where is home?" the lieutenant demanded, as he slammed his hand on the desk trying to startle the boy.

"Litzmannstadt, I told you before. I was sent east during the invasion, and did not want to stay in Russian territory. I want to be here," Pants proclaimed in Polish, then repeated, "I want to be here" in German hoping to make his case more believable.

"I think you are a spy." The officer accused Pants with his finger pointed centimeters from his face then reached forward and pulled his left ear to the right and after letting go, slapped him with his palm against his head that spun it back to the left.

The sharp sting made Pants reach up and cover his left ear and blurt, "I am not a spy! I am nothing! I just want to go home."

The German picked Pants up by his jacket 20-30 centimeters then dropped back onto the chair in what appeared to be disgust. He then ordered, "Take him out of here, and place him in the holding tent where the sergeant can continue the interrogation. I will continue the questioning later." The guard pulled Pants out of the chair and pushed him towards the door. He picked up the backpack, and with another thrust pushed it against Pants's back as if it was a boxing glove. Pants lurched towards the ground as he fell off the platform from the top of the steps hitting the ground in a heap. Before he could stand up on his own, he was pulled up by his collar and taken to the holding tent where he was shoved hard, causing him to again fall to the floor on his head, hands, and knees. He rolled into his side and tried to get his knees under him but only managed to stay on his knees and elbows. His heavy coat protected him from most of the damage from the falls but he was slightly dazed, and slowly rolled his head side to side on the floor to ease the pain.

A couple of minutes later, a soldier without his tunic on burst through the flap of the tent holding a flat leather strap in his hand. He paused for a moment as Pants stared up from his knees at the towering figure in horror, as he focused on the menacing belt. The man stepped up to Pants quickly, and grabbed him with one hand that was powerful enough to bring him up onto his feet. With cold piercing eyes he looked into Pants's soul and said, "So you are a spy? Well this is what I think of a spy." With that, he dropped the boy to the floor and began to whip Pants with the strap all over his body and legs. Pants covered his head with his hands for protection, but the strap cut his arms and stung his head where the leather penetrated through or around his defenses. The impacts seemed to come in five to ten strikes followed by a pause as the soldier caught his breath then the beatings would start again. "Are you a spy?" he yelled when resting; then he would strike Pants again.

Pants cried out in anguish and terror, in almost a shrill tone "No, I am not a spy! Please stop!"

"Oh you're a crying spy. Are all Polish spies babies?" He was trying to taunt an unintentional comment or protest from his victim.

Rolling side-to-side trying to spare the same body parts from the onslaught of the guard, Pants curled into a ball and absorbed the strikes. Then, just as suddenly as it started, the punishment stopped. Pants stayed on the floor in the corner alone for the next three hours, stunned by the pain caused by the assault. He drifted into a foggy numbness as his body tried to cope with the beating.

By late afternoon, Pants became more conscious, and as he did, he became uncomfortable with his bladder being very full. Pants called to the guard in German, "I have to pee." There was no answer. "Please, I have to pee right now or I'll wet the floor." The guard looked inside and motioned for him to come out. He was taken to a slit latrine not far from where he had come down from the hill early that morning, but felt like days ago. The guard only accompanied him half-way to the latrine area where other soldiers were also doing their business. With great satisfaction Pants was able to relieve himself and returned to the guard. While doing so he noticed that it would not be very far to run to reach a place that would take him to the trail he had used before, but there were so many soldiers. Could it be done? He noticed that the guards were being changed in an informal manner. He was returned to the tent and fell asleep during the reprieve in his interrogations.

Two hours later, Pants was taken back to the trailer where the lieutenant was waiting for him. Pants become anxious about going before the officer who suspected him of being a spy. He was bruised and sore from the beating in the tent, with several welts raised on his head and shoulders. The backs of his hands were turning blue from the bruises, and his fingers were swollen. He was placed in the same chair as before and this time the officer challenged him with, "Are you going to tell me the truth, or do you need more convincing that to lie to me is not a smart thing to do?"

Pants looked at him with apprehension, but repeated, "I am not a spy. I just want to go home."

"I don't believe you. Whom are you spying for?" he continued, and once again Pants insisted that he wasn't a spy but he was a trader of things as he worked his way home.

After 30 minutes more of the stalemate where Pants was slapped, pinched, and hit with the rubber stick, the German became inpatient and said, "I am going to send you to talk to people who know how to ask questions better than I can." The lieutenant grinned, with cold unemotional eyes. This started to terrify Pants all over again.

The officer reached for the identity papers on the desk and gave them to one of the clerks at the desk near him. "Photograph the papers and this spy's miserable face for the files." The clerk took them and went to a small desk to retrieve a small 35 mm camera and took Pant's picture front and side views. He then took a picture of the papers Pants had given, and finally returned the document to the officer, who placed them in his uniform pocket and buttoned the pocket closed. "I guess that's all I have time for. You can talk to the Gestapo later."

The sound of that sent chills up Pants spine, and he felt an unreal, dazed sensation overcome him as he was escorted back to the tent. Without a further word he was returned to the tent and as he entered his saw his backpack leaning against the inside of the tent at the doorway.

Just before 20:00, hours, darkness and some evening rain had begun to fall Pants asked to go to the latrine to pee once again. During the preceding time he had quietly worked himself to his backpack and removed his extra shirt and pants, bread, and some string but his pocketknife and his compass were gone. Putting on the extra shirt and baggy pants over his pants he waited for the guard to escort him out. As before he was taken about half way then the guard stopped to talk to another soldier who was standing under an overhang to be out of the rain. Pants used the latrine and observed that there were very few other soldiers in the area as he returned to the tent. When he got to the guards, he stopped to tell them, "I have to go back to take a crap." The two guards looked at the boy and told him to go ahead, and not take too long. They did not notice the relatively larger boy standing in the light rain.

Pants nodded and headed for the latrine, but when he had reached a shadowed area he scanned to see if there was anyone watching him or in the area. Finding none, he ran for the spot where the slope allowed him to climb up to the trail further up the hill. He worked his way up the wooded trail in the fading light. He knew they would come looking for him within minutes, so he had to get as far away as fast as he could.

As he suspected, the guards became suspicious of the long absence by the prisoner and went to investigate. Not finding him there they blew their whistle summoning more guards. Six guards spread out around the latrine looking for any sign of where the boy had gone. One found what looked like a trail and with their lanterns they started to climb up the hill in what was total darkness. Beating bushes and kicking piles of leaves looking for the escaped boy they covered a vast amount of the hill without finding him. They walked almost within arms length of each other as they scoured the area around the trail but to not avail. After several hours the search was called off for the night and the soldiers returned to their camp. One by one, they left the area that included the perch Pants had used in the morning as well as where the horse had been, but there was no sign of their prisoner. The guards knew that there would be a price to pay for letting the boy run away.

Two hours later, after being sure that none of the soldiers remained, Pants worked his way down the tree he had climbed, and in the light of the rising moon slowly worked his way to through the woods to the ridge and valley he'd tried to cross fourteen hours before. This time, by morning he was through the forest and working his way to the fields beyond what he hoped was the range of the patrols, and before the arrival of the spotter planes.

At dawn, Pants was only four kilometers away, moving towards what he hoped would be the safer valleys in the Holy Cross mountain range, and away from Kielce. The darkness and lack of a real path had greatly retarded his ability to cover distance in the thick woods. Often he found himself circling rather than going forwards, his directions confused in the thick woods. Once out and on the road, he was sure that he might find a safe drop location for his information and where he could also rest. He was sore in all his extremities from the beating he received yesterday, but kept moving, knowing that if he stopped he would be too sore to get up again. Walking for safety was the only option, and had to be done.

A light foggy morning had broken. Pants was able to pick up the pace now that he could see a path he thought he needed to take to find the road away from the camp and Kielce. Without his compass he was guessing where he was. As the morning light filtered through the clouds, he still wasn't sure which direction he was traveling. He was afraid that he was still vulnerable to capture and listened for danger between his own footfalls when the air was free of covering sounds. His fatigue was great as was his hunger. Whatever food he had in his pockets was consumed hours ago. He had been walking or crawling nearly non-stop for ten hours. His hands were covered with dirt and leaf debris, while his clothes were soaked through from the rain and mud he had been crawling through. Those ten hours he worked during the night were after getting only two hours sleep in twenty-four. Add the time riding in the morning and he was reaching exhaustion. He desperately wanted to sleep, but had to keep moving.

Soon Pants reached the edge of the forest that he had struggled to clear all night. He found a creek where he washed his hands and face and rinsed his hair to decrease the panic that he felt. As he worked his way out of the woods, he spotted a road further down the hill. He watched many travelers moving up the road, as he had seen before on what he thought was a different road, some distance away. Unlike what he saw yesterday, there was a marked increase in the number of soldiers in sidecars patrolling in and around the lines of people. Pants carefully watched the line of slow moving humanity that spread over three km long ribbon of road to the far hill and beyond. The soldiers herded the crowd with their motorcycles, slowing and speeding up as they came to clumps of people and studied them. The passenger in the sidecar was holding a short machine gun that was generally aimed at the people to his side, but it seemed more as an incentive than an ongoing threat. With the crowd moving slowly, without much energy, Pants thought that this was perfect for him to blend in and be hidden within the mass of humanity.

Pants climbed out of a shrub when there weren't any soldiers in the immediate area and drifted between groups of people listening to hear conversation to give him a clue as to where they were from and where they were going, but the journey was a silent one. He spotted a middle-aged woman with a large pillowcase on her back and slowing worked his way to her side. She was wearing a nice long blue wool coat with an embroidered edge, indicating a happier and wealthier time in her past.

When the time was right he asked her, "Where are you going?" The question was under his breath and done with his head down.

She replied with a little suspicion, "To Kielce, where we will be put into a camp for our safety," she said, with little emotion.

Pants breathed in deeply, and had trouble breathing out. *I'm on the wrong road. They're going to a Ghetto like the one in Łódź, and I'm in the line this time, just like Jakob.* He now knew this was not where he wanted to be and immediately started looking for a place that would allow him to slip out of line and back into the woods. His stress increased as he looked forward and saw no place that would allow him to hide. The road ahead was flat, lined with one row of trees on either side as it led to Kielce. Behind Pants, one of the motorcycles cut into the line of weary souls and blocked a family group almost in mid-stride. The small wooden cart pulled by two men nearly spilled its contents when they dropped the yoke. The soldiers inspected the group and their papers, especially those of the older boys. As they did this Pants picked up his pace slightly to stay close to the woman with the pillowcase, trying to look like he was with her and would not be questioned. The steps the woman took were labored, and she was bent under the load on her back. Pants asked, "Can I help you carry your bundle?" He hoped that he could do her a favor while at the same time adding a disguise to his presence.

The woman stopped for a moment and with little thought turned the pack over to Pants who hoisted it onto his shoulder and back. He immediately began to labor under the new weight that added to fatigue that had already worn him down. The new challenge was almost too much for him as he questioned his judgment in volunteering his service to the woman, but it was his only recourse at the moment. Within a dozen steps the rain that had been only a drizzle since early in the morning, became heavier adding to the weight and gloom. They walked for several hundred meters as the soldiers finished what they were doing with the group behind them and remounted the motorcycle.

Pants could hear the engine start and accelerate behind him. He dipped his head down and held the bundle's handles against the side of his face where the motorcycle would pass. Slow heavy steps were made mechanically as his ears estimated the distance between him and the motorcycles' position. 100 meters, 50 meters 25 meters, 5 meters, and he prayed to God as the sound reached him and continued on. 25 meters, 50 meters the motorcycle continued up the road and Pants began to feel excitement, but suddenly they stopped as the passenger pointed backwards to the driver and they both turned to look at Pants. 25 meters, 10 meters Pants walked closer to the idling motorcycle, trying not to look suspicious as he attempted to walk past them. He never looked up and never changed his pace only his heart rate was changing and the urge to run crept over him.

The passenger got out of the sidecar with his machine gun slung under his right arm and stood waiting for Pants to come to him. "Halt. Papers." came the order. The woman stopped and reached into her blouse and pulled out her identification then handed it to the soldier.

The driver had also gotten off the motorcycle and approached Pants. "Papers." He ordered. Pants searched through his many pockets several times each knowing that he would not find them but the exercise bought him a little time to think. "I can't find them. They were here yesterday." He stated with a bewildered voice as he shrugged his shoulders and put his empty hands out towards the soldiers. "They must have fallen out of my pocket during the night." He offered as an explanation.

The soldier looked for a moment at Pants who was becoming anxious and wide-eyed as he pleaded his case. The soldier, after a couple of seconds, reached down and pulled the pack away from Pants, and then examined his hands, which were still red and with welts from the previous days beating. Letting go of the boy's hands the soldier called to his partner who came over and was told of the problem of missing papers. Pants watched them closely, knowing that others have lost their papers in the past, and maybe they would leave him alone, but the examination of his hands left him with a knot in his stomach.

The soldiers walked to the edge of the road, and while still looking at Pants, one waved his arm to another soldier down the road who in turned waved behind him to a third soldier. Shortly after, a staff car came up the edge of the road. Not making any effort to avoid the people walking on the road, it nearly hit several while others dove out of the way.

When the car came to a stop, the driver got out to open the back door to let out a lieutenant, who was the one that had questioned Pants the day before. A heavy sick feeling took over Pants, his stomach cramped and he felt spent. Another man in a long coat, the trademark of the Gestapo, accompanied the officer. The lieutenant grabbed Pants by the arm and sarcastically asked, "What are you trading for today?" as he lifted the bundle Pants had next to him, and then dropped it to the ground.

"Nothing, I was just carrying the pack for a while," Pants stated innocently.

The woman stepped over and said, "That is mine, he was helping me carry it."

The lieutenant looked at her with his cold and judgmental eyes, "Do you know this boy?"

"No, he's one of the boys from my town and just happened to come and help me," she offered, with no emotion or energy, but clearly she did it in an attempt to give him a cover story.

Her answer was something that Pants and the lieutenant knew to be a lie, but she failed to anticipate it as being of serious consequence in her effort to help the boy. Pants, on hearing her statement, stepped towards her and placed himself between her and the lieutenant stating, "I took her pack thinking that I could sell what's inside of it. I was about to run away with it when your soldiers came. She has obviously mistaken me for someone else," Pants offered as his version of the truth, trying to separate the woman from his activities and the danger he presented to her.

The lieutenant looked at Pants then told the soldier closest to him, "Put him in the car. Watch him, not only does he stink, but he tends to disappear."

The soldier, who knew what had happened the night before, saluted, and with a swing of his rifle jabbed Pants in the side with the rifle's butt then added a push causing Pants to fall onto his already bruised hands and knees. Before he could recover, Pants was pulled by his sleeve then half dragged and thrown into the back seat of the car. On the other side of the car the Gestapo agent slid into the back seat where he sat back and adjusted his leather gloves.

Once in the car, Pants turned and looked out the back window to see the lieutenant talking to the woman who was shaking her head and gesturing gracefully with her hands. Then, as if in slow motion, the lieutenant pulled his pistol and without hesitation shot her squarely in the chest. The impact threw her chest backwards, with head dropping down and forward as her arms swung across the front of her body too late to block the deadly bullet. She hurled towards the ground like a heavy flour sack. Her head snapped backwards making a horrible sound as it cracked on contact with the pavement, a thud that was audible even in the back seat of the car. She was dead before the hem of her long coat stopped moving. A hole in the nice fabric slowly turned the blue coat to purple and the rain added more sadness to the scene where her life ended suddenly on the road to Kielce.

Pants let out a cry at the sight of the murder. His fist came to his mouth and he bit it to prevent a longer scream. He turned abruptly to the front of the car, guilt ridden by his part in this person's slaughter. The lieutenant returned to the car and got into the front seat. Turning and looking towards the backseat with his head turned half way towards Pants, "One less piece of garbage to deal with in Kielce," he said.

The Gestapo smirked, and chuckled in agreement.

A long 20 minutes went by as the car drove into Kielce. The time passed with pain for Pants as the Gestapo asked Pants questions that were not answered. A gloved hand would hit Pants on the face or twist his ear after every question that was left unanswered. "What did you see?" No answer. "Whom do you report to?" No answer earned a sharp stinging blow to the face.

Pants rolled onto his side on the back seat, bringing his knees up towards his chest and covered his head with his arms once again. Only "agh" or "ow" was called out in response to the menacing and malicious assault onto the boy. He was pulled up by the ear to sitting, and then beaten back down with a fist or open hand, again and again. The blows often landed on areas that were bruised from the day before. A point came when Pants stayed down on the seat waiting for the next level of pain the Gestapo would inflict. The only delay was the time it took for the agent to identify a vulnerable spot to probe, and was refreshed enough to start again.

Pants did not move. The blows were weakening as the agent grew bored. The agent looked at his gloves, noted the stains from hitting Pants, and with disdain rubbed them on Pants's jacket to remove the "filth". He decided that his assistants would have more room to swing their fists or stick at headquarters and would complete the interrogation correctly. There he would get his answers with the boy talking, or have the boy die, there was little preference for one or the other. Once he decided that, the agent turned and looked out the window as if he was on a Sunday drive in the country admiring the colors.

Upon entering the city, traffic began to plug the streets with cars, trucks, soldiers, and people moving to no place quickly. Herding people into the ghetto, along with the beatings of the slow ones, produced a panic within the crowd, and sudden gridlock where the car stood. There were hundreds of people being pushed and funneled down the main street in the small city, overwhelming the physical capacity of the street to handle this much humanity at once.

The commotion and chaos seemed to catch both the lieutenant and the Gestapo agents off guard, since it suddenly appeared to demand their attention and intervention. The ancient town had dozens of small alleyways and curved streets merging with the one they were on. All of those side streets were congested, as well. The lieutenant became impatient at the delay in crossing an intersection that was blocked by a horse and wagon. He reached over to the driver's steering wheel and pressed hard on the ring below the Mercedes emblem, causing the horn to blare. When that did not result in a passageway, he decided to get out and tell the soldiers around the car to move the wagon and horse, giving personal directions and pointing as how to clear the congested area so his car could get through. The Gestapo tried to open his door but people being pushed against the door blocked it. A forceful effort created a space for the door to open and he leaned out to see the progress and glowed in the success of controlling this large of population with relatively few soldiers.

Pants noted that the activities and the mass of people produced a surprising amount of quiet chaos in front of the car. He slowly raised his head and looked out to the side and saw an alley that almost immediately curved away from the street. With the agent half way out his door and the lieutenant away from the car, Pants grabbed the door handle and opened it, and as it did he jumped, then rolled away from the car, tripping slightly as he tried to escape his pending visit to Gestapo headquarters. He dashed down the narrow alleyway, bumping into or weaving between stopped cars, bicycles, horses, and people who were trying to take an alternate route around the intersection. As he bolted from the car, it took several seconds for the Gestapo to move through a group of people blocking his door and around the car in the direction that Pants had fled. As he gave chase, he yelled to the lieutenant but was not heard as the lieutenant was yelling orders of his own over the commotion in the intersection of two streets. Unable to wait for a response, the agent raced after the boy who had a precious short head start.

The several seconds was all Pants needed to place time and distance between him and his pursuer. In spite of his many layers of wet clothing and dull gnawing pain in his muscles from the bruises, he ran at top speed for several blocks ducking into other alleys and between houses and cars to see if he was being followed. When the crowds failed to keep moving, Pants sensed panic from being slowed, and the Gestapo agent gaining on him. At one corner he desperately tried to decide which way to go and pressed on a couple of doors without success in opening them.

At the third door, a boy came running by and grabbed his sleeve and said, "Follow me." Pants did not hesitate and ran behind the other boy. From behind him two other boys "clumsily" bumped into the Gestapo as he ran, breaking the agents momentum and distracting his view of Pants. Within an additional block, Pants and his rescuer dropped into an open door, and closed it behind Pants and himself. They sat on the floor of this dark room in silence, breathing heavily, while they listened for danger.

After ten minutes of waiting and listening, the boys looked through a peephole and sat back down, more relaxed than a minute before. The rescuer looked at Pants and shook his head as he asked, "Who are you and what did you do to get that pig to chase you?"

Pants looked at the boy, and with a little surprise at the queries, said. "Do you know who that was? He was a Gestapo who was going to question me at their headquarters. Thanks for helping me."

The boy smiled, and looked at Pants and his filthy clothes. "That's Heinrich, the local agent. He thinks he's Himmler himself. Only he's bigger, stronger, but dumber than the real one. What did you do that made him want to question you? He usually lets the flunkies beat up the kids."

Pants was thrilled to be away from the Gestapo but did not know who his "savior" was and did not want to disclose his mission. "They thought I was a spy and were going to send me to the Gestapo headquarters for questioning, but I escaped last night. They caught me again this morning, and were taking me there when I jumped out of their car. They shot a woman who tried to protect me." He added the last statement in anguish.

"We have to go to a safer place, now," the boy declared. "I have some friends who can help you." Not knowing any other alternative, Pants followed him to another door, through a cellar and out a basement window. Both boys moved carefully through the narrow alleys and the slow-moving people until they reached an apartment building. They climbed to a second story room, and after an asynchronous knock, the door opened. Pants hesitated before entering and the first boy noted his caution and said, "I think I can trust you. You don't look like a traitor to me." Pants was surprised at the comment as the boy continued, "I am Wart and I am a Scout. This is where my Hive meets. Go inside and wait while I bring my leader."

Pants furrowed his brow and almost burst into tears of relief, as he was able to relax briefly, knowing he was safe, for now. He grinned in thanks for his good fortune, and put out his left hand. Wart smiled and returned the Scout handshake. As they shook hands Pants stopped and held Wart's hand and smiled broadly. Wart asked, with a puzzled look on his face, "What are you smiling about?"

Pants answered, "I am called Pants. Your codename is as bad as mine."

Wart was barely able to stifle his own laugh, then pumped Pants' hand a little harder. "Nice to meet you Pants," and from that, a kindred spirit was found. For the rest of the afternoon Pants and Wart became fast friends and each enjoyed the company of the other. Each had a sarcastic sense of humor and tried to outdo the other on any subject. For a brief time, they played like teenage boys would, as they mimicked the Gestapo agents and told outlandish stories of what they would do to get even with the Germans when they got their chance to fight.

In a quiet moment, Pants asked, "How did you get Wart as a codename?"

Wart smiled and said, "It was nothing spectacular. Look here." He pulled back his hair from the side of his face near his ear where there was a birthmark.

Pants said, "It kind of looks like a Rosebud, but I can see a Wart too."

"Well that's the problem. They wanted to call me Rosebud or Wart. Rosebud did not sound like a good codename, so I went with Wart."

Both laughed at the face that Wart made when he said, "Rosebud."

Pants told Wart how he got his codename. That story had Wart nearly in tears from laughing so hard. "No one could make up that kind of story so it must be true!" Pants was angry at first, at the unbridled laugher from Wart about the attack that lead up to the codename being given. But then he laughed with him. After all, in hindsight it was quite a story.

By the end of the evening, Pants had met the Scoutmaster who explained what was happening in Kielce and the surrounding areas where the Germans had been collecting and storing all kinds of vehicles and horses for some time. The tanks and half-track trucks that Pants saw were not as well known or located. Pants told them about his need for a safe place to send or pass on his information. It was determined that shortwave radio would be the fastest and safest method to post the details, as it was broadcast and picked up by all the underground groups. Pants gave the list of vehicles and his observed details to the Scoutmaster, who confirmed the information to his contact, saying that it matched what other observers had seen in other areas.

The Germans were trying to round up Jews and quarantine them in most of the larger cities in the area. They had stepped up their pursuit of informers, as well as having swept through many areas in the Holy Cross Mountains for partisan fighters, in essence sterilizing a large part of the eastern part of Poland from potential saboteurs and spies. This explained the extra effort to catch Pants during the past two days.

Farther east, they had established marshaling centers where thousands of soldiers had been assembled. It was June 19th, and from other reports it was clear something was about to happen. It was thought that Pants could not stay in Kielce because they would surely be looking for him. They decided that he should immediately be sent back to the Konskie forest, where the Opoczno headquarters was last located. Pants was shown a map and given local information about German-patrolled areas, as well as those where known resistance groups were camped. He was given general coordinates for directions for his return to his group. Pants said he knew the area, and if they could get him close to the town he would be able to make contact there again.

Since Pants did not have his papers or his compass, he needed replacements. Within a couple of hours Wart was ordered to take Pants to another apartment's basement were he was given another set of documents that had a new name for him, and a replacement compass. He was taken to a garage where he was placed with an older man who would be driving a large produce truck towards Konskie. Pants would pose as his helper. There he would be sent to a contact and be given supplies for his return to Konskie's Underground company's camp. Wart and Pants said goodbye and swore that they would meet again.

Within 24 hours of being spotted and arrested on the road to Kielce, Pants was in a truck filled with vegetables and was heading west. His information had been sent up the command chain. That gave him a feeling of deep relief, and very little more. He did not appreciate how tired and scared he had been until the noisy truck was on the road. The rocking of the heavy truck and engine sound gave him a sense of security for the time being. He leaned against the door and immediately fell asleep in the seat of the truck.

Four hours later, the sudden downshifting and the heavy braking of the truck awakened Pants. He sat upright as the driver said, "We're coming out of the woods at the bottom of this hill. We will be on the main road to Konskie soon."

"How long before we get to Konskie?" Pants asked, as he tried to adjust his vision to the darkness and the winding tree-lined road that was barely illuminated by the partially covered headlights.

"Several more hours at this speed; certainly before daybreak, which is at 5:30." The driver patted his pockets as he looked for something. Finding an apple he handed it to Pants, who thanked him, savored the first bite and sucked on the sweet juice before swallowing the pulp. Slowly, with appreciation, he ate the seeds and all, not wanting to waste any morsel of food. The driver produced a second apple and made short work of it; clearly being a man who did not dwell on the finer points of food.

An hour later, they stopped for a stretch and some relief. They pulled several carrots from the back of the truck, and several more apples to eat later. The driver had bread and butter, with milk that he shared with Pants, and they ate as the dark of night began to lift. The colors were always special to Pants this time of day and he watched the purples turn bluer minute by minute. They had cleared the trees and were on a narrow long road heading for Konskie when the driver pulled over again. When stopped, he looked at Pants and asked, "Do you know how to drive?"

Pants was startled by the question, and answered, "I know how the gears work, but I haven't driven a truck." (For that matter he really hadn't driven anything.)

"Well it is never too soon to learn, and I need a rest, so slide over here." The driver waved towards the driver's seat as he got out of the truck driver's door and walked around the front to sit as a passenger.

"First, move the seat closer so you can reach the wheel and the pedals." He pointed to the handle near the front of the seat. "Now push in the clutch on the left down to the floor while you hold your foot on the middle pedal, which is the brake." Pants did as instructed, and found the left pedal hard to press, but he did get it down to the floor.

"All right, do you see this knob? This is the gearshift, and you move it in the shape of an H, with the top left spot the 1st gear. Every time you want to change gears, you push the left pedal down, move the shifter to the next gear then let up the clutch pedal. Got that?" Pants automatically nodded again not really knowing what needed to be done from the brief instructions.

"Good. This is the hand brake," as he pointed to a lever next to the gearshift. "Pull it back slightly and push down on the button on top, and as you do that push the lever forward." Pants, with a long reach and hard pull, disengaged the brake while a sense of panic took over him.

"You're doing fine. Now let up the clutch slowly, as you step on the gas pedal slowly until you feel the truck start to move, then step harder on the gas." The driver waved the back of his hand limply in a forward direction, as he settled against the door.

Pants did as he was told, but got excited and stepped too hard on the gas. The motor roared from the flood of gas going into the engine. When the gears engaged, that caused the truck to nearly leap forward under the high torque that was generated. The lurch surprised Pants and he had to grab and squeeze the wheel with all his strength to not fall out of the seat. He let up on the gas, and the truck slowed suddenly, which also caught Pants off guard. He floored it again, and again the truck lurched forward, throwing both Pants and his passenger forward and back into the seat.

The driver began yelling instructions, "No, too much g…" the truck lurched already was slowing down as he spoke. "More gas; keep it steady!" Gears wound up quickly and loudly. "Clutch in quickly, push it into second gear. NO! All the way down, now let it up. MORE gas, NOT that much. WATCH WHERE you're going, keep the wheel straight!!" The driver generated orders faster than could be comprehended by the boy. "Now the clutch again, easy on the gas. Third gear, third gear now, do it now–KEEP the wheel STRAIGHT."

Then, magically, the truck was rolling along at a steady pace. "That's it, one more time, clutch in, gas pedal up, shift to fourth." Pants completed this last gear change, and realized that he was moving smoothly, and for the most part straight, on the road. A big smile came over his face, and he looked at the driver who was also smiling. "Okay, that's good." The driver sighed. "The road is fairly straight for 20 km.

Keep the truck on the road and wake me when you get to the big curve to the right."

"Wake you up?" Pants blurted out. "What do you mean wake you up?" His eyes were wide in disbelief at what his ears had heard.

"I'm tired and I need a nap. If you have to stop, push down on the clutch and press the brake until you stop. I will be here if you need help."

Pants looked back toward the road and stared into the distance that hinted of the predawn light. "But…" Pants started to say as he looked at the driver to slightly protest being abandoned, and found him already snoring. Pants turned back and focused on the road. A moment or two later, he thought, *I'm driving*, in a very self-satisfied manner. *I'm driving, this is easy.*

That was true for about 35 minutes. That was when Pants saw the lights and swinging lantern in the distance. Pants strained to see into the source of the lights and then it was clear to him. "Crap! Germans." He reached over to the driver and shook him. "Germans, Germans are on the road! What do I do?" The driver was instantly upright and was nearly awake.

"Nothing; just keep driving." Pants immediately pressed on both pedals at once and nearly threw the driver onto the dashboard. "No, keep driving." The older man said softly. As they approached the blockade, Pants again started the deceleration sequence and this time brought the truck to a stop some 20 meters short of the soldiers. Pants put the truck into first gear with the help of the driver and slowly raised the clutch as he revived the motor. The truck lurched slightly then stopped closer to the blockade.

The man and Pants rolled down their windows and listened for the orders from the soldiers, who told them to get out of the truck. They obeyed this order without a word offered in protest. The soldiers demanded their papers and explanation of their purpose for being on the road.

"We are going to deliver this produce to Konskie, see?" The driver swung his arm towards the canvas-covered vegetables on his truck. "The boy is learning to drive, since my other boys are in the German Army. "Heil Hitler!" He said crisply as he raised his arm up and forward. This startled Pants but made one of the soldiers look at the man closely. Pants tardily raised his arm in the Nazi salute, but without conviction, as he watched the driver talk to the soldiers.

Another soldier went back behind the barricade and talked to what appeared to be an officer in a car beyond the roadblock. Upon his return he walked around the truck and examined the contents of the truck cab and the bed carrying the produce. He pushed his rifle's bayonet into the vegetables and between the boxes all around the truck without hitting anything of interest to him.

When he and the other soldier returned from the inspection, he went to the staff car and the officer handed him a piece of paper. This was in turned given to the driver as the second soldier began to climb into the cab of the truck from the passenger side.

The old man looked at the paper and in the improving light read the note written in Polish and German. "Your truck and produce is being purchased by the General Government for the amount of 110 RM. You can collect the amount indicated at the Postal Station in "Litzmannstadt.""

The driver looked at the paper and grumbled, "Litzmannstadt? You are giving me only a fraction of the value of my truck and merchandise and you want me to go to Litzmannstadt to get it? How do you suggest I get there if you take my truck?" The old man furrowed his brow and stared at the soldier but tried not to raise his voice too much.

The soldier quickly grew inpatient with the driver and answered, "I have other options if you do not wish to be paid." He glared back at the man making his message clear. "As far as getting to Litzmannstadt, it is that way." He pointed nonchalantly to the west. "As to how you do that, is not my concern. I suggest you start walking now." With that comment the soldier waved to another soldier, who got into the truck and backed it up and eventually drove it back in the direction Pants and the driver came from. As the two watched the truck leave, the convoy that was behind the roadblock also began moving. For the next 15 minutes trucks filled with freight and men drove passed Pants in the direction of Kielce.

In the light of the morning the sound of the Germans diminished into the distance. Pants turned to the driver and asked, "Now what do we do?" His comment was as much of a statement of relief as it was a question.

"I still have to go to Konskie to deliver my information. You have to get to Opoczno for your instructions. We will travel this way until Konskie. We should be there by midday," the old man said, matter-of-factly.

The sun was coming up, and it was warm. Staszek was tired but the heat felt good which made him really want to go to sleep in the grass along the road. His skin began to itch again under the layers of clothes he had been wearing for weeks. The irritation took him out of his relaxed mood. Without saying a word, Pants turned and started to walk to Konskie. The old man, after looking one more time in the direction of the Germans, turned and followed Pants, and hoped that he could hitch a ride soon, which he knew was not going to happen if the Germans were commandeering vehicles behind him. Walking was his only option now. "Better than being shot. Damn Germans," he mused as he adjusted his belt and pants up and tighter.

By late afternoon, they had arrived in Konskie and parted ways, as the driver needed to find his contact and Pants was directed to the road to Opoczno. As they said goodbye, Pants thanked the old man for the driving lesson.

He replied, "I wish it would have been all the way to town. My feet are killing me." They shook hands and wished each other well knowing that their travels were far from being over.

The walk to Konskie was hard on both of them. The old man was fatigued and sore from the prolonged hike he was not prepared for, while Pants was using muscles that were still sore from the beatings he'd undergone in the past couple of days. The bruises were large, tender, and were beginning to itch as the blood clots were being broken down.

For the next several hours, Pants made a stop at two farms and looked at the clotheslines for colored aprons that were his signal to pick up a message. Either there were none or one of the other couriers had collected them for the clotheslines were empty of aprons. Just at dusk, he arrived at the farm of Samuel and Gertrude, and in the dimming light he saw two aprons on the line. He sat at the edge of the tree line and watched for 15 minutes for any activities around the farm that would put him or Samuel's family at risk. The windows were covered with dark curtains, and it was difficult to tell if anyone was even at home. There was a tattletale wisp of smoke from the chimney that indicated that at least someone was in the house. After the allowed time, and not finding anything suspicious, he approached the farm and knocked on the door in the pattern that was his code.

Through the slightest crack between the curtain and the window Pants could see that a dim light was extinguished, and a moment later the curtain moved as someone peered out at him. Several seconds later, the door opened and Pants heard Gertrude's voice invite him in with a soft but firm "Quickly!" Pants stepped into the darkened room as the door closed behind him. His eyes were still adjusting to the darkness and the very dim glow from embers in the fireplace, when a match was struck and a candle lit. The soft yellow flame reflected on Gertrude's gentle round face, her blonde hair pulled back and under a blue bandana. Her smile was sincere but her eyes did not share the moment. They were red and lightly ringed by dark shadows under them. "You're Pants. Is that right? I haven't seen you for some time," she said, as she blew out the match.

Pants was slightly embarrassed, and said shyly, as he stood before this nice woman, "Yes I'm Pants. Thank you for letting me in, but I apologize for looking and smelling so bad." Pants reached up and pulled his cap off his head and held it uneasily with one hand in front of him while the other tried to press his dirty disheveled hair down onto his head. He removed his jacket and dropped it against the wall near the window with his cap on top of it.

Gertrude's eyes adjusted to the dim light and gestured for Pants to sit on the chair. Pants bowed slightly, as young gentlemen do, in acknowledgement of the offer and sat on the wooden chair at the small table. He looked around at the modest but neat room and asked as he noticed his absence, "Where is Samuel?"

Gertrude sat on the chair opposite Pants, looked at his face, and could see the bruises and red marks. She stood up without saying a word and went over to a large basin and water pitcher where she dampened a cloth and returned to Pants. She started to wash the dirt and dried blood out of his hair and around his ears, dabbing the cloth to moisten the area, then wiped to clean it.

Pants was startled at how tender his face was, but quickly started to relax at Gertrude's skillful, gentle touch. He asked again, "Is Samuel here? I have to see if there are any messages for me to take to Opoczno." Gertrude did not say anything; just continued to clean his head and hair. Feeling awkward Pants added, "I saw the aprons, and thought there must be a message for me." He waited for an answer, but none was coming.

Gertrude went to the basin, rinsed out the cloth, returned to the table, and said, "The aprons have been up for over two week. No one has come to pick up anything. They are almost completely bleached by the sun when they are not being rained on." She showed some impatience with the comment and continued, "I don't know what is happening. Yesterday, one of the milk cart drivers told me that the Germans have been buying or stealing food and vehicles, because they have begun an invasion of Russia."

The news surprised Pants, but made everything he had been observing seem to fall into place.

"Are they so powerful that they can invade and beat the Russians?" Gertrude gently stroked her cheek with her slender fingers as she looked blankly into the fireplace. She continued, "I don't know what's going to happen to the world or to me." She looked at Pants, who was sitting straight in his chair, his mind running through the things he had seen over the last couple of months and it all started to make sense when she asked, "What are you thinking?"

"Of course, that explains everything," Pants replied. He told her what had been happening to him over the last several months, and especially the last several days. As he relived the tale of his capture, Gertrude scrambled some eggs and gave him bacon, bread, and some fruit juice.

Pants continued to talk as he ate, and tied in what he had seen with this new information. He punctuated his story by pulling up his sleeves to show the welts and bruises on them. Gertrude looked at the multiple marks on the boys' body and sighed deeply and said, "Those look painful." Pants, sensing a sympathetic ear from a pretty lady, impulsively pulled up his shirts to show her the marks on his back and ribs. This time Gertrude was stunned, not by the marks, though numerous, but the rash and skin sores from the lice on his body.

"Take off your clothes," she ordered to the speechless boy. "Take them off outside and put this on." Gertrude went into a cupboard and pulled out a man's shirt that was too large for Pants. "We have to take them out of here and take care of your skin."

Pants did as he was told. After leaving his clothes in a pile, he returned, wearing the shirt that provided enough modesty for the situation. "Sit here, and put your head in that basin." Gertrude ordered and pointed to a basin on the chair in front of the first chair.

As he leaned forward, he asked, with a little concern, "What are you going to do?"

As she rolled up her sleeves, Gertrude brought the oil lamp closer to Pants' head increased the brightest by increasing the wick size and looked closely at his hair. "Just as I thought," she said, as she went to a drawer and pulled a razor from it. She paused in front of Pants for a moment and said, "We have to shave your head. Then you will wash yourself with this vinegar." She placed a bottle on the table.

"Why?" Pants asked again.

"If you don't get rid of the lice on your body and the eggs in your hair, you will never be free of the little monsters."

Pants nodded, but still wasn't sure about the treatment.

Over the next 30-45 minutes Pants was soaped and scraped clean of any hair on his head, and the few hairs on his chest were also sacrificed. The hairs were few, but they were his and he was upset to lose them. After all, he was 16. Gertrude said, "You have to do the same to your groin and man parts." She handed him the straight razor and dish of soap.

Holding the razor in his fist, he sat frozen at the instructions. First looking at the blade then towards his crotch and back again. "I can't do that! What if the blade slips? I could be seriously hurt." Pants was quickly weighing the harm of keeping the lice where they were versus causing harm to himself and the chance of never having children.

Gertrude offered, "If you're afraid, I will do it for you." She started to reach for the blade.

"No! I'll do it." Pants mind raced. He hadn't tried shaving his face more than once or twice, because the scraping hurt, and he'd cut himself. Now, to shave a part that men don't shave, or have a woman do it, were his options. He opened the shirttails and looked at himself. He could picture the blood flowing all over if something went wrong. He had never been with a woman, and having one take a razor to his manhood was not acceptable, so he'd do the task. Upon further consideration and visual inspection, he found that this stressful situation had been more effective than sitting in ice water in reducing the chances of harming himself. Slowly and carefully, he scraped the hair that would provide a nest for lice if they were to go there. Ten long minutes and two to three nicks later, and he was done.

Just when Pants thought the worst was over, Gertrude came to him with another cloth that was soaked in vinegar. She rubbed his head and back, poured more vinegar on it, and handed it to him to finish the job. As it he did that, he let out a howl, as the stinging was HORRIBLE! Not only from the nicks and bruises, but the sores from the lice on his body produced a pain that was like thousands of hot needles piercing his flesh. He yelped several times as the fire on his skin put him into contortions, standing, then squatting and squirming, as he pressed the cloth on his skin. His eyes, red and watering, sadly reflected and recreated the pained look that had been inflicted on him during these weeks.

Finally, when he was totally exhausted, Gertrude came once more with a cloth. This time she said, "This will soothe your skin. It is lanolin, from the sheep, and it will smother whatever monsters are left on your body." She rubbed the cool oily cream over Pants' back and shoulders. Pants finished the job, and felt much better. Gertrude gave him a fresh shirt and pair of pants to wear. She gave him a couple of blankets and pillow to sleep on. Pants took them and placed them in the far corner near the fireplace. Gertrude had placed a couple of logs into the fire to grow it from the ambers that were going out when Pants arrived. The light and heat felt wonderful. Gertrude asked, "Are you comfortable?"

Pants nodded and said, "Yes, thank you."

Gertrude headed for a curtain that separated the main room from her bed. "You'd better get some sleep, and I have to get up early tomorrow."

Pants paused, and asked again, "Where is Samuel?"

Gertrude stopped but did not turn around. Softly, she said, "Dead. The Germans killed him earlier this year in a round-up of people in town in retaliation for the killing of a German by someone. He was delivering milk and was at the wrong place at the wrong time when he was taken to the town square and shot with 19 other people."

"I'm sorry!" was all that Pants could think of saying to the woman who had just taken care of him, and by doing so risked her life. Pants flashed on the shooting of Artur, and the suddenness of death and the end of someone's future.

"Thank you, Pants. You are a good boy for doing what you are doing for all of us," said Gertrude.

"Staszek, my name is Staszek," Pants told her, impulsively.

"She looked back at him and smiled, "Staszek is a nice name." She stepped behind the curtain and pulled it forward. From behind the curtain, she said "Goodnight Pants." In her mind she could never forget that they were still at war with an enemy that did not care about life or families, or the pain they inflicted on the innocent. Even if the innocent are middle-aged crippled men or teenage boys who were brave enough to fight back any way they can.

"Goodnight Gertrude." Pants rolled over, and in seconds was asleep in a clean bed, with a clean but stinging body, for the first time in months.

The next morning, Pants woke in the pre-dawn light to the sound of footsteps around him. His first thought was to listen to tell if they were friendly or dangerous, but quickly realized where he was sleeping and relaxed at the soft sounds of Gertrude going by. She was starting to make some oatmeal, fruit, and coffee for herself. Pants reached to the top of his head to rub his hair and froze for a moment when he did not find any on his head. That memory came back to him. He rolled onto his knees and flinched when he applied pressure to a bruise but still said, "Good morning."

Gertrude smiled and replied, "Good morning to you, too. Would you like some coffee or tea?"

Pants thought about it for a moment, as his mother always made him tea, and that traditionally was the usual warm drink at home. But coffee always smelled good to him as he passed cafés near their shop, and was popular with the men he knew. "Coffee please," he answered, with some enthusiasm. He got up, and found it hard to squat down from the soreness in his legs from the now maturing blue and brown bruises. He rolled up the blankets and placed them in the corner before sitting at the table. As he watched Gertrude make the coffee, he tried to make conversation by saying, "I don't know many women that drink coffee." He thought that was a dumb statement, for surely there were many at the shops and cafés that liked it. The reality was that he did not know that many women in the first place, but it was conversation.

Gertrude looked at him with a little smirk and answered, "It's a habit I learned when I lived in America. It's very popular there. The stronger the better."

Pants perked up at the comment and asked, "Do you speak English?"

"Yes. I lived there as a teenager before coming home to Poland after the Great War. I do not have anyone to speak with, though Samuel spoke it a little."

"Well, I speak English a little. I learned it in school from my Scoutmaster," Pants added. For the next hour, they made small talk as they brushed up on their skills. Gertrude spoke English fairly well, and corrected Pants' grammar and sentence structure. Pants had a gift for language, and caught on quickly.

Finally, Gertrude said, "Your English is good, and I would like to talk more, but it is getting bright and I have a lot of work to do. I'll get you some more clothes so you can be on your way. I'll wash your clothes to kill the lice. Then I'll hot iron your wool pants to kill those hiding in the hems and seams. I will get them done later today, and you can pick them up the next time you come through this way."

Pants asked, "What do you have to do? I can help, and I would like to repay you for what done for me. I can stay one more day. It will not make any difference, since I have nothing new to report."

Gertrude thought about it and found that the extra help would be a blessing, especially since she had been behind on chores. "Very well. I would appreciate help with chopping some wood and raking out the stable for the goats and cow, and replacing the straw. Could you do that?"

"Yes, of course I could do that for you." Pants said, without hesitation.

"Wonderful! Eat some food and drink your coffee, and we'll go to work. I'll get you some clothes and sheets to put into your boots."

Once dressed and oriented to the tasks that needed to be done, Pants went to work. His arms were sore, but over time they loosened and he quickly sawed or chopped enough wood to last for several weeks. Raking, carrying straw, and fixing a gate made for a long day. By afternoon, the sun was warm to the point where Pants had to take his shirt off. In the full sun, he could see how infected by the lice he was, and the signs that they had been killed, and were off his body. The little monsters must have infested the bed in the partisan hut, all those weeks ago, so he was pleased that they were no longer feeding on him. The down side was that it felt funny without hair, and by the end of the day he had a slight sunburn on the crown of head.

As evening brought an end to the day's labor, nightfall would soon cover the farm. Pants and Gertrude had finished their work and shared the dinner meal. They continued their conversation in English about a variety of items, including music and folk dances that Gertrude loved to do. Pants had learned some folk dances in school, but never had the opportunity to improve his ability. Gertrude had a phonograph, played Mazurkas, and taught Pants some of the basic steps of the regional dance, which he learned quickly. Pants had a good sense of rhythm, and they had a wonderful time. As the evening grew late and they had danced to fatigue, they sat to rest on edge of the bed and listened to one more record play its tune. Gertrude thanked Pants for his help and said, "Since Samuel was killed, I never thought I would smile or laugh again. Thank you for what you did around the farm today. It has saved me days of work."

Pants blushed, and said with a smile, as he looked down and rubbed his arms "I haven't been this tired, yet happy, since the war started. I'm glad I was able to do the work for you." He tried to make a joke of his soreness, but when he looked back up he could see that that Gertrude had moved closer and was looking into his eyes and lightly touched his scalp. Her touch was gentle and warm, and he immediately forgot about his shoulders. Gertrude moved her hand down his neck onto his back, stroking it gently. Pants felt a surge of warmth race through his body, as his breathing became deeper. As he looked back into Gertrude's brown eyes, his urge was to touch her as she was touching him. His hand touched her arm and awkwardly rubbed it nervously, too fast. That made Gertrude smile and giggle as she took his hand and directed it to her breast. Pants marveled at the feel and symmetry of Gertrude's body and slid his hand to her waist to pull her closer and kiss her awkwardly. She returned the kiss then looked at him again.

After a pause that seemed to be hours to Pants, she kissed him again. This time it lasted longer and was slower, as she gracefully directed him how to hold and touch her. They slowly gave up the tension that held them to the edge of the bed and leaned, then reclined in each other's arms onto the bed, one improvising on instinct, while the other guided with confidence and encouragement. The loneliness and fear that had followed each of them for so long was forgotten as the boy became a man and the woman knew she had taught the novice well, and felt pleased.

Pants left the next morning for the area where the Opoczno partisans were to be found and he was to give his report summary. He hiked through the woods until he came upon a railroad track that hauled coal across the mountain and into the valley below. He waited in hiding on a blind bend that just passed a bridge where the train would slow down for safety. At the right time, he came out of the brush and ran up to a ladder on the coal car and climbed up between the cars and sat on the knuckle for an hour or so, when the train would slow before entering a station near his destination. Coal trains were seldom guarded and getting on and off the train was relatively simple, though the ride was very uncomfortable and dirty. Once on the ground, he spent time looking for possible trails to a camp, or until, as in this case, a lookout spotted him and after being quizzed, brought him into the camp.

The information gathered was passed up the chain of command, and eventually to the Allies. Thanks to his actions, as well as those of many dozens of other Scouts, the Allies were provided with a complete list of German units, their markings and approximate composition, including units down to battalion size, and where they had been and where they were going. By the end of that day, Pants had given his report summary in great detail about all that he had seen and done during the past eight weeks. He told the commander all the details of each encounter and situation—that is, all events except for one.

Author's Notes: Chapter 13

On June 22nd, 1941, Germany invaded Russia in operation "Barbarossa". This was the largest invasion force in the history of warfare, with over 4.5 million German troops being sent into Russia, followed by 900,000 other Axis troops. It is estimated that Axis forces suffered over 4 million dead. This turned out to be a tactical error on Hitler's part, in that the invasion split his forces and had the Germany army fighting on two fronts at once; something Germany could not sustain.

The Russians are suspected of losing over 8.7 million casualties during the war.

Picture #1: Modern day view from Zamek Checiny in the Holy Cross Hills

Chapter 14
October 29th, 1941: Radom, Poland

IN THE GROWING shadows of late afternoon, Pants leaned back against the corner of the building at the far end of the alley. He nonchalantly brought one boot up and placed it on the wall, his hands thrust deep into his coat pockets as he scanned the area to see if anyone was watching him. Looking to the opposite end of the alley that emptied onto the street, he watched people walk quickly with their collars up against the wind. Streetcars rumbled by, with their pro-German slogans plastered on their sides. The ever-present red flags with the Swastika fluttered at an angle against the walls of the buildings across the street.

Pushing off, after being satisfied that he was not being observed, Pants turned the corner and passed two buildings before he slipped into the back door of a tavern that was doing a brisk business at the front door. Once in, he went down narrow stairs into a storage area and was greeted by four other boys, and one girl with the codename of "Cotton."

Cotton was a big girl, who had come from a farming community where many of her friends and family were killed. She wanted to fight, and it appeared that she could if she was made mad. Otherwise, she was very jovial and always smiled at what was now her new family. Some of the few times when Pants felt totally relaxed and happy were when he and Cotton would tell stories of their adventures of country life, Cotton as a farm girl and Pants as a city boy going to Babiak.

Cotton seemed to enjoy Pants' company as much as he enjoyed hers. On more than one occasion, after the class was dismissed they would go to a park and sit and talk as if there wasn't a war to worry about. Her laughter came easily and was honest. Pants would tell jokes or humorous stories, and they would laugh until they cried. It was a time when Pants acted like the school boy he should have been by showing off for a girl, while Cotton blushed at all the right times. In the quiet moments Cotton longed for the simpler life of the country, and the only thing that she really missed were the ribbons that she braided or tied in her hair. Ribbons were always worn at festive occasions, and reminded her of better times. Pants talked about soccer, and how he missed running for fun and not watching out for Germans. In those moments of solitude they would kiss and hold hands. They became very good friends.

Today, Cotton arrived at the meeting and sat down at the table between Fist and Pants. Fist was one of the teachers from the Battle School, who was also one of the Grey Ranks highest-ranking Scout leaders in the Hive. Pants was leaning against a beer barrel and when Cotton sat down he pulled out of his pocket several red, yellow and white ribbons and handed them to Cotton. "Here I traded a packet of sewing needles for these. I thought you would like them." With a sparkle in her eyes Cotton pulled one red and one white and quickly tied one on each of her braids then swung her head side to side in a moment of fantasy trying to see the ribbons sail around her head.

They both laughed, and Fist commented on how nice they looked. As Cotton started to settle down for the beginning of the lesson, she quickly leaned over and gave Pants a kiss on the cheek. Pants could not stop the grin from spreading over his face while he wrote down the title of the subjects for the day on the small table in front of him. "Franck," one of the Scouts, leaned forward over the table towards Pants, making small talk that was punctuated by off-color innuendos, and loud enough for everyone to hear. Everyone was giggling at the comments except Cotton and Pants. Fist called the class to order before he lost control of the direction of the class. Pants was still blushing at the kiss as he tried to ignore Franck's quip. Inside, he was beaming.

Since Pants returned from his assignment to Kielce, he had been ordered to return to school, specifically to the "Battle School" (Bojowe Szkoly B.S.). In the B.S., the students received schooling in Polish history, literature, mathematics, and basic military organization, tactics and functions. In addition, they learned techniques for the use of small arms/pistols and organized "small sabotage." Small sabotage was designed to challenge German citizens' lives by distribution of propaganda, destroying German symbols and flags, and disturbing German activities and gathering centers. Notably, stink bombs in German-only theaters, restaurants, and businesses, and setting off fire alarms. The Battle School would also disturb train station activities by running through the German sections, knocking over newspaper stands, stacks of suitcases, and disabling loud speaker systems. Pants had already participated in much of this while he was in Łódź earlier in the year. They were also given basic introductory instruction in sabotage and guerilla warfare skills that were advanced further as the Scouts/ Grey Rank members reached seventeen years of age.

Concurrently, Pants continued to run as a courier between cells, carrying the copier stencils for one of the underground newspapers, and copies of the newly formed project called "Operation N." (The "N" stood for Niemcy, the Polish word for Germans.) This organization targeted German civilians and soldiers with newspapers and bulletins that looked like existing publications, but selected articles were reprinted with an anti-German slant. These focused on the tremendous loss of life, and how many German civilians were dying because of the Nazis. Pants had a special fondness for getting on streetcars or trains holding one of the Operation N newspapers written in German. After he had read it for a while, he'd put it down, change seats, and watch from a distance as someone else picked it up and read it. Watching them become engrossed in the stories, and obviously wanting to question the statements, yet because they assumed the articles to be true in well-known German-titled newspapers, they would become confused and carefully look around at the other passengers. This amused Pants, especially when every once in a while the braver ones would point out one of the planted stories and start to argue with the person next to them, spreading the propaganda that much faster. It was important for Pants not to be seen leaving the paper, for fear of being asked where he got it. Any questions that brought attention to him, even for a moment, could be fatal. Since it never had, the mischief remained amusing to him and encouraged him to push for a larger challenge and more risks.

The number of participants in this Battle School had increased, along with their skill and coordination abilities in completing acts of civil disobedience, but so did the risks and penalties they faced. Many of the boys and girls who were caught during these activities were sent to Germany as slave laborers, beaten severely for information, or for some offenses were shot after being captured and interrogated. Pants lost several friends from the Battle School during these months of resistance. On two of his missions he was nearly caught, while his partners were not as lucky. Being fleet afoot was his salvation in at least two of the episodes. In the past three months he had seen four Scouts trapped on the streets and taken away, while another was arrested one night from his bed, and was taken to jail along with the rest of his family. Later Pants learned that the Gestapo beat two Scouts to death, while the other two were beaten but released, for whatever reason God had granted.

The boy who had been taken away at night was never heard from again, though the rest of the family was allowed to return home after questioning. It was presumed that spies and traitors in the community told the Gestapo of the Scout activities and pointed out the boy. Night arrests were common methods of operations for the Gestapo, and were effective in instilling fear in the people, no matter where they lived, not only by the shock value of breaking into a house at night, but by the violence and brutality of the arrests themselves.

Each time Pants survived a mission, he learned more about the way the Germans operated, reacted to events, and, more important, he learned about his own capabilities along with the risks he was willing to take, which were also growing. His rage and contempt for the Germans had hardened by the fire of life experience around him. He felt that he had to continue to fight, if for no reason than to get even with the Germans and the traitors who plagued his country. He was willing to do this for as long as it took to get rid of the invaders. As with others in his group, his name was not known to any associated group, for fear of being identified if captured. This anonymity would protect him from discovery, but it also gave him the feeling of being alone. The loneliness was often deepest at night where he missed the kiss on his forehead or embraces from his sisters, the very things he found annoying in the past. This loneliness produced bonds between Boy Scouts and Girl Guides, as well as with those who would help them. This level of loyalty and dependence was between people who did not know each other's names. Pants had been told that there were many "swarms" throughout the city holding secret classes and planning actions against the occupiers so they were definitely not alone in spirit or in numbers.

As Pants settled into a chair in the basement of the tavern, two more Scouts arrived and shook each other's left hand in the Scout tradition. In many ways, the title of "Family" for the squad of teenagers meant a lot to him, and to the others.

Tonight's lessons were on geometry and hand grenades. The connection was the difference on how far you can throw the German 24 "Stick grenade" versus the English Mills, or "Pineapple," using the geometry of a throw to determine how the increased length of a persons arm became useful when using these weapons. Using both algebra and geometry, it was determined that the German weapon, which had a long wooden handle with one end being heavier due to the explosives in it, could be thrown further than the English grenade that filled the whole hand with metal and explosives. The long handle would, in essence, lengthen the arm of the thrower, giving it more range by 10-15 meters. That was good, because you could engage the enemy from a greater distance and not be in danger of blowing yourself up by a short throw. Something that definitely had to be considered when throwing the Mills was that its blast radius was greater than the distance it could be thrown. The need to get down low was an important thing to know when using the Mills.

Pants was doing the calculations, which he was fairly good with, in his head, and determining how far the fragments could go, when he turned to the Scout next to him, called Shark, and asked him, "How far do you think you can throw one of these?"

The boy was caught off guard, and said, "What?"

Pants repeated the questions and added, "What's wrong? You haven't been paying attention since you came in." Pants noted that the boy was looking at his watch several times, and was looking at the other Scouts rather than concentrating on the teacher.

"The streetcar was delayed, and I had to make sure I was alone getting here," was his answer to Pants, who accepted the response with a nod.

Pants tried again, "All right then, but how far can you throw it?"

"Farther than you," was the glib comeback.

Pants smirked and confidently replied, "Impossible. I definitely can throw it better than you." The boys verbally jousted about their prowess at such things.

"Bat," one of the older boys, turned to Shark. "I can throw a real melon farther than you could throw that Pineapple," taunting Shark's declaration of skill.

"Well, I would like to see you prove it," Shark retorted.

Bat became irritated with Shark, who was smaller, but somehow was always able to put everyone, especially Bat, on edge with his arrogance.

The same basic lesson was done with the accuracy of a bullet at different muzzle velocities, and the trajectory of the bullet over time to hit a target at set distances. The Scouts worked on the math for nearly two hours before getting the concept and the math right. This was a useful skill when shooting a target from a long distance away. The plan for the following day was for them to meet in a remote open field and practice shooting pistols and rifles to prove their math correct. Then they would throw the grenades, both a practice and a live grenade. Pants and all the other Scouts were eager to try their skill at throwing bombs.

Before leaving, there was a question and answer period, where they would discuss problems or concerns among themselves and the leader. Just as they were about to start, Shark said he had to go to the toilet and went up the stairs to the latrine outside. Not more than a minute later the door opened at the top of the stairs but rather than the footfalls of a Scout there was a sudden descent of two much heavier individuals rushing down the steps. All heads turned towards the steps and the first sign of trouble were gray fabric covered legs with black boots coming down the steps. "Hande Hoch!" came the order to raise their hands from the SS officer who had squatted down to see and cover the room with his gun. He was followed by the distinctive black suit and overcoat of a Gestapo agent. Each had their pistols out and swung them across the room at all the Scouts there, covering them as they went down the last two steps.

As the SS officer reached the bottom of the stairs and moved his pistol to the far side of the room, Fist went for his own pistol that was on a table off to his left. The SS officer swung back and fired his pistol twice at Fist. Fist's forward motion away from the stairs and sudden jerking shots by the officer had only the second bullet strike Fist in the hip, causing him to fall forward on to the top of the table as he grasped his gun. The Scouts had ducked for cover as one muffled shot was heard above them then five more shots were fired from at least three weapons popped in rapid fashion inside the basement followed by a groan and the sound of a body falling down the steps; then silence. Pants started to look over a barrel of beer that was stood next to him and had been a shield from the bullets when he heard more footsteps but this time slower. He saw that the SS officer and the Gestapo were in a pile at the bottom of the steps and the legs coming down the steps were men's trousers and the tip of a machine pistol was held at the ready at the knee level.

"Fist?" came the call from the steps.

"Over here." Came the reply as Fist started to get up from the floor. The heads of the Scouts also started to come up and each looked to the other in disbelief when they thought that everyone else was all right. Pants turned to Bat on one side of him, and Franck, who was just getting up. The room was slightly gray with the smoke and dust that lifted into the air with the sudden commotion. The barrel next to Pants had a hole in it, and beer was flowing from it in a soft foamy stream down the side. The odd smell of gunpowder and aged beer filled the room.

The man with the machine pistol came down and pushed the Gestapo agent over and found him dead with a bullet in his neck while the SS officer was shot twice, with one bullet in the stomach and one in the chest. He went over to Fist and saw him splattered with blood and asked, "Are you hurt badly?" He looked at the wound in the hip, but found no other holes to explain the amount of blood on him. As he said this, he looked under the table behind him and saw Cotton on the floor, not moving. Fist pointed to the table, and immediately Pants and one of the other boys moved it out of the way as the guard turned the girl over and saw that she was dead. The first bullet the SS officer fired struck Cotton on the side of her head, and shot off a part of her face, killing her instantly. Pants looked at Cotton and felt deflated and mournful to be so helpless at that moment. The white ribbon on her braid was slowly absorbing blood, turning it a darker red than the matching ribbon against the ground. On the verge of total despondency, he turned to Fist for an answer, but saw his leader being attended to by two of the Scouts who placed a tight dressing and bandage to the hip and thigh.

Pants looked at the bloody face of Cotton, and felt crushed inside. The exhilarating moment after her last kiss has turned so dark, cold, and painful so quickly. He became incensed at the sight and grew angry. *This is wrong!* His anger needed a channel to be released, but in the tight confines of the basement he capped his rage and frustration with great effort in order not to make a bad scene worse. He went over to the bodies of the Germans crumpled at the bottom of the steps. The SS officer had his pistol still in his limp hand. Pants looked at the body, then to the gun, and with a sudden thought, impulsively reached down and took the pistol from the SS officer. Pants looked at the Nazi markings on the 9 mm Walther P38, and with a slight pulsing nod as if to confirm his decision, he thrust it into his jacket pocket. After doing so, he attempted to punctuate his action by spitting on the S.S. uniform but his mouth was too dry to produce any moisture. A dab of salvia was all he could produce, and he couldn't get it out off his lip after failing to launch it at the body. Frustrated by the lack of saliva, Pants just made the noise as he spit air in partial vengeance at the corpse. Pants turned back to the others looking for something to do.

Fist was able to get up and hobble over to the stairs. He surveyed the bodies and looked around the room. Apparently the S.S. officer was shot last, since he was the furthest from the door. The moments between the Gestapo being shot and the fatal wounds to the SS man allowed him time to squeeze off two more rounds after hitting Cotton and Fist. Those stray bullets punctured the barrel that Pants was hiding behind and the table where they had sat. The security guard that had been posing as one of the taverns customer had seen three Germans come into the building walking briskly as they headed directly for the back room, apparently thinking there were only unarmed Scouts in the basement. The German, stopped at the top of the stairs and the two who went down expected a simple arrest of the Scouts, not thinking they would have a guard in the tavern for just such an occurrence. The Scout guard wasted no time when he heard the shots downstairs. He shot the German at the top of the stairs, and quickly went to the top of stairs, shooting the Gestapo and then the SS officer from the door as he entered the stairwell.

Fist looked around and told the Scouts, "One at a time, go up the stairs calmly and leave the building normally, some through the front and the others by the back door. Go to your safe houses tonight, and make sure you are not followed. You will be contacted there when it is clear." He looked at each and said, "Go." Then he said, "Wait." He grabbed several bottles of wine giving one to each Scout and said, "If asked, you were here bringing wine for your friends."

Taking a bottle each, they exited the basement and disappeared into the evening and headed for their night shelter. As Pants left, he looked back at Cotton once more and clenched his teeth. Moisture finally came to his mouth, in the form of a tear from down his cheek. As had happened all too often in the past two years, Pants felt alone, and that made him lessen his fear of death and gain more determination not to let the Germans beat him. If they did, he figured that he would have let down all of those friends and family members. Pants had the same sense of heightened awareness as he had after he shot the German last winter, and after his escape from the holding tent near Kielce.

His mind raced as he replayed the sudden arrival and outburst of gunfire, something he was sure was not the plan of the Germans who had found a gold mine of potential information from this cell of Scouts. He could still see the two bodies at the bottom of the stairs and he thought, *Good! The sons of bitches deserved it.* He reached into his pocket and squeezed the pistol grip and swore to himself that the next bullet from this gun would kill a German. After a brief moment, he thought about the bullet hole in the barrel next to him. *That could have been me.* Then he pondered, *How did they know? We have been changing meeting places regularly. How did they know?* A chill came over him when he asked, *Where was Shark?* He did not like or believe the answer that came to his mind. He could not determine if he was right, so for the time being he let the thought go.

As Pants came to the top of the stairs, he looked left and right, deciding which way to go. The Scout in front of him turned left to the front of the restaurant, so he turned right towards the back door. As he opened the back door to leave, the light over the back door surprised him with its brightness forcing him to stare past it into the dark. He did not remember the light being on before, and if he had thought about it, why it was on at all. As Pants headed out into the darkened alley, a figure in the storage shed just outside the back door advanced the film of his camera and waited for the next person to come out.

Two days later Pants got a message from a drop point that said, "Hive compromised after meeting. Go to camp B for further orders." The coordinates were then given. Pants knew that Camp B only meant that whatever the coordinates were, the first two numbers would be reduced by "2" as the letter B was the second letter of the alphabet. That way, if the note was found, the reader would not be able to find the camp, since it would be off by a kilometer. His password was Gdansk.

The fastest way for Pants to get to the area was to either hop a ride in a truck or sneak onto a train. Since he was carrying a pistol now, he would be safer riding the train, as inspections were less thorough when done on the train. He packed what clothes he had and was given some extra heavy wool sweaters and a winter jacket to take with him to the camp by the old woman in whose house Pants had been staying. "Give two of the sweaters to whoever might need them, when you get to where you are going." She gave him a grandmother-type kiss on the forehead and said, "Be brave, but be safe."

Before leaving town, Staszek stopped in to see his mother for a couple of minutes and told her, "I will be gone for some time." He gave her a kiss on one cheek then on the other cheek just before she started to cry.

"I'll light a candle and say a prayer for you to be safe." He smiled and carefully left the house. His care in leaving was very good but the vision of Mrs. Von Rupp across the alleyway was excellent.

Once into the outer area, where he was past the boundary of occupied Western Poland and the General Government that was just east of Łódź, Pants entered the heavily wooded forest and followed his compass heading to a place equally distant between several small towns and the junction of railroads and major roads.

Deep in the woods, he came to the place that was indicated by the coordinates and was met by two perimeter sentries, who stopped him and demanded a password, which he gave properly. From there he was taken to the camp commander, codenamed "Stone," who was in a hut built into the side of a fern-covered hill. A blanket hanging over an opening acted as a door. Pants identified himself as a Scout and courier and why he was there. The commander said, "I can use you as a forward scout. The Germans are sending a lot of troops into Russia, and I need to know where they are gathering and what they are up to. Can you do that?"

Pants nodded and told him about being captured in Kielce. During the explanation, Pants mentioned that he tried to get out of the problem by speaking German to the interrogator, but was not successful. "He still beat me up pretty good."

The commander perked up his head at that information. "You speak German? How good are you?"

Pants shrugged. "I can get by, and I know swear words." As Pants said that, it did not seem as important as it did when he was in the first partisan camp, in what seemed such a long time ago.

"Can you describe and translate military titles, units and equipment?"

"Sure, those are easy," Pants answered, knowing that they were the majority of what he had done during the summer.

"Come with me," the commander said, as he stood and pushed through the blanket door, and headed for another hut across the tree-dotted campground. It appeared that there was room for at least 50 men at this camp by its obvious size, though only about 10 could be seen at any one time.

They crossed the compound to where an armed guard sat next to another hut that had a wooden door made of five cm saplings, which in turn was also covered by a blanket. The guard stood up and looked through a slit in the wall above his seat and then opened the door for the commander.

Pants followed Stone into the hut and he looked upon a German soldier sitting on the ground leaning against the wall with his hands and feet bound and a mask over his eyes. Stone sat down on a stump near the soldier who sat up on the dirt-floor.

Stone explained to Pants, "We caught him after he had taken a crap while patrolling through the woods on the other side of the valley. He was so slow and clumsy at shitting in the woods that his company probably still hasn't missed him."

Pants grinned slightly, but remembered how scared he was when he was held prisoner. *At least I wasn't tied up.* He became grateful for that as he looked at the dirty hands tied behind the soldiers back. They looked blue from the tight rope that must have added to the pain and fear.

Stone told Pants, "Tell him word for word what I say to you."

Pants looked at Stone and nodded.

"What is your name and rank?" Pants repeated it in German.

The soldier froze a little as he heard the German words and twisted his head towards the German voice and tried to see through the mask that prevented it.

"Grenadier Albert Flohr." He said, quietly and with hesitation.

"He is Private Albert Flohr" Pants translated.

"That is better. What is your unit number and designation?" Stone continued.

For the remainder of the next hour Stone asked questions about where he had been, what work he did, what did he know about his unit's destination, all of which Pants repeated in German then back to

Polish. Several times the private refused to answer and each time he was threatened with death or was beaten by the guard before he divulged the information, but in the end he gave all the information that Stone wanted to know.

After the interrogation was over, Stone took Pants back to the command hut. Once there one of the sentries came in with a cup of coffee for Stone, and Stone ordered some bread and a cup of coffee with milk in it for Pants. "I assume you drink coffee?" He asked Pants as he sat down.

"Yes sir," Pants responded sharply. He was cold, and anything warm would be helpful now.

"You did a good job in there. It was a big help getting the information. It seems the Germans are sending all their first-line troops to the Eastern Front and keeping these types of soldiers on occupation duty. This gives us more targets to attack, and more ways to keep the Germans from hurting our people if they are out here chasing us while still trying to take on the Russians." Stone grinned slightly at the thought. "We can make a difference and get some revenge, all at the same time. You will help us with this process. Do you like that idea?"

"Yes Sir!" Pants said, without hesitation.

"Very good. Tomorrow we will send you to one of the other groups where they have other prisoners and you can help translate for them too. Do you have a gun?" Stone asked.

Pants pulled out his P38 and showed it to Stone. Stone took it and held it clearing the chamber and removing the clip. "Nice, where did you get this?"

Pants went briefly through the story of the basement, and Battle School classes he had been taking, plus the math of a grenade toss. Stone listened intently and could see that he had a dedicated soldier in front of him. "How old are you?" Stone asked with some curiosity, thinking of himself at that point in his life.

"I'll be seventeen soon." Pants answered, and assumed that five months would qualify for the word 'soon' in some dictionary.

"Have you fired this pistol, and did you ever throw your stick-grenade?" Stone asked, from the information that Pants had just given him.

"No, but I would like to, some day." Pants volunteered.

Stone nodded, and called the sentry to come in. "Get our Scout here ten rounds of 9mm ammunition, a Mills and a potato masher to practice with." Stone laughed and said, "Let him see if his math was correct."

Pants was taken to a small clearing, a distance from the camp and surrounded by the forest. The sentry, code named "Ox," paced off eight meters and placed a cloth against the trunk of a tree and continued another twenty meters placing another large piece of cloth on a stump. When he returned, he took the pistol that Pants had and reviewed the features of the gun, most of which Pants knew and was impatient to do himself, but he learned a couple tricks to field strip the gun and reassemble it quickly. Loading the magazine with bullets, Pants was instructed in a better functional stance to shoot his weapon at the first piece of cloth, first shooting individual shots, then three series of two shots each, using both hands, and then only one. When all the bullets were shot, they went to examine the cloth for holes. The pattern was not very tight but all the rounds had hit the cloth, for which Ox congratulated Pants.

As a reward for doing well with the pistol, Ox took his STENS 9 mm submachine gun off his shoulder and gave it to Pants. Pants held it and examined the gun, holding the magazine that stuck out from the side of the gun like a handle. "I've heard of these, but I haven't seen one. It's lighter than I thought it would be."

"It has a nasty habit to misfire, and it's only good for 30-50 meters, but it will put bullets out there quickly," Ox said with some frustration, as he pointed out the features and firing mechanism of the gun. "There." He pointed to the cloth on the tree again. "Try hitting the cloth again," Ox encouraged Pants.

Pants grinned as he shouldered the curved metal butt of the gun. He slowly pulled the trigger, and about half way to where he thought he would fire the gun came to life and sprayed bullets at the cloth initially. Then they worked their way up the trunk of the tree. Pants released the trigger and smiled.

"Fun isn't it?" Ox added, "Now try it again, but in short bursts."

Pants took partial aim and squeezed the trigger firing three to four rounds at a time. On the third pull of the trigger, the gun jammed. Ox grumbled as he took the weapon and showed Pants how to clear the chamber. Pants cleared the chamber once by himself, before firing the gun again. "The English have started dropping these to us, and they are mostly better than nothing." He took the gun and put it over his shoulder and across his back.

Ox produced two grenades, the "Pineapple," or Mills, and the Stick-grenade or "Potato Masher." Ox gave Pants instruction on how to hold each weapon and allowed Pants to practice throwing each one with the pins still in. His distance was not as far as he thought he would throw, but the Potato Masher indeed went further than the Pineapple. Once Pants became comfortable with the technique Ox asked, "Do you want to try to pull the pin and throw it?"

Pants paused for a moment still holding the Potato-Masher and moving it up and down like a hammer several times testing its weight. "Well yes. That's why we're here, right?"

Ox nodded as he pointed to the German grenade, "Okay then. One more time, let's walk through the drill: unscrew the bottom cap, let the string fall out. When you are ready, pull the string and heave it towards the stump. Then duck and cover."

Pants got his footing the way he wanted, and went through the steps. When he got to the pull the string, he paused ever so slightly to say a prayer that he would not blow himself and Ox up, and finished the step before letting it fly. Five seconds later with his face in the ground and hands covering his head there was a loud explosion. He got up when he heard the dirt stop falling and looked to see if he had blown up the tree stump. His throw had been short of the stump, but there was an impressive hole in the ground.

Ox patted him on the back, and said, "Now that one." He walked Pants through the drill for that grenade, and again Pants prayed not to blow the two of them up as he let the grenade fly. He hit the ground again to protect himself. This time it seemed forever before the blast occurred, but when it did he seemed much louder and the falling dirt was more intense. When he got up, the damage from this grenade was much greater, but also closer to him. Ox looked at the hole in front of them and commented, "You'll have to get stronger if you are going to throw one of those without hurting your comrades. Pants was amazed by the noise, dirt displaced, and the hole he made. He knew that he would do better next time. He had to, or it might be his last effort. The awesome power that fit into his hand unnerved him a little.

For the most part, he hadn't given much thought about his death while in the woods, but the noise and the hole in the ground brought the possibility of death closer to him than any time since the beginning of the war. Being blown to bits out in the woods and no one knowing what happened to him seemed so much worse than a bullet. He thanked

God for still being in one piece. Today's lesson was better than the day at the tavern; a much better day.

In the morning, Ox, Pants, and two other partisans headed out to the next camp. That camp was much larger and also had captured a group of German soldiers as well as citizens who were with the Germans. When Pants arrived he was taken to the tent of the commander of that camp and introduced by Ox. Ox related the message from Stone that Pants did a good job in helping the interrogation of their prisoner. On hearing this, the commander said, "My boys call me Root, and it so happens I have a special need from you right now." He pointed to a bench in his tent and Pants sat down. "He turned to Ox and asked, "Did you come in over the mountain trail in the north?" Ox nodded. "Good. The prisoners could not have seen you. I am going to have one of my men take you into the prison compound as if you were a prisoner. I want you to listen to the conversations and see which of the civilians are working for the Germans and whatever other information you can collect. We had captured them during a fight in the nearby village, where the Germans were surrounded and surrendered after a stand-off of several hours, where we killed most of them. When it was done, there wasn't an officer among the soldiers, so either he got away or is still among them, acting as a civilian."

Pants thought about the situation for a while.

Root continued, "I know we have a bunch of people in the cage who are not sympathizers of the Germans and were Poles caught because they were at the wrong place at the wrong time, but I need to know who is who. You'll fit in with them. Find out what you can. Don't let them know you speak German. Is that clear?"

Pants nodded, but was not clear on the exact mission. The crux of the issue was to listen and not be found out as he looked for the leader of the Germans. It was apparently an important mission for him and the commander, but he was extremely anxious about how he would act and not be spotted as an imposter. He could not tell his new commander that he was afraid, but he was almost shaking at the risks he was about to undertake.

He was tied firmly by Ox out of sight of the cage. The cage was a small tight area surrounded by tree posts and lots of barbed wire. Half dozen guards patrolled around the cage at all times. He was escorted to the gate and roughly thrown into it. His hands were untied, and he was left on his own. The cage, he estimated, held approximately forty people, fifteen being soldiers, and of those, ten had been injured during combat. As he was placed in the cage and began to move around it was clear that no one was talking to anyone. He wandered around, trying to sit in a group, but no one would talk to him. He was there the rest of the day and night, sleeping next to several older men for warmth on a pile of straw and leaves that were thrown over the wire fence. During the next morning all the civilians, and then all the soldiers were to be taken one by one for interrogation.

Pants was the first civilian to be taken for interrogation. Root was waiting, and asked if he had learned anything. "No, they don't know me and no one is talking about anything. There doesn't seem to be any reason to talk. They just sit and wait."

Root acknowledged the challenge and said, "I have an idea. I will tell them that I am going to send all of them to the Russians, who have a way to get information from them if they don't talk to me. Before they come in here, I want you to tell them that I'm looking for the spy in the group, and for the officers of the soldiers. That should increase their motivation."

Pants was led back to the cage and another man was taken out. As he sat down next to a group of civilians he said to no one in particular, "This is stupid. I don't belong here, and I don't want to go to Russia." He waited for a while. "The Russians are worse than the Germans I can't go there, I'll die!"

Finally, one of the boys close to his age asked, "What are you talking about? What has Russia to do with us?"

Pants looked around to the others, lowered his voice, and leaned towards the boy, "They told me that if I don't tell them who is the traitor in the group, or who is the leader, I will be sent to Russia. All of us will if they don't find out. I'm just a farmer's son, and I don't want to go because someone is hiding a spy." Pants started to get agitated as he felt the part coming from within him as he allowed his fear to surface for real. "We have to give up the officers and spies here. I don't want to die because of a German who wants to live. I was on the God-forsaken road heading for Konskie at the wrong time. This isn't right." His passion began to stir among the men from the village, but they were hesitant to say anything.

As the morning went by, all the civilians were taken through the interrogation process again. After each man came back, Pants pressed, "See, they are going to send us to Russia, right? Do you want to go?"

Pants looked at each man and boy for an answer. None came. After the 14th man was taken away one old man who wore a knit sweater sat down next to Pants and said slowly as he squeezed his arm, "You be a good boy and not get so worked up over the lies these forest criminals have told you. Keep your mouth shut, and you'll be able to go back to your potato planting soon. They're not going to empty a Polish village of the men and let women and children starve. Do you understand boy?" Pants flushed red and nodded as the man squeezed his arm harder.

The last civilian man returned and he announced that he was told the commander of the camp believed all of us to be villagers and were not involved in any conspiracy of silence or a cover-up. You all know me, and believe me when I say that our worrier here," pointing at Pants, "can rest, knowing he'll be home tomorrow." The man patted Pants on the top of the head. Pants really became frightened. He could not believe that Root had changed his mind, but he had to continue with his role for the time being. Pants paused and smiled at the man and said, "That's wonderful news. We would be killed like so many bugs if we went to Russia. We will all be all right." One of the other teenage boys came over and shared that he was scared too, and he was happier knowing he would be going home soon.

The energy was calming around the group and conversation began to loosen among the civilian group. Pants sat quietly, waiting for something to happen as he watched the activity among the prisoners. He did not have to wait long. When the last soldier went through interrogation and was returned to the cage, several of the partisans came down the hill and into the cage. Three of them guarded the gate while two more went over to Pants, picked him up, and started to drag him away from the group.

As he started to protest, the man who had called Pants a worrier, stood up and said, "I told the Polish commander that this boy was the problem. He wasn't from the area and was the spy for the Germans." He triumphantly pointed in the direction Pants was being pulled and ceremoniously slapped the dust off his hands as a gesture of victory.

Pants protested louder after hearing the proclamation, and was soon out of sight and sound of the cage when he was pulled into Root's tent. For a moment he wasn't sure whether things had gone terribly wrong, and Root really changed his mind. Did the old man really convince Root to let everyone go, and did he think he was a spy? He sat down on the bench he sat on the day before. Roots sat down opposite Pants while he held a cup of coffee and stared deeply into Pants' eyes. "What have you to say?"

Pants thought about the facts, as he knew them and asked Root, "Did you change your mind about the story?"

"No. I kept with the story as we discussed."

"Then why am I here?" Pants asked.

"The last man swore that you were the spy and you were trying to panic the rest of them against us." Root slowly spun the cup of coffee in his hands. "I'm afraid you might have played your hand too much. They have marked you as the spy. If they believe that, you would not make it through the night." Roots leaned forward onto his knees as he sipped the coffee. "Putting you in there might have been too big of gamble. It was better to pull you out."

Pants sighed, a long breath out. "Good. I think I know what you need to know." Roots looked at him and handed him the cup of coffee. Pants smiled, took a sip and took another long breath out to calm down more. The coffee had milk in it, and he smiled, a tight-lipped effort.

Root was slightly surprised at the statement and asked, "Well what do you know now?"

"Since, if you did not change the story, the last man is the traitor of the village, as he lied to isolate me from the rest of the people as well as place suspicion on me. The one with the knit sweater is a German officer."

Root suspected the old man as the traitor, but was not sure about the officer. "What makes you think that one is the German?"

Pants relayed the intense conversation where the man had squeezed his arm and told him to keep his mouth shut and he would be able to go back to planting potatoes. "His Polish was very good, but he used the German word, Kartofel, for Potato rather than the Polish word, Ziemniak."

Root smiled, but asked, "Is that your only clue?"

Pants shook his head. "I saw him going by one of the German soldiers who had his back turned towards him and they accidently bumped together. When the soldier, who was knocked off balance, turned suddenly around and saw him, he started to salute him before he caught himself."

Root smiled broadly. "Do you want more coffee?"

Pants smiled, and nodded with delight.

###

As the snow started in November, Pants stayed with this group of Partisans, where Pants was assigned to horseback travel through the forested areas once again. He carried messages between this unit and others in the Radom, Konskie, and Opoczno areas. When needed, he would be present for interrogations, and served as an interpreter whenever there was a need. He also was able to help translate German maps and identify papers taken from prisoners or dead soldiers after a mission. The job of the courier however, was fraught with danger when, over time, a transient person would eventually catch the eye of someone who was watching for just such a pattern. Being mobile and having the ability to drop out of sight by relocating was a good strategy to follow for a courier.

During one such opportunity, Pants had to go to Gertrude's farm for a message pickup. He had traded some honey that he had been given by a farmer near Jozefow for some red embroidered fabric. He wanted to give the fabric to Gertrude. Once he reached her farm, he sat and watched to make sure the area was not a risk to him. He watched Gertrude do her chores that she seemed to be laboring with in the snow and mud-covered yard. Even doing hard labor Pants could see that Gertrude was a graceful woman by the way she moved during her work. The colored aprons were on the line as a sign that a message was to be collected and Pants carefully moved towards the farmhouse giving his horse a light rein.

When he thought he was clear, he rode to the gate of the house where Gertrude recognized Pants and came with a faster step than just moments before while she was working. As she came towards Pants she wiped her hands on her skirt. When she came close, she opened her arms and gave Pants a hug and kiss on his forehead. She pushed him back at arms length and took off his cap and smiled, "See, I told you it would grow back."

He rubbed the short hair on his head and they hooked arms as she escorted him to the door.

"Wait," he said as he reversed direction and retrieved a package from his bedroll. "This is for you." He handed the bundle of fabric to Gertrude.

She accepted the package and said, "Go put your horse in the barn and attend to his needs while I make some food for you." Pants took the reins and led the horse to a stall in the barn and threw some straw in front of him to eat. He returned to the house and savored the smell of the food and the warmth of the room. During the rest of the afternoon and into the evening they talked in English about the war and what was happening around the areas. Gertrude said, "The Germans are coming more often, and cleaning out the storage bins of all my food stock. I can't dress a chicken without figuring that there's a good chance I won't be able to eat it myself because the Germans will take it."

She reflected on how she should have stayed in America, where the Germans could not scare her so much. To change her dreary mood, she put on one of her records and reached out to Staszek, "Do you remember the steps?"

Staszek nodded and said, "Of course. I had a wonderful teacher."

Gertrude smiled at the compliment, and they spent the better part of an hour swaying and kicking and whirling to the sound of the Polish folk dance. Staszek had a talent for folk dance, and loved to show off his improvisational steps and deep squat kicks. When they sat to rest, they sang the words to the songs, which were popular after the last war.

Afterward, they drank some homemade fruit juice that Gertrude had blended with a small amount of Polish Vodka, "Just for flavor." Staszek sipped the beverage, which reminded him of his uncle Jozef, who had bragged about getting his father, Felix, drunk for the first time, and did the same for him the last time he had visited Babiak. Staszek sat quietly as he remembered his uncle and the Babiak area, and his family, who he was starting to miss more often while on the trails. With Christmas coming, being away was harder at this time of year. He sat on the chair staring at the fire when Gertrude called, "This is beautiful!" Staszek turned and Gertrude was holding the fabric around her waist on top of her skirt and looking at it against her right leg, which she had posed forward of the left. "I can't wait to make a skirt from this. I will wear it proudly." She spun around slowly and watched it rise up slightly from the twirling. "It is very Polish," she continued to say, in English, "When it's balanced against a white blouse, it looks like the flag." She showed him, as she pressed a white blouse against her chest.

They talked into the late evening, when Gertrude said, "It has been a long day and I need some sleep." Staszek stood up and said, "Of course. Can I sleep here near the fire like before?" The memories from his last visit caused a pounding in his chest. Gertrude, who from the daily grind of farm work done alone, seemed to have aged a great deal over the past months. Yet, she was still a beautiful woman, and her voice, smile, and laugh were overpowering for the young man. He dared not take advantage of this woman, but he wanted so much to hold and be with her again. "I am much better now and the floor would be fine to sleep, or I could be in the barn or ..." Staszek started to ramble, and blushed from the awkward monologue.

Gertrude smiled and walked over to him. She touched his face, and took his hand. As she pulled him to the bed, she quipped, "I need sleep, but being warm is good too." They found the bed to be cold, but it was not long before it did not matter.

For the most part, the Partisans were mostly interested in acquiring weapons and supplies from the Germans, especially with the group in the Radom/Kielce area, of which Opoczno was the northwest part. Direct attacks on individuals had been few and far between, because the Germans would retaliate by killing 10-20 innocent bystanders for every German that was assassinated. The hope of the Partisans, as well as the general population, had been that by this time in the war the Allies would have been marching towards Berlin, which would draw troops away from Poland and back to Germany to protect their own homes. In reality, the Allies were trying to save England, and the Poles were on their own.

The Germans were battling on two fronts, west and east of Germany, with Poland in the center. The German supplies and troops demands had become stretched thin from the escalation of their war effort. Along with that came intolerance for anti-German activities by those caught in the middle who dared to fight back. In Opoczno, where there had been a protest over the treatment of the Jews in the town, a speeding car that was trying to get away from the Gestapo hit a German officer as he fired at the vehicle. The officer's death resulted in the rounding up and shooting of 100 people in the town square. Pants entered the town just after the shootings, and the people on the streets who walked past him were sobbing. Some were even vomiting in the street.

As he came to the square, there was a conspicuous absence of Germans, but the corpses gave proof of their recent presence in town. The murders of those who were in the wrong place at the wrong time was committed to show all who broke the rules that any incident against a German would not be tolerated, and would be revenged at the severest level. The Germans' lack of respect of the lives of Poles extended to their pets. Among the murdered was a dog that was also shot, still attached by a leash to the owner lying silently next to him.

When Pants heard of the massacre and came upon the scene of the atrocity he thought of Samuel, Gertrude's husband, who had been one of those victims somewhere else, but under similar circumstances. Pants became outraged at seeing the bodies that were left for all to see, but no one was allowed to touch. If a body was moved before permission was given to do so, that person was shot. Pants walked by slowly, but did not dare to stop. He could see blood still draining from the dead and pooling in the gutters. Old men, women, and even children were crumpled on the sidewalk like so many piles of clothing. Their faces for the most part were contorted by the last sensation of their lives; pain with horror and disbelief of how terribly wrong it was that their existence had been ruthlessly snuffed out. The Germans continued to prove that they needed to be stopped, and stopped as soon as possible, in any way possible. Pants reached into his pocket, squeezed his pistol, and fought the urge to shoot the next German he saw. His common sense stopped him from a futile gesture, and he walked on. His maturing and ability to control his rage, unlike his habit just a year ago, stopped him from making a deadly mistake. He did not look back as he headed for his meeting place. He did not have to. The memory was burned into his brain and would never leave.

With the German invasion of Russia, greater opportunity for sabotage activities against German materials became possible. Between missions, Pants continued with the Battle School instruction, where he continued learning about explosives and the manufacturing of these materials at clandestine shops, with other Scouts. They learned to make the explosives from raw materials, but especially from explosives liberated from the Germans. In these manufacturing sites, Pants and other Scouts made pipe bombs, electrical primers, detonators, and wire relays. They also produced smoke bombs, stink bombs, and incendiary devices. The primary targets were railroad tracks, telegraph and telephone lines, and German-only shops and businesses. They placed spiked strips across roads to flatten tires and metal "jacks" with long sharpened points that would be placed directly in front of tires of cars that were parked, causing those tires to be flattened when the car was moved again. To slow down and complicate the German's war efforts in the absence of a large standing army was still possible. Through small-dedicated groups of Partisans, each making thousands of cuts, that would bleed a giant to weakness until the Home Army was ready, was the plan.

Of all the actions, railroad tracks and locomotives were highly prized targets, since they were moving massive amounts of war materials to the Eastern Front, and on a very frequent schedule. Derailing one train would tie up tracks and delay deliveries for days or weeks. Railroad workers loyal to Poland assisted the Partisans' intelligence service by giving train schedules and material lists to them. They also told of the number of guards who would be protecting the train and the risk in attacking it. Derailing a train was fairly simple, and materials could be picked up and repackaged for future use. Actually destroying the train became the next goal during this new phase in the war.

Meanwhile in a command bunker in northeast Poland that Hitler called the "Wolf's Lair", the German Führer was handed a dispatch by one of his aides. Until this moment he had been sullen and frustrated by the failure of capturing Moscow as his army stalled just eight kilometers from the Russian capital. The sabotage of his supply lines and the historically cold winter had stopped his troops in the -50 degree below zero Celsius temperatures. There the poorly prepared soldiers were freezing to death next to equipment that were no more than blocks of frozen metal that could not be moved. Hitler could not believe that his general's could not do the job he ordered before the winter snows had started. After all he gave them six months to secure Russia. Until the paper was read, his look was one of anger and frustration over the incompetence of his Field Marshalls.

In moments this all changed when Hitler read, *"December 7ᵗʰ Japan has declared war on the United States and had bombed Pearl Harbor where the American's Pacific Fleet was destroyed."* He was almost giddy with excitement over the news, something that he did not except to happen. Although he wanted the Japanese to invade Russia to distract them from his own offensive, he thought the bombing of Pearl Harbor would draw the resources of America away from England over to the Pacific. For Hitler this was good news. Earlier today he released new orders for his S.S. called, "Nacht und Nebel" (Night and Fog) that gave the Gestapo instructions to arrest and detain any political activists or suspected activists as well as "resistance helpers" that would harm German security. This meant that they would arrest anyone who **might know** or was **suspected of knowing** where resistance fighters were. More to the point this decree would make anyone suspected of the slightest anti German activities simply disappear without a trace.

With the new events in the Pacific he was certain that Germany would win the war. Turning to one of his military advisors who read the dispatch he said with glee, "After all, the Japanese have not lost a war in 3000 years, they will not lose this one as well." His mood had instantly improved. The military advisor thought differently but was not foolish enough to give a dissenting point of view.

Hitler had planned to give a speech to the German Reichstag on December 10th to denounce the American President Franklin Roosevelt, but now decided to postpone the speech in order for his embassy in Washington D.C. to destroy all documents that might be seized if the Americans invaded it. On December 11th in an eighty-eight minute speech he declares war on the United States.

Ten days before Christmas, Pants delivered 10 kg of explosives, primer, wire, and detonator to a group that was ordered to blow up munitions trains heading east just north of Opoczno. He rode a horse from the fabrication safe house to the rendezvous point for most of one day, being extra careful to stay away from roads and places where he could be discovered. Upon arrival he met with the new group, led by a sergeant from the Polish demolition brigade, who now was with the ZWZ. The rest of the team included two brothers, "Jay" and "Robin," plus "Butcher," "Edwin," and "Nail".

The leader "Nail" started with introductions and then the news that Germany had declared war on America and that the Japanese had attacked and sank the American Navy at Pearl Harbor. All the members of the team sat with heavy hearts and in disbelief. The allies had not advanced to help Poland to this point and with the American's drawn to the south pacific the timeline for liberating Poland has most assuredly been pushed back if not totally forgotten by the west. More than before the team felt alone in their mission and therefore placed the urgency to take the fight to the Germans even further onto their shoulders. Pants looked around at the older men. Pants thought that Nail was the oldest one and must be 21. Nail looked composed but deep in his own thoughts as the news was absorbed by the rest of the team. Pants watched the others and tried not to show his fear and anxiety from the grim report. No one looked more confident than he did, which really worried him almost to the point of distraction.

After more logistical matters regarding the target area, Pants focused hard on his orders that were to go with this team, plant the explosives under a selected section of tracks, and wait for a specific military train to come. When the ammunition cars from that train were over the charges, the team was to blow it up and escape to a safe house several kilometers from the site. Setting the charges had to be done at 4:30 PM the next day, between scheduled passenger trains. They had to be ready for a train that was to come by just after dark, at 5:00. This place and time of day gave the group time to see which car was in the center of the cars, and to blow up the train while being able to hide from the guards and any pursuit by soldiers that were on the train after the blast.

At the rendezvous point, Pants presented the explosives for inspection by the sergeant. All connectors and materials were carefully examined and repacked by him. He and the six men were to ride by horseback through the woods to an isolated area of the track to plant the bomb. The night before and day of the planned attack the group went over every part of the plan many times, trying to anticipate any problems or unforeseen dangers. Scout teams had identified areas along the track that would be suitable staging areas for the attack. Preliminary spots were decided, and escape plans and routes were drawn out.

They planned not only a primary location, but also a secondary spot on the rail line, if the snow or other issues prevented setting the explosives in the first target. It became clear that the mission depended on the train coming through at the right time, to make sure that it was not mistaken for a lower-value military target. To know what other trains would be moving on the tracks, it was determined that Pants would go to the train station a kilometer from the attack point to get more details on civilian traffic and an up-to-date time schedule. Pants was instructed to talk to a ticket agent at the station named Henryk, and tell him that he was a nephew from Warszawa. Henryk wore a monocle on his left eye. If he moved it to his right eye, that would be the signal that he understood that Pants was from the Underground and accepted the code message, whereupon he would give any details or extra information that would be vital.

Pants rode his horse to an area 100 meters away from the small country station north of town, where he tied it to a tree off the road. He walked to the kiosk at the station to get a time schedule and asked about a ticket to the next largest city to the east. When he got there, a train was sitting on a spur at the station with some passengers on the train while many others were still on the open platform, moving around in the chilly air trying to keep warm slowly making their way onto the passenger cars. The platform was crowded; more crowded than he expected due to the many German soldiers being transported, and some guards on duty who were also waiting on the platform. They had backpacks as well as their weapons with them. Pants estimated that there were 150 men waiting to board a train. Most were sitting on the platform on their packs or sprawled out and trying to sleep. He worked his way through the line to the clerk and when there was no one close to them he asked, "When is the next train to Radom?"

The clerk said that the 3:30 train was already here but no one was to board until a special train had gone through. "Which would be anytime now."

With that said, Pants added, "Uncle Henryk you don't recognize me, but I am your nephew from Warszawa." Henryk, with little emotion, moved his monocle to his right. He pretended to sort through tickets as he said, "There has been a delay for the supply train. It has not arrived yet. We are waiting for a handcart for inspection crews to clear any bombs hidden under the rails. They will go first for several kilometers ahead of the train, before the train is allowed to proceed. The passenger train will be kept for a diversion, if the commander feels it is necessary." Pants turned around and looked closely at the train on the other track and could see that it was a passenger train and the engine was idling. The locomotive was a larger German model with German lettering on the side. Most of the trains running passengers were smaller Polish commuter engines. Nonetheless, civilian passengers were already in it, waiting to leave the station, while the soldiers continued to wait on the platform. There were no German guards on the tops of the cars, which was the usual clue for being a military transport of some kind.

This news was a surprise, since the plan was for it to come at 4:30. This probably wasn't the one the squad wanted. Pants thanked him for the information and knew he had to get back to his horse. He pulled the small scarf tighter around his neck against the chill and tried to walk slowly so not to draw attention to himself. Speed was important, because the charges might not be planted in time if the ticket agent was correct, so he had to hurry. As he stepped off the platform he started to walk quickly in an unnatural way to his horse that was tied out of sight of the train station. His stifled jerky steps were being watched by one of the guards at the perimeter of the station who was curious about the boy without a suitcase or backpack walking quickly away.

"Boy!" He called out. Pants did not stop nor turn around. "Halt!" The guard ordered with some irritation.

Pants looked over his shoulder and slowed then turned around when it was clear that there was nothing he could do this close to the station, and the need for him to be inconspicuous. "Heil Hitler! Yes sir." Pants said crisply as he stood at attention and arm outstretched to show respect to the guard.

The guard came up to Pants with his rifle cradled under his right arm and said, "Papers." Pants produced his forged document that the guard thumbed through as the guard asked in deliberate but adequate Polish, "What is your hurry? Jerzy Broc." Looking at the picture and name then to Pants.

Pants managed to relax on one leg and explained, "My uncle needs to go to Radom, and wanted to know when the train would be here. So he sent me to find out." He watched the guard's eyes who was mulling over the answer. Pants added with some urgency in German, "The train is supposed to leave very soon, so I have to get back to the farm to tell him." The guard tapped the document on his thumb then handed it back. Pants raised his arm in the Hitler salute to acknowledge the return of the papers, and turned to walk back to his horse and give time for the guard to head back to his post.

Once on his horse and out of view of the guard, Pants heeled his mount to get to the attack point as quickly as possible. He rode swiftly to the place the other horses were tied just off the road that paralleled the tracks by some 300 meters. He hurried through the trees to the attack point to tell the group about his information.

Pants found the sergeant and told him the news. The sergeant looked at his watch and climbed out of the woods near the tracks. He climbed carefully up the snow and dirt covered embankment, then onto the tracks on the outside bend, where the brothers had started digging a trench between the ties to bury the explosives. He stopped them. The sergeant sent Butcher and Edwin to either end of the attack point as sentries. They each had STENS machine guns, while Jay and Robin had two pistols and one rifle each. The sergeant and Pants unpacked the charge. While the sergeant prepared the primers for the explosives, Pants was told to run the wires clear into the woods on a line of sight from the tracks, hopefully far enough away not to have the sergeant blow himself up when he detonated the charges. It was possible that if they hit artillery shells or mortars, the blast could flatten the area for 200 meters. The problem was that they only had 100 meters of wire.

The trap was set, but the sergeant did not place the charges pending the passage of the handcart. Several meters from the track, the explosives and wires were covered with snow and dirt to hide them from the watchful eyes of the soldiers on the cart when it went by. Any disturbance that could be seen by the soldiers might make them stop to investigate possible sabotage. Considering they were the first to enter the trap, they were very vigilant in regards to possible attacks.

The sentries were called in and told that it could be any minute and they should be near the horses to protect them from any patrols and plan to get away quickly.

They waited with excitement and anticipation, but neither the handcart nor the train came. They waited another hour and still no train. It was dark and cold in the woods. The sergeant looked at his watch. The radium dial glowed 5:00. The nerves of the whole group were on the edge of short-circuiting themselves, waiting for the train, listening for patrols, and keeping the horses calm. Trying to remember the path out was becoming too much for the group, they mumbled that they should leave, since the longer they loitered the greater the chances they would be discovered.

It was then that they heard the sound of an engine and the vibration it produced. The sergeant could see the tracks from his nest. He had been digging a deeper hole to stand and then to squat in if the explosion was too great. However, there was no handcart yet. If the train was the supply train it would get by and the mission would fail. He could see the tracks but now needed his binoculars to see exactly if this was the train. He swore at the need to decide. Run and place the bomb or wait for the handcart. "Shit!" he whispered again.

His plan was to detonate the fourth car past the coal wagon, which was his best guess for a successful explosion of a munitions car but it would be impossible to get to the tracks and do this it if this was right train.

Pants was with the other men preparing to flee after the attack when he began to wonder, *What if the transport train did not come and the passenger train was on the tracks first after the handcart? Would they be accidently blown up?"* The thought sent a chill up his spine and he decided to go back to where the sergeant was and to tell him of his concern. He ran as quickly as he could, but the light was almost nonexistent, other than his small flashlight with a red lens that helped him avoid severe hazards as he went forward. He got to the foxhole just as the train noises became closer and louder. The sergeant listened to Pants and said, "I thought about that already, I will wait to make sure that it is not a passenger train." It was too late for Pants to retreat to a safe distance further away so he squatted down next to the sergeant to watch. The sergeant placed the detonator on the dirt in front of him. It was in easy reach and all it needed was the lever to be pulled up and quickly pressed down to set off the bomb. The train appeared, but it was going slower than normal speed on these tracks but it was here. The sergeant looked through the binoculars for a clue but only got questions. "Is there something wrong? Do the Germans suspect something? Were the trains changed?" His eyes strained into the blackness. The train was dark and cars started to move by, and they were dark too. "From the sound it has to be the munitions train, it has to." The Sergeant muttered, "We've missed it." He gave the binoculars to Pants who pressed them to his eyes.

Pants called out, "Stop! It's the passenger car." For an instant he saw a light through the black out curtains of the passenger car. "I see the letters on the engine, and I see passengers but no guards on the roof posts."

The sergeant cursed then grabbed the binoculars back to look for himself and he too could make out flickering lights as the curtains moved slightly. He swore again as he put down the glasses and fell back onto his butt at the bottom of the hole.

He swore again. "We have to get the explosives out of here. We can't have them know that we were here and we can't wait much longer. They could set a trap for the next time we try."

Pants nodded in the dark and could not think of anything else to say except "I'll help you." The sergeant unhooked the wires from the detonator before climbing out of the hole followed by Pants. They were about 20 meters from the edge of the woods when they heard a sound. They heard it at the same time and froze in place. It was the subtle clacking of a handcart. They approached the edge of the woods and watched the flat car with a manual drive where two soldiers moved the handle up and down to propel the cart. The cart had a huge light mounted on it that illuminated the tracks and scoured the tree line. Any disturbance to the normal look would alert the soldiers of a problem and they would surely spray anything suspicious with the heavy machine gun mounted below the searchlight. Since the charges were never set, the track looked clean and the cart continued past the target point.

Now the sergeant and Pants ran up the embankment and shoveled out a long slot between to rail ties and stuffed the explosives into the hole. As the started to cover the charges they heard a noise. "A train, another train," Pants muttered. They looked at each other in the red light glow, and immediately started back to the foxhole. The little flashlights gave them enough to see where they were going as they jumped into the hole then scrambled to rewire the detonator.

Pants used the binoculars to follow the train and started counting, "Engine, coal car, first car, second car, third car." He looks at the sergeant, who was holding the light with his teeth and trying to tighten the wing nuts on the detonator. The weather was cold but he was starting to sweat.

"Fourth car, fifth car; hurry." Pants urged, with teeth and jaw tight.

"Get down" the sergeant yelled as he stood slightly to get leverage on the detonator's handle.

Pants ducked and covered his ears as he heard the whirling sound of the detonator being pushed down, followed shortly after by a rumble through the ground and in an instant a very bright light got to him before the blast sound pierced the night. The heat from the explosion immediately heated the air around Pants and the sergeant, even as they ducked under the ledge of the hole. The fireball ignited the trees immediately around the tracks and flattened many of them as if they were pencils being dropped. The heat from the first explosives set off the cars on either end of the target car, and they, too, went up. Further forward, the power of the blast pushed the engine off the tracks and onto its side. The back cars that had a barracks car among them were also burned and knocked off the tracks sideways. Screams from the soldiers who were not killed by the blasts gave testament to the pain and damage caused by the flames.

Small secondary explosions were going off and sending flares or mortars into the air as the heat triggered their primers. Orange and red balls of flame reached into the dark sky overwhelming the stars and their light.

"Let's get out of here." The sergeant called to Pants. He picked up the detonator and scrambled out of the hole. The firelight was enough to see where he had to go, and they were going there in a hurry. As they made their way towards the horses they could hear orders being called out to the soldiers and soon Germans were setting up a perimeter to protect the scene and at the same time they were looking for the bastards that did this to them. Everyone in the group knew this, and they were not planning to waste time getting out of the area until they got to the rendezvous point and found that the horses were gone!

In the dim light of the flames they stopped where the horses were supposed to be and turned in puzzled circles looking into the darkness and not knowing which way to start moving. Rifles at their ready and trying not to speak above a whisper then strained to see into the darkness. Finally a set of sharp eyes said, "There!"

The blast must have scared the horses off, but finally one could be seen some distance away, all heading away from the flames. By this time, the Germans had started into the woods using their lanterns and flashlights to search the area near the tracks. The sabotage group had a large lead on the searching soldiers, and eventually the saboteurs caught four of the horses, which forced them to ride double to get away. The soldiers fired in the direction of the horses whinnying but the group was beyond the range where they could have been truly seen and targeted.

As they cleared the woods on the trackside of the road they heeled the horses so that they could reach the getaway route at the next trail into the woods. The fire from the train and trees gave enough of a glow for the group to make good time on the road and were seconds from the trail when the headlights of a motorcycle as well as a car illuminated them head on from the road. A split second after being seen the riders were showered by machine gun fire from the soldier in the motorcycle sidecar. Jay seated in front on one horse was hit by two of the bullets and slumped onto the horn of the saddle but held onto the mane of the horse for support- but was weakening quickly. The horse froze in the headlight of the motorcycle and did not budge for the moment. Robin, behind Jay returned fire at the motorcycle and hit his mark, causing it to turn violently to one side and roll into the ditch. Shots came from the car behind the motorcycle and they hit Butcher and Edwin who were also sharing a horse. Butcher was able to hold on to the reins but the horse was hit next, and it went down in a heap throwing both men to the ground.

The sergeant poured bullets from his STENS into the car, hitting and shattering the windshield and windows on the driver side. The car went off the road, stopping short of a tree. Jay and Robin's horse came up behind Pants and the sergeant when the sergeant shot into the car at the stunned and slowly moving passengers.

The sergeant dismounted and opened the doors firing two shots into the passenger who tried to move. He and Robin pulled the bodies of the driver, a second soldier and one apparent Gestapo agent out of the car and left them on the road.

Edwin ran up to the car after he had shot the motorcycle driver who had shot at him with deadlier accuracy. Edwin collected their submachine guns, as well as a couple of potato mashers throwing the weapons into the front seat of the car. He returned to Butcher but found him dead.

The sergeant jumped into the car and put it into gear. After several attempts he was able to get it onto the road where Robin and Edwin jumped in and piled onto the back seat. The sergeant looked back at Edwin with a questioning stare, Edwin shook his head. "He is dead," was the answer that the sergeant hoped not to hear.

As the car was working its way from the ditch, Pants was scattering the two remaining horses. Pants took the reins and pulled them away from in front of the car and slapped one of them so they would run into the woods and could not be used easily by a pursuer. One of them was badly wounded and was whinnying as it suffered in the middle of the road, barely able to stand. Pants pulled his pistol out and fired one shot into the animal's head where it dropped on the right side of the road. As he started to run back to the car a German soldier came up out of the woods and across the ditch. He cleared the ditch at the spot where Pants was running and saw Pants who turned and aimed his pistol at the soldier but did not fire as the headlights shone upon him. Pants recognized the soldier as the guard he talked to earlier. In that moment of hesitation the soldier aimed his rifle at Pants, but was dropped by a burst of shots that came from the car. Pants turned and ran to the car as Edwin yelled, "Get in Pants!!"

The car, with its full load, jerked forward and picked up speed away from the train station and ambush site, but it wasn't fast enough. In the rearview mirror the Sergeant saw headlights behind him that were gaining. A large truck with several soldiers in it was barreling down the road at full speed as the car pulled away from the ditch. The soldiers on the truck fired at the car but missed as the truck swerved violently around the body of the horse. The truck returned to the control of the driver and the soldiers in the back regained their balance and fired again at the car. This time the shots hit the car many times in the trunk and peppered Edwin and Robin in the back seat. Edwin fired back with his submachine gun through the broken back window, his left hand and arm bleeding from a wound. The noise of the gun and spitting bullet casings all over the backseat added to the chaos of the wind blowing straight through the car from front to back. Pants, in the front seat, could not fire without hitting the men in the back seat. Another shower of bullets came through the car hitting Robin again and he dropped to the seat. The bullets hit the dashboard next to Pants making him lean towards the door reflexively. The sergeant, with his foot pressed hard against the floorboard, was trying to stay in the middle of the narrow road while erratically weaving to avoid being hit by the stream of bullets. The barrage of lead was flying by and regularly puncturing the sides of the car when the sergeant barked to Pants, "the grenades get them, they're on the floor."

Pants looked around and saw the Potato Mashers rolling under the front seat. He picked them up as the sergeant yelled over the noise, "Pull the cord and drop one out the window and toss the other back over the roof of the car when I say so."

Pants twisted off the safety cap from both of them exposing the detonator cords and said, "Ready".

Just then another series of bullets came through the car's passenger-side window, just missing Pants but scattering glasses fragments into Pants' right ear, shoulder and back.

The sergeant swerved to the left and as he did so he screamed above the howling wind in the car, "Now." Pants dropped the first one onto the middle of the road as the car severed hard to the left side of the road. He quickly pulled the cord on the second and tossed it out the window with an up and backward motion allowing it to land behind the car as it swerved back to the right. As he pulled his arm back into the car, the first grenade detonated and caused the truck to veer sharply to the left then over-correct slightly to the right. That brought it directly over the second grenade that exploded and destroyed the truck's front right tire and puncturing one of the fuel tanks, causing it to tip over the missing wheel support and crash violently in flames.

Pants looked out the window to see the truck catch fire while in the distance there was a glow of fire from the train and trees that were burning. Edwin reached forward with his right hand and patted Pants on the shoulder, "Nice throw," he said.

Looking over at Pants, the sergeant, as he maneuvered the car over the rough country road yelled at the top of his lungs, "Good job! But if you ever hesitate in shooting a German like that again, you will be dead. Either he will have shot you or I will." Pants, using his flashlight, looked back at Robin, who was not moving and towards Edwin who was bleeding. Pants leaning back over the front seat, took off his scarf and wrapped it tight around Edwin's hand. Pants did not feel any pride at the moment for the success of the train's destruction, as half of his team members had suffered wounds or died in the effort. He touched his ear, and in the minimal light he rubbed the blood between his fingers, and then unconsciously wiped them on his trousers. There was nothing that he could do about any of it now. He turned and faced the strong cold breeze coming through the broken windshield on this Christmas Eve morning that meant nothing to him right now. The sky was clear and still, with the temperature quickly dropping to zero, but he was sweating and uncomfortable. He knew that the price he was paying was nothing compared to the others. He sat quietly and wanted to be home. Slowly he noticed that his shoulder was aching too.

By dawn, they were in a second safe house, where the unit leader debriefed them. The first house just gave them warm food, replacement clothes, and the location of the second safe house, and took care of the dead and injured. Each of the squad members gave whatever information they could about the event. The explosion was massive, and surely would have the Gestapo and police looking for those responsible.

Pants was congratulated for preventing the attack on the passenger train that would have killed more civilians and would have allowed the munitions train to escape. However, since Pants had talked and shown his papers to the guard who was shot, there was a good chance that they would be looking for him if the guard had reported the contact, and the leader could not take that chance. The decision was made to immediately send Pants back deeper behind the German lines into Łódź, and for him to keep a low profile by being lost in the large population. He was ordered to return to his Scout Hive and get new identity papers and orders, while continuing in Battle School.

Before going, Pants asked if it would be all right to visit his family. The leader reminded him of the danger his family would be in if he were to be caught with them, let alone the danger he would be in. Pants assured them, "I will not be observed, and I will not spend much time there. I just want to see them. It has been a long time since I have been home." The leader agreed, and arranged for some gifts be given to Pants to take home.

Within an hour of getting to the second house, a very tired Pants was driven to a train station to the west of Opoczno, and he boarded a train to Łódź. Were he collapsed on a bench and fell asleep with his backpack under his heels.

In a German field hospital, a doctor was about to sedate the guard who was shot on the road near the explosion. A Gestapo agent stopped the doctor from continuing with a hand placed in front of the surgeon.

"Tell me anything you can remember about those who shot you." Pulling out a small notebook he paused for the answers.

The guard began, "I came out of the brush onto the road where I heard a car motor then I saw a boy carrying a pistol. I recognized him as someone I had questioned earlier in the evening. His name was Jerzy Broc. From his identification papers, he was 15 years old, and his hometown was Kielce. He said he was checking the schedule for his uncle who lived on a farm. Everything seemed in order, so I let him go. When I came up out of the ditch and saw him I raised my rifle and was about to shoot when I got hit." The soldier coughed and groaned from the painful wound in his side.

The Gestapo wrote the information down and asked, "Would you recognize him if you saw him again or saw his picture?"

"I might; I did not look at him very long, but I did get a good look at him."

The agent wrote himself a note. "Is there anything else you remember?"

The guard paused and sighed, "Someone in a car shot me, but I could not see him. As I lay on the ground he called out to the boy, and said, 'put on your pants' or 'get in pants'. Something like that, I don't remember exactly. I do not remember much after hitting the ground but he did have pants on." The Gestapo underlined and placed a question mark after the word, "pants." Looking down at the word, he scratched his head and muttered, "pants?" Then said with a different tone, "Pants".

###

It had been only six weeks since Staszek had seen his mother, but he was homesick. He had not seen his brother or sisters for nearly a year. He was deep in a day dream of his home when there was a jolt to his right shoulder that made Staszek sit up suddenly on the hard bench with pain from the sore shoulder. He had slept for the past four hours, and could have slept for eight more. The train he was on had made its way from Opozcno to the eastern train station in his hometown, making two dozen stops in the process. It now was approaching the station and the conductor was announcing the station while a soldier was inspecting papers once more looking for suspicious names or people that were wanted for questioning. The sabotage of the ammunition train had surely sent local German officials into a rage that was felt by communities all around Opoczno. Anyone that had a check mark next to their name on the persons of interest list at Gestapo headquarters would be questioned, not just once but two or three times, but even German efficiency could not have gotten to Litzmannstadt as fast as Staszek had.

When Staszek handed the soldier his identity papers he watched him flip to the back of the book where stamps from out of the area were placed. Staszek was still carrying his ID that stated that he was Jerzy Broc since there hadn't been time to make new papers for him. It was a risk, but it would be several days before new names were circulated, and by that time there would be more incidents that would add still other names to whatever list the Gestapo may have. Staszek looked at the soldier with his dirty face and red eyes that the soldier ignored and did not say anything about and he just handed the papers back to Staszek.

When the train stopped, Staszek got off with his backpack that had some food, including a slab of bacon, some honey and jams for his mother and the family as gifts. He had his pistol in an inside pocket of his lightweight undercoat, a death sentence for him if the pistol were to be discovered during a spot search. He made his way through high mounds of snow that had been pushed to the gutters after a severe storm hit two nights before. Only a soft flurry of snow was falling as he left the station at just before 1:00 PM. He wanted to go home and felt that under the cover of snow he would be less likely to be bothered or spotted by any of the many German citizens of the town that might have known him from the past. He walked past his home once, to look at the door and the access into the store. The store was still boarded up, so that meant that he would make another pass but then he would slip into the alley and enter the house through the back door. As he continued away from his home his thoughts turned to anger as he observed dozens of red flags dangling from homes and business all along the streets. The black broken cross on the white background was everywhere and as such attested to the complicity of the Polish citizens who wanted to be liked as Germans by virtue of their actions or their ethnic background. In any case, Staszek became more disgusted. On the streets were men, women, and children, laughing and smiling as they played in the snowdrifts along the street. Well dressed, and apparently well fed. Most were speaking German, though they were Poles until that infamous September 1st. They were now Germans enjoying his city as if it was theirs. He pulled his backpack straps a little tighter; suddenly in a way he felt colder than he had earlier. He worked his way through the light traffic angry with those who did not seem to care that there was a war going on and people were living and dying out in the woods.

He could not stop at his home yet as he had to check in with the contact that was given to him, a butcher several blocks from his home. After the German customer in front of him left, he approached the man and gave him several passwords in a sequence. Without expression or hesitation Pants was given an address some distance further from the shop.

Staszek, walking with his head down to protect it from a sudden bitter cold snow flurry, turned the corner a block from the shop and nearly tripped over legs powdered with snow. He paused to see that it was several people who appeared to have been shot earlier that morning. Lying on the sidewalk where they fell, probable victims of German revenge action. Death did not seem to bother him anymore. He was seeing and being close to it more this past year than in his entire life, or for that matter anyone should in a lifetime. He stepped around the legs and puddles of frozen blood and continued on.

He crossed past the gates to the Ghetto where he had seen Jakob for the last time. On the other side of the street, German civilians walked arm in arm. One even had a Christmas present sticking out of a canvas bag. Their only awareness of the Ghetto was some apparent joke about the stench that wafted through the air from the cage that held so many people. Some of the dead could be seen through the fence and in the snow and dirt looked like mannequins. Some of those were naked skeletons with their skin shrunk tight over the bones. The bodies had been stripped of their rags to protect other skeletons from the same fate, for now. Staszek looked back across the street. The Germans continued to laugh. Staszek's hand was itching for his pistol but he stopped the impulsive thoughts with the patience of a war-hardened man.

He reached the safe house after 30 minutes of walking through town, after doubling back several times, and going into a café in order to make sure he wasn't followed. Once at the house he gave still another password to the person who opened the door, and he was eventually let in.

The house was decorated with some ornaments and a Nativity scene on a small table to celebrate Christmas. He was shown a room for him to use while in town on assignment, and then was given warm food. The woman showed him a German newspaper that proclaimed three hundred priests had been arrested during the last two weeks. The headline was a quote from Heinrich Himmler, the head of the German Police, proclaimed, "All Holy Joes; warmongers, have been deported with similar scum." The meaning was clear to Pants; anyone, even priests who stand up against the Nazi's will go to concentration camps. Pants thought about the priests from the church where his family had been baptized for generations. The priests of the Church of St. Stanislaw Kostka were all gone too.

He was debriefed and his information verified to the satisfaction of the woman who ran the safe house before she gave Pants the final instructions on the location of the Battle School. Classes would restart the next day in an apartment near the Ghetto. After repeating his instructions Pants said that he was to run an errand and would return the next day. No questions were asked, nor explanations beyond that were given. He would stay at this house for only a couple of days before moving on. The fewer individuals knew about each other the better.

As Staszek walked back to his home he again looked at the streets and shops that showed activity and commerce. The multitudes of Nazi flags and pictures of Hitler were placed in windows and in public places. The German slogans that were everywhere, either by billboard or spray-painted onto surfaces sickened him. Every once in a while, there would be one that was defaced and the meaning changed or altered. He smiled to himself, knowing that the Grey Ranks were still at work in and for Łódź while resisting "Litzmannstadt".

Finally, after dark, he reached the back stair well at his home. He paused for a long careful moment out of habit to check for others who might be able to observe him going in. Step by familiar step his heart began to beat faster as he anticipated seeing his family again. Looking around to make sure that no one was watching, he scanned doors, windows, and the alley. He turned back towards the door, paused, listened and finally knocked slowly on the peeling green paint, then waited as the door knob slowly turned.

Early the next morning, Staszek disappeared into the darkness of the predawn, heading for the safe house, using shadows and the snow to conceal his journey and the start of a new page in his education.

Christmas morning came and Helena worked her way through the slow-moving crowd, entering the church for Mass and heading for the rack of red glass candleholders that were glowing brightly this morning at the foot of a statue of Jesus. Nearly all of them had been lit and for a moment she was worried that there would not be one to light for her Staszek. Helena dropped a couple of coins in the poor box near the box of kindling that would be ignited by an existing flame to light the next available candle. She dropped to her knees and said a prayer for her children, and especially for Staszek, thanking God for allowing him to come home for even that brief period. When finished she did the sign of the cross and stood as she slowly turned away from her favorite place of solace. As she did she found herself looking to the face of Mrs. Clara Stefonovich, the church's cleaning lady, who was dressed nicely for her own Christmas celebration, solemn though it was under the circumstances. Clara was many years younger than Helena, but always asked her about the children every time she saw her at church. "Have you already gone to confession today?" Clara asked Helena, then added, "Fr. Bruno is in his confessional and there isn't a long line over there." Helena knew that Clara was single, and thought sharing special family moments would good for her. So she said, "The Christmas meal was made special by having all the kids together again." As she said that she stopped short, knowing that it was risky to say things where others can hear her. She thought she would have to ask for forgiveness during confession for putting her son at risk like this. Helena, to change the subject, said, "Thank you. I will go to see Fr. Bruno now. Merry Christmas," she wished to Clara. Clara stood and watched Helena head for Fr. Bruno's confessional. After watching her go in, Clara turned and watched other people who were lighting candles in thanks and prayer.

Author Notes: Chapter 14

On February 14, 1942, new orders from London changed the ZWZ into the *"Armia Krajowa - AK"* (Home Army). The A.K. had 300,000 members by the end of 1943.

The civilian population assisted the AK as they increased anti-German activities. Secret meetings and training were part of the plans for a future uprising. Secret schools trained officer cadets and non-commissioned officers to lead the restructured army. The Supreme Commander in England was able to arrange for air supplies of weapons to the AK as well as trained commandos called "the Silent and Dark".

In April, 1942, the German army was engaged in heavy fighting inside Russia.

During this time the Supreme Commander of the Polish Underground issued an order to switch from sabotage to armed diversions. These were directed particularly at the transports that were heading to the Eastern Front. The destruction of railroads, bridges, troop-trains, warehouses and telephone installations were the highest priority. In addition, actions to free prisoners wherever necessary were initiated. Such actions took place mainly in central Poland around Łódź and the Holy Cross forest and the area of Warszawa.

Chapter 15
June 12th, 1942: 50 km East of Litzmannstadt

EXHAUSTED, PANTS DROPPED onto his blanket after taking off his saperki, or field boots. At one time, the roomy wide-topped boots were easy to put on and take off, and when he had some pieces of fabric to wrap his feet before donning the saperki, his feet would be fairly comfortable. That was true until his youthful body started to mature and his feet got bigger. The consequence tonight for the seventeen-year-old soldier was that his feet were cold and sore as were his back and neck. He rubbed his feet to increase the circulation to the calloused spots that were now very red from the tight boots. Finally he nested himself into the pile of reasonably clean straw and sank into a shallow rut made by his wiggling body. With a large sigh, he tried to release the tension of the long stress-filled day.

He worked at distracting his thoughts from the terror he felt under the truck this morning. Slowly he won that battle, and drifted to sleep. The blanket and straw acted like an insulator that blocked the cold in this far corner of the barn. The five other Partisans that were with him also found places to sleep, except for one who was to be the lookout for half the night. This had been long, difficult day for Pants, a day that had actually started months ago.

During the past six months, Pants had participated in Battle School classes, as well as field sorties with his fellow members of the Grey Ranks.

In February it was announced that the Union for Armed Struggle (in Polish *"Związek Walki Zbrojnej*; ZWZ) organization had been renamed the Home Army or the A.K. (from the Polish *"Armia Krajowa)*. This change stepped up the level of activity to include armed combat, small sabotage, and engaging the enemy after long grueling marches.

The task of perpetrating propaganda and sabotage against a well-organized, ruthless enemy required tremendous amounts of work, timing, and organization. Everything from messages being carried between Swarms either by hand, word, or by instructions received over hidden radios; all needed to be coordinated tightly. The results had been successful in producing confusion and pessimism among the German civilian population and the German troops. Though the actions to date had primarily been short, quick contacts or actions, the cost of failure at any one of those levels could be fatal. Until today's mission, Pants and his group had been successful.

Today had been a beautiful summer day, and Staszek was very happy to have lived through it. To protect his cover, he had been given a new set of identity papers, with his new name being "Tadeusz Gora." He was also given an excellent forgery of a health certificate that stated he had a heart condition, which effectively gave him a reason for not being in the army in case he was stopped for any reason. The new papers gave him more freedom to travel across the new border of Germany, which once was Poland and included his hometown of Łódź, to see his family for brief periods. At the same time, reality was that Łódź/Litzmannstadt was not a safe place to go, because the walls had more and more ears and eyes that were connected to the Gestapo and SS, so the fewer the encounters with those he loved, the safer for all of them. He still went to see his mother, usually very late at night, hiding in the shadows and alleyways before climbing up the stairs to see her.

Helena had been given a job as the housekeeper for the Zajfert family. It was not hard labor, but she was responsible for keeping the house in order and clean. When Stazsek came home on those rare occurrences, his mother would be overjoyed but overwhelmed that Staszek was still alive. Death surrounded her and absorbed her thoughts. She told Staszek that every time he left she had dreams that he would be killed and she would never see him again. "I dream of you being killed and when I find your body and hold you," she rotated her hands and arms as if to examine her skin slowly, mesmerized at what she thought she was looking at, "my arms, they turn black." Staszek found her words morbid and grotesque and deeply unsettling.

Staszek would respond, "But look, Mamusia, here I am, whole and warm. Touch me. Your arms will not turn black." He would hug her, but that never relieved her fears. Her only solace and strength came from going to the church, lighting candles, and going to confession. When Staszek left, she felt that going to confession would help her prayers to be more worthy of God's attention. She would spend hours on her knees, praying the rosary on her son's behalf.

At the other end of the spectrum was her employer, Herr Zajfert, now "Major" Zajfert, who had become an administrator at one of the government offices that oversaw the local prisons, including the infamous one called Radogoszcz. This prison, located less than a kilometer from the Niklewicz home, was where the Gestapo sent the most "difficult" prisoners for interrogation. Very few people left the red brick detention center alive. Most were "shot while escaping," or "died of fever." The major's son, Kurt, (Staszek's former schoolmate) had been sent to military training camp prior to his army induction on his 18th birthday in August. The major had many pictures of Kurt that Helena dusted regularly, which also brought memories about the days the boys were inseparable.

Staszeks' sister Fela had been sent to Germany as a laborer in a uniform factory and would regularly send a heavily censored letter to her mother and siblings to keep her own spirits strong. Her conscription would supposedly be over in one year, at which time she hoped to return home.

Zdzislaw continued to work in the floor mill in Babiak, six days a week. His days were routinely fourteen hours long, and he suffered chronic back and neck pain, as well as respiratory distress from the flour dust and weight of the sacks. He participated in the war effort by short-changing the sacks of wheat heading for Germany and giving the surplus to the underground or starving Poles in the community. This action was punishable by death if discovered. He did not care, because he was doing something to thumb his nose at his oppressors.

Basia worked locally in two restaurants to earn extra income. Jan Szymański owned the primary restaurant where she worked. It was quite busy, and frequented by German officers and citizens because of the German cook and German pastry chef, who provided exceptional German dining there. Jan spoke excellent German, and made the guests comfortable in his eatery. Staszek could usually get a meal at the back door of the restaurant when Basia or Jan was there, but he tended to avoid Jan because his coziness with the Germans made Staszek suspicious of his loyalty to Poland. Basia was the only member of the family who knew where Staszek had gone and what he was doing. She also knew his code names, in case anything happened to him. Staszek did not care for Jan, because of his fraternization with the Germans but Jan was nice to Basia and respected her, which balanced the scales ever so slightly in Staszek's eyes. Nonetheless he had remained suspicion about Jan and his motives and allegiances.

Staszek's primary activities were to become more competent in fulfilling the clandestine activities of the Battle School group in the city, and into surrounding areas as much as five hours away. The Battle School group's assignments were generally ones of liberating food, clothes, fuel, and other vital materials from the Germans for use by the resistance. This morning the next older level of Grey Ranks, the Assault Group, was to liberate food and trucks from a warehouse outside of town. Fifteen soldiers and German civilians guarded the storage area.

A group of twenty-five Grey Ranks and older partisans; soldiers known to each other by codenames or first names only, were ordered to get to the location just before 4:00 AM, and be ready to strike just at the breakfast time for the soldiers. Among the Germans were Polish patriots who had gotten jobs at the warehouse through their ability to speak German and swearing loyalty to Germany; an oath they took under false pretenses, with no intention of keeping, and as such placed their lives at risk at all times. The attack was aimed to liberate six trucks and their cargo, which was scheduled to go to Germany the following day.

The plan this morning was to enter the compound, rush the building with the soldiers in it, surprise then disarm them while they ate. Once they were relieved of their weapons, the trucks would be driven away. The leader of the assault group was a young man of twenty-one called Hammer, a veteran of the Resistance, and now responsible for twenty-five men, of which Pants was one. Pants spoke German best, and had driven a couple trucks, so he was made the driver and drove the canvas-covered truck to the gate. Lurching the vehicle as he missed one of the low gears and stopped short of the gate was not part of the plan. The sudden jerking of the truck made the sentry stare at Pants intently as well as at Hammer who sat in the passenger seat and was trying to suppress the cringing sensation that came over him at the faulty maneuver.

Pants gave the password and passage papers to the German sentry, and engaged him in some conversation. As the guard examined the papers, Pants got out of the truck and became animated with the problems getting through checkpoints in the mornings. Without missing a beat he complained about the weather, and other random things, like the "lousy clutch" in the truck. As a diversion, Pants chattered away with grandiose hand gestures, while Hammer quietly slipped out of the cab and came around the front of the truck. He was about to use a knife to overpower the guard. Looking through a seam in the canvas the rest of the squad waited for Hammer to take out the sentry, which was their signal to jump out of the back and attack the barracks.

Just at that moment, a second soldier came out with a cup of coffee for the sentry and saw Hammer coming around the truck with his knife and sounded the alarm. Seeing the danger he dropped his cup and brought his machine gun to his waist and began to fire. The first soldier turned at the warning and had just enough time to bring his machine gun up towards Hammer who had his knife down low ready to strike. Pants saw the plan falling apart and the imminent attack on the exposed Hammer. In a heartbeat he jumped at the sentry and knocked him down before he could fire his weapon. The second guard sprayed the front of the truck with bullets, hitting Hammer once that sent him spinning down to the ground.

Hammer got up slowly but started to move to the protected side of the truck. The sentry rolled, and then stood up after being knocked down by Pants and fired at Hammer during his retreat, causing him to fall and not move this time. Pants ran towards the sentry who was now turning back for him. Pants slid into his legs and knocked him down, hard. The sentry rolled onto his back and from the ground turned his weapon towards Pants. Pants saw the unfolding danger and dove under the truck, a ribbon of dust geysers followed him as the sentry fired.

Meanwhile, the squad in the back of the truck had burst out from under the canvas and returned fire at the guard as he retreated to the barracks. As the burst of bullets from the retreating soldier hit one of the squad members, there was a sudden shower of lethal fire from the barracks that scattered the squad. An intense firefight ensued, as projectiles filled the air. The noise of gunfire was deafening. The barracks windows were shattered from both outside and within, as bullets traveled through those portals. The flashes of light from the guns contrasting with the morning darkness momentarily blinded the shooters with every burst of fire.

From under the truck Pants instinctively continued to roll to the other side of the truck as the sentry ran to the front to get a better shot at him. Pants got under the middle portion of the truck and pulled out his pistol while he watched in terror the shadow made by the gate's light of the sentry going to one side of the truck, then coming around to the front of the vehicle searching for him.

The terror intensified when the sentry suddenly stopped to kneel down and pushed, without looking, his weapon under the truck, and blindly began shooting in the general direction of Pants. The poorly aimed shots ricocheted off the under carriage of the truck and punctured the tires on the driver's side of the vehicle. The gun flashes and noise almost overwhelmed Pants with the bright light flashes and deafening sounds. Pants and his young reflexes and focus had him react in that instant to protect himself. From his stomach and with arms outstretched, Pants fired his pistol, hitting the sentry in the knee that was on the ground, causing him to scream from the pain and twist off the knee onto his side. The bright light and loud, echoing report from the pistol stunned Pants for a moment again making him blink to clear his vision. As his eyes quickly adapted, Pants could see that from the ground the sentry looking at Pants as Pants looked back at the man's wide eyes glaring in rage from under his helmet. The sentry brought his gun back under the truck, pointing it nearly straight at Pants. Both were surprised at the sight of gun barrels aimed at each other. Pants hesitated, but it was not longer than the guard's in pulling the trigger. When Pants fired, he hit the sentry in the throat, ending the danger for the moment. Not wanting to spend any more time under the truck Pants rolled and crawled out from under the truck to Hammer's side and found him bleeding from several wounds. He placed pressure on the wound in Hammer's side with his left hand to stem the bleeding. His pistol at the ready in his right hand while his head swiveled side-to-side looking for danger as well as for help.

The squad had advanced on the barracks that suddenly became quiet as the patriots called to them saying not to shoot, because the Germans were dead. Cautiously they entered and found the situation to be true. They found seven Germans and one patriot dead, and another two injured. Outside a squad member was dead and two were wounded as they ran from the truck.

Without wasting a moment, the squad sprang back into their plan and Pants moved the truck with the flat tires out of the way of the gate to allow the food-laden trucks to get out. Those valuable trucks and cargo, including weapons from the dead soldiers would be distributed to the resistance fighters and to those who had helped the resistance members when they needed food. The whole process took less than 15 minutes, but that was too long.

Hammer was alive, but barely. Members of the squad took him to a car that was in the compound and decided that they needed to drive him away for medical care rather than the planned distant meeting place, which he might not survive due to the time element. The trucks were started and began to move away from the warehouse as the car carrying Hammer, a driver and two wounded squad members turned south towards a village where there were known places to get medical help. Pants drove one truck while five others headed for the rendezvous point to the east. Each truck carried a Partisan in front with the driver, with the others in the back, guarding the rear. Their mission, being compromised right from the start, only promised that trip to the meeting area would have everyone on their highest level of awareness looking for pursuers. Over the winding tree-lined roads, everyone had their eyes open, hands on their weapons and their hearts in their throats.

As the car carrying Hammer and the others sped south, several kilometers from the warehouse, it was intercepted by a truck of SS guards that received a partial message from the warehouse about an attack. The speeding car should not have been on the road at all at this time of morning and therefore drew fire from the truck and men standing in the back. The onslaught of bullets riddled the car killing the driver causing the vehicle to swerve several times and crash into a ditch against a tree. It's wheels continued to spin at high speed as the dead driver's foot was wedged against the gas pedal.

The SS dismounted their truck and retrieved the body of the driver and the weapons of the men inside. The three remaining men, including Hammer, were injured but alive. Except for Hammer, who was unconscious, the others were immediately taken to Gestapo headquarters for interrogation. Hammer was taken to a medical unit where he would be stabilized, then questioned the German way.

By 10:00 PM that night, the liberated trucks had been emptied at a dozen locations. Several hours later, the trucks were taken to a transportation center hidden in the forest east of the city, to be used to move partisans, as needed. The remaining six members of the squad went to a safe farm where the barn was used regularly by Partisans who past through. Pants, as he had done so many times in the past, found his way to a place to sleep in the barn, much like dozens of barns he had visited on his routes. Unlike most cases, he was not going to sleep hungry because of the good fortune of having smoked sausage in the back of his truck, which each man helped himself to. Tired, and with food in his stomach, Pants settled into his blanket on the straw for some sleep. He was still reliving the fight that was not suppose to happen that morning, but did anyway. As he fell off to sleep, the voice of the sergeant from Kielce came to him about hesitation at shooting a German. The emotion of having shot a person that was about to shoot him was tempered by the short sentence that came to Pants' lips, "Thank you, God, and thank you, Sergeant."

His imagination saw a different ending to the shooting, as Pants thought he could feel the bullet going into him. He forced his mind to think about being home and safe. He did not want to be here in the straw, but his exhaustion finally had him doze off to a deep but not restful sleep. His rest was complicated by correctly fearing that a list of towns had been radioed and phoned to their small garrisons in a seventy-five km circle from the warehouse to be on the lookout for any unscheduled truck traffic that evening.

Near Piotrkow Trybunalski, one of the garrisons had heard that several trucks had been driven through town in the middle of the day and thought suspicious by a good German citizen, who gave the Nazi salute to the trucks. In return a boy in the truck had returned a disrespectful hand gesture. On the outside chance that his information would be crucial as part of the alert, ten teams of six men left the garrison to check out farms and businesses that had suspected ties to the partisans. There were many farms over a large area, but headquarters said it was a high priority, so it promised to be a long day and night for the soldiers.

In the deepest part of his sleep, a hand suddenly covered Pants' mouth and whispered, "Germans are coming," then the hand let go of him as the lookout went to the next man in the near corner. Pants fumbled for his boots and the pieces of cloth to wrap his feet, but they were not only still damp but also cold and gritty. The damp and cold made getting the tight boots on impossible; his struggle to get them on proved to be futile and he gave up in frustration. He was about to try once more, but he could see the shadows of the other men heading out the back of the barn through loosened planks in the wall and knew he had to get moving quickly. Failing to get the boots on, he picked them up and ran for the hole in the wall carrying them, his blanket, and small backpack. The awkward bundle was difficult to carry, but in spite of the weight and the cold mud on the ground Pants, with his speed, quickly caught up with the others. They took up firing positions just past a wooden railed fence, their backs to the east and the pending morning light.

Pants slid in next to one of the squad members. His feet stung from the sprint through mud, rocks and weeds. He reached for his pistol and pulled back and released the slide that chambered a round. Placing it on his backpack in front of him, he tried once again to get his boots on over his muddy feet. After great effort, he got them on, due to the lubrication from the mud. He retrieved his pistol just as a salvo of gunfire zinged over his head and those of the other squad members, but the shots were not particularly well aimed though they were plentiful, and far too close for comfort. The soldiers had cleared the barn and were spreading out towards the field. They were looking carefully around the area in and around farm tools, pig pen and chicken coop. Six of the soldiers, who must have been on patrol alone, played a hunch that they would find someone in the barn. If they were expecting the squad that raided the warehouse, they did not bring enough backups with them, for as they cleared the pens they began to spread out along a line that was good for looking for one person, but not for seeing anything dangerous in the very low light of the pre-dawn. The shots they did take were at ghosts or their imagination, since they were wild and poorly aimed, as if they were not sure how many men were out there.

With all the Germans in the open and silhouetted by the predawn light, the squad opened fire on the soldiers, dropping two of them immediately. The other four retreated behind a water trough and one of the coops. The firing became intense as the squad fired their rifles and one of the machine guns taken from the raid earlier. Pants emptied his pistol and tried to reload it with loose bullets in his pocket. The effort frustrated and scared him, as he fumbled to place the bullets into the slender magazine with cold fingers in the dim morning light. Once loaded, his frustration cleared as he took aim at the kneeling soldiers and squeezed off several more rounds that mostly missed their marks. One shot seemed to have hit one soldier as his arm came suddenly off his rifle that was leaning on the water trough. He fell backwards and grabbed his left upper arm with his right and tried to crawl to the barn. The other soldiers began to be move backwards from their protected positions towards the barn door as well, as the men at the fence were getting closer with their shots. The Germans, sensing that they had entered a trap, tried to withdraw to the barn but as they did so one of the Grey Ranks squad members ambushed them from the back, after quickly circling around the other side of the barn. The intense exchange of machine gun fire from the squad member, and from the four soldiers resulted in the killing of all soldiers and the squad member as they literally ran into each other, firing at point blank range.

At the sudden silence, the Partisans approached cautiously, and quickly searched the dead soldiers pockets for papers, maps, or other useful items, as well as taking their ammo belts, backpacks, and weapons, all the while scanning the trees and the road for any sign of more soldiers. The remnants of the squad looked to the next senior member of the squad, who decided to head for their alternative camp some twenty hours away on foot. As they were leaving, Pants stopped and looked at the legs and boots of one of the dead soldiers. As he stood there staring, the partisan next to him at the fence, who had watched Pants struggle with his boots, walked up to him, nudged him with his elbow and said, "Take the boots. He certainly won't need them." Pants looked at the man, and then at the boots. In an instant, he dropped to the ground and pulled off the German's boots and, after a brief pause, pulled off his socks too. *"Germans have great socks."* Pants mused. In thirty seconds, his feet were suddenly in warm dry socks and boots that had growing room. As Pants walked away, he noticed that he was not tense but rather strangely calm as he carefully turned and walked backwards to the woods looking for anyone behind him and his squad. The retreat into the woods necessitated leaving the body of the courageous squad member who died in the final seconds of the ambush. Pants was concerned about what the Germans would do to the body of the fallen squad member. He had the leader stop and change his exit plan. The squad returned and each grabbed a piece of shirt, arm or trouser and together they carried the slain partisan into the woods and quickly covered him in a shallow grave, away from possible revenge of the German troops.

Once into the forest, they selected whatever was needed from the German backpacks, and quickly buried the packs under a thin layer of dirt and leaves. With this unexpected battle, it was clear that they needed to leave before their scheduled ride back to the partisan camp arrived. At least they had some extra blankets and rations to help them on the way. Pants, fully awake and in a slightly heightened mindset, followed the others away from the barn. Looking back into the distant barnyard that now revealed the sprawled dead, in the overcast dawn light, they looked like only small lifeless mounds in a flat muddy yard. Pants was occupied by the thoughts of how fast everything happened tonight. Just minutes before, he had just been asleep for a short time, but now was walking in mud, in pirated boots. His squad member who was asleep in the straw minutes ago, was dead, first in a puddle, then under a few centimeters of dirt where he now began a sleep that would last forever.

Into the breaking grey haze and filtered sunlight, the five men headed into the trees that would shelter them until they reached their next camp; a camp that gave Pants mixed emotions, because it was Mr. Olechinski's cabin. This visit did not carry the excitement as it had in the past. The sun filtered through the cold rain clouds that had drenched the farmland overnight, leaving a fresh smell to the air that was completely overshadowed by the sadness he was going through after another death of a Grey Ranks scout. The hike through the forest near Mr. Olechinski's cabin began to bring back good memories of scouting events. Except for some shadowed areas, the snow was nearly gone, replaced by the cold rain and damp fields. When Pants reached the valley where the cabin would be found, the heaviness of his wet clothes became slightly lighter. The five men reached the cabin and found that it had been used recently. Cigarette butts and fresh ash in the fireplace told Pants that they were not scouts that had used it. Especially Scouts that had known Mr. Olechinski; they would never have been so disrespectful of their scout leader's property.

The five occupants of the cabin today were full members of the Resistance, except for Pants, but all in their own ways had been hiding and fighting in the woods since the war started. Like Pants, they lived one day at a time by taking orders, doing their duty, and living off the land and what it offered. Usually sleeping under leaves or branches covered by a wool blanket and oilcloth shell, was the only shelter they would have for weeks at a time, months for several of the men, who, like Pants, were couriers at times. A common bond gave them spiritual support and comfort.

The cabin was wonderful, and having a fire to dry clothing and cook warm food was like Christmas and their birthdays all wrapped into one. Ravens, pheasants, blackbirds, and farm-raised chickens were the basic meat source for the partisans. Pants was getting tired of fowl, so the sausage he had been eating all day, cooked in a warm dish, was welcomed. The plan was to dry out, eat, and get on the trail to Opoczno the next day, but for the time being, this break and shelter was greatly needed.

Just before dawn, Pants went to get a pail of water from the creek that his patrol had built their bridge across just a few years ago. The defeat of the Oaks still haunted him, but the sting had subsided. His thoughts flashed on Mouse, Artur, Jakob, Karl, and the other boys in the troop. He wondered where those that were still alive were at this moment. The silence of the forest was different than the silence of the city, as he stood still and listened to nothing in general but the whole world at once. In the distant bush, he could hear small animals moving slowly and the rustle of birds leaving their nighttime nests. *The forest was coming to life*, he mused for a brief moment. Then it occurred to him that there seemed to be a lot of animals moving all at once. He put down his pail and knelt down on one knee and listened into the silence between the sounds.

"Voices...I hear voices." Pants strained to hear what he wasn't sure of. Then one was clear. "That way," were the words, and a jolt gripped his heart. It was a German voice coming from the direction the squad had come the night before. The Germans had been able to track them to this spot. Pants turned and started to run in a squatted position until he was clear of the low branches then sprinted to the cabin. His large boots were not a good enough fit for running, but that did not deter Pants from sprinting flat-footed the entire distance to the cabin along the edge of the tree line.

One of the other men was in front of the cabin lighting a cigarette when he saw Pants running full stride through the mud and snow, obviously in distress and waving his arms in warning. He dropped his smoke and went into the cabin where the others came out to find out what was going on. When Pants was within 20 meters he called in stifled voice "GERMANS!"

The four men dashed back into the cabin to retrieve their weapons and gear. They always slept in their clothes except for jackets and boots, and each man was donning that piece that was missing, but it was too late. Machine gun bullets and rifle fire ripped into the cabin through the open door scattering wood chips and men in different directions. Staying in the cabin was not an option, since the walls might slow some bullets but would not hold against repeated grenade attacks. There was only one door and the squad needed to get out of it if they expected to live another hour. Ten to fifteen meters away from the door was the log lean-to where group campfires and cooking was done. Pants yelled to the others, "Follow me!" Sticking his head out the door and seeing the Germans closing on the cabin some seventy five meters away, Pants rolled out the door to the left and headed behind the lean-to, with the others close behind him. There was the trail that took the new scouts on their first ceremonial hike out of the forest and now would give this squad a chance to get away. Machine gun bullets chased the last two men who were crawling and scrambling on their bellies to get behind the logs.

One of the older Resistance members, trained as an officer in the Polish army, with the codename "Wire," was an accomplished courier and horseman in his own right. He also was an excellent shot, and like Pants had gone through the Scouting program as a youth. The five men ran along the winding trail, dodging in and around the trees with gunfire trailing them, but slowly fading into the distance. Wire gave orders to crawl under a large berry bush whose bare canes were covered with thorns much like barbed wire. They were growing over and around some large boulders that flanked the trail on one side while the trail continued up the other side of the sloped hill. The boulders gave a clear line of sight for about thirty meters, while the bushes acted as a barrier to the Germans.

Pants crawled under the bush where his clothes were caught then torn, as he pulled them off the needle sharp tips. Pulling a rifle along with him, he worked his way to a point where the ground fell away towards another creek and he was free of the bush. Once there he looked for Wire, who was on top of the boulders a meter above Pants. Wire bent down and handed him two stick grenades. Wire signaled Pants to move along the creek in the direction that the Germans would come from. From there, he circled back towards the camp about twenty meters. The squad hid in their positions, hoping that the Germans had turned and gone home, but kept a vigilant watch towards the trail, knowing that they would not give up that easily. There they waited for fifteen minutes, and soon patience became their enemy.

By thirty minutes, one of the squad members signaled that he was going to go back towards the clearing to see if the Germans had left. Going forward, there were mostly heavily wooded and tangled pathways that only courageous deer and scouts earning badges would cross. If the Germans were still in the area, they were still in the clearing and someone had to find out. The soldier quietly and carefully retraced the path from the cabin, working his way past Pants location, off the trail and below the rim of the creek. The water running down the slope covered any sounds that Pants made but also covered sounds from below. Pants had been breathing heavily from the sprint across the clearing and then up the slope. The stress and anxiety of being pursued had faded by the end of the first half hour, and now he was impatient and looking for a end to this deadly game.

The wait ended with the sudden return of the squad member running back up the trail. A moment later the drone of an airplane engine was heard producing a sound that Pants knew all to well. "*Stuka!*" his heart cried out. His head turned towards the sky and through the treetops he could see the shadow of the plane racing down towards the spot where the squad was hidden. Then there was an explosion as one of the bombs hit the top of a tree and rained wooden fragments and shrapnel down on his position. The ledge of the creek protected him from the falling materials but not from the return of the plane, which opened fire with its nose-mounted cannon. The 20 mm shells exploded along the trail on the opposite side of the squad and their hiding places, but mostly hit and damaged the trees high up on their trunks. There were no sounds, which could be good or bad, but neither Pants nor the others would know for sure at the moment. Another pass by the plane sprayed the trail along the same side as the squad, wide but close enough to force them to bury their heads into the loose soil and leaves. A moment later the Germans came up the trail, first with grenades to clear the path, and then one at a time leapfrogging up the trail, covering each other. Approximately eleven soldiers were unable to fan out due to the terrain, but they had ample firepower to get their mission completed.

The squad held its fire, and waited for the Germans to move further up the hill to have it appear that the Poles had escaped over the top of the trail or were killed by the bomb and strafing, and make them drop their guard. The ruse worked. One by one the Germans started up the trail until the eleventh man was slowly moving towards the top of the slope while sweeping the forest with his eyes and his machine gun. A fine shot from Wire dropped the last man in line. The others dove for the ground upon hearing mostly an echo from the shot. They could not determine which way it came from, and it took them time to figure out that one of their own had been hit.

The first man stood quickly and made a dash for a pair of trees off the trail for cover, but was shot from the squad member under the bush. This kill caused the rest to turn back down the hill and start to run. The ambush took out three more Germans and six others began firing into the surrounding trees and bushes as they came down the trail. Two more Germans went down, one of who had pulled the string on a grenade and was tossing it into the thorn bush when he got hit, exploding on top of the occupied area. The last four were in full stride, firing their weapons in a defense pattern, and were heading for Pants' position. Pants could see the fear in the eyes of the Germans coming down the hill and was sure that he'd look the same way to them if they spotted him. As if by the power of thought, the German at the point coming down the hill saw Pants and fired at him. Pants slid down the creek wall and rolled to a point behind a stump where he pulled the string on his grenade and tossed it towards the line of running Germans. The grenade however, hit a low branch and bounced back at Pants landing behind the first German and ahead of Pants. The explosion killed the closest soldier but missed the ones behind him. The dirt rained down on Pants, while he brought his rifle to the edge of the creek wall. Using a branch as a rest for the barrel of his rifle he fired at the next gray overcoat he saw running at him. The shot had the soldier start to stumble and his efforts to regain his balance had him trip and fall in front of Pants. The squad killed the remaining Germans within moments of the grenade and Pants' shot.

Though shaken, the German that Pants shot was not mortally wounded, only dazed, and was less than a meter from him. He looked up at Pants who was scrambling to get on his feet and away because he was too close for the rifle to be aimed at the soldier. The soldier, still holding his machine gun, pulled on it but it was tangled in the sticks and branches where Pants had been hiding. Moving away, Pants slipped on the wet ground but caught himself with the butt of his rifle that he jammed into the mud, stopping his momentum down as he landed on his knees. Once balanced, he pulled the rifle from the dirt and in one continuous motion swung the butt of the rifle with two hands, down onto the head of the German stunning him as his helmet was knocked from his head. The German pulled his weapon up in a defensive motion, with his arm that was still caught in branches, but was able to pull the trigger shooting a dozen shots widely in the general direction of Pants. Pants reversed his grip on the rifle, which allowed it to be brought down to the level of the German chest and without hesitation he pressed it into the fabric of the German's coat and pulled the trigger. The German lurched up with the impact then fell silent. Pants froze for a moment then dropped his head down onto his arms trying to catch his breath and to bring his heart down and out of his throat. Then with a burst of adrenaline pushed himself up and onto his feet as he scrambled up the slope and on to the trail.

The squad slowly regrouped and found that the member who was under the bush was dead from a grenade explosion. Pants walked up the hill to see his fallen squad member. Looking at the mangled body with most of his left side missing and the rest of him in pieces chilled Pants, and brought back his fear of being blown up. Wire came to Pants and slowly stroked his back and said, "Let's go, we can't stay down here anymore." The remaining members took what they could from the Germans, and the dead member's weapon, and headed back to the trail they needed to get to their headquarters.

###

Wire was a graduate of law school, though he was never able to practice law, due to the war. During their trek from the cabin towards Opoczno, Wire passed the time by giving Pants history and civics lessons, especially about politics and the different forms of government. The differences and similarities between capitalism, socialism, and communism were contrasted and discussed for kilometers to make the time pass faster. Pants enjoyed the lectures and pondered the topic constantly, though they often frustrated him by the virtues and evils of all of them, which often overlapped. Wire gave in-depth histories of Karl Marx, Lenin, Hitler, and Stalin, power-seeking despots, one and all. It became clear to Pants that Poland was in the wrong place when it came to the tyranny and greed of her neighbors. The many influences and variables of the current situation were frustrating to Pants. When he told Wire, "I'm confused about all this. Why can't Germany and Russia just leave us alone?" Wire smiled and said, "If anyone had a solution for that question, they would probably become king, and that would present its own set of problems."

As the next day progressed, the remainder of the squad broke up and some opportunities arose to gain transportation to their assigned safe house in Opoczno. Using the back of a couple of farmers' trucks, as well as a small delivery wagon, the group reached their destinations one by one late the following day. The rendezvous was at the church where Father Bird gave shelter and food to the partisans. A gesture that would end his life if the Germans knew what he was doing.

While there, Wire and Pants were ordered back to Pincow, near Kielce, where intense sabotage was being carried out behind the Germans rear guard, targeting train and military transports heading for Russia. Wire had contacted his superiors and made his report. In it, he highlighted the abilities that Pants had displayed and asked that Pants be attached to the A.K.'s Infantry Regiment with him in the Radom-Kielce area.

After a day at a safe house, where plans and assignments were provided to the contingent of partisans, they were to be sent to four different areas. Pants found that he and Wire were going to travel through the area where Pants had served as a courier the previous summer on their way to the Kielce headquarters. Pants was warned to be careful, since there had been an increase in German raids on the farms and business in the area that were suspected of being cooperative with the partisans. The Germans' raids were based on information gathered from traitors and collaborators. Based on seldom more than an accusation, the Germans had taken many retaliatory actions against Polish civilians. Pants was not to take anything for granted, and made observations of any contact point before proceeding further. He would make contact with the farms and businesses that he had not seen in many months, but only if he was certain it was safe to do so. In his heart, he hoped to see Gertrude as they traveled through Koneski. Pants and Wire started their trek on horseback, since the woods were thick and they needed to get to Pincow, and then Kielce, as soon as possible.

There were no sign of problems at the first several stops, but there were also no signals that there were messages to be picked up. Pants and

Wire spent nearly thirty minutes at each stop to observe the actions of the people. One of the farms and one small shop was abandoned, with no signs of their occupants to be seen. The night was spent in the woods with an open campfire for warmth and cooking a chicken that was taken from one of the abandoned farms. The travelers shared the meal and talked more about politics and what the destiny of Poland might be after the war ended. Wire made it clear that Russia, though fighting against Germany, was anything but a friend to Poland. Their history of treachery toward Poland was long and well known, and would certainly repeat itself, given a chance.

By noon of the following day they reached Gertrude's farm. Pants was excited about coming back to the farm to see Gertrude and introduce her to his companion. He was sure that the afternoon could be spent in spirited conversation and good food, as Gertrude was a fine cook and was very smart. As they neared the edge of the trees that circled the farm, Pants and Wire dismounted and crawled to the tree line to watch and see if everything was as it should. Within minutes, Pants spotted a woman wearing a red skirt, white blouse and babushka coming from the barn. "There, that's Gertrude," Pants whispered to Wire. He pointed to the clothesline and the once colorful but now faded aprons fluttering gently on the line. "That's my signal that something needs to be picked up," Pants told Wire and started to stand.

"Hold on. We've only been here a couple of minutes. Let's wait for a while longer." Pants became irritated at the hesitation but grudgingly knelt back down to watch Gertrude. As he watched the figure moving back and forth between the house and barn, it struck him that there was something wrong about what he thought he saw. "This isn't right." He said to Wire, who looked over to Pants with a quizzical look on his face. "The babushka covers her face, but her walk is wrong."

"What do you mean?" Wire asked as he looked back to the woman.

"Gertrude was not young, but not old. This person walks like a much older person. She doesn't act like Gertrude, the way she picks up things and throws them. It's wrong." Pants started to feel a little panic inside, but didn't know why. He desperately wanted to go and talk to Gertrude, but this wasn't right.

Wire said, "I'll wait here. Go to Gertrude and see what's happening. I'll stay here to cover you." With that said Wire pulled his rifle off of his back and laid it in front of him.

Pants nodded and got up slowly as he scanned the farmyard for anything that would alarm him. Walking towards the barn where Gertrude had entered several moments before, he was suddenly confronted by the woman coming back out carrying a large armful of hay. He could now see her face and saw that it was not Gertrude though she was similar in size.

Thinking quickly Pants asked, "Are you the owner of this farm?"

The woman abruptly said, "Yes, and who are you and why do you ask?"

"I am a traveler to this area for the first time who is very hungry and is looking for something to eat," Pants asked in his nicest tone of voice, with emphasis on 'something to eat.'

"I have only enough for myself and nothing for you," was her curt reply.

"But I'm very hungry. Can't you give me something? You must have something in the house." Pants started to take some steps towards the porch.

"I told you already that I have nothing for you and you should leave now." The woman stated again with more firmness and moved to put herself between the door and Pants.

"Very well then. I will not bother you again." Pants apologized and turned partially away. He stopped and asked, "Since you have no food for me, do you have a message?" He looked at her face, which had suddenly tightened and looked at him strangely.

"What do you mean?" She asked cautiously and squared her body towards Pants, her arms crossed on her chest. Pants looked towards the clothesline and pointed to the aprons.

"I was told that when you put aprons up there, I should pick up a message. Do you have one for me?" Pants watched her expression and her mind working quickly at the new and unexpected development. He slid his hands into his pockets of his jacket gripping his pistol as he waited for an answer.

"You must be one of the couriers from the Resistance. Why didn't you say so? I am Gertrude and I have the message in the house. Come and you can get it." She turned and waved her hand towards the door. "I have food for you too." Gertrude added.

"Thank you but I'll wait for the message if you would please bring it out to me." Pants knew that all messages were in the secret hole in the post of the stable. A message would never be in the house.

"You must be hungry and I can give you some food if you come with me." Gertrude placed her arm on Pants shoulder and just as she started to hold him with her other arm, Pants saw the door of the house open. He spun away from the woman and dashed back towards the tree line. As he did so, he saw two soldiers came out of the house armed with rifles that they were bringing to their shoulders. Pants immediately started to sprint in a zigzagging fashion, darting left and right as he headed back to where Wire was hidden. A rifle shot rung out from the trees in front of Pants as Wire fired at the men at the house. The second man fell as the first man paused at the sound of the shot, not from his rear but from in front of him. He aimed his rifle at the place the sound and flash came from in the woods, and fired his own shot. The bullet buried itself in the tree trunk to the side, but in line with Wire who had reloaded his rifle and squeezed off a second shot that dropped the soldier as he crouched to move away from the door.

Pants looked over his shoulder and saw the woman running for the barn. He slid to a stop on the moist soil, turned, and ran after the woman, pulling out his pistol as he sprinted towards the barn. Wire, fearful of others being in the house, stayed low but yelled after Pants "Stop! Don't go in." But his advice was ignored or too slow in coming as Pants ran to the barn door and dropped down behind a wooden cart that was stored there. Cautiously he stood up from behind the cart and looked into the shadow of the barn and froze as he saw a woman in a red embroidered skirt and peasant blouse hanging by the neck. The neck was grossly angled and the skin was dark and swollen but he recognized the fabric that he had brought to Gertrude last year. As he stared in horror at the lifeless body of the woman who had made him a man, a high pitch shriek had him turn suddenly to his left to see the imposter Gertrude coming at him with a pitchfork poised at her shoulder level and ready to lunge at him. Stepping back at the sudden appearance of the screaming woman Pants tripped backwards and fell to the ground. The woman was quickly upon him as he fired a shot at his attacker. The bullet hit her in her thigh but it did not slow her down. Pants raised his pistol higher, but hesitated as looked into the face of the enraged woman.

She jabbed the pitchfork at Pants, as he fired again, this time hitting her in her side, which slowed her as she twisted to that side to touch her wound. Pants crawled towards the cart to get away, but the wheel partially blocked his motion allowing the imposter time to recover and jam the fork down into him. A quick motion that moved his leg away from her at the last moment had three of the prongs hit the ground but the fourth penetrated into and through the side of his thigh.

Pants screamed in pain as the imposter pulled out the fork to try a second effort at impaling him. Pants pulled his gun up for the third time and fired, this time hitting her squarely in the stomach that doubled her up but did not drop her. She paused for a moment and weakly tried to lift the fork once more. As she did she was hit with a bullet from Wire, which sent her sideways onto the ground with a fatal shot to her right side.

In a moment Wire was at Pants' side, looking at his wound. "Are you well enough to travel?"

"Yes, I think so." Pants nodded, as Wire pulled him up.

"Good. We can't stay here." They headed back to the trees, with Wire moving backwards as he made sure that there were no others to deal with. Pants, pushing on his thigh for added support and to slow the blood from the wound, ran and skipped to the trees. Once a fair distance into the covering, they stopped and dressed the wound with some honey that Pants had for his meals, and bandaged the puncture wound.

"Depending on what she had stabbed before you, the infection should be mild. The honey should take care of most anything else," Wire observed, with no other real comments to be made.

Pants knew that if the fork was recently in manure or dirt instead of the dry hay in the barn, he could have a problem with a dangerously infected wound. But as Wire had stated, they could not stay there, so they were on their way quickly. Mounting and dismounting the horse wasn't comfortable, but much better than walking. Within three days they had stopped at several more contact points, but only retrieved one message to be delivered to headquarters.

Once they arrived at the designated camp, Pants could see that this was a bigger operation than he had ever seen. The camp was made of many pine log structures built into the side of the hills. The logs were stacked only one and a half meters high. They were so low that you had to climb into them almost on your hands and knees, through a small opening in the bottom two logs. It could sleep twenty people. However, a person could not stand in them because the bunkers were intended to keep the warmth in and the profile from the air to a minimum. A man could sit inside to play cards, but could not throw his arms up to celebrate a winning hand without hitting the logs that made the roof.

To some, it felt like they were crawling into a crypt. There were well over two hundred men in the camp, six kilometers from Kielce. The wound in Pants' leg was cared for. It would eventually heal completely. Wire took him to the commander's headquarters and introduced him to the officer in charge.

After the report Pants gave, and the recommendation that Wire provided to the commander, Pants was told that if he wished to stay in the camp he would be allowed to take the oath of a Soldier in the Home Army of Poland. "What is your real name young man?" the commander asked Pants.

Hesitating for a moment he answered, "Stanislaw Niklewicz, Sir." Staszek was elated at this opportunity and accepted almost instantly. The commander had Staszek raise his left hand with his index and middle finger pointing upwards. He swore the oath to fight for God, Country, and Family. He did this with pride, and a sense of strength and achievement. "Congratulations, Private. You are the newest member of the Swietokrzyskie Gory Armia Krajowa (Home Army of the Holy Cross Mountains District).

Staszek could not have been more proud and eager to be a soldier.

The commander called one of the sergeants and instructed him to get Staszek an appropriate coat and cap and prepare him for training. "Get him a White Eagle for his jacket too."

A couple of minutes later he was handed a heavy leather coat, that was slightly too big, but had room for a good sweater to be worn under it. He also was given a beret and a metal pin of the Polish White Eagle standing upon the Kotwica (the anchor looking P/W emblem) for his jacket. He was also given a long white over red strip of cloth with the Kotwica hand drawn on it to be worn around his upper arm. In essence this was the uniform of the Polish underground. Staszek could not be any prouder than at this moment holding the symbols of his beloved country.

The ability to live and survive alone in mud, dust, sun, or snow while on missions had been a strong trait for Staszek, but it was time to work and fight as part of a larger unit, where he depended on someone else and they depended on him for their lives. Staszek was excited about being in the army where he could fight and not just engage in diversionary or small engagements. As part of the A.K., he could start to push the occupiers out of his country. The tide was starting to turn, and he wanted to be part of it.

What he did not expect nor imagine was that he would not go home for more than a year. The life he had as a courier and a Grey Rank scout was to be taken to a new level. He would now be living exclusively on the food that was liberated from the Germans, donated by farmers or shot, trapped, and harvested in the woods, and, when necessary, the salvaged remains of horses that were ridden into battle, and killed as casualties of war. For days and even weeks at a time, the food Pants would eat would not be more than soup that was not always warm. His home would be where he placed a blanket on the dirt, or straw or leaves. Extremes in cold and heat during the seasons, and always the ever-present bugs and parasites of nature were to be dealt with and endured.

By fall, he would be serving as a forward lookout and reconnaissance scout, which allowed him the opportunity to run distances when horseback was not an option. Marching from camp to camp and battle to battle with his backpack and weapons, covering hundreds of kilometers, hardened the boy into a man during the following year. That year he turned eighteen and he distinguished himself as a soldier in the A.K. and experienced many hardships and loses of more friends. Among the hardship was being away from home for that time but as difficult as it seemed to Staszek, it was to become a blessing in disguise.

###

In a Gestapo office many kilometers away, the information about the raid on the food warehouse two weeks before was collected and inspected by the agent there. Information provided by the injured raiders of the warehouse gave a variety of pieces of information. The agent wrote down names and places that were provided by one of the "bandits" before he was shot in front of the others, "while resisting arrest." None of the names were real; they were all codes that had almost no meaning, except a couple that he had seen before somewhere else on another piece of information. He thumbed through a box of index cards, "There it is," he mumbled, "Pants. Opoczno train sabotage." He put the card on the desk on the side of his pile of papers next to the card that said, "Hammer, Boy Scout, Litzmannstadt." On the card that said Pants, the agent wrote the word "Scout?" Since he was on the raid with Hammer, it seemed logical. The agent smiled as his mind tied two strings together. He pulled out another stack of cards labeled Litzmannstadt Scouts, and compared those names to the new ones. This time he smiled with his eyes, too. The word "Ja," came to his lips that were going into a grin. He picked up the phone and called a number. It rang several times and when it was picked up the Gestapo said, "Seig Heil, Father. This is Ruback, I need some information that you can find for me."

For the next eleven months, Staszek learned the ways of the soldier and participated in train sabotage, as he had some skill in that area already. The largest event was a massive attack on troop trains south of Warszawa, as they headed for Russia. He participated in roadside ambushes on truck convoys, much like the one where he was introduced to combat two years before. He was always deep in the woods, except for the sorties along the roads, always staying under cover and learning to fight. The Gestapo had information, but no activity to complete the net that was already being set in Litzmannstadt. They arrested thirty-three scouts and forty-six A.K. members in Litzmannstadt in August 1942 but they were tracking more. The only thing that the Germans needed was patience and a little luck.

Author's notes: Chapter 15

The invasion of Poland in 1939, was part of a plan to fulfill Hitler's dream of taking all of Eastern Europe, as described in his book *Mein Kampf*. Taking the land was called Lebensraum, or "living space". To acquire this *living space*, the German army was ordered to "send to death mercilessly and without compassion to men, women, and children of Polish race and language." This was quoted from a speech in Armenia in 1939. What Russia, Hitler's ally at the beginning of the war, did not realize or want to believe was that "Eastern Europe" included the Soviet Union.

March 1942, found the Russians releasing Polish prisoners that were captured during the beginning of the war. This was done in order to show good faith to the Poles and as a gesture of their good intentions and need to fight together against the Germans. However, the hate that Russians had for Poles was exemplified when they released seventy thousand men into a tent city in northern Russia, but only gave them enough food to feed forty thousand. Temperatures dropped to -50 degrees Fahrenheit. The seventy thousand were only a fraction of the one million five hundred thousand that were deported to Russian Gulags from 1939 to 1941.

The "White Eagle" is the national symbol of Poland. Either a patch or pin worn on the clothing would designate the wearer as a member of the Polish military. In case of capture, it would place the soldier in the position of being a combatant, and he would be due the rights of a prisoner of war, rather than a spy who could be shot on the spot. For the Germans such a medallion or patch was not much more than a technicality. The punishment was what they felt was appropriate at the time, rather than what was the expected behavior of a country at war.

During the initial invasion of Poland the Polish Communist party had been silent because of the alliance between Germany and the Soviet Union (Russia). However, they became active again after Germany attacked and went east into the Soviet Union. The pro–Soviet organization "Polish Workers Party" formed a military organization called People's Guard, later to be called the People's Army *"Armia Ludowa (AL)"*.

In 1943 when Germany floundered in its invasion of the east, the Soviets switched to the offensive forcing Germany to retreat back into Poland. This put Poland in a very difficult political position as to who to fight for their survival. It was clear that there were now two enemies on Polish soil. Poland was at war with the Germans and would continue the fight to the end. Russia was also at war with Germany; therefore technically Russia was an ally of Poland. However when they entered Poland they would also become a danger to Poland's independence. If Russia occupied increasing amounts of Polish territory, they would also be able to influence the decisions of the Allies in the post war period. Instead of an independent republic as the people wanted, the Russians wanted a Polish subservient state organized by Russia. Poland's situation was becoming critical.

Poland 1939

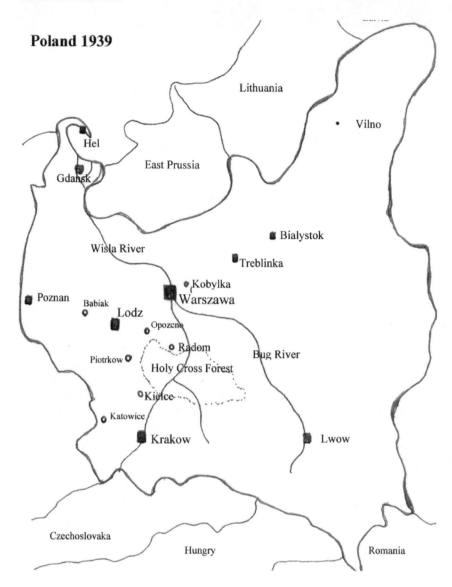

1.0 cm =80km. (50 miles)
Picture# 2: Location Map

Chapter 16
July 1st, 1943: Kolo, Poland

AT FIRST, CORPORAL Pants became aware of the slow footsteps compressing the dry leaves several meters away from him. Next he passed from a dream state to light arousal and started to reach for his pistol when his shoulder was slowly shaken. Even this gentle pressure felt like a jolt to his shoulder and made Pants sit up suddenly from his blanket that covered a pad of leaves. He had slept deeply for the past four hours, and wondered how time managed to go by so quickly. After long marches during the two days and nights before, where he covered 16–24 km each day, every moment of rest was priceless. The private who had been on guard duty for the past four hours knelt next to him said, "I'm sorry to have startled you, Corporal, but it is the time you told me to awaken you."

"Thank you Private," was all that Pants said as he pulled off his beret and rubbed his face for stimulation, and ran his fingers through his black hair, scratching the top of his head briskly, only slightly aware of the dirt and oily grime feeling of his skin after several months in the forest. Pants had been promoted to the rank of corporal after taking part in a series of raids and train bombings in October and November of last year, near Warszawa. Now he was returning from a mission where his squad and two others attacked a German district office that held the records of grain and dairy quotas that the local farmers had been providing.

Setting fire to the building and the file cabinets, and making it look like an oil lamp was the source of an accidental conflagration was key to the assignment.

The significance of these records was that they were wrong; they were fraudulent, and if they were to have been audited, as had been the German plan for this coming week, many farmers would have been shipped off to labor camps deeper into Germany or shot. The farmers in this area had been shorting sacks of wheat as well as tubs of butter and honey that had mislabeled weights. The labels made it look like the quotas were being met, but the skimmed amounts had gone to the underground resistance and locals who were starving. A traitor had tipped off the Germans that documentation was being altered somewhere along the line, and an auditing committee was on their way to compare weights that were received by the Germans with what was supposedly sent. However, a person in the German administration, who was sympathetic to the Polish cause, informed the underground that the audit would be made, thus saving the lives of many farmers and workers.

What made this mission especially important for Pants was that one of the mills that were to have been investigated was the one where his brother Zdzislaw worked, in the town of Babiak. If the numbers were discovered to have been wrong, as they surely would have, Zdzislaw would probably have been shot. Neither Zdzislaw nor the rest of the family knew of the pending raids of the government workers, or of Pants' involvement to foil it. With a successful escape into the forest near Babiak, Pants was doubly pleased. He was slightly disappointed that he could not stop to see his uncle Mieczyslaw, his father's oldest brother. The last time Staszek saw his uncle was just before the invasion. At that time uncle Mieczyslaw, who was known for making high quality alcohol drinks, had gotten Staszek drunk for the first time. Staszek fondly remembered Mieczyslaw saying, "I got your father drunk for the first time, and your uncle Josef drunk for the first time, and last year I got Zdzislaw drunk for the first time, so today it is your turn to become a drinking man." All Staszek really remembered from that point forward was that he was very sick from the cherry-flavored vodka; so sick that he barely made it out the back door when he vomited a large quantity of alcohol on an unsuspecting chicken, which made his aunt yell at him and Mieczyslaw. There was a slight smile on his face as he reminisced, but he had little interest in experiencing that feeling again.

When they had returned to their headquarters, Pants was called into the lair of the commander. Pants was pleased to see Wire, the lawyer-solider that he had worked with the previous year. They shook hands and gave each other pats on the back during a strong, sincere hug. Since their last duty together, Wire had been assigned to work with the KEDYW (Kierownictwo Dywersji, or Directorate for Diversion). Wire was now working for the Polish Underground State and its justice system. His duties involved not only the sabotaging of rails and trains, but also the executions of Nazi collaborators and traitors that were sentenced to death by the Underground Court system for crimes against the Polish people. He came to this camp to recruit Pants to help him at this strategic level of war.

The commander pointed to seats for them and started the meeting. "Corporal, give me a report about the raid into Babiak."

Pants sat up slightly straighter on a box, and gave a detailed report of the mission and the results while the commander and Wire listened. At the conclusion, the commander looked at Wire, and Wire nodded his head slightly. The commander then said, "Good job Corporal I knew that this was an important mission, because of the danger that your brother would be facing. Leaving the Agricultural Directors office burned without being spotted or the citizens involved will assure the sabotage by the farmers will continue safely for a little longer." He paused as he pulled out a pack of cigarettes and pushed the pack towards Wire who took one, and gave the pack to Pants, who accepted one and slid it into his coat pocket.

"For later," he said knowing full well that he was going to trade it for food, candy, or anything else. The commander took a cigarette and held it unlit between his fingers as he continued his thoughts after standing up. "I was told by the captain that you were someone that he wanted on his team. A team assignment that has a lot of risk, and it's very important for it to be done correctly. Moreover, it is to be done in Łódź. Are you interested in this mission?" The commander leaned back against the log-reinforced wall and lit his cigarette, blowing smoke towards the ceiling while watching Pants' reaction for the moment.

Pants leaned onto his knees with his elbows and back straight, while he looked at the men and said, with little hesitation, "What is it that you need me to do?"

Wire turned to him and leaned forward, first looking at the commander then to Pants. He looked into Pants' face, studying his eyes, and said, in a soft voice "The mission you started is not fully done, and we have to complete it."

Pants was stunned for a moment and said, "I thought that we completed the mission fully and successfully as planned. Did I do something wrong?" Pants became slightly stressed, thinking that he had failed his assignment in an area that he was not aware of.

Wire continued, "Your squad stopped further damage by destroying the evidence against a lot of loyal Polish patriots. What we have to do now is to stop the traitor from getting another chance at harming them. I have been assigned to carry out the orders of the Polish Republic's Underground Justice System and execute the traitor of his country who gave the information to the Gestapo in the first place." Wire looked at Pants who had been listening intently to the statement and continued, "And I need your help."

"What is my part in this assignment?" Pants asked, firmly and pointedly of the importance as well as the risks seemed to be heading to a much higher level.

"The Underground Court has prosecuted this case against the agent, Marek Strezowicz, and had found him guilty of crimes against the Polish Republic and the Polish people. He is the traitor who has collected the names of the farmers and mill workers, like your brother, loyal merchants and gave them to the Gestapo for favors for himself and for money. My orders are to interrogate and then fulfill the orders of the courts against Strezowicz in the next three days. Your assignment is to be one of two of my bodyguards and cover me while I complete the sentence on Strezowicz. I need your knowledge of the city and loyalty to our country to make this successful. We will be going deep behind enemy lines into your hometown, are you able to do this?"

Pants had been living and fighting in the woods for a long time, and he was concerned about danger of going back into the city once again, but to be asked to do this important assignment was something he could not turn down. Slapping his knee in a decisive manner he said, "When do we go?"

Wire smiled and said, "We leave tonight for a safe house where we will clean up and I will get the details from the observation group that has monitored Strezowicz's every move and habit for the past month. There we will get the final details and some backup support. Are you ready for this?"

Pants stood up and said, "Let's go." He reached for Wire's outstretched hand, and shook it firmly. The commander shook Wire's hand, and then the hand of Pants, the eighteen-year-old corporal, soldier, Grey Ranks member, Boy Scout from Łódź and now a new KEDYW operative.

Pants and Wire arrived at the train station in Litzmannstadt very early the next morning. After departing the train, Pants handed his ticket and his identity papers to a soldier who was inspecting documents. Pants glanced at the soldier and thought for a moment that he looked unexpectedly young. The soldier flipped to the back of the book where stamps from out of the area were placed. Staszek was still carrying his ID that stated that he was Tadeusz Gora. This name had been clean and was the name of a teenager that had been killed during the invasion of a nearby town.

Forged papers were always a risk, but with things turning bad for the Germans in Russia, the traffic on the trains and for that matter on the roads had increased as the Germans desperately tried to reinforce their army in the east. One of the ways they seemed to be doing that was to put younger and younger men in reserve positions that allowed more veteran warriors to move east. Pants took back his papers from the boy soldier who appeared overwhelmed by the mass of documents that were being held out to him. More people had started moving west, anticipating the Russians coming back to Poland. The civilians were not only Poles but also the ethnic Germans who had moved to the east on Hitler's promise of the open land, and his assurance that it would be theirs for a thousand years. Now they too seemed to be pushing to the west. This was a good thing in many ways, but in particular it made it easier and faster for Staszek to get through the checkpoint.

During the weeks prior to his last mission, there had been more sabotage incidents that had added other alias names, codenames, actual citizen names and pictures to whatever list the Gestapo may have made and had to keep current. Staszek hoped, or more accurately he bet his life, that the name Tadeusz Gora was not on one of those that made a list. The young German soldier guard did not seem too interested in dirty Tadeusz Gora, whose dirty occupation was listed as "Mason." He had already checked several hundred people on the train this morning alone, and was becoming careless. Staszek continued on with his backpack, which had some food, including a slab of bacon, some honey, cigarettes, and a sack of coffee for his mother and the family as gifts. He also had a carton of cigarettes for bribes or barter as well as his pistol inside his waistband that was secured by a cord that hung around his neck.

He made his way through the crowd of German-speaking people who laughed and joked amongst themselves as they continued to think that they had done the right thing by being, or trying to be, German. As he left the station at just before 1:00 PM, he hoped to get to Basia's restaurant for a real meal. He wanted to come home, and felt that since Łódź was far enough behind the German annexation line, he could blend in a little easier than in Radom or Kielce where fighting still raged in and around those towns. His German had improved, and he felt that he had been gone long enough and changed physically enough that if he were spotted by any of the many German citizens of the town that might have known him from the past, at best they would not be sure that it was indeed him.

An hour later he reached the safe house and went to his room, where he was given a fresh change of clothes, towels, and soap. He had enough time to take a bath and shave the thin crop of hairs from his face and the dozen or two more on his neck. It wasn't a lot, but looking into the mirror he thought that it was a good start. Soaking in the tub for a long leisurely experience was like heaven to him. He actually bathed twice, by letting all of the water out from the tub, and refilling it with hot water from a boiler in the corner of the room. This room was used as a utility closet, and the boiler served the needs of the entire house. When he came downstairs, he talked to the large-framed but very fit landlady, who had given him the room and clothes. With an exaggerated motion of her head and trunk, she looked at him up and down while she placed her hands on her hips. Smiling, she said, "Even if there isn't any warm water left in the house it was worth it to see you without a crust!" She gave a hearty laugh.

Pants looked down at himself, and felt slightly embarrassed and had a sense of being undressed without the layer of body oil and dirt he'd collected out in the woods.

The landlady gave Pants information where to meet Wire for their meeting with the third member of the team. The location was in an apartment above a row of businesses that Staszek knew well. As he approached the apartment he was especially alert, because it was directly above the restaurant where his sister Basia worked. He became extremely cautious as he climbed the stairs knowing the patrons below him were mostly Germans. *This could be a trap,* he thought, as he climbed the stairs slowly, looking for the number five on the apartment door. He placed one hand on the handle of his pistol concealed in his coat pocket while the other knocked the assigned code pattern. Wire opened the door and allowed Pants in. When he entered, Pants was immediately on the defensive when he saw Jan Szymański sitting at the barren table in the middle of the room. Wire went over to the table and sat down next to Jan. "Have a seat Pants, I think you know Bear."

Pants just stood and looked at them and wondered if this was a trick or a prank that was being played. He stood still as he stared at them for a moment longer then cautiously reached for the chair to sit, never letting go of the pistol in his coat pocket. He looked at 'Bear,' then back at Wire, and said, "Do you know that this man called Bear is also the owner of the German restaurant downstairs and this could be a trap?" Pants never took his eyes off of Szymański.

Wire turned to Bear with a smile. Bear also smiled. Wire gently placed his hand out towards Pants, waving up and down, as if to say "calm down" while declaring, "Pants I know that you know that your sister works downstairs, and that Bear, here, is the owner, and that the Germans come here for the food that is served as well as the social life. What you do not know is that Bear is one of us and has been an asset to the cause since the beginning. This restaurant has been a wealth of information to the Republic in fighting our oppressors."

Pants could not believe that this very German-friendly and privileged restaurant owner was on the side of good; on the same side as Pants.

Bear leaned forward on the table with one elbow as he partially reached towards Pants with the other hand that was open and slowly twisted upwards in a relaxed gesture to explain, "Your sister has told me about you and how proud she and the family are of you. She worries about you all of the time, but has kept her secret to herself, and I have not asked anything that would put her or the family in harms way." Bear paused as he watched many unanswered questions and thoughts go through Pants' brain. "She had not told me your codename, and I was only guessing that it would be you coming through the door, but there was also a chance that you were not you. You could also be someone working for the Germans carrying Stanislaw's name. Wire had your real name. I had to make sure it really was you."

Pants was dumbfounded for a minute, thinking that "they" were thinking that *he* might be a fraud. After a long minute he came to the conclusion that he would have done the same thing if his life were being placed at risk on a mission for the Polish Republic.

With a slightly red-flushed face and needlepoint eyes Pants asked,

"How is my sister? Is she well? Have you been good to her? I know she works very hard for you." The tone of the questions were given in a slightly offensive way.

Bear grinned and said, "She is doing well, and yes, she works very hard. She is able to bring leftovers to your mother and sister Fela regularly," Bear said, with sincerity. He added, with firmness, "Basia is very important to me, and I would never harm her or allow any harm to befall her. One of the safest places to work is in this restaurant, and she is respected here, though she is known to be a Pole." He paused as if to think whether he should continue, and did, "She is also a very brave woman who has a sharp mind and good ear. She has heard a lot of things from overly-friendly drunken German soldiers that have been useful to our country."

Pants nodded, and asked, "She is not in danger is she?" With a slight tightening of his stomach at the thought of Basia in danger and so close to the volatile Germans.

Bear who was a former boxer and 10 years older than Pants, took a deep breath, loosing his smile for a moment, and in a somber tone said, "We're all at risk, all the time. Your sister knows that as well as you or I. I'm doing everything I can to keep ALL of us safe. I cannot say more than that."

Pants knew that to be true, but it did not really make him feel any better. Becoming resigned to that truth, he said, "All right, what is the plan?"

Bear started the description of the mission that was to kidnap, interrogate, and then eliminate a German informer. Bear stated that, "The informer is a Polish businessman who has been distributing beer and wine to restaurants, and as a Pole had gained the confidence of many of the shop owners who were still loyal to the Polish government in exile. He gave their names to the Gestapo, who arrested them, and shipped them off to a camp for political prisoners. We believe that he has an extensive, well-placed, network of contacts. He not only had been identifying businessmen, but also members of the Grey Ranks and members of the resistance. This mission is to turn the tables on this man." Bear watched Pants start to clench his teeth, as he became angry at the thought of someone, a Pole no less, doing this to his own people.

Bear continued, "The three of us will pick up Strezowicz under false pretenses of him being rewarded for his service to the German government. We will be in a German staff car, with you posing as the driver and Wire being the Gestapo agent. I will be a bodyguard. We are to take him to what he thinks is a Gestapo sub-headquarters for a debriefing and to receive an award for his loyalty to the Reich. We will have some backup help at the warehouse, if needed. This will not end well for the traitor."

Pants said, "Where will I have to drive? I've driven trucks, but not cars, I might not be very good at a car's gears."

Wire interjected, "We'll practice a little before going for the pick up. The route will be a long indirect one, but if you know the area it should be an easy drive. We will be starting the interrogation in the car, while his guard is down. We will continue in the warehouse, if it becomes necessary. We will complete this mission out of sight of any passersby. If for some reason there are witnesses, stay calm and head for the safe house. " He added, with clarity, "If we are out in the open and we have completed the mission assignment, just walk away calmly. The people will be looking at the body. They won't see or remember you."

Pants nodded in agreement, but his heart rate had increased with this information as the three completed the details of the plan. At the end Wire leaned towards Pants once more and said, "You are very clear on the concept that Strezowicz will be executed in the name of the Polish Government in Exile. This has already been judged and granted. You understand what is going to happen and that there is no alternative."

Pants mulled over the statement. He had shot and killed soldiers in battle and had been mad enough to have shot in cold blood, but had restrained himself. With a false sense of confidence, he said with a little arrogance, "Absolutely. I can do it."

Wire, stopped and analyzed the boast and repeated the message, "We will shoot this traitor without exception. *Do you understand?*"

Pants let his breath out, realizing that his moment of posturing was not appropriate. This was going to be an execution, and he was to be part of it. Reflecting for a moment, he confessed, "I don't know what I will think at that moment, but I know that this is necessary and is for the greater good if Poland is to survive. I am ready to do my part."

Wire took a deep breath and let it out completely, "That is what I expected from a soldier and the Grey Ranks KEDYW member. I think you are ready for the mission. Your job is to be vigilant, act with determination, and execute the plan as we have made it. Above all, you must stay calm." Wire stood and said, "I'll leave last, the two of you leave immediately after the assignment is carried out. Pants, head for the safe house-understand?" Pants nodded and said, "Completely." He then asked, "Before I leave here, can I see my sister?"

Bear looked at Wire for direction who answered, "No, we're too close to the start of the mission, and I don't want to take any chances of something going wrong at this time. Maybe later."

Pants was disappointed, since he was directly above the restaurant where his sister was working, but accepted the decision. He shook hands with Wire and with a moment of hesitation took hold of the massive fist of Bear and grasped it very firmly making Bear smile from the force of the grip. Without saying another word, Pants left the apartment as instructed.

The next morning the team arrived at a warehouse where they would bring Strezowicz back for interrogation. A staff car with all the correct markings was ready for the team. Pants was given the gray tunic of a German sergeant, and a soft cap to wear, while Bear and Wire had the omnipresent black long coats and hats. After about fifteen minutes of practice, Pants was sufficiently comfortable with the gear pattern that he was driving easily around the district.

At the arranged time Wire arrived at the office of Strezowicz and went into the office to announce his arrival. The secretary, upon recognizing the uniform of the "agent", though not the man himself, quickly stood and went to Strezowicz's office and informed him of the Gestapo agent's presence. Strezowicz closed his briefcase as he added one more page to its contents before leaving for the car. As he left he waved to his secretary in a dismissive way, "I will not be back today. If there are calls, take messages and I will call when I have time tomorrow." He then left the office with his briefcase tucked high under his arm and strode with his head proudly held high as he walked ahead of the imposter to the imposter's car. He climbed into the back seat of the sedan through the door that was held open by Pants. Strezowicz looked past the "soldier" without a word, like he had so many times in the past with other cars. Once in, Wire sat in the back with Strezowicz while Pants got behind the wheel of the car and drove away. He did not see the secretary coming out to flag down the car. Upon failing to do so, she returned to her desk phone and said, "I tried to catch him but he has left with the Gestapo agent." Listening for a moment then answering, "He did not say, but it was an agent that I do not think I have seen before and they headed west on Herman Goring Street in the black staff car." The caller hung up abruptly as the secretary said into the phone, "Hello? Hello?" to no avail.

Pants drove a long circuitous route to extend the car ride, which would give Wire time to develop a rapport with Strezowicz. As Pants drove his eyes moved from the traffic ahead of him to the rearview mirror to look at the traitor behind him.

Wire explained in Polish, "As you know from the letter delivered to you yesterday, the director's office in Babiak was destroyed by a fire caused by an oil lamp, and all the files were destroyed."

Strezowicz, holding his satchel on his lap repositioned himself in the seat, and with some enthusiasm said, "Yes, yes, I did hear that. What a stroke of bad luck."

Wire continued, "Well, we do not believe that it was an accident and that is why we asked that you bring the information you had with you so we could recreate the files to the best of our ability to restart the investigation at a higher level. Since we had sent everything to Berlin initially, there may be something that we missed that would give us a clue about the sabotage in the field office. You can imagine how eager Berlin is to have us investigate this information further."

"Sabotage? I did not know that." Strezowicz pondered for a couple of seconds. "Of course, I will be happy to recreate whatever you need. You know that I have been very cooperative with the Gestapo and will do what I can to help. Of course those records destroyed at the office will be hard to recreate, but I have everything the Gestapo needs to look at more closely at other offices. Perhaps Berlin would be appreciative of my efforts in the same manner as before? It is a lot of work to keep track of my contacts and to pay them." Strezowicz was boldly suggesting further financial compensation for his traitorous behavior and treacherous activities against his country.

Wire, with a curious smile and tone quizzically asked, "I'm curious as to how you got so many names of those involved in the crime against the Reich. You must have a wonderful network of informers in the city. I'm sure Berlin would be very pleased to reward your network, and you for your efforts for the cause. Maybe they could learn something from a man of your skills." Wire threw in the compliment to stroke the ego of the traitor.

Strezowicz stated boisterously, "There was only one main contact who was extremely good and several strategically placed ones, but from there I did the research and investigated the names that were given to me while arranging for liquor deliveries." He smiled broadly, "Many of the merchants were proud of their crimes against the Reich, and I want to make them pay for that treason." He laughed proudly. "And they will, I assure you." Strezowicz became distracted at the route that they were driving and looked out the window slightly puzzled. Wire noted the increased awareness of his passenger and leaned back into the seat as he said in German, "Driver, when will we get to Headquarters?"

Pants, on this prearranged question said in German, "In a couple of minutes, sir," as he started in the direct route to the secret warehouse selected for this mission.

Upon arriving, a man wearing a large-brimmed hat opened the tall warehouse doors and allowed the car to drive in. He promptly closed the doors afterwards and strolled a short distance away. Once in the warehouse, Strezowicz got out of the car and watched with some puzzlement as the two ancient big doors closed behind him and the car. He suddenly became suspicious and asked, "When did you change locations? This is not Gestapo Headquarters," as he looked around at the barren walls and painted-over windows. As he did this he spotted Bear and looked at him closely and with a gasp said, "You are not a Gestapo! You're Szymański and have that restaurant..." Bear simply walked up to him and punched him in the face, stopping the revelation in mid-sentence.

Wire and Bear grabbed the stunned Strezowicz by the arms and wrestled him to a chair that was just in front of the car's shining headlights. Pants now had his pistol out and aimed at Strezowicz who was shocked at the sudden change in his situation. Moments before, he was expecting monetary rewards for his information, if not a medal from the Führer for his work. Now he was held at gunpoint in an empty warehouse.

"You will not ask the questions. We will." Wire said, with a hard slap across the face of the now terrified traitor. "Who was that informer who gave you the names?" Wire pressed a pistol with a silencer on it into the chest of the now very anxious and suddenly odorous collaborator.

Pants noted the stain that had appeared on the seat of the chair and wicked down Strezowicz's pant legs as he identified this dire situation that he was now embroiled, and its imminent life or death option.

"Who are you? I don't have to tell you anything." Strezowicz announced in a shaking voice and paled color to his skin, which attested to the fact that he was failing at holding his composure.

"Wire demanded, "Who are your informants?" Bear hit him across the face with his fist. "Who are they?" Wires pressed.

Strezowicz continued to refuse to answer the questions. Blood was running down from a cut on his forehead and into his eye. Wire raised his pistol and demanded once more, "Who are your informants, or I start to shoot you in every joint of your body."

"I won't tell you, and when the Gestapo..." he didn't finish the sentence as a bullet tore into his left knee and he shrieked out in pain.

Pants, who stood near the big door watching for trouble outside, was startled by the muffled gunshot and looked to see what happened. The sight of the blood running onto the floor did not faze him, and he noted that to himself with trepidation though tempered by his distain for the traitor.

Strezowicz, wracked with pain, tried to scream as he grabbed his knee but Bear restrained his arms and Wire shoved a rag into his mouth.

"Who are they?" Wire pressed the gun against Strezowicz's hip and groin.

Strezowicz whimpered through the gag and his eyes showed submission.

"Let's try this again." Wire calmly stated, "Who are the informants?" there was a pause and he jammed the barrel of the pistol hard into Strezowicz's groin, and then slowly took out the gag.

"All right, all right! I'll tell you!" Strezowicz now fully appreciated his position and what he had done that warranted this pain. His sense of self-preservation started to take over from his posture of defiance. "There was one main one, it was the Russian, a Russian man who had been in the Grey Ranks. He infiltrated them posing as a teenager, but he was a Russian double agent. He worked for me and I thought he was a Pole, but he actually was a Russian."

"What was his name?" Wire pulled back the hammer of the pistol and pushed it harder into Strezowicz's groin.

"His name was Sukolov."

"What was his codename!" Wire screamed the question at Strezowicz.

"He called himself Shark, and he provided names and pictures of managers, delivery people, and contacts with the mills and breweries where the Polish loyalists were to be found." He stopped, and with a snarled grin at Bear, "and he has one on you, too."

Bear hit him again, but Strezowicz smirked as he spit out some blood, and tried to stall for time hoping to stay alive a little longer to give the Gestapo time to find him. Strezowicz boasted, "The Gestapo have been watching over me and they must know that you have taken me. If you were smart, you'd get out of here now. They have everything they need to close down your weak organization in Litzmannstadt. Let me live, and you'll have a chance yourselves. More than a year ago, Sukolov and I exchanged addresses of the mills and meeting places of the Grey Ranks and other reconnaissance. He needed me and I needed him. Then he disappeared last year, and I found others to follow up on the information. The money was very good for all of us." Stopping, he looked at Wire and Bear and said, "You need me alive to save your miserable skins." He scanned Wire's face for a sign that there was hope to stay alive. Finding none he desperately added, "I am a Pole, and I can work for you and our country by getting information about the Germans for you. Isn't that worth anything?"

Wire looked at Pants, who was wide eyed and becoming enraged. "Where is he now? Where do we find him? I have to shoot someone and it can be you or the Russian. Which should it be?" The barrel of the gun was slowly brought up to his temple so that he could see the cocked hammer and Wire's finger on the trigger.

"He is gone. I didn't know he was a Russian until much later, those sneaky bastards." With absolutely no sense of irony, Strezowicz shook his head in contempt at the fact that Shark was a sneaky Russian rather than a traitorous Pole like him. He continued, "He has gone to Lwow, I think. When things got too intense on the eastern front, he left and he said he was going to join the A.K. near there." Strezowicz tried to read the face of Wire to see if his information was worth his life.

Wire got very close to Strezowicz and asked, "Who else?"

The terror in his eyes found no harbor of hope in Wire's face. He thought to stand to get away but the fire in his leg stopped him from moving. "That is what you wanted, right? You do need me, right? I was just making a living. I have a lot of bills to pay. This was business. I don't know the others. The Gestapo set them up and I don't know who they are."

Wire stood up and dropped his arm and pistol to his side. Across the garage, Pants watched, as Wire seemed to relax for a moment. *He isn't going to let him go, is he?* Pants wondered, with some alarm. *That bastard has killed a lot of people with his treacherous deeds.*

Pants started to turn towards Wire to make sure that he would complete the assignment, when Wire pronounced, "In the name of the Polish people and government, you have been sentenced to death for your betrayal of your country." With that last word said Strezowicz tried to protest by raising his hands up towards Wire but Wire's arm and his gun came up to Strezowicz's temple as the final terror gripped the traitor. A split second later, Wire pulled the trigger and the 9mm bullet exploded into the greedy man's head, the echo muffled by the silencer and the head itself. The lifeless body peeled sideways off the chair and unceremoniously hit the floor, only being moved by gravity as it settled in a heap that befitted the traitor.

Pants looked at the blood flowing quickly from the gaping wound that looked like so many of the martyrs' wounds who died at the hands of the Nazis on so many streets in this town, as well as the rest of the country. Pants looked at Wire and said, "Shark, Sukolov; he knows me. He knows all the members of the Grey Ranks here in town. He must have all our codenames and aliases. If Strezowicz had them, then the Gestapo will have them. " Pants felt worried and alarmed partially for what he just witnessed and the reality of this being repeated across the country by Nazis against Poles, because of Shark and people like Strezowicz. "We have to find Shark. If the Gestapo has this information, Shark has given even more to the Russians," Pants declared.

Wire paused and took his own deep breath and let it out. He looked at Pants and in a calming gesture leaned towards him and said, "Sukolov may know codenames, but he doesn't know much more than that, which is why we use them. What he doesn't know is that we know who he is and that we will find him."

Pants looked at Wire, reassured. Wire said, "We have to go. We will go to the Kielce headquarters and make plans to look for Sukolov. Pants, change out of that uniform and was to get to the train station as soon as you can. Bear, you are to return to the restaurant and report to your contact. We will see you again, hopefully soon."

Bear went to Pants and gave him a hug. "I will watch out for Basia, I promise."

"You'd better," Pants said flatly as he returned the hug and slap on the back.

They were about to leave the warehouse and its mess to be cleaned up by the Germans who would surely find this spot when Wire said, "If Strezowicz was right about the Gestapo watching him, we need to discourage them as much as possible from following us. Bear, give me a couple Potato Mashers from the car." Bear went to the truck and brought out three of them and gave them to Wire who gave one back to Bear and said, "Keep this one." With the other two, Wire took the grenades and placed one handle through the handle of one of the large doors and wired their detonator cords to the opposite handle. He repeated that for the other large door on the side of the building. "There. If the Germans storm the building, they go through the big doors and these will slow them down. We'll go out the small access door on this side." Wire motioned them on to the small door and they split up with Bear going one direction and Wire and Pants the other way down a different street.

As Pants and Wire turned the corner from the warehouse they watched a transport full of soldiers coming quickly down the street towards them. Pants made no effort to change his pace but turned down between two buildings just fifty meters from the corner where he stopped near several garbage bins and a pile of bricks that were stacked against the wall, a remnant of the debris from the invasion. Wire delayed a moment and looked to make sure there were no others coming. He was able to see that the first trucks had stopped in front of the warehouse and soldiers jumped out near to the side door where he had placed the grenades. Several of those soldiers started towards the alley. Pants watched from the alley and mumbled, "They knew we were there." His stomach knotted at the thought that a matter of minutes could have caught him and the team still inside. He squatted behind one of the bins when the two soldiers from the truck entered the alley and walked slowly towards Pants and Wire with their rifles aimed from their shoulders.

"Audstehen. Komm' heir," (Stand up. Come here.) One of the soldiers ordered. Pants stood as ordered but kept his hands down trying to figure out how to get to his pistol in his waistband before the soldiers found it. "What's wrong?" Pants asked in casual German slang. Wire had his hands in his pockets and did not move.

The first soldier gestured upwards with his rifle for Pants to raise his arms, but Pants did not move his arms but started backwards towards an alley door some 10 meters away from him. "Halt!" the soldier announced with a firm order. Pants started to raise his left hand but also began to turn to the right to block the view of the soldier as he reached for his pistol. Wire pulled his hands up and stepped slightly forward to block the view of the soldiers of Pants. Wire sensed what Pants was trying to do and tried to distract the soldiers.

"Halt, arme hoch!" (Stop. Arms up!) Pants stopped turning but he continued to slowly reach for his pistol.

Suddenly machine gun fire erupted from the direction of the adjacent warehouse then an explosion from a grenade echoed into the alley coming from a half block down the street, followed by a second and moments later a third blast in the area of the truck unloading its soldiers. The concussion from the street side behind the soldiers had Wire lunge for the pile of bricks as Pants drop to a knee while the soldiers dove to the ground; face down. As Pants recovered from the blasts he pulled out his pistol and fired it twice at the soldier closest to him. Hitting him from five meters away in the side of his chest. He turned his pistol towards the second soldier, but missed as the soldier rolled sideways behind the far end of the pile of bricks making a shot impossible for Pants or Wire. Pants went to the alley door and kicked it trying to break in and give himself some protection, but the door was barred and would not budge. Turning his back to the door, he held his arm out straight at the pile of bricks waiting for the soldier to expose his position when a burst of bullets rained down on the hidden soldier from a window above them, hitting him several times. The soldier fell sideways from behind the bricks and laid motionless.

A moment later, Pants swung his gun around towards the alley door as it was unbarred and opened. He held his fire as two armed men peered out and called, "You two, come quickly." Pants, seeing no other choice ran into the building with Wire close behind. They continued to run the length of the warehouse until they were led down some stairs and then through an underground tunnel to a building a block away. Pants emerged with Wire and their guides in an abandoned and badly damaged store. Catching his breath he thanked the men for their help, "Thanks, but where did you come from?"

"We are your shadow," one of them said. "We were to watch the warehouse until you left and thought we were clear until the SS showed up."

"Bastards, they're everywhere." The other cursed. "We will wait here for a while, until it is safe to leave. Do you know where to go?"

Pants nodded. "I know my way around here." He looked closely at one of the men. "You're Bat from the Grey Ranks, aren't you?"

The man turned and looked into Pants face for a moment and said, "Pants? I did not know that it was you. Good to see you." They shook left hands with its familiar gesture. "I thought you were long gone from here. Why did you come back? This is not a safe place, as you found out."

Pants did not give any details of the mission, but asked, "Do you remember Shark?"

"Shark?" Bat repeated, and then turned to the other man with them. "Franck what happened to him?"

Franck just shrugged.

Bat added, "He was around for several months after the ambush at the tavern." Bat recalled slowly. "He said he went to the latrine when the shooting started and was afraid to come back afterwards. He bounced around for several missions but I don't remember when or where he went or what happened to him. Why?"

Wire stood up, looked around and said, "We have to get out of here."

Pants also looked around while he added, "If you hear of anything about him, or anyone that has seen him or knows where he is, tell the Chimney leader, because he was the traitor that got Cotton killed and the rest of us nearly captured."

Bat was stunned with the news and asked, "How do you know that to be true?"

Pants answered, "I can't tell you, but on my mother's life, I know it is true. If I get a chance, I will kill him."

Bat took a deep breath in, and sighed. "Okay, I will be vigilant," giving the Scout motto new purpose. "We will make sure it is clear for you, and watch your back while you get away." Once again Bat and Pants shook left hands. Over the next thirty minutes, they waited for the right time to leave under the cover and watchful eyes of the other two Grey Ranks members.

Pants and Wire split up once they were out of the hideout. Rather than heading for the train as planned, Pants went out of his way to stop in to see his mother if even for only a minute; he had to see her. Using caution, as had been his method before, he made his way up the back stairs and turned the knob to the apartment. It was not locked and he entered quietly, surprising Helena. The short period of joy and tears were heartfelt and badly needed by each of them. Within fifteen minutes of entering the house, Pants was leaving for his next report and assignment. Forty-five minutes later he was on the train heading east, and Helena, in her joy, headed for the church to give thanks before it became dark. No confession was being heard, but Clara was arranging flowers and the two women talked for a minute or two.

Picture# 3: Corporal Niklewicz

Chapter 17
February 16th, 1944: West of the Bug River

THE CAMP WAS covered with a soft white blanket of snow. The morning light gave a quiet beauty to the trees that surrounded the tarpaper and log shelters built at their bases. The camp's priest was saying Mass to the 180 men and women who made up the 25th Regiment of this A.K. unit on the far northeastern edge of the Holy Cross Mountain range. At the high point of the Mass, the group sang several spiritual songs, which, despite the cold and the location uplifted the souls attending the ceremony. Pants loved to sing and the songs lifted his spirits and bonded the men and women in the camp to the mission they had undertaken away from their families. Having love for God and faith in the righteousness of their cause was as much a certainty as their hatred for the Germans and the ever-present Russians, both of whom lusted for the land of Poland. This unit was determined to evict the invaders with God's help or, if necessary without it.

At the end of the Mass, a captain called the group to attention and called out for NCOs (non-commissioned officers) and higher-ranking personnel to report to the command shelter. The rest of the troops were dismissed and headed for the cooking area for their breakfast. Eighteen-year-old Sergeant Niklewicz and fifteen other NCOs and ranking officers slowly entered the tight quarters, where they were served coffee with milk and sugar. The warmth and calories were greatly needed and appreciated in the harsh weather and rugged terrain. The coffee, a mix of coffee beans and some kind of nut, was thin, but it was dark and warm. Among the officers was Wire, who had been the intelligence officer for the group for the past several months, and was to whom Pants reported.

Pants had been on several missions with Wire over the past months, where they had Scouted and observed German movements to the east. Pants had been given a squad of 12 men that had participated in ambushes and attacks on German positions, transports, and materials, which earned him his sergeant stripes in combat. Just as important, they also had monitored the retreat west by the Germans and reported the numbers and conditions of the troops. In the majority of cases, the Germans were in poor condition, which was a good sign that the Germans were losing the war.

Wire, after officer training school, had further training by their commanding officer, Colonel Jan Pinwik, who was a Polish "Cichociemni" (silent and dark), commando. The colonel trained in England, and was dropped back into Poland to do counterintelligence and sabotage. The Cichociemni were elite soldiers, who used the Grey Ranks and the KEDYW for many of their assignments, hence Wire's interest and use of Pants and other former Scouts for his missions.

As the heat from the twenty-plus bodies warmed the shelter, Wire stood at one end of the group and called them to attention. He looked over the assembly of four-pointed military hats and a collection of berets that the NCOs wore, as was the case for Pants. All looked toward the front table where their leader stood with his hands behind his back, inside his bulky unbuttoned coat.

The colonel placed the troops at ease as he took several slow steps to the side of a table and removed his coat, head down slightly in thought. He stopped and sat on the corner of the table with one leg up on the rough-cut wood. He looked over the fixated group, and wanting to choose his words correctly he began his statement quietly and deliberately, "Boys, more than five years ago, our country was assaulted and raped by the Hitlerites from the west. For all these years we have endured their atrocities and brutality with strength and determination to throw off their yoke of oppression. We have fought in large groups as well as in numbers of one and two. We have fought physically alone at times, but in the millions in spirit. During these years, we have struck German propaganda efforts, prisons, railroads, and factories and with bombs as well as pencils. We have shed blood, tears, and lost lives. We have stopped tanks in their tracks with pits and hand grenades. We have interfered and stopped the Germans everywhere by not allowing them to control our hearts and spirit. The hundreds of thousands of men they had sent to hunt us down were men they could not send to France or England. Unselfishly we have sacrificed for the Allies by holding on and waiting for our time to fight back. We have waited in the cities, towns, and the many forests of our country for the day when we can cut out the German cancer that has grown on our country, and eliminate it from our lives. We have all sacrificed much, and we will have to sacrifice still more for our chance to win that day of our victory." He stopped and let his words take effect as heads were turning side-to-side looking at each other or down to their rough and dirty hands in reflection of the words. Pants in that moment relived the first days of the war, and felt the frustration of being helpless, boil up inside of him.

The colonel continued, "Boys, with much pride and great hope, I believe that pivotal day is upon us. We now have orders to take the fight to the Germans like they have not seen for many years. As of the 15th of January, Operation Storm (Burza) has been put into place, and we have orders to take it to the Germans and attack their rear guard to slow their ability to continue into Russia. We know full well that Russia continues to be a snake with two heads, one striking at Germans now, but without warning the other head will strike at us; we will have to defend our country from two foes by working with the lesser of the two. With that said, our orders are to attack the Germans on the Eastern Front and give support to the Russians wherever we can."

There was a rumble in the room at the thought of siding with the Russians, since many of the men knew that they were every bit the barbarians that the Germans were, if not more so. They had proven that when they invaded in September 1939 and collaborated with the German bastards for 15 months, and from their infamous massacre of Polish officers in the Katyn Forest.

"Boys," the colonel tried to calm the crowd, "we have been ordered to do this; it is not a suggestion, and as soldiers we are bound to do our duty as ordered." The commotion in the room increased further, but stopped when Wire yelled, "Quiet!"

The colonel rolled down a large map and pointed on the map. "Here in Vilno, the Russians have already attacked the German troops there, by pouring over onto our side of the border. Polish troops have fought with them, and we have beaten the Germans back off of our land. Starting today, we will study and make plans for the support of the Russians west of Kowel. It will be a three-week march to get there, and set up camp at a to-be-determined site in order to make contact with the Russian Army and plan our attacks. We will march primarily at night and camp during the daylight hours. We must not engage the Germans until we are ready, and we don't want them to know where we are going. We will start preparation for our departure tomorrow night. Prepare your men for the march. They need not know where we are going, yet. That is all; dismissed."

The men in the room immediately starting talking amongst themselves, with their anxiety reflected in the rapid motions of hands and arms punctuating the comments. One strong voice rang out, "It's bad enough to march for three weeks, but once we are there we have to help the Russians? God save us."

Another calmer voice insisted, "Maybe some of those German bullets in the air will find Russians instead of us!"

The other man moaned, "It will be hard to shoot a German when one of your eyes is looking behind you, watching to see if one of those sons of bitches from Moscow is actually shooting at a German or you."

The NCOs exited the room and went to the kitchen area for a meal of chicken broth and potato soup, a meal that they would definitely need.

Wire called to Pants as he was about to leave the room, "Pants, wait a moment." Pants turned around and went back into the room where the colonel and Wire were standing. The colonel turned to Pants. "Sergeant, I need you for a special project. I will put your corporal in charge of your squad for this assignment to Kowel." Pants was puzzled, and was about to protest about how his team had been waiting for this chance to have open combat with the Germans, but wisely held his thoughts to himself. "I am sending you and Wire, and three runners to Kowel in advance of the rest of the company to Scout out and determine the situation there. The Russian partisans have been absorbed into the regular army, and have formed a formidable regiment. You are to report anything suspicious or out of the ordinary that would adversely affect this Company. You and Wire are to avoid contact with the Germans or the Russians, but you can defend yourselves with deadly force against either side."

Pants looked at Wire, "Either side?"

Wire nodded, and explained, "The Russians have been proven to use Poles for as long as they served their purposes, and then disarm and arrest them the next moment the Katyn massacre being the most hideous example. We can't let that happen to us or to the Company. We will leave in the next several days, march to a campsite that I will determine, and communicate by runner. We can not take the chance of having a radio signal intercepted."

The colonel added, "This action is on my authority and has not been sanctioned by London. This is a difficult situation, and time is of the essence to get the job done and get back to us. Any questions?"

Pants looked at Wire who impassively returned his gaze. Pants turned back to the colonel and said, "No sir."

"Good," the Colonel acknowledged. With that word and a firm pat and shake of Pants' shoulder he declared. "You are dismissed Sergeant." Then, in a moment of reflection, he called, "Sergeant, one more thing." Pants turned and came back to the Commander. "Wire told me of the information that was gathered during your mission in Łódź, and that your codename in all likelihood has been compromised by the Russians as well as by the Germans."

"Yes sir," Pants nodded. He then stated with some apprehension, "I do not know where or when the Russians or the Germans will make the connection, but I know that they will, sooner or later."

"I agree, and have given a great deal of thought to when your codename should be changed, and I think this is the time." The colonel pulled out a bundle of papers from his jacket and shuffled through several pages. "Wire has given me a history of your duties and missions that you have taken on. Your passion for your country from the beginning seems to have been without compromise. Even as a scout and courier your performance has been exceptional." He paused and watched Pants sit a little straighter with his eyes a little wider at the comments. The colonel continued, "One of our finest operators, who had been able to confuse and frustrate the Germans with his behind the lines activities and missions, much of them like yours, was killed in of all things an accident at a camp several weeks ago. The lose has been a difficulty one for us in that the Germans have spent a lot of time, men and energy trying to track him down. I believe that it would be good for the cause and for you if his codename were to continue." Staszek looked a little puzzled, and was waiting for more details when the colonel added, "I have talked with Wire and gotten his opinion on this matter and agree that your new code name will be 'ZNICZ' (the Eternal Flame or Flame). The captain, from his work with you, feels that the name is appropriate by deed and merit. From now on you will be called by the codename 'ZNICZ (Flame)".

Pants, now Znicz (Flame), was taken by surprise and was nearly speechless, though his chest rose with pride and honor of being given a new codename. A codename that reflected his service to his country as a man, rather than a reminder of his embarrassment suffered as a boy. "Znicz" (Flame)" he tried out several times. He liked the sound and puffed up his chest a little and smiled. "Flame." he said as he tilted his head with pride, and smiled at the Colonel.

The Colonel added for emphasis, "This codename is not to be taken lightly or in a negative way, because if your codename were to be compromised it would take some work and time for the Gestapo to figure out whether the codename was for the same person, thereby buying you time while they investigated. Extra time is always a good thing in those situations."

Pants, now Flame, stood straight and with his right hand brought his index and middle fingers to his right eyebrow and saluted the commander before he left the room. A moment later Wire came out and said, "Flame." He paused for effect, and smiled, "We have work to do. Meet me at my hut in 20 minutes, after you get something to eat."

Flame looked slightly glazed, but exhilarated in a way, knowing that the time had come where hit and run attacks and the destruction of materials and men through sabotage had now become open combat that would put the Germans on their heels.

During the meeting with Wire, over a small table drinking coffee by candlelight, Flame learned that they would travel by horseback to a location that had been determined as a marshaling area for the Germans. This would be the area where the Russians would more than likely pick for an attack, after blending partisan groups and A.K. regulars with their forces.

Once there, Wire and Flame would observe and tally the numbers of men and types of equipment that would be available by the end of March, at which time they would return and meet the forward elements of their Company.

Wire added, with some solemnness, "Flame, there is more you should know about this mission not disclosed by the commander earlier.

The utmost importance of the mission is to gather hard, indisputable information about the Russians and their treatment of Poles under their command. The commander did not tell the other officers because of the possible consequences for the future. It will be our task to find out if our Russian *'allies'* are indeed allies."

Flame looked puzzled, with still another twist to the day's events and his pending mission. Accepting the statement by Wire, Flame studied his face intently hoping to read what Wire felt was the gravity of the assignment.

"We have to find more information about the way the Russians treated our soldiers after the battle. After defeating the Germans in Wilno, with our help, the Russians disarmed our men and offered them the choice to join the Red Army or to be shipped to a retraining camp in Russia. In essence, they were sending them to prison. This does not bode well for Poland. If the Russians are disarming our soldiers, we have to find out whether this is true, and that information needs to be sent back here." Wire was quiet for a long time. "If the Russians are doing this treachery, Poland will not come out of this war as a free country but rather as a slave to Moscow. The Russian Bear will have its big paw on our throats for a century."

Flame did not know what to say. He was almost overwhelmed by the thought of having to fight on two fronts against two of the largest armies in the world. "What do we do to stop that from happening?" He finally asked, without forming any kind of answer himself.

"We will do what we have to do as soldiers and Poles. We will find the truth and act accordingly. Have no doubt this will be a dangerous mission." Wire paused to allow the sentence sink into Flame. "Our fate is in God's hands," Wire explained, fully believing in what had to be done then ended with, "Get your gear and we will saddle up within the next 30 minutes."

Flame raised his fingers to his forehead in a sharp salute, and left the room.

Within a day, Flame, Wire, and three Scout couriers whose jobs would be to run information back to the commander as Wire determined necessary, left for their journey to a place between the German and Russian lines. It would be a deadly place that had little room for errors, if discovered by cither side.

###

The journey was slow, as the group traveled mostly at night or through densely forested areas, using compass and flashlights as the main navigation system. The availability for food and shelter rested on farmers or small communities that welcomed the partisan fighters. For some reason, every stop for meals or travel supplies consisted of chicken. Sitting around a small campfire trying to keep warm, and beginning his meal of more chicken, started to weigh on Flame. It was not just eggs that he'd been eating, but smoked chicken, dried chicken, shredded chicken, chicken sausage, chicken roasted, raw, fried, old, cold, or boiled chicken and even chicken preserved in a jar. Though Flame had liked chicken; between the crows, quail, pheasants, and pigeons he trapped or shot over the past years, he had started to detest fowl and occasionally wondered whether going hungry would be better than eating more of these birds. He had mixed grubs and other bugs into his soup more than a few times while riding as a courier, and right now that sounded better than chicken. He had eaten squirrels, rabbits, dog, and horse. Each had a stronger flavor than the one before, and right now they sounded better than chicken. After two months of almost exclusively eating fowl, Flame's facial grimaces during meals where chicken was the only thing available made Wire laugh as he watched Flame force himself to eat a meal. "I have never seen a man so hungry have such a hard time eating something."

Flame looked at Wire and shrugged. "If I eat any more birds, I swear I will grow feathers and lay eggs."

The small group laughed, and teased Flame by clucking and flapping their arms like they had wings.

"Go ahead and laugh," Flame retorted, "but you'll stop doing so when I start laying eggs, and I wonder whether you will have the appetite to eat them."

They laughed and groaned at once at this rather grotesque image.

Several days, or rather several long nights, later the group reached what Wire believed to be their objective, and they reconnoitered the rolling hills that were thick with the tall pole pines common to the area. Leaving one of the runners with the horses, the four men proceeded on a course that would place them at a bluff where they should be able to see several roads, railroad tracks, and open fields from some distance.

Their objective proved to be their last stop, where contact with two local villagers and partisan supporters, said there had been increasing activities of both German and Russian forces for the past two to three days. The Russian trains had been moving men to the east, but no one knew why. There had also been rumors that a company of Polish partisans had been seen with the Russians during an aggressive battle against the Germans further to the east just the week before. The rumor was that the Germans were nearly destroyed and had retreated in tatters to the west.

This news caught Wire's interest, and he decided to look for the camp of the Russians that had Polish soldiers with them. Wearing white oiled fabric as overcoats they walked slowing and cautiously through the forest, watching for both Russians and Germans. Flame and Wire carried STENS machine guns deeper into the woods, while staying low and using drifts of snow for camouflage, stopping every several steps to listen for anything that would warn them of danger, or of guards or the activities of a camp. After two days of stalking and following trails or signs of foot traffic, early one afternoon Wire and Flame found a path that was fresh from a creek into a clearing dotted with camouflaged huts and tents.

From a distance, they watched the camp, and over the course of the rest of the day they slowly circled it to get an accurate count and description of the encampment. "I think there has to be around three hundred men and women in the place." Flame said, putting down his binoculars, "but for so many buildings there were very few visible people in the camp. Almost like a ghost town," he concluded.

Wire agreed that it was a minimum number, and that there would be patrols outside of the camp, which had heavy machine guns and mortars, visible in areas around the perimeter. At the east side of the camp was a road that lead to a separate area where horses and trucks were kept, and it was surprisingly quiet there. They crawled over a slight rise when Wire touched Flame's arm and pointed to a barbed wire enclosure guarded by two Russian soldiers on foot and one perched on top of a truck with a mounted machine gun. Inside the enclosure were about 100 soldiers, apparently prisoners, walking or hunkered down in the open or under a flimsy lean-to where a fire was burning. What caught the eye of Wire was that the soldiers were not in German uniforms, but Polish.

Wire whispered to Flame that he was going back to give the information as to coordinates and conditions to one of the runners. This would also warn the company that Poles were being held in an enclosure at gunpoint. Flame was to stay in place until he returned, and was to stay unseen. Flame nodded, took out his binoculars, and scanned the camp to see if there was anything else that needed to be noted. He was able to identify the headquarters tent, as well as the tents for the commanding officer. From the epaulettes they wore, it appeared there were four junior officers; lieutenants, and one major. Flame did not see any higher field grade or company grade officers, indicating that the force was a company of close to 200 soldiers, or less.

Flame watched the enclosure for about three hours when the snow started to come down lightly, adding a calm but cold feeling to the scene, making it harder to see activities, but at the same time it also would hide him from a closer range. The area was cleared around the wire for ease of patrolling guard to circle the prisoners, but the patches and drifts of snow mixed with mud and dirt paths and many open areas, gave many areas that could be used for hiding. He noted that the guards would make a rotation around the wire fence every 15 minutes or so. They did not appear to be in any hurry to complete their rounds. The rest of the time they were sitting near their fire pit. After watching four such trips Flame decided to move closer to the backside of the wire cage, and perhaps get information from one of the prisoners.

He crawled 50 meters from his vantage point, and circled deep into the trees in order to have a straight line to the portion of the fence that was near the fire. The evening twilight was quickly covering the camp, due to the tall tree shadows that darkened the camp, with their wide branches making Flame almost invisible from any distance. Carefully, he listened, watched, and crept half a meter at a time, on the alert for any danger, looking like dirty snow and mud oozing towards the fence.

Making his way ever closer to the fence and seeing if he could contact one of the prisoners who were far enough from the group near the fire, yet his actions would not be conspicuous to the guards. He watched for some time, to target one man, hunkered against one of the tree stumps near the wire as a possible information source.

When the time was right, he approached the man from behind. "Polish Soldier," Flame whispered, "don't turn, just listen." The soldier was startled by the voice behind him, and started to turn, but stopped with the order. "Are you prisoners because you are Poles?"

The hunched-over figure nodded, which knocked off a thin layer of snow from his thick hat that exposed the metal white eagle of a Polish A.K. soldier.

"I am too," Flame said. "Did you fight with the Russians before they put you in this cage?" Flame asked after looking over his shoulder.

Again the man nodded.

"How many Russians are there in the camp? One hundred? Two hundred? Three hundred?" Flame queried.

The soldier placed down four fingers.

"*Shit*," Flame mumbled. *We'll be outnumbered two to one*, the numbers ran through his brain, and they weren't good if the company came in unprepared and unaware. But the numbers did not match up. He leaned in closer and asked, "Where are the rest of them? I see no more than a hundred."

The man slid backwards towards the fence and answered, "They left on a night mission to ambush the Germans north of here. The guards and the Russian officers in those tents have been interrogating us one at a time, so they stayed in the camp." He looked around to check if the guards were still in their area as they were before he continued, "There is an NKVD officer in there, and he has records on everyone."

What is the Communist secret police doing out here? They're usually further back behind their lines. Flame was puzzled for a moment before he realized that the Russians were on the move, and their secret police were on a faster pace to control dissidents and other anti-Soviet factions as they moved in after the Germans.

The man called back, gently speaking to his armpit while his eyes scanned for the guards, "They will either ship us to Russia tomorrow or shoot us in the woods. A dozen trucks were coming and going most of the morning, moving prisoners out of here and coming back empty in the afternoon. Whatever is happening, it isn't far away." As he said this, the guards stood up from their campfire and started their rounds of the cage. One of them climbed up on the truck to man the machine gun while the other went on foot patrol with the first man.

Flame saw the motion of the guards and thought about the situation the prisoners were in. The fact that Poles were being taken to the trains to be sent to Russia was a very bad sign. What was more, he couldn't let these soldiers be held prisoner. "I have to go, but I will be back." Flame whispered to the man, and added, "Be Vigilant."

The man turned towards the fence and looked at Flame and smiled in recognition of the motto, staring at the shadow of the face inside the white hood. Unfortunately his acknowledgement of the motto was noted by one of the guards, who was working his way along the wire and became suspicious of what had caught the prisoner's interest in that moment. He pulled the strap of his rifle off his shoulder and picked up his pace slightly while straining to look into the darkness of the trees. A lantern he held for light was reflecting off the snowflakes back at him and illuminated his heavy steps and his struggle to see clearly.

Flame watched both guards heading to the back of the compound, and to where he was hiding. He tried to crawl slowly but the distance between him and the guards was diminishing too quickly. *I have to tell Wire,* was his focus, and he started to crawl back to their observation point. As he crawled he started to move faster when suddenly he saw the shadow near the base of a tree that was not a natural shape for a tree, and knew that Wire was watching and stopped his crawl. In a voice that was no louder than he dared he cupped his hands over his mouth and said, "They will be shipped away tomorrow by the NKVD. Three hundred Soviets have gone to attack Germans, north, only three guards." Flame fell silent and pressed his head down into the snow and hoped that the guards would not see him and waited.

It was not to be, within a minute he heard, "Встаньте руки вверх!" (Standup – Hands up!) Flame looked into the shadow and decided what to do. He quickly stood up, turned and marched towards the guard that stopped them from advancing while saying. "Не стреляйте!" (Don't shoot!). The two guards grabbed Flame and took away his machine gun and at gunpoint lead him to the commander's tent. Wire, deep in the shadows, watched the capture and did not move as he watched the Flame sacrifice himself for the prisoners and Wire.

Inside, Flame had his heavy jacket pulled off of him, exposing the white over red armband with the Kotwica painted on it. He was patted down and ordered to empty his pockets, where he placed his A.K. identity papers, compass, flashlight, knife and a brown-shelled hard-boiled egg on the table. The identity papers identified him as a member of an organized army, and therefore he was to be treated in a manner consistent with the Geneva Convention. During the pat-down, they found his P38 hanging from his neck. Watching this was a Russian major who crushed out his cigarette on the dirt floor when the guards were finished with Flame and ordered him to sit on a small stool. He then picked up the pistol and skillfully dropped the clip, and cleared the bullet from the chamber, but replaced the clip before putting it back down on the desk in an empty and safe matter. The major reached for the identity papers and thumbed through them. He then asked in passable Polish, "What is your codename?"

Flame knowing that his true name was already known and that his codename needed to be protected said, "I don't have one. I'm just a soldier."

The muscular, heavy-set major smiled calmly, walked over, and hit Flame across the face with an open hand that was almost as thick as it was wide, his ring cutting a wound on his nose. First in Russian, but correcting himself back into Polish, "Now why would an ally want to lie to a comrade in arms?" He hit Flame again, with his fist. This time he knocked him to the floor and added a cut to his left cheek. The two guards picked Flame up and placed him on the stool again. Flame defiantly swung his arms to have them let go of him. "You," the major snapped, pointing to one of the guards, "go get the lieutenant and have him bring his books with him. Then return to your post."

Four minutes later a young officer came in carrying two large journals under his arm. As he entered the major dismissed both guards. He pointed to Flame and said to the lieutenant, "He says he doesn't have a codename. Here are his papers. What do you have?" The lieutenant looked at the bloody face of Flame then sat behind the table and opened one of his books. The major sat on the front edge of the table looking at Flame and glancing at the journal occasionally, waiting for any information that might be found.

Under the light of the single lamp hanging over his head, the lieutenant after a minute, looked surprised at what he read then looked at the dirty, wet, and swelling face and eye of the man in front of him. He cross-referenced what he found in the second book and leaned back looking forward without expression. He stood and walked over to Flame and looked at him closely trying to see through the mess that was his face, but Flame already knew what he would find. The lieutenant stood up and said, "Pants, I didn't recognize you, what a surprise."

Hello Shark. Or should I call you *'Lieutenant'*?" Flame snarled at the Russian.

The lieutenant turned to the major and said, "Comrade Major, say hello to one of my old Grey Ranks classmates. We called him Pants, but now we can call him Stanislaw Niklewicz, or Sergeant Niklewicz, if those bars are real."

Flame stared at the double agent who sat on the edge of the table with a look of satisfaction on his face, and said, "The sergeant has been a busy fellow. According to the Gestapo records and my own, he has been involved in sabotage against Germans trains, rode horseback as a courier, participated in attacks on food storage areas, and has generally been a thorn in the side of the Germans." He laughed and continued, "He has been a problem from Radom in the north to *Katowice* in the south."

Flame was stunned and slightly shaken by the information that Shark had provided, but he was also puzzled with one error regarding *Katowice* the town he told his mother about as a decoy. He asked, "You have done your homework. I know you could not have done this alone. Who helped you plot against your friends in Łódź?"

The lieutenant thought about the question and felt empowered and satisfied with his work behind the enemy lines of two opponents. He was especially proud that he had fooled so many people, not only the Germans who thought he was a Pole informing on Poles, but the high and mighty Scouts and Grey Ranks.

"You were not smart enough to do all of this yourself, what stupid godless stooges did you convince to help you? They must be very despicable vermin that would help Russian scum." Flame quickly stood and leaned forward and from across the table spit at the lieutenant, delivering a moist, well-formed, wad of mucous directly under his right eye. The major stepped up from the corner of the table and hit Flame once more, knocking him to the floor.

The lieutenant pulled a handkerchief from his pocket and wiped the spit from his face, while his disdain for the boy he knew as Pants, and for that matter for all Poles came to a head. His disgust for the Poles and hatred exploded in a wave of profanity and rage as he blurted out, "You son of a bitch, you are the fool and stooge! You had no idea to the extent your pathetic life was chronicled, as had those others who resisted the Germans and now think they present a threat to Russia." He leaned back and picked up the P38 pistol that was on the desk and moved it around in his hands then he held the grip and slid his finger onto the trigger. "It was easy to get people, many '*loyal Polish citizens*' to inform on anyone and pretty much everyone that I needed for all those years." Then to punctuate the statement, "I even got people in your own church to inform on the naïve God-fearing imbeciles that knelt at that altar. Stooges? It is you and those worthless other Poles that should be looking in mirrors for the fools and traitors of their country."

Flame was pushing his luck, but did not care. If he were going to be shot, he would die fighting this traitor if it were the last thing he would ever do. He started to tense his legs and to lean forward into his chair thinking that he could choke this son of a bitch with his bare hands before the major could stop him. Just as he was about to lunge forward, a burst of machine gun fire was heard and suddenly stopped followed by rifle shots while a great commotion was started in the camp. A soldier burst into the tent and said to the major, "The prisoners are escaping!"

The major jumped up and grabbed his heavy coat and hat and stormed out into the darkness towards the wire cage that was outlined from within by the campfires. His exit, watched by both Flame and the lieutenant, broke the tension between the two, but not for long. As soon as the major left the tent, Flame sprang to his feet at the table separating him from the traitor. But the table was too big and it gave time for the lieutenant to grab the P38 and aim it at Flame. "You are as reckless and foolish now as you were when I knew you in 'Litzmannstadt,' your German home, that will soon be ours once and for all." His voice was heavy with sarcasm while his eyes showed glee in having the power over another Scout. He came around the table arm extended and without hurry or hesitation but with apparent pleasure he pulled the trigger to the 9 mm aimed at the center of Flame's chest. The sound of the hammer hitting but not sending the bullet surprised Shark. It had clicked on the empty chamber. Shark, not thinking that the gun could be not loaded was briefly frozen. Not being familiar with the pistol, Shark looked surprised and puzzled as he looked down at the gun in order to pull back the slide and quickly chamber a fresh round. As he pulled the slide back and released it, Flame sprang on him, knocking him backwards over a chair and onto the floor. The two men struggled and rolled around the floor trying to control both the gun and their opponent in the small space of the tent.

The lieutenant had passed as a younger boy because of his small frame and weight. That worked against him as Flame rolled over on top of him pinning him to the floor. The P38 was held between them with no one in total control of the muzzle. Flame had his body weight pressing down on the lieutenant, and they both had their hands between them trying to hold the gun. Flame reached his left hand up and gouged the right eye of the lieutenant forcing him to stiffen in pain, and as he did so Shark released his grip on the gun to protect his right eye. In that moment, he released his pressure on the gun to grab at Flame's hand, was when Flame quickly controlled the lieutenant's left hand, which was still on the gun. Lying on top of the Russian and adding weight by pushing his feet and toes against the ground, Flame looked down from five centimeters and while a drop of his blood dripped down onto the face of the lieutenant, a.k.a. Shark, Flame said to him, "This is for Cotton and the people you helped murder." Flame squeezed Shark's hand and the finger on the trigger that sent the bullet, muffled by the two bodies, ripping up through Shark's right lung and out the top of his shoulder, spraying Flame with blood and tissue. The lieutenant's head lifted from the floor in a painful spasm effort, but in less than two seconds it dropped hard to the dirt floor. Blood rose up in his mouth like a tide pool, while his empty eyes gazed at the lamp hanging from the bar at the top of the tent.

Flame rolled off the corpse and looked at the gun, and at his hand, that were both wet with blood. Flame wiped his shaking hand and pistol on the Russian's tunic in a final gesture of disdain before he got up onto his knees and listened to the shouting and running outside of the tent. Lifting the flap slightly, he looked out the front of the tent. There was no exit to be made from the front, as men were running around the camp, heading for the wired compound. On the other hand, the commotion distracted them from the eye peeking out of the commander's tent.

Flame put the lanyard around his neck and the P38 into his pocket as he grabbed his machine gun and the other contents of his pockets that were now scattered on the floor. He grabbed the two books from the floor and tucked them under his jacket. Looking carefully into the dark through the back of the tent, he slipped through the snow and mud in the direction where he came early this morning, to the opposite side of the cage. Quickly getting into the trees that were ever so slightly lit by the lamp glow from the tent, he crawled into the darkness on his hands and knees. He pulled his sleeves down over his hands to protect them from the sticks and patches of snow. Going as fast as he could in his crouched-crawling posture, he worked his way around the camp and in the general direction of the horses, hopefully to where Wire had gone after Flame surrendered to the guards.

For more than an hour, he worked away from the camp, feeling his way through the trees, heading for the darker shades of gray where there was no reflection off trees or bushes, stopping for brief moments to flick on his flashlight to read his compass and orient himself in the direction he had to go. As he increased his distance from the camp, he took deliberate steps into the darkness, trying to be invisible or like a ghost until he looked down at himself and suddenly realized that his white overcoat was reflecting whatever light there was, like a beacon. He quickly removed it; he crumpled it up, and shoved it into a mound of dirty snow. Soldiers were running closer to the edge of the camp with their own lamps, looking everywhere, yet continued to fail in spotting Flame. They were moving further out into the trees.

With the Russians using their lamps openly to see where they were going, they started to gain on Flame by sheer numbers and luck of the search. Flame heard and saw the pursuers closing in on his direction. He reflexively went off on a tangent from the deer path that he had been loosely following, into the thickets. Moving sideways when the path became difficult to distinguish, he hunkered behind a fallen log and waited for the closest patrol to pass his hiding place. As they came to the end of the path and decided that he must have doubled back, they turned and headed down to a clearer path several meters back.

Flame watched, and waited for the group to get far enough away to continue on undetected. He watched from under his log as his heart pounded and he tried to hold his breath for fear of being heard. He was anxious to get going, but through experience he waited a little longer before leaving. His patience was rewarded as a limping soldier that had been a straggler of the group slowly worked past the hiding place of Flame. *The fox was not found by the hounds this time*, he took a deep breath and let it out, while he thanked God for protecting him, and had him listen a little longer.

When it was safe, he crouched down and ran for short distances as he continued onto a different path towards Wire. He knew that he had to find Wire, because Wire would not abandon his fellow soldier. He had to find him, and their well-trained mounts. Flame knew that they should leave the area towards the route they came on, which would decrease the chance of running into the returning Russian forces or stumbling into the opposing German army.

The path was long and slow, but Flame seemed to have escaped from the Russian searchers. After what seemed like hours Flame saw a small red light from a distance 50 meters blinking three times, then staying on, giving just enough light to speed his steps: a recognition code they had arranged that allowed Flame to reach Wire and the two horses that were waiting.

Wire was as glad to see Flame, as Flame was to be there. They knelt near the horses and debriefed each other about the encounter at the camp. Flame told Wire of what happened to him and that he'd killed Shark. Wire told Flame that he had ambushed the two patrol guards with his pistol and silencer and then shot the guard on the truck but not before being shot at himself. He then opened the gate to the wire cage, where the prisoners stormed out and into the camp, gathering whatever weapons they could, and fought with the Russians while escaping to the trucks parked near the cage.

Flame and Wire stayed silent in the dark, waiting for the hint of morning light as it crept through the fog enveloping the tall trees. With the light came a chance to ride away faster, but also made them more visible to anyone still looking for them. The heavy dew was like light rain floating in the air as they mounted the horses and made their way down a slope to the edge of the forest. Wire was wondering if they would be seen as they broke through the last group of trees.

He found out quickly, as rifle shots rang out from a distance. They were indeed spotted. To gain speed, they rode down the slope towards the marshland at the bottom of the hill. The snow was sparse, but the ground was still wet but level. It was also in the open. Hoping their speed would get them to safety they were suddenly taking fire from their right side, mostly small arms but that was enough to make them dodge back into the trees.

They were no more than two to three strides into the tree line when Flame's horse reared to the left and fell down on its crumbling knees, throwing Flame against a bush and a tree. The impact knocked his breath away, causing him to get up slowly and painfully. He hobbled towards the horse, which was on its side. Its front legs were flaying furiously in the air in an effort to get back up, but a bullet had penetrated its back just behind the saddle, severing the spinal cord. Getting to the animal and seeing the fear the animal was suffering, Flame pulled out his pistol and dispatched the brave animal with a shot to the head. He then fired a string of ten or more shots from his STENS in the direction of the shot that hit the horse, hoping to slow down any pursuers.

Wire turned around and came back to pick up Flame, who climbed up behind him, and they rode double away from his fallen mount. As they rode away more shots tore into the trees and bushes around them. They could not ride deeper, as thickets were too high to climb into by the horse, causing them to stay along the tree line. Flame looked to the side, and could see German soldiers in the morning mist trying to get a shot at them. Chased by the Russians, and now shot at by the Germans, Flame leaned forward on Wire and waited for the burning sensation of a bullet to enter his body that was surely to come. Being paralyzed by a bullet as had happened to the horse made him shudder at the thought. While his thoughts were consumed in the fear of being wounded, he was unaware that the impact with the tree had shaken loose one of the books under his coat and it had fallen to the ground.

They rode as fast as they could on terrain that took skill from both rider and horse to navigate, often stopping and doubling back to get around obstacles or steep creek banks. Forty-five minutes after being shot at, a new sound became audible. It was the sound of a plane engine overhead. The trees were thin and the marsh was opening up as they approached a large river with the fog starting to burn off.

The plane circled for a while then came down for a closer look as it skimmed above them and the trees by only fifty meters. Wire knew that they were seen and looked for a place to shelter and cover, but the trees were too thin and the fog was nearly gone as a slight warm front came through the area. They were exposed and vulnerable from the sky. The plane turned and came down again, this time with its guns in line with the horse that was weaving through the sparse trees. It fired a volley of shots that hit a couple of the trees, but fortunately only sprayed the ground as the horse turned away from the path of the plane.

Seeing a small grove of trees, Wire encouraged the horse to head for them with a hard kick to her flanks. As they reached the clump of trees, they heard a second plane above them. The sound of the engines of the two planes suddenly changed as they both climbed back to altitude. Hiding among the trees, Flame and Wire watched as the two planes maneuvered above them. Wire called to Flame, "The second one is Russian!"

It appeared that both planes were on patrol over the battlefield from the night before. When the German plane went after Flame and Wire, it was unaware of the Russian plane's approach. Simultaneously, upon seeing the ground attack by the German, the Russian assumed that it was targeting Russians and attacked it, giving Flame and Wire an opportunity to escape, of which they took full advantage. They remounted the horse and worked their way to flat land to give themselves a longer lead on the Russians who were still following them.

After several minutes, the dogfight ended with the Russian plane spinning into the forest in front of them. He was no match for the faster and more maneuverable German. The momentary reprieve quickly became a nightmare as Wire had led the horse to faster but more exposed ground, which also made them clear targets for the German. Turning the head of the horse hard back into the cover of the trees, Wire kicked the horse many times to gain speed and the protection of the trees. Wire was able to zigzag the horse on the first pass of the plane, which fired its machine guns, cutting nearby trees to shreds and barely missing the two riders and horse.

On the second pass Wire and Flame dismounted and ran for the cover of some large boulders and a stand of trees for cover. This time the plane, a Messerschmitt 109, used its 20mm cannon to shear the trees down and to fracture the rock-hiding place. One of the boulders near Wire took a direct hit that shattered the stone sending fragments deep into his chest and mangling his left leg just below the knee. The pilot circled the area and could see that one man was badly wounded and the other was not moving at all and flew back to protect his men from the Russians, who were on the march in that direction.

Flame lay motionless but unharmed until the sound of the engine diminished. He got up and rushed to Wire. The bleeding from the leg wound was great, so Flame ripped up his shirt for strips of bandage. Placing a tourniquet on the thigh to control the bleeding, he could see that the leg would not survive. Flame worked quickly but became more anxious as it became clear that he could not do enough to save his mentor. The multiple fragments in the chest were too many to manage individually. Using Wire's shirt as a wide bandage for compression, Flame wrapped it tight and used a stick to twist the fabric in order to hold it in place. The pressure that was applied slowed the bleeding from Wire but not the tears and helplessness from Flame as he sat down hard in total frustration.

Wire, knowing that he was mortally wounded and would not be able to walk, let alone ride, ordered Flame to return to the camp with the information that they had gathered. Flame protested vehemently, but was ordered again to leave. "Get to the camp and don't get caught! They need to know what the Russians are doing to us, and about Sukolov's book," Wire insisted with clarity and finality. Flame said, "No, I will not leave you alone." Flame was just as adamant to stay and protect his leader and friend at any cost. Wire choking on some blood in his throat, weakly spoke, "I order you to go now. Leave me here."

Flame knew he had to follow the order, and agreed but stayed for a short time as he put together a lean to shelter that would protect Wire from sight and from the rain that started to fall, for as long as he needed. Flame looked in disbelief as the light snow that had been all around was now being melted by rain that was coming down in a noisy deluge. Flame had been in all kinds of extremes in weather from high humidity to double-digit cold. Of all of the elements, the downpour of rain made him feel the most vulnerable. The rain quickly penetrated his clothes and down his neck, as he sat next to Wire. He sat there for some time listening to the rain and through it for danger. He felt tired and heavy.

Flame watched for any sign of approaching danger, while holding his STENS at his side. Flame knew that Wire was firm about the order, and that he knew the danger of the mission. Both knew that he would be dead soon, and Flame did not want Wire to die alone. Wire gathered up all his strength and said, "Soldier, you are ordered to leave and get back to headquarters. If you fail, many more than one man will die out here." Flame understood the order, and finally agreed, but before leaving he left his machine gun and a hard-boiled egg. When Wire looked at it and shook his head Flame responded, "You know I don't like chicken." Wire smiled through his pain. With reluctance, Flame tracked down the horse and mounted it for the ride back to the Polish forces. As he cleared the grove of trees, he could hear in the distance behind the sound of a STENS firing and rifle shots in response. Flame would never see Wire again.

It was not until later, when Flame stopped to get water from a creek that he realized that one of the books were gone. What he had was a journal that had code names of people, and towns with addresses that covered three years of information from the Łódź area. It did not have information from any time forward of that, but what was there was a treasure trove of information that could be used by the underground justice system.

By the next afternoon, he had worked his way to where the Polish troops had camped and reported the events of the past several days. With the information, he was to continue back to Kielce to brief the commanders who were prepared to march to Lwow. After that, Flame was ordered to Opoczno to talk to the Polish Underground court to determine what was to be done with the information Shark inadvertently provided about informants being in the local churches of Łódź. The book was copied to microfilm and was to be sent to the Łódź A.K. headquarters, where the top intelligence agents inspected the information.

Flame was kept in Opoczno for the rest of the spring and into late June, where under the command of K. Zaleski a.k.a. "Boncza", he and the 25thRegiment saw extensive action against the retreating Germans around Opoczno. Flame distinguished himself, along with his platoon of A.K. regulars, finally being able to engage the enemy with strength in numbers and the blossoming realization that the Germans would be driven out of their homeland.

As spring turned to summer, the Polish Underground court system identified more traitors and decided upon actions needing to be taken. Many Polish collaborators had been investigated and tried in the underground court system, which found them guilty. One of those marked for execution was identified as a co-conspirator with Shark, and therefore was a high priority case to be dealt with. Flame was once again ordered to Łódź to be part of the team assigned for this new mission.

Traveling exclusively by horse, cart, and foot along back roads, Flame was able to sneak back into Łódź a week after leaving headquarters. It was imperative that he not get caught, and time was sacrificed for a safe trip. He knew that he would be getting a chance to be on a mission that involved someone in his church who was the informant to Shark and the Gestapo in Łódź. He was again to be given an assignment that placed him in danger in his hometown, and in his own neighborhood.

The war was quickly turning bad for the Germans. Łódź was a major town, which the Russians planned to take as soon as they could. If that happened it would stay a town of prisoners, the only difference being the name of the country that would be the jail-keeper. If the Russians were kept out as the Germans retreated, the town would be free once more. The direction would be decided in the next several months. Flame wanted desperately to be part of the effort to make Łódź free again. His fate was tied to that of his hometown. The war started for him while he was there and if possible it would end there too. And, if necessary, he would die trying.

Author's notes: Chapter 17

In April of 1943, diplomatic contacts were broken off between the Exiled Polish Government in London and Stalin's Russia. The dispute was over the Katyn Forest Massacre of Polish Officers by the Russians, on Stalin's orders. As such, the Polish Underground was ordered to stay separated from the Red Army, since they were presenting themselves not as liberators but as invaders, as were the Germans.

German causalities from Polish Underground actions were estimated to be nearly 150,000 troops. Approximately 930,000 troops plus their supplies and materials, were locked into battle with the Poles, and were not available to fight the pending Allied invasion of Europe in June 1944. A fact that saved countless lives during the invasion of France and Italy and possibly saved the war for the Allies.

Chapter18
July 23ʳᵈ, 1944: Łódź

DURING THE MONTH of July, Flame studied and trained in stealth covert activities in the urban areas, specifically in Łódź. He trained with Bat and Franck, so they all knew the process of following through with the orders from the underground court decisions. Pistol use, with and without a silencer, was practiced, as well as diversionary techniques. Because of the assignment, he was not allowed to visit his family, though they were no more than a kilometer away. He was not allowed to visit Jan (Bear) or his restaurant, or to see Basia.

Flame was instructed to move around to several safe houses, and Bear would contact him for further orders. Headquarters worked at a high level of secrecy, since the head intelligence officer, H. Klab, had been arrested in May. Her arrest had all activities doubled-checked for possible informers or double agents working against the A.K.. HerHer arrest had occurred after three couriers for the A.K. were captured and hung in the courtyard of Sterling Street prison, on May 6th. In this case, the girlfriend of one of the boys boasted that her boyfriend was in the underground. The boys were arrested the next day, along with their families. The information extracted from them lead to the execution of Klab.

One assignment had Flame watching train traffic as it came and went, from a vantage point in a warehouse loft near the tracks. He checked to see whether the military traffic was moving east or west and what was on the train. From the loft he could see that there were many prisoner trains leaving Łódź. Most looked like families with their belongings in bundles. The exodus from the direction of the Ghetto reminded him of his capture on the road near Radom, with the woman who was shot protecting him.

Later he learned that the Germans had ordered the dismantling of the Łódź Ghetto, which still had 76,551 people in it. The tragedy was that the prisoners were being sent to the death camp in Chelmo, not far from Łódź. Chelmo was certainly where Jakob and his other friends who had been in the Ghetto for the past two years, had been sent, and very likely were murdered in the camp. Staszek thought about these Scouts and friends and felt a pain in his gut and emptiness in his heart. It also left him in a somber state of mind where he withdrew from his normally gregarious demeanor and dwelled on dark thoughts and the injustice of the world around him. The thoughts of being in captivity and being under someone's total control, as was evident in the Ghetto's population and to a lesser degree in Łódź in general, consumed a lot of his time. This was especially true at the safe house, when he was alone in his room cleaning his pistol and thinking of the tyranny of both the Germans and the Soviets. He lived day-to-day doing his duty and waiting for new orders, adrift in a sea of people trying not to be noticed. In some ways he was more isolated now than when he rode alone in the forest as a courier.

Flames' next assignment was to become part of a three-man team for the Underground Justice Court. Flame along with Franck and Bat, all with Grey Rank backgrounds, and each having full trust in the other two. Flame and his team trained in tactics, scouted routes, and practiced skills that they would need for their mission. Being part of a team helped Flame overcome some of his loneliness but the three functioned covertly to avoid capture or exposure of the team, leaving few opportunities for leisure or social time. His permission to go home, even for a minute, was denied for safety reasons. The limited number of people Flame could contact, were screened in advance for safety. The world was at war and these were desperate times, and any carelessness could court disaster for many people.

During the rest of the month and into early July, the news from the Eastern Front was almost nonexistent in the German papers, but was easily found in the underground bulletins. Flame was cleared to make contact with some of the workers that he remembered from before the war, but all the information he found was that they were all dead or held in the infamous Radogoszcz prison for political prisoners. His friend and pressman for the bulletin that Flame worked for before the war had become Chief of the Bureau of Information and Propaganda for the A.K. in Łódź. His codename was Grot. Grot continued some of the newspapers, like the "Trybuna Łódźi" that Flame distributed as a courier and messenger for the A.K. They had the chance to meet briefly when Flame visited a group of Grey Rank Battle School students. The meeting raised Flame's spirits tremendously, and gave him a boost in his spirit. The Grey Ranks were still active in the Łódź area, and Flame was allowed to assist the local Battle School by sharing his experiences about the situations that they might find themselves in. He was aware that he had lost friends because of a traitor, and was cautious about sharing too much information and details of events, even with this group.

###

By the beginning of July, Flame had been given the final details for his next assignment, where he would be the lead on the team with Bat and Franck. He would be serving the sentence of death on an identified traitor, who was convicted in absentia by the Underground Court. This individual had sent the names of Poles and Germans living in Łódź to the Gestapo. The names were of people who had been providing safe houses for the Underground. This assignment hit close to him from his personal experience with so many fine people who helped to hide and feed him when he was on the run.

The execution teams were always made up of three individuals, who were responsible for no more than three missions, where each member was personally responsible for the completion of the sentence 'the execution'. Shooting Shark was considered an act of combat and self-defense, and did not count as part of his assignments. This case would be his first actual assignment as the primary player. His team was with Bat and Franck, the Grey Rank Scouts who helped him escape from the Gestapo agent on his assignment, months ago.

The subject of the capital crimes was a woman in her 40s who had betrayed over two dozen people directly, before she was set up and identified as the traitor. Flame had not expected to be assigned to a woman. He did not know if he could execute the sentence on her, though he had shot the woman who had impersonated Gertrude and saw this as much the same situation. They were given a picture, the address, and the written order for the sentence, signed by the Underground Court.

The day of the assignment, Bat drove the three players to the home of the woman. Bat stayed in the car as a sentry. The woman was observed entering the building with her elderly sister in the late afternoon. Franck and Flame entered the apartment building and quickly climbed up the stairs listening for and trying to avoid any other residents. Finding none, they knocked on the door and identified themselves as strangers looking for a room. When the door was opened it was the older sister who stared at them for a moment as they pushed past her and swept through the house looking for the subject. Both Flame and Franck were wearing brown clothes with their collars up and hats that partially obscured their faces; a crude technique to make them harder to identify if a witness was questioned later. Franck stayed near the front door with the older sister and had her sit in a chair facing a wall as Flame continued in.

Using a pistol with a silencer, Flame held it at his side as he found the traitor sitting at the kitchen table eating soup. Startled, she looked up at Flame as if he had materialized from thin air. The window light at his back made the woman squint as Flame dropped the decree in front of her and she stared at it as if she was not surprised. She knew that this day could come, but did not expect it like this. Flame waited for her to read it but she read only a sentence or two when she crumpled the sheet then swept it off the table with the palm of her hand. She slammed down her fist and looked up at Flame with her brows furrowed and her lip open slightly showing her clenched teeth as she sat in defiance.

Her posture hid any sense of guilt for the terrible deeds she done. Flame started to give the decree, "You have been found guilty of..." He didn't finish the sentence as she tossed the bowl of soup at him and reached for the knife she had used to slice her bread and swung it in quick succession. The hot soup, missed his face, but splashed his neck and coat as his reflexes moved him sideways out of the way of most of the scalding liquid. Almost instantly he straightened up while he simultaneously raised his right arm to full length and shot her above the right eye. The shot snapped her head backwards, and her arms at first jerked straight out as her body went limp in the chair; the knife she was swinging at that moment had lost its momentum, yet still hit his left sleeve that he had raised to block the strike. The knife fell harmlessly and clanged twice on the floor, though it made a slice into the coat's fabric before it was dropped.

Flame turned without looking back, and walked out of the front door while Franck, who kept the older sister from entering the kitchen, stepped backwards as he exited the apartment. They went downstairs to where Bat had the car idling, and were quickly taken to another safe house. Sitting in the back seat, Flame wiped the soup from his neck, collar, and shoulder then looked at his sleeve and the partial cut. He noticed that he was clenching his teeth but otherwise he appeared to be perfectly calm. This outwards appearance was diametrically opposed to the true anguish he was feeling. He repeatedly wiped off his hands with a hankie though there was no visible blood on them. Franck watched the stress that manifested itself in Flame, though he was not smiling, he patted Flame on the shoulder in a gesture of appreciation and support.

That night, the face of the woman came to Flame as he lay in bed. He also saw the faces, or imagined the faces, of a dozen people he may have known with the Grey Ranks or the A.K. that possibly could have been imprisoned or killed because of her. By morning his nightmare was over and he felt steady. He did not like it, but this was war, and he did his duty. He tried to think of fun times as a boy playing soccer or going to the movies, but those thoughts never materialized. He was nineteen and all those things seemed like a thousand years ago.

Shortly after this assignment, the plans for the start of the Warszawa Uprising were unveiled to the local A.K. units. Most of the men who served in the capacity of justice enforcers were immediately sent north, in anticipation of the final thrust to remove the Germans from the capital. On July 20th, the A.K. reformed the 25th Infantry Battalion, to which Flame would be assigned, returning to his duties as a sergeant under commander Boncza and would go to Warszawa for the uprising.

Concurrent to the completion of his first primary mission with the Underground Court, the microfilm that Flame brought in had been printed and analyzed for content and leads to other traitors. Flame had also provided information about an informer who told Shark that Flame had been in Katowice, a city that he had not been to. He had told his mother that city name only as way to calm her and protect himself. There was no doubt that she had innocently given the name to someone she trusted. Other than the immediate family, he knew she trusted no one... except perhaps her priest.

A common thread was slowly teased out of the information. It was matched to other intelligence that had been collected from hundreds of single sources that were ultimately woven together and pointed to a single source. The results were not a surprise, and were indisputable. There was a traitor at the Basilica Cathedral in Łódź.

This new event complicated placement of soldiers in the region. The time had come for the Polish Government in exile to go on the offensive to regain control of Poland from the invaders. The plans were set for the pending uprising in Warszawa, and all available Partisans were being mobilized for that operation. The Underground Justice ruled to serve sentence on the church traitor with the next team available. Because of the reassignment of the other teams to Warszawa, the team that was available this time was again to be Flame, Bat, and Bear. Franck had to be replaced as he had been assigned to command a squad of his own with the 25th Infantry Battalion, and would be leaving soon. Franck would have been the lead for this mission if he had stayed. Both Bat and Bear have been on two previous missions, therefore the lead was passed to Flame.

After the "safe house traitor" mission, Flame had been allowed to visit his family. Upon his arrival home the family had a big surprise for him, which was that Basia was pregnant with Jan's child, and the baby would be born sometime before the end of July. There was never a good time to have a child during war, but Fela and Zdzislaw gave praise about Jan and how he had helped everyone secretly without asking for anything in return. The war was changing, yet life continued for Staszek's family.

While he was with the family, he took advantage of the little time that was allotted for his visit home. Staszek knew that he and Jan would have to go soon and do their duty, which made the moment especially powerful to him. He made a point to sit for a time with Zdzislaw, where he wanted to tell him of the trip to Babiak, but could not. He talked to Fela and told her that things would be better soon, and how much he appreciated her strength to work in Germany and to return home. Basia was always special to him, and he sat and listened to her dreams for her baby and her anxiety over Jan's duties in the Underground.

For some deep unexplainable reason, as he was saying goodbye to everyone, Staszek somehow sensed the danger that was waiting for him.

A heavy sense of foreboding lay over him like a heavy blanket, but he ignored it, or worse, did not feel that this danger was any more intense than so many others times he had felt this warning.

Of all of the moments of privacy with the family, the time he had with his mother was especially meaningful, as she was not as emotional as was customarily her way when Staszek had to leave. "You are becoming such a young man. Be careful when you are away, doing what you must. I have you in my prayers and thoughts everyday. I light candles for you nearly each day, and several on Sunday." Staszek kissed her cheek and hugged her. He asked, to change the subject of the church, "How is your work at Major Zajfert's home?"

"He is not a mean man, just a little impatient. I can never do anything the way he wants." Helena paused, and added, "I am lucky to have a job."

Staszek said, "Have you heard anything about Kurt?"

"Only that he had been wounded while on the Eastern Front. He hasn't been home." Helena added, "The major has been sad and troubled with things, and often looks at his pictures on the mantle of the house."

"Mamusia, I will be leaving right after the baptism, and I will not be back for some time," Staszek told his mother as he stood up from the chair next to her.

Helena started to cry a little, and reached out towards him, her short arms reaching only far enough for her fingertips to pat, and then slide down his arm in a gentle way. "I still have my nightmare with you gone, and my arms become black from not holding you."

This was the third time his mother had told the story, and it left him uneasy and unable to think of anything else to say. "I have always come back, and I will do so again." He offered as a counter to her concern. "Because the Germans are being run out of Russia, and soon we will have them out of Poland too. I will make sure of that myself!" He boasted, and slapped the side of his thigh for emphasis. Helena looked up and smiled, as still another tear ran down her cheek and into the corner of her mouth.

The risks were great in coming to the city on a mission, but the planning was excellent and as thorough as it could be. The reality in the extremes of life did not escape Staszek, as the baby's birth would be celebrated in a church with innocence and joy. Yet it also harbored the antithesis of that day in the being of the betrayer of Poles and his impending death.

On July 26th, Basia gave birth to a boy and named him Stanislaw, after her little brother. He was given the middle name of Kazimierz, which was mandated by the Germans to be given to every male born in Litzmannstadt who was not Jewish, to distinguish between Poles and Germans citizens. The baptism for the baby was to be done on the 5th of August at St. Stanislaw Kostka's Church, the name "Stanislaw" for the godfather and godson as well as the church itself was thought to be a good omen for the family. The family was thrilled at the arrival of the newborn, and was celebrated with friends in the community.

Helena had gone to the church to make the arrangements for the sacrament. Fr. Bruno scheduled the baptism for the following Saturday, to be done by Fr. Sebastian, who had baptized the rest of the family over the years. She told Fr. Bruno that Staszek was very proud of the honor of being named godfather to little Stanislaw, and Fela would be the godmother.

This normally joyous event was quickly becoming problematic for Flame, as he was selected to be one of the enforcers of the mission against a priest; something he hesitated to do, since his godson was possibly to be baptized by the traitor. They decided that the mission would be before the baptism and completely secret, leaving no clues as to who would was involved. Urgency to close this case and evacuate personnel to Warszawa was the priority. Flame was ordered to leave immediately after the mission and report to his headquarters by the fourth day afterwards. Flame decided that the word "immediately" could mean two days before leaving, so he would stay for the baptism instead of going into a safe house to hide.

Several kilometers away, the phone rang at Gestapo headquarters. "Seig Heil, Father. Who? No I did not know he is back in town. Are you sure? Do you know why? I see. No matter, I'll find out." The Gestapo agent wrote a few notes and said, "I'll check around and get back to you. Seig Heil." The agent ended the call while looking at his notes. What he did not notice was that there was a third click on the phone when the caller's receiver was replaced.

On the morning of the Thursday before the baptism Saturday,

Flame, Bear, and Bat walked steadily towards their designated streetcar stops; their heads holding steady toward the front but their eyes darting up and down the streets for any sign of trouble while working hard to look normal and casual. Three city blocks and one trolley car spaced them, Poles were allowed only in the second car of the trolley, and were watched by the conductors. They were dressed in work attire, with Flame in a cloth jacket with soft cap and dark trousers, while Bat had a lightweight soft brown leather jacket, and beret. Bear was wearing a business suit. They looked much like dozens of other men walking on the street at this given time. Flame, carried a carpenter's box with a dowel handle, but also a rope acting as a shoulder strap to allow it to be slung over his shoulder. The ancient crate held the typical tools of a carpenter, all showing years of wear. The only difference between this box and many like it was that it had a false bottom in one of the drawers where two pistols, one with a silencer and the other without one, were hidden.

As Flame approached the station stop he noticed that his hands were damp and he sensed that his heart was beating quickly. He was uncomfortably warm this late July morning. Flame's body's heat made him want to unbutton his jacket and take it off, but he knew that he could not. He had to look like the others, the typical worker, to make it hard for anyone to identify him. The box was becoming noticeably heavy on his shoulder as the streetcar arrived and he climbed in. On the two other cars, Bear and Bat did the same thing within a minute of each other.

Father Sebastian and Father Bruno were saying their morning prayers in the small chapel at the rectory. Today would be slow day, with no confessions or Masses, except for the one that morning. Father Sebastian was in his 80s and was doing the work of three priests, just as Father Bruno needed to, since the Germans had sent the majority of priests to concentration camps earlier in the war. Father Bruno had been at this parish since March of 1938, while Father Sebastian had been there for decades. The parishioners had joked that Sebastian had been a priest since Jesus was a child, which helped cover their awareness of his progressive dementia, which was taking their favorite priest away from them slowly.

Father Bruno Buski was a short but square-framed man of about 50, who walked with a slight limp. He was born and raised in Łódź, but attended seminary in Germany. He went to Germany, since his mother's family was German and it was her wish for him to go there before she died of her progressing tuberculosis. His face showed wrinkles around the eyes, and his short blond hair hid many strands of gray that gave him a worldly and compassionate appearance. He was known to be jovial and quick with jokes that never were delivered correctly, but nonetheless always made him laugh at his own punch lines. He was always available to hear confessions or for private counseling sessions whenever a tormented soul or worried parent needed to share their pain. His Polish was perfect, and his Polish last name endeared him to the members of the parish. His crueler side liked to tease Fr. Sebastian by asking for the location of items in the sanctuary that Bruno would have moved or hidden to watch the old man struggle to remember something that he could not have known.

What was not known about Fr. Bruno was that he had been sent to the parish by the orders of the Bishop of Łódź. This transfer was a favor for one of his counterparts, the German Bishop from Munich. The transfer was done under the auspicious purpose of tending to the German Catholics in Łódź in their own language; a language he supposedly learned while in seminary but was actually the language he spoke to his mother.

Bruno had been in the seminary just after the Great War, where the instructors, among them the now Bishop of Munich, had a very strong hatred for the Poles, based on their belief that it was the Poles who had always started the conflicts between the Germans and Slavic countries, and housed high numbers of Jews in their country. A country they felt should be German. The indoctrination and his love for his mother helped set the allegiances that had skewed his loyalties.

He agreed to come to Poland as a priest in order to provide information to Germany about potential conspiracies in Poland aimed against the Germans. His goal was to right the wrongs done by the Poles in past. For nearly five years, he had discreetly sent information to Germany, via Gestapo agents, about activities in the Łódź area that he was privileged to know through the confidential counseling meetings he held with the families of Underground members, those who aided anti-German activities, or from naïve patriots who totally trusted their church, and therefore their priests, about their burdens and fears. Sadly, many people disappeared in the middle of the night due to their names or the names of others being passed to the Gestapo by Fr. Bruno. This outrageous behavior was a breach of his vows that he would have to justify to God someday in the future; a time that was closer than he could have ever imagined.

When they were sure they were not being observed Bear took a position near the rectory door as the lookout. Bat and Flame went into the building and quickly went through the house looking for Fr. Bruno and to make sure that no one else was in the building. Sweeping through the rooms they found Fr. Bruno in the library hanging up the phone when the two came in with their pistols at their sides. Bat took his place near the door while Flame pulled out his pistol with the silencer on it.

Flame walked with his arm out straight at the priest who was behind the large ornate desk. Flame was about to pronounce the sentence of the Underground Justice court when he was stopped by Fr. Bruno, who said, as he looked at the young man near the door, "You must be Bat." Bat turned and looked back with a shocked look on his face. Fr. Bruno continued, "Staszek I like the codename Flame better than Pants don't you?" The speech stopped the men cold in their thoughts and purpose. Fr. Bruno knew that he had unnerved the two, and felt that he had the upper hand at the moment.

Bat looked at Flame with hesitation, then back to the priest who leaned forward upon the armrest of his chair his fingers interwoven on his chest, hoping his aggressive statement may have saved his life. "Yes I know all about you." Then his face grew stern and he slapped his hand flat on the desk for emphasis, "How dare you come into the church with guns? Have you no honor or decency? This is a house of God." The statement made Flame furious and snapped Bat into a defensive mode. Both men wanted to argue vehemently with this hypocrisy, producing the reaction that was the purpose for it being said, as talking was Fr. Bruno's only weapon. The priest continued as he though he had the upper hand, "I have just talked to the Gestapo to let them know that you were here and to arrest you for being traitors against the Third Reich for no other reason than for you being the cowards and ungodly men that the partisans are."

As he finished his statement, Clara came in haste through the side door that led to the back of the church. "The Gestapo are here! They are just pulling up to the church right now." Bat and Flame had turned their pistols on her as she burst into the room but held their fire. In some anguish after a moment's hesitation she continued, "I am a Partisan working undercover here. He is stalling; you must finish the mission now."

Fr. Bruno turned crimson red and exploded verbally at Clara's revelation, that she who had taken care of the household business for the priests for the past three years had been watching him. Bruno slammed his hands on the desk and began to stand up.

"Get the job done and get out now!" She demanded.

Flame's spine stiffened and he raised the pistol and said, "For the Polish people!" and fired two bullets into the dumbfounded traitor who dropped forward onto his desk blotter. Flame paused for a fraction of a second as he looked at the motionless body then turned to Bat and Clara and said, "Get going," and without hesitation, they dashed for the side door. Flame did not look back.

As they cleared the door, they heard gunfire from the side of the church where Bear had been on guard. Clara stopped and held her arms out to stop the two men from continuing out the side of the church. "Over there, through the dressing room behind the altar, and then out the door behind the confessionals. As they ran for the door Fr. Sebastian came shuffling towards the dressing room in confusion, "They are shooting outside, be careful."

Clara responded, "We will!" and continued running towards the door while the two men kept their faces turned away as they darted passed the old priest. At the door they stopped and carefully peered outside. They waited for 10 seconds before seeing that there were no obvious dangers on this side of the building. In those seconds Clara told the two men, "Last night Franck was captured, and he had given up the codenames of you and several others before they killed him. You have to get away immediately." Looking once more out the door, she stood tall and walked several steps outside then motioned for Bat and Flame to follow. "Go. I will stall the Gestapo for you."

Flame started to grab her arm in order to pull her with them, but she yanked her arm back and said, "GO!" Flame opened his mouth to protest but Clara added, "Be vigilant!" Flame and Bat knew why she was sacrificing herself, and they turned and started to run.

They were no more than three meters out the door when several SS soldiers and a Gestapo came from around the corner; they broke into a run when they spotted Bat and Flame. Seeing their pursuers, the two bolted across the street through traffic, trying to get to an alley and the protection of the maze of service roads behind the buildings.

As they headed for the street, the soldiers open fire and hit Bat, who dropped in a heap onto the street. Two bullets, and several more, ended his life, and the life of an innocent man who happened to be next to him. Flame, who was ten meters ahead of Bat, jumped onto the running board of a passing truck and held on until he was around the first corner, then stepped off into a full sprint for the alleyway. Flame got past the front of another truck, and by so doing reached the alleyway while the truck shielded him from the view of the soldiers who had shot Bat. Using his speed and familiarity of the neighborhood, Flame zigzagged between the garbage containers, boxes, horses, and people heading for the far end of the alley and hopefully to the nearby safe house. As he made the decision to go right, he saw a truck pull up slowly at the far end of the alley searching for him. He was spotted, and several more soldiers jumped off and started to run towards him. Again turning on a burst of speed he vaulted over some crates and then up a fire escape, through an open window, through an apartment, downstairs to a shop below, and into the alleyway once again. Bullets hit behind him and echoed between the tall brick walls of the narrow alley.

Two stores further, Flame recognized a shop that he did business with years ago, run by a friend of his father's. He ran sideways between two delivery trucks for four steps and hammered the back door of a store with his shoulder and burst through. He ran to the front of the store and past customers of the store who started to run out the front door at the sound of gunfire in the back. He stopped when he saw the owner standing tentatively, his arms braced against his counter; he could see the gun inside Flame's belt. Upon seeing him, Flame said, "I am Felix Niklewicz's son Staszek, please help."

As he stepped slightly backwards the owner pointed to a stairwell into the basement and said, "Quickly, down the stairs," a moment later the owner started to scream "Partisan, PARTISAN!" at the back door and signaled to get the attention of the running soldiers. As they ran towards the store, Flame headed down a flight of stairs that took him to a storage area below the store. There, from a basement window, he could see soldiers searching and looking towards the roof and upper floors of the building. One soldier, thinking he saw something, fired four or five shots upwards that rang out as they struck the walls and windows of the back of the building above him. Chips of red brick rained down on several delivery trucks behind the store.

From the top of the stairs he could hear the store clerk say, in passable German, "He went across the street and climbed on the back of a streetcar." This was followed by the running and heavy footfalls of the German soldiers' boots.

Flame waited for his pursuers to rush into and then out of the store. In the basement he removed his hat and jacket and donned a white store clerk's jacket that was hanging on a nail. He climbed up the stairs, his hand on the handle of his gun and came through the door. There he bumped into the storeowner who gently held him back as he scanned the front door then the back. He pointed to a 20 kg sack of flour he said, "Pick that up and come with me." They walked to the back of the store and out into the alley. Seeing some soldiers in the distance looking in garbage bins, the store owner said loudly, "Put the flour in the back of the truck with the other items, and take it to the bakery on Himmler Strassa, and this time don't forget the money, you foolish useless boy." He pushed Flame towards the driver's door where he climbed in. The shop owner handed him the invoice and whispered, "Show the invoice at the road block, park the truck behind the bakery shop, and leave it there. Good luck."

"Thank you," was all that Flame could say, as he felt pride, relief, and some tears well up inside of him. Flame placed the truck into reverse, and then slowly drove back up the alley and eventually passed the roadblock to the bakery.

That night Flame laid in his bed and he replayed the mission over and over in his mind. His heart raced each time he remembered squeezing the trigger. Then the pain and sadness he felt for Bat would balance the deed that was done. Once totally fatigued, he slept well and felt blessed to be alive while he mourned for his lost friends, from today and the years before. All of them had been real heroes of Poland.

Their trip to the church would be a short 15 minutes by horse-drawn cart, as most streetcars were forbidden to Poles, and getting the whole family onto one trolley car was difficult. Staszek was delighted to be with his sister and her son, who was named Stanislaw in his honor. He was so excited that he took an extra bath and put on a shirt that belonged to his father, and one of his ties, so he could look the part of a godfather. He was strangely relaxed, and his old laugh and teasing of his sisters began to reappear. He knew that his orders wanted him out of town immediately, but he did not wish to miss this special event. Especially since Jan would not be there and he could not let on that he knew why. He was confident that his bold return to the church would not be noticed until after the service and his journey out of town.

Along with Staszek and his namesake, Basia, Fela, Zdzislaw, and Helena rode in the stiff cart. Staszek was caught up in the excitement of the pending baptism but still had to keep vigilant, since Jan had not returned from the mission two days ago. That was not a good sign, but his name had not been printed in the German newsletter that listed all the "criminals" that had been arrested in the past several days. Staszek was afraid that Jan was either in prison or dead. If alive, had he revealed what he knew about the Underground in Łódź? Or did he somehow manage to keep his knowledge secret? In either event, he could not say anything to the family, for letting them know who had been responsible for the death of Fr. Bruno would only add more pain to this supposedly happy time. Basia was distressed because of Jan's unexplained absence, but suspected it was related to a mission he would never have talked about. She had no options other than to pray that he would meet the family at the church.

The walk into the church was careful and deliberate, as the family went to sit in the front pew. They sat near the baptismal, and each said prayers for the events that were to occur this day, as well as for Jan. Staszek was saying prayers but they were different than everyone else's. Sitting in the church brought back his stress and heightened his level of alertness, as he knew that this church was hostile territory for an A.K. fighter right now. He was betting that he had time to participate in the sacrament and still be able to get to the Regiment's headquarters in Opoczno, as ordered, on time.

He was startled when he saw Fr. Sebastian walk through the side door to the Baptismal but kept his composure as the old priest came to stand in front of the family that had taken up the first pew in front of the sanctuary. Fr. Sebastian scanned the group with his eyes resting momentarily but noticeably on the disguised soldier. Staszek had a sudden further heightening sense of tension with the priest's presence and his inspection of the family. Staszek had the feeling that the priest knew what he had done on Thursday, which had the hair on his neck stand up slightly in a moderate alarm.

Fr. Sebastian's gaze passed over the family. He apologized for being late, because he could not find the right sash. He accepted the well-meaning smiles for his explanation, and focused with his recognition of Staszek and said, "Staszek, I hear you will be the godfather. Is that correct?"

Staszek nodded sheepishly, suddenly being aware of the responsibility of the title and wondering if coming to the church was a good idea.

"I have not seen you in church for some time, I hope this visit will help you get closer to God." Staszek bowed his head, but instantly stiffened up at the sentence, "...help you get closer to God." Staszek shook off the comment as a coincidence as he thought, *how ironic,* since Flame's mission earlier was for Fr. Bruno to get close to God briefly, before being sent to Hell for his misdeeds.

Staszek said proudly "Yes Father, I am." Then, deflecting the conversation, "Isn't he the most beautiful boy you have ever seen?" He held little Staszek in the air for the priest to see. After a moment's pause, he added, "That is why they named him after me." A big smile and laughs came from everyone, as he looked to Basia for confirmation and approval of his humor while at the same time trying not to stare at the priest and still calm his own nerves. Basia smiled, but her heavy heart wasn't in the church as she was desperate to know what happened to Jan, and sensed the worst. What she did not know was her heart had not reached the bottom yet.

As the polite laughing calmed down and the atmosphere in the church changed, Fr. Sebastian also seemed to transform from the stumbling old man to thoughtful scholar. "Child Stanislaw Szymański", looking at and then gently touching the head of the baby with his warm palm then turning to Staszek, "And Godfather Stanislaw Niklewicz you have both been given the name of St. Stanislaw, a martyred Saint who was dismembered for his beliefs in 1257. Through a miracle of God, he was made whole once again. Since that time he has been the symbol of a divided Poland; and a partner with God in her miraculous reconstitution. This miracle has been taken as a prophesy of Poland's eventual resurrection and reunion against sinister and overwhelming odds." He looked directly at Staszek and continued; "Some of us will pay dearly for living this prophesy in the ongoing history of Poland. It will be our strength and belief in God that will carry us through the trials and tribulations that will surely face us because of our determination to do the wrong thing for the right reason." Staszek was absorbing the lecture and looking directly back into the eyes of the priest. Fr. Sebastian ended the lesson with, "It will be God who ultimately will judge a persons actions, not I. May God have mercy on all of our souls." He blessed the family as they sat pondering the unusual message. Staszek looked straight ahead at the Baptismal fountain and vassal reliving the events of the past several days through his mind and became even more convinced that what had happened was for the greater good of the country. His part was the price he'd pay to do his duty, some day in the future when God examined his life.

For nearly 30 minutes, the pomp and solemnness of a tradition that was centuries old carried the ceremony to a spiritual place. The baptism went well and was focused on the joyous coming of this infant and the best wishes and hope for him to have a bright future. This was in stark contrast to the present where he was brought into a world drowning in turmoil. Fr. Sebastian finally made it through the sacrament; though awkwardly after becoming embarrassed and apologetic for losing his place once in the missal and needing to repeat himself from memory. The baptism was completed and for the moment, had everyone in a happier state of mind, hoping for a brighter and freer future. The post baptism plan was for everyone to return to Basia's apartment, which she shared with Jan, for a meal that was to be shared by all. Helena was sad because she knew that Staszek would not be coming back afterwards, though she had not asked why, so she prayed extra hard.

As they stood from the pew and prepared to leave the church, the sound of quick steps from a dozen pairs of boots came towards them. The family was blocked in the pew from both ends by a group of armed soldiers and a Gestapo agent who entered swiftly from the front of the church. "Stanislaw Niklewicz?" he asked, looking directly at Staszek.

Flame looked at the guards and how vulnerable he and his family were, and cautiously answered, "Yes, that is me."

The agent moved sideways to reveal Clara standing behind him. She had been beaten severely; as her face was disfigured and she was being held up by two of the soldiers.

Helena cried out and covered her face with her hands at the sight of Clara and the results of her beating. "Is this one of the murderers of Fr. Bruno?" He reached out and pulled her hair from the back of her head so that her eyes and face turned up towards Flame.

With one eye swollen, but able to see through, Clara paused, looked at Flame, and said with a slurred voice, "No, that is not one of them. He is about the right height, but he is not one of them. The man who shot him was wearing a leather jacket and beret." Clara tried to add doubt to the matter. She knew that Bat was wearing those items. Flame looked up at the stained glass window above the altar seeking help but not finding any from the colorful stained glass pastoral scene.

The agent appeared to expect this answer and said, "Very well then, bring both of them." The Gestapo stated, staring directly at Flame.

Fr. Sebastian protested, "What is wrong here? This is a baptism. You should not be here now in this church." Then looking at the woman he grieved, "What have you done to Clara, and why?"

The Gestapo looked at the old man and said, "Father, this church has already lost a priest this week, it would not be wise of you to force it to lose the other."

Not having any option to get away without harming his family, Flame nodded and came out of the pew. As he started to move there were outcries from his mother and sisters who protested loudly and tried to block Staszek's removal with their own bodies and grabbed at him as he was pulled away. The guards broke their grip on him as they forcibly separated Basia and Helena from Staszek. Fela, holding the infant turned her back to the commotion to protect little Staszek. As Flame was whisked towards the doors, he called back over his shoulder to the family, "I love you all." He was promptly grabbed by the arms and quickly escorted out of the building, leaving everyone stunned and sobbing.

Once on the street, he was pushed into the back of a car with Clara and a guard on his other side. The car sped off to the Radogoszcz Prison to deliver its newest resident. Clara never looked up nor said anything. Her slumped posture allowed Flame to see the top of her head and it appeared that she had a severe gash on the top of her head, and her skull may have been broken. With the amount of caked blood in her hair and the smell of stale sweat and urine, she had been like this since Thursday. Only her moans showed any signs of life. At the prison, Flame was taken out of the car, which continued on with Clara still in the back seat. She was never to be seen again.

Flame was taken to a room where he was questioned and registered by the German agents at the prison. The soldier took down vital information from him, including name, age, birthday, nationality, religion, and occupation. The Germans had a profile on Flame, but wanted to see whether he added anything different. It was noted at that time that he listed his occupation as "Zimmerer" (carpenter). At the end of the registration Flame was taken to a chair and was given a clean wool stripped jacket that he put on over his shirt and tie. A photograph was taken of him as if he was modeling the prisoner's jacket.

"For your file, so the Red Cross can see how well-kept you are," was the sarcastic comment from the soldier with the journal that had the vital information entered in it. "Now take off the jacket and your clothes. They are too good for you. Put these on."

Flame did not understand the significance of the comment, but removed the jacket and clothes and gave them to the soldier. He was given a pile of old worn-out clothes that barely covered him, let alone would keep him warm. The July heat made that fact insignificant for the time being, for thinking of his comfort in the coming winter was very likely a waste of time. Radogoszcz was a converted shoe factory, four stories high, made of red brick walls and massive wooden beam floors and stairwells. From the registration area he climbed to the top floor where the political prisoners of the Gestapo were placed in one large cell with about five hundred other men. The cell took up the whole fourth floor.

As he entered the cell, he was struck by the foul smell of tired bodies, urine and fear. Flame was assigned to a top bunk on the south wall and climbed up slowly. The four men seated at a small table at the foot of the bunk looked up from a chess game that was near the small window. They were playing with chess pieces that were roughly shaped from small stones and wood. When Flame entered, they said "cześć" (Hi). Flame looked at them without saying a word but gave a slight nod of his head.

"What are you here for young man?" one of the older men asked. He looked Flame over from head to foot. "You must be a special inmate to make it to the fourth floor." He smirked and continued, "The third floor is for ordinary criminals and the second floor is for prisoners of German ancestry. Since they would not be safe on the other two floors, it is better that they stay with their own kind."

Flame was leery of the sarcasm of the comments.

"Did you meet the commandant? He usually visits the movie stars that come in."

"Movie star?" Flame asked, with a strange look on his face.

"They take pictures of most of the new prisoners for the fourth floor in a striped jacket before they go through the Welcome Beating," said one voice, with a sincere tone. "When the Red Cross comes through they want to see the roster of prisoners, and that they are being respected. Therefore the pictures."

"Yeah," came another voice, "The beatings will come later because you tried to escape."

From still another bunk a voice offered, "I have heard that those pictures are morale boosters for the Gestapo, where they post them as victories over their enemies to other agents who were working on cases."

Flame looked at the man in disbelief and shook his head and hands in denial.

"Sure, think about it. You are a prize that they wanted to catch for a long time. The picture proves they did it." Flame thought about it for a while. The voice from the bunk continued, "Then they get their Welcome Beating afterwards."

Flame dreaded asking, but had to know what to brace himself for, "Welcome Beating?"

"Either the commandant or Bloody Joseph greets everyone that comes in with their own form of hospitality." The speaker turned away and looked at the chessboard that was roughly drawn squares on the table. His thoughts drifted to his own welcoming, and he unconsciously rubbed his shoulders. Flame just looked around at the men and the cell itself. He saw a bucket that was nearly full of urine and three bunk beds with only boards to be used as a mattress. Two of the four men already in the cell that quizzed him, turned back to their game and daydreaming. A third man looked at Flame and said, "Ignore them. They're trying to amuse themselves at your expense."

"I haven't done anything. I'm just a carpenter," Flame responded.

"Well, the Germans do not think so. Either you are lying to me and to yourself, or the Germans' information is wrong, but in any case you have been marked as a troublemaker. That's not a good thing, and is why you're here instead of a simple jail cell at the police station," the man continued.

Flame was concerned. If they knew everything, his life would not be worth much. If this was a bluff, since he did not know this person giving the advice, this could be a trap, so he had to be careful. "I don't know what they think or why, but I am just a carpenter. It is a mistake for me to be here," Flame stated nonchalantly from his perch on the bunk.

"Very well then. You will probably meet the commandant; he greets the movie stars personally. You would be well served to avoid him." The man paused and looked at Flame and saw the conflict within him. "Believe me or not, do as you will, and know that you may be here for months. Not being conspicuous is a good plan." He was about to give up on the conversation when he stopped and told Flame frankly, "There is a saying here, 'We are not afraid of death, but only of prolonged agony.' We have all met Bloody Joseph, Mateus, and Pelzhausen himself. Your turn will come."

Flame stared into the distance trying to think of the unthinkable. *Who are these people that seemed to revel in producing agony?* It seemed too hard to comprehend and rolled onto his back resting on a blanket over the hard boards. That night his brain turned and twisted around the things that he had seen and heard that day. The fear of the unknown has always been great, but this level of torment was overwhelming. Waiting through the night, he hoped that the promised horror of tomorrow would not come. The mental visions could cause even a cocky nineteen year-old to pull the covers up over his head to cover his cry, and it did.

Before noon the next day, the guards returned. Without saying a word, they pulled Flame out of the cell. He was hurried to another room where he was stripped naked and placed on a very sturdy wooden chair. Again he was asked questions that were repeats from the day before, and as before Flame continued to claim that he had always been working as a carpenter and that they had arrested the wrong person.

That was enough for the guards, who pulled Flame's arms back and tied them behind the chair and proceeded to flog him across the chest and front of his legs. With every stinging blow he strained at the binders that held him firmly leaving his body an open target for the strap. He yelled in pain as strike after strike of the strap cut into his legs and chest. His skin and muscles quivered from the pain and shock. When Flame passed out, he was doused with water to revive him. The stinging and pain absorbed all of his attention and left him feeling like a trapped animal. He whimpered at not being able to move and protect his battered flesh.

This interrogation lasted into the evening before Flame was pushed down and forwards onto his thighs, and his hands were now tied down to his lower legs. The heavy gauged wire held him bent and strained his back muscles but relaxed his chest. His sweat found its way into the open wounds of his chest and legs, burning and stinging him severely in every pore of his body. The pressures from his chest on his thighs made the cuts on his bruises hurt and burn even more. He desperately wanted to rub the painful places, but was frozen by the wires and binders and could not move.

He sat there throughout the night and into the morning dozing off into a painful sleep and stupor. Hungry, thirsty, cold, bruised, and aching to straighten out, he sat or slept while he waited for the next encounter that would be something he could not or would not imagine. Awakening many times from the pain and in his exhausted haze his bowel and bladder emptied, soiling the chair and himself, just centimeters from his face that was pressed against his knees. In this subconscious state he was dragged back to his bunk and tossed onto the floor next to it. The men in the immediate area tended to him as best they could, primarily by getting him onto the bunk and covering him as he shivered in spite of the heat of the day. They gave him water and portions of their food as his head cleared enough to eat. Desperately he tried to not focus on the pain. He tried to think of the road to Babiak, imaging each curve in the road as the wound through the small towns. Trying to escape and conquer the physical with the mental. Then two days later the process started again as he was dragged to the interrogation room and the questions started again. After being tied for several hours, the heavy metal and wood door to the room opened some time in the morning. Flame tried to look up but the angle of his head only allowed him to see the boots of a large man come towards him. The man in the boots spoke to a guard that came in with him and asked, "Is this the runner?"

"Ja," was the answer.

Suddenly a large hand grabbed Flame by the hair and pulled his head up sharply backwards. There was such force that he could look into his assailants eyes all the while having a painful strain applied to the muscles in the front of his neck making it impossible to close his mouth or swallow.

"I am Commandant Walter Pelzhausen. You have made the Gestapo very mad and unhappy by being so difficult to catch. Apparently you run very fast, so they have asked me to give you a special welcome to Radogoszcz. Do you want to tell me now who are your handlers? Or do you want to wait until later to tell me?" the commandant taunted Flame.

Flame looked up at the round head with a smirk on its face, and studied the features for that moment. He saw a face he would never forget, a face of sadism revealed in its purest form. He did not speak, as he knew instantly his fate would be the same no matter what he said. "I did not think so," the commandant determined, and with that statement Flame's head was dropped down towards his knees again.

The commandant said to the guards, "Get him ready."

In an instant, the two guards took a wooden dowel, 10cm in diameter, and placed it through the space made by Flame's tied arms and legs and his bent-forward trunk, at the level of his pelvis. In essence, he was wrapped around the wooden pole. Then, with a sense of lightning hitting him in his tortured spine, Flame was sharply hoisted by the dowel and placed on the backs of two heavy chairs that faced away from each other. He looked much like a piece of meat about to be rotated over a fire pit, with his head slowly moving around the dowel as his relatively heavier shoulders rotated him into a head-down position. He was asked if he was "Pants?"

With what strength he had, he protested vehemently, "No! I am a carpenter! I have been doing small jobs for the past several years around the district. You have the wrong person." With that answer he was beaten with a leather strap across his back, buttocks and hips. As he caught his breath he let out a cry and whimper as the sting of the belt felt like it penetrated from his back clear to his stomach, and then against the dowel.

"ARE YOU THE SHOOTER OF THE PRIEST?" came the question.

"No! I did not know anything about the shooting of the priest until Saturday. He must have been someone else they were interested in." With each of these denials he was hit across his naked hips, back of his thighs and scrotum with a willow shaft several millimeters in diameter. His nose filled with mucous and tears, as gravity pulled the fluids from the inside of him to the outside. A puddle was forming on the floor between the chairs, but his eyes were too swollen to see it.

"Are you called Flame?" they asked next.

Flame groaned a "No," and was rewarded for his answer with blows so painful he passed out.

Until late into the night, he was left hanging helplessly upside down on the dowel. The dowel cut into his pelvic bones, crushing his skin against the wood, causing tremendous pain that made unconsciousness a blessing. Every half hour, someone would come in, ask him questions, and beat him no matter what he said. Sometimes they would spin him so that the dowel bruised his ribcage and arms as he slammed down on the pole. With the changing contact points of his spinning body, the dowel loaded and unloaded contact points on skin and bone by the motion against the wooden hangar, exchanging relief to one place with pain in another.

After midnight, he was cut loose and allowed to fall to the floor. He stayed there until morning, when the commandant came in and said, "So our runner still has no manners and is silent." Lifting Flame's head up again from the floor by his hair and looking at his swollen face the commandant dropped it and watched the head slowly rock to a stopped position on the floor. The swelling of his face was made worse due to the head-down position that he held for so many hours, making his eyes very red and causing his nose to bleed.

"Put him on the Mare." The Commandant ordered. "This should stop his running habit for awhile." With that Flame was again hoisted up, but this time it was onto a wood box with his chest on the top of a wooden crate like someone placed stomach-down on the saddle of a horse. His knees were placed on a small shelf. His knees at the crease, and arms were tied together by wire that ran under the box, exposing his naked back, buttocks, and the bottoms of his feet.

Pelzhausen, using a stiffer and larger willow shaft, laid his strength into beating Flame's thighs and legs. When Pelzhausen had warmed up, he laid the stick to the bottoms of Flame's feet and especially his heels. The blows sent electric, searing shocks through Flame's body. The bonds that held Flame in place restricted any physical withdrawal from the pain, forcing him to strain against the wire bonds that now were cutting into his wrists and brought blood through the skin. The quick, intense pain generated by the whipping stick produced an endless cry of horrible agony from Flame that slowed only to be asked more questions that produced more denials, which again led to the shaft coming down on his bare feet.

Pelzhausen paused for a moment and made sure his victim was conscious and could hear and understand him. He then added an even more sadistic pain to the process. He smirked and said, "Your friend Franck told me everything I needed to know before he died trying to escape. There is no need to keep any secrets since they are already known."

Flame cried out in a tormented shriek that became wilted as he lost his strength to react to this cruelty and inhumanity. As the wooden shaft landed on his heels and soles of his feet over and over again, he vomited mucous. In minutes, blood ran from the wounds in the tattered skin of his feet, and he passed out. His fading thoughts were that this animal knew everything that he could have provided, yet still did this to him anyway.

Eventually, even Pelzhausen became tired, so he told two of the guards to take the prisoner back to his cell. Flame was pulled off the box and his arms were wrapped around the necks of two large soldiers who dragged him to a cell. Reflexively, Flame made stepping motions, but his damaged tendons, fractured right heel bone, and the battered and shredded skin of his heels prevented him from taking weight so his legs buckled with each step as if they were made of rubber.

Flame was tossed into a dark cell that held sad shadowy figures, landing like a sack of sticks against the floor. His clothes followed, landing on top of him. When the door closed, as had happened two days ago, two of the figures rolled him over and slid him to a place where Flame could recover while in his pain-induced sleep. His cellmates, who examined his wounds and marveled that he was still alive, carefully placed him on a bunk. As Flame tried to stretch out, one of them asked, "It looks like you met the commandant. Get whatever sleep you can."

It did not take long for him to lose consciousness again, and melt away in the sanctuary of sleep. A sleep where a school girls' blonde braids, the back of the logging truck, his mother talking to him, and the campfire from a Scouting outing floated through his mind, sparing Flame from the harsh reality that made him suffer. A reality that would come back many times to leave it's mark.

Shortly after Staszek was taken to the prison, Helena walked the two kilometers to Major Zajfert's home and sought out the major. "They have taken Staszek to Radogoszcz." In near panic she sobbed and pleaded her torment to her boss and influential administrator.

"I have nothing to do with the prison. The Gestapo has little time or interest for a manager like me." He looked troubled at the posturing and pleading of his cleaning woman. "I can do nothing for Staszek. Now go home. You are no use to me in this state." He escorted her to the door and closed it behind her. Helena, in her first episode of defiance, turned and hammered the door several times with her fist, once, then twice more with each fist. In frustration she resolved to herself that her son might never come back unless she did something herself.

From that point on, every day she would go to the gate of the prison and ask the guards on duty if they knew her son, and if they would give him a message or could have him come to the fence so she could see him. Though it always fell on deaf ears, she continued to return nearly daily, asking for assistance from anyone who was in hearing range of her passionate begging.

One day in late October, during one of her visits she asked a familiar guard walking his post the same question, "Have you seen Staszek Niklewicz? If you do, tell him that I love him and I am praying for him." The same message that was given dozens of times before, but this time the response was different. The guard, without breaking stride turned his head toward Helena and said, "Tell him yourself." He pointed to a hunched figure dressed in dirty worn clothes and a worn blanket over his shoulders, hobbling along a path not far from the fence.

Helena did not recognize the figure, but in desperation cried out, "Staszu!"

Staszek turned towards the familiar voice and limped to the edge of the wire barrier and called back, "Mamusia."

Helena looked at the crumpled shape and gaunt figure and burst into more tears of joy as well as pain at the sight of the ill-looking caricature that was once her robust son.

Their eyes met, and Staszek broke into tears upon seeing his mother, who lifted his spirits from across the wire fence. Their fingers touched through the small spaces in the wire. Without hesitation, Helena reached into her deep purse, pulled out 250 grams of bread, her ration for two days and tried to push it through the fence in the direction of her son. Her effort failed as a larger man pushed Staszek away and grabbed part of the bread. Staszek, who had lost his balance and fell, could not stop the thief, who hurried away to eat his prize.

The dejection at the loss of the bread enraged Staszek, and he swore an oath to himself and to God that he would react quicker the next time he had the opportunity to eat something fresh. Helena pushed the rest of the bread through and reached into her purse, pulled out a smaller piece of bread, and pushed that through the fence as before. This time Staszek was on top of it in an instant. He let out a short yelp as the pain in his right foot returned with the sudden burst of motion. When he had consumed half the bread he pushed the remainder into his shirt, at which time Helena pulled out a hard-boiled egg. In the one moment before she pushed it through the fence, Staszek recognized what it was, and for a brief second thought ruefully about his bold and brash statements about chickens. Before the egg cleared the fence, Staszek was already mentally eating the unborn chicken.

Helena, after watching her son devour the food, asked him "What can I bring you?"

Without hesitation he said, "Anything you can." Staszek paused for a moment then added, "Especially cigarettes." Helena was surprised at the request and looked puzzled.

Staszek clarified, "Food I will eat quickly and it will be gone. With cigarettes I can buy time and food."

During the remainder of October and November someone from the family would visit the prison to make contact with Staszek and give him extra food to build his strength and cigarettes that he traded for extra food and favors from guards.

Their efforts paid off, as he continued to grow and get back his strength despite recurrent and often severe beatings from the SS's Bloody Joseph the staff Gestapo, and for good measure, regularly from Pelzhausen himself.

In mid-December, as the snow returned to Łódź, things changed. The prisoners were not let out of the prison to walk freely in the compound but only to run up and down the four flights of stairs where guards on each landing would whip the prisoners as they went up and down dozens of times. This was a sure way to have as many as possible die from exhaustion and hunger. The Russians were closing in on central Poland, and there were far too many prisoners that needed to be removed from the rolls of the prison. The prisoners could not be left to be witnesses against the Germans, or turned loose to fight again.

The German war machine was being pushed back into Germany, replacing the suppression and murder of the Fascists with the murder and suppression of the Communists. The German Eagle that had its sharp bloody talons in Poland for five years was being replaced by the Russian Bear, which was consuming people and land as it invaded from the east. Poles were being slaughtered from bullets and politics from both sides of the compass.

All German functions and offices were being withdrawn, and they expected the Russians to be in "Litzmannstadt" by the first or second week of the New Year. Select prisoners were to be transferred to concentration camps outside of Poland for continued interrogation, but time was running out for the Third Reich in Poland, and the nearly 2,000 prisoners packed into Radogoszcz had to go away. However the Germans had a plan, they always had a plan and whatever it was it never bode well for the Poles.

Authors Notes: Chapter 18

Radogoszcz Prison at one time was the Samuel Abbe shoe factory. It served as a transit camp for accused criminals in the early 1940's. As it grew larger, it became known as one of the toughest men's prisons in Poland.

Prisoners who were sent to concentration camps from Radogoszcz often found conditions better in the concentration camps than the horrible prison they had been transferred from. In Radogoszcz, prisoners died every day from starvation, disease, exhaustion, and the sadistic behavior of the guards. The death toll numbered 60-70 per day with a population of over 2,000 men at any given time being held there.

Picture #4: Scale model of Radogoszcz Prison Only the 5 story stairwell remained after the fire.

Picture # 5: "Hollywood Picture"

Chapter 19
January 17th, 1945: Łódź

THERE WAS A pounding on the door and someone yelling from outside, "Helena! Open the door, come quick!" The pounding continued harder and faster.

The darkness was still thick in the apartment as Helena swung a robe over her shoulders and headed for the door. Fela and Basia were coming out of their room and turned on a light. They asked, "What is it Mamusia?" Helena shrugged helplessly and shook her head as she reached for the door. The heavy wooden door was vibrating from the fist that was assaulting it.

She opened the door, and there was a neighbor and friend, with a shawl over her shoulders covering her robe, terror on her face. "They have burned down Radogoszcz! You must come with me." The neighbor, Kasia, had a son in the prison, as did Helena and the terror in Kasia's eyes chilled Helena to her soul.

Helena still was in a slight fog from her deep sleep said naïvely, "Burned down the prison? Now? Where did they put the men?"

Kasia started to pull on Helena. "They did not put them anywhere, they burned them inside the prison. Almost no one has gotten out!"

As if a club hit her Helena grabbed her stomach and bent over and placed one hand into her mouth to stifle her scream. Fela was snapped into action and ran back to her room for clothing and bundled up for the snow that had been falling on and off for days. She told Basia to stay with little Staszek, as she grabbed her boots, and yelled to her mother, "Get your clothes on Momma; we have to go!" Helena, in a daze, spun around on wobbly legs, got a pair of pants, pulled them on over her nightgown, and wrapped her heavy coat over it. Donning her boots at the door, she followed Kasia and Fela down the stairs as she wrapped her scarf around her neck and head.

The sight of the prison in the early morning light was ghastly and surrealistic. Gray fog, gray snow, and dirt on the gray-looking building surrounded the red, orange, and yellow glow of the main building, which had collapsed into itself. The wooden floors, stairs, and roof had fallen to the base floor in a massive pyre, glowing from within the red brick-walled crucible.

Hundreds of frantic people surrounded the prison, crying, yelling, and calling out names of their loved ones who were inside. Some spread rumors that the building must have been empty; not even the Germans could be so callous as to kill 2,000 people like this. There were no guards around the smoldering building so people started breaking down the fences and gate to get closer. The heat drove them back. A fire brigade had arrived earlier to quench the thirst of the building, and slowly gained control of the inferno.

By early morning the heat had dissipated to a great extent, but was still glowing red-orange from the central stairwell. The water from the fire brigade caused steam and smoke to rise through the collapsed roof. Slowly there was enough morning light to see the worst of their fears. The flames had gutted the building, and piles of corpses encircled the stairwell and were scattered around the outside of the building. Hundreds and hundreds of bodies littered the area outside the walls marking the places the men landed after jumping off the roof to avoid feeding the hunger of this hell. Last night death was assured, how it came was their choice. At least their families would have a body to identify and bury if they leaped far enough away from the engulfed roof.

The crowd fell silent in waves a block away from the prison but erupted in screams of sorrow and outrage as they neared the courtyard and witnessed the results of the conflagration. The wailing and sobs burst from the old men and women who wanted to find their fathers, brothers, and sons who were hopefully not part of the mound of charred remains scattered all around. Their howls would start again and taper away with disbelief but returned with the horror at what they saw.

There in the courtyard, where prisoners were once forced to run for hours while being whipped, was a pile of unrecognizable twisted and mangled figures, all in contorted tortured postures frozen in black and gray death. Men who had jumped from the lower windows to escape the flames, were dead in a massive pile that was in turn set afire by the guards who left last, burning the survivors of the fall with the flames they tried to escape. Some of the bodies that were away from the burned corpses had bullet holes in their backs or their heads in addition to the broken legs from the jump. This told the townspeople that the guards did not all leave at once and never showed mercy, killing those broken men who tried to crawl away.

The heat lasted for many hours before the snow allowed a wave of family members to wade into the pile of charred remains to look for their loved ones. Helena was among the first to start to search. At first, she methodically went from one corpse to another turning them over and looking to see whether it was Staszek or not. Or perhaps it would be Jan, who had not been heard from for months. Hours went by, and the smell and sight began to overwhelm her to where she was mechanically turning over one body after the other and crying. Well into the evening she searched with Fela, and then with Basia, who brought little Staszek with her. The women sorted through whole as well as portions of bodies looking but hoping not to find Staszek. Mercifully Zdzislaw never knew what had happened, as he was working in Babiak.

Helena was finally pulled away by Fela and said that they would return the next day to look some more when there was light. In total exhaustion, her mournful daughters led Helena back to the apartment. Once there, she sat in the light of the small lamp, dazed. Her ash-dusted face had several lighter streaks on her cheeks where her tears washed away the soot. Helena sat fully clothed and smelled of burnt flesh and wet charcoal, still in disbelief at the enormous number of bodies that she had handled. She knew that Staszek was in the pile somewhere, and she could not reach him. She would find him or she would die looking. Suddenly she froze in horror as she looked down at her arms and hands resting palms up in her lap. They were black; her recurrent nightmare had come true. She lifted her arms and stared at the charcoal-like paste that was covering her arms and sleeves to her elbows in disbelief.

Unable to sit and do nothing while her imagination tortured her about what Staszek must have gone through when there was no place to escape, she got up and left the house. Fela, upon hearing the door close, went to see who had come in but instead found her mother gone. She went to the window and could see her mother walking slowly down the street. Fela quickly dressed again and ran out into the street to catch her mother and bring her back; not knowing what she was intending to do in her devastated frame of mind. When she caught up with her Fela asked, "Where are you going? What are you doing?" Fela pulled on her sleeve and spun her around to look at her.

Helena pulled her arm away from Fela and said in a voice foaming with rage, "The major has to be told what he and his people have done. I want him to see Staszek for one last time." With that said she pushed her ash-covered arms and spread fingered hands towards Fela's face for her to see. "This is what he has done. This is what is left of my son, I will not let him forget it." Helena turned away back towards her original path and over her shoulder she proclaimed, "After that, he can do what he wills to me." Fela, almost hysterical, begged her to stop, but was unable to sway the determined woman, so she went with her mother pleading the whole way for her to stop.

From the city limits, there were the sounds of artillery firing at the approaching Russians. In the dimming daylight the flashes of light in front of her, marked the direction in which the Russians were coming from. Helena was either oblivious to the sounds, or just did not care, as she approached the major's home.

Arriving at Major Zajfert's home, she rang the doorbell and waited, but no one came to the door. She could see some activity inside, so she rang again. Not successful with the second and third ring of the bell, she reached for the doorknob and found it unlocked. She went in and found the major clearing out his desk and burning papers in the fireplace. He twisted to look at his housekeeper for a moment and then turned back to the fireplace, tossing in another file. With his back to her, he said, "What are you doing here Helena? You should not have come."

From across the room Helena stood staring at the major's back. His contemptuous posture raised her anger to a higher level. For her whole life, she'd avoided confrontation and asserting herself, but at this moment her meekness was forgotten. She started to hang her head at the dismissive comment he made. Then it boiled up and over when she looked again at her blackened hands and arms. In a rage, she stomped up to him and when she was a step away, she yelled, "You murderer! You murdered my son Staszek! Look and see your handiwork." She pushed her hands towards the major.

The major was caught off guard at the sudden explosion of hate and venom from his normally sedate and passive housekeeper. But he was quick enough to turn and catch her arms with his hands as she thrust them at him. She tried to reach for his face but he towered over the small woman by more than a head and held her firmly. She began to sob in exhaustion and melted to her knees.

His anger and stress met hers. Using all his strength not to slap her as she knelt on the ground, he squeezed her wrists until she started to withdraw from the pain. Holding her arms up and at bay, he clenched his teeth, looked right into her eyes, and spoke in a firm level voice as he regained his composure. "You stupid woman, what are you talking about? I did not kill your boy, I saved him."

"You saved him by burning him in that hellhole of Radogoszcz?" She spit at him as she tried to get up and start her struggle anew.

He pushed her backwards towards Fela, who caught her mother and held her, knowing that the major controlled her life, and that of the family.

The major let out a long breathe and leaned forward at the waist with his head slumped down, placing his hands on his knees to compose himself. Upon standing, he saw that his hands were black from holding Helena's arms. He slapped his hands three times to wipe the ash from them, and reached for a handkerchief to clean them some more. Once done, he looked at the two women and said in frank disappointment, "This was not how the world was to be. For weeks now I could see that the worst of everything was happening. I had little power to change things, so I have to leave my home, never to see it again, and probably will not see my son again, too." This was the most candid that the major had ever been to Helena and she was now the one caught off guard.

He continued, "You have worked hard and honestly for me, so the one thing that I could do, I did two weeks ago. I sent an order under my general's name to have Staszek sent to Austria, to be away from the prison and the plans that were being formed to deal with the prisoners. By tomorrow he will be arriving in Mauthausen. There he will have a chance that he would not have had here if he stayed."

Helena and Fela were dumbfounded the news. "He is in Austria? Alive?" They turned and hugged each other, and now their tears were of joy.

Helena turned to the major and tried to think of something to say, but he put his hand up to wave them away and said, "I have much work to do, and you must leave now and not come back here again. Go, leave now." With that comment, he gestured them towards the door as he turned his back on them for the last time.

Both women turned and slowly headed for the door. Helena stopped at the threshold and was about to speak, but did not. Fela closed the door behind them as they headed home. The cannon fire was getting louder in the distance as Helena muttered, "He is alive."

Fela nodded and asked, "But what is Mauthausen?"

The rolling and swaying of the boxcar had placed the 75 riders into a deep sleep as the train rolled through the flat Danube River Valley heading west towards a place that no one in the car knew. Staszek had seen through a slit between two boards the names on signs change from Polish, to Czech and eventually German or Austrian over the past several days. It was strange to Staszek how not being able to do anything made him tired and had him napping whenever he could. Staszek, deep in his exhausted sleep was curled up with several threadbare blankets, between two other men on a wooden bunk, his inverted metal bowl serving as his pillow. He dreamt of the magical time of Christmases past, which contrasted sharply to the dark, dismal days and nights of the current January. In this thin-walled wooden icebox that was his rolling cell, Staszek remembered the days at home when the tree was decorated and food lovingly prepared. He longed for the Oplotek (a large unleavened wafer, blessed by the priest) that was shared before Christmas dinner. Breaking of this bread between his parents, brother, and sisters, was an opportunity to wish each other good luck and happiness for the coming year. These memories were truly only a dream today.

He awoke from the dream when there was a sudden change in the speed of the train. From over the shoulder of the man in front of him, Staszek could only stare at the cold dark door and lament that the men on either side of him were the only sure signs of life and hope that he had experienced so far, in this new year. Their gift to him was the same as his to them; the warmth their starving bodies generated in a small quiet place. The other men were like shadows each drifting around in their own worlds. Their contribution to this journey was an occasional sob or whimper followed by a string of profanity aimed at everyone or no one. This place was not only hundreds of kilometers from his home, but millions of kilometers from any happiness.

A year before this, and the year before that, he had also been in the dark and cold while he dreamed for hope in the next year. A wish of being in a home with family and friends contrasted greatly with the smells and cold of the present. The new year of 1945 did not promise anything different, and at nineteen, in prison, cold, and hungry, he wondered if those happy days would ever come again.

A week ago he may have been in prison, but at least it was near his home. Then one early morning 75 prisoners were ordered by name to move out of the building and into the roll call yard. One of them was Staszek. He still had trouble walking due to the pain from his feet (as promised by the commandant, he would not be a threat to run again). It was only now that he was able to put his feet completely flat on the ground. His gait was still painful and awkward but functional, though complicated by poorly fitting and badly worn out shoes. But he could walk which meant he could stay alive a little longer.

Staszek and the others were broken into groups of five and given a kilo of bread and some salted meat or fish per man, and then were marched out of the prison. Staszek asked one of the men closest to him if he had any idea were they were going.

"No," was all the man said without turning or lifting his head as he devoured his bread before even leaving the gate.

As they marched, or shuffled, through the dirt and mud, some women ran through their ranks looking into their faces with excitement looking for a loved one then in an instant becoming devastated in not finding whom they were looking for. Staszek looked back at several hoping to see his mother, or at least a familiar face that could tell his family that he was being marched away. He did not see one, which made the chill seem that much deeper and the loneliness that much more profound. The guards used their rifles to hit or push away the women, who desperately looked for husbands or brothers. It was earlier than the normal transfer of prisoners, so there were few witnesses to this exodus. When small groups like this had left the prison in the past, it was clear that they would not be back. His fate and that of the others was unknown for now, but whatever it was, it could not be worse than the last four months.

As the seventy-five men walked slowly, in a disjointed rhythm of swaying or lunging to keep from falling, it was clear to Staszek that they were heading out of town to the train freight yard north of the city. They walked for three hours, not stopping for any reason. His feet, though no longer swollen, were painful, and each step stabbed his heels. The men were, as a whole, the healthier of the prisoners, and by some small mercy at least they weren't hurried along.

The weather was cold and dry, and since no one had anything to drink, their thirst became powerful, as water had been withheld from them for some time. The small patches of white snow on the streets were few and far between. They did not last long as thirsty men would lean down and pick up the frozen crystals and consume them at any chance they could, snatching a handful or even a fingertip full of the precious item. Those who could not reach a morsel of snow, because the guards would beat those who showed a thought of reaching out of the ranks, resorted to dropping a sleeve into a mud puddle and wringing out drops of fouled water, but water just the same. By mid-morning, they had reached the rail yard and marched to points in front of open cattle cars that were part of a train that already had cars filled with miserable people from other despicable and horrid places.

Staszek stood without shelter in the glow of large lights near the train. A light snowfall began, and seventy-five heads turned up towards the clouds. The dry mouths of the standing men tried to catch flakes of snow as if they were baby birds waiting for a worm from their mothers. Staszek's legs felt like lead and his knees were sore as he stood at attention for another hour before being allowed to climb into the car in front of him.

The merciful dusting of snowflakes had moistened his mouth and eased his thirst, but began to melt on his shoulders and back, which began another type of misery. A small, personal satisfaction came from being able to suck the moisture off of his wet shoulders once he was on the train. One by one, the prisoners were marched up a ramp into the car that was already filled by men from other towns and other prisons, filling it quickly, and finding bunks spaced apart at 70 cm high and stacked to the ceiling. The warmth of these many bodies reduced the chill in the air, but the collective smell of the tired, and many sick men wafted over and through the cattle car. Staszek was able to get close to a barbed wire-covered hole that functioned as a window and vent that gave him some relief from the stagnant air. Near his knees was the slit between the boards that he could look through to see a line of landscape appear then disappear from his sight.

The mobile prison headed south, towards Czechoslovakia. The ride took most of two days and nights. In the morning of the third, it arrived at a transfer depot, where the cars were emptied. The human cargo was moved to another train that had more cars, and many of those were already filled. One by one, the prisoners were marched up a ramp into another car, filling it quickly to where there was standing room only. Fifteen more were pushed in before the door closed and the heavy latches were secured with squeaky sounds that ended with a definitive metal clank.

Several prisoners had died while on the train, and the prisoners around them "shared" their things. Staszek was able to take part in the "sharing" when he out-wrestled a larger, but older, man for a pair of leather shoes that were a larger size than he needed. Staszek had been using two sheets of cloth wrapped around his feet for nearly four months. Staszek estimated that the leather shoes, if lined with the sheets of cloth, would provide warmth and protection for his still-healing feet. Not getting the shoes was not an option, and he got them. He also got a large jacket that would fit over his own, adding more protection from the cold. The most amazing thing of all was that in the pocket of the jacket was still some of the bread and salted fish from Radogoszcz This food was worth at least a day of extra life, and that was the best he could hope for.

It had been nearly five months since his capture, and many of the men had grown substantial beards, except for Staszek, who had barely enough growth on his neck to pass for anything more than a deep red-shaded shadow. His hollowed cheeks made his face look longer than it normally did, but still had some shape to it, unlike those whose faces were sunken to a point where their eyes looked like deep bowls with only pale cherries in the center.

On the fifth day, the temperature had fallen to 10 degrees below zero Celsius (about 20 degrees Fahrenheit) as the train arrived in another large train depot. The morning light showed that this depot appeared to be primarily a freight station, with hundreds of boxcars, and bin cars carrying everything from coal to gravel. As the train rolled to a stop he could see into one of the bins. He had to look twice, because sitting on benches, open to the elements, were corpses frozen in place much like snowmen, sitting alone and forgotten like grotesque figurines from some distant land.

Staszek looked through the space between the boards and could see a small town up the hill about six kilometers from the depot. As the train doors opened once more upon a plain rural platform, there was a sign above an arrow pointing right and towards the next hill. The sign boldly said, "KZ Mauthausen".

Between the tracks and the village were large open fields that reminded him of Babiak to a great extent. Many muffled questions were being asked, "Does anyone recognize this place?"

To a man, no one knew, nor did anyone know where they were to go next. They would not find out for eight more hours.

By late afternoon the answer came with the order to get out. Those near the doors made their maximum effort to keep their footing and not fall from the car. Slowly and orderly, the train disgorged its soiled and miserable cargo. As the forlorn masses left the train, they passed through a line that ended with each man getting a cup of water and a plate with some horsemeat and oatmeal on it. Before most of the men had returned to their place in line, they had consumed all the food and water that had been given to them. The plates had been licked clean, and they were instructed to keep the plates and cups.

Five of the prisoners protested that they needed more food and water, and were unable to walk any more. Those men were told to return to the train car and ordered to strip and fold their clothes on a pile and sit down to rest. One of the Kapo guards went into the car and, without a word, shot all five, returning with the pile of clothes that he threw in the direction of the remaining prisoners. The braver and coldest of them snatched at the articles that they could reach quickly without being harmed. Staszek pushed and pulled to get one of the blankets and was victorious. The warmth outweighed the stink of the fabric.

The officer in charge asked if there were any questions. No response was heard, "Good," was all he said. He ordered the guards to move the men to the road. Five across, they started walking up the gentle slope over a curving road. After a half hour, they reached the outskirts of the colorful town. Staszek looked at the well-manicured gardens and very clean houses lining the road. The few people that he saw did not stay visible for long. Disappearing into doorways or behind window curtains, the residents observed the marchers from protected places and spaces. Only an occasional child standing at a gate or along a fence would be seen staring at the shuffling mass of people, looking expressionlessly back at those who did the same.

Joining the seventy-five men, actually seventy, as five had died on the train from Radogoszcz, were several hundred more that had boarded it earlier. Some were from jails and prisons in the outlying areas of the district. The Germans thought that if these particular prisoners were released, they would cause mayhem on Poles and Germans alike. Many were criminals of the basic kind, who this day walked up the slight slope to KZ Mauthausen. Even in the time of war, there are bad people who steal, assault, and/or murder, because that's what they do as part of their personality. These individuals had no loyalties to any thing or person other than themselves. As such, many had no difficulty becoming operatives of the Gestapo and were called Kapos (prisoner guards) who sold their loyalties to the Germans. These dregs of the earth did the bidding of those who were stronger and meaner than them. Therefore, the Germans quickly approached these types of people and offered them privileges like food, quarters, and even sexual favors, plus power and control over others. These were the kind of men that met the car and were responsible for moving the prisoners out. They did so with rubberized pipes and long sticks that fell on any straggler, for any reason they wished. They were chosen because they seemed to enjoy their work.

During the six-kilometer trek, the men were subjected to the bludgeons of the Kapos. Their sand-filled rubber hoses regularly knocked down the person they assaulted, and almost as often broke a bone at the same time. As they came over the last rise Staszek's breathe looked like a locomotive's exhaust expelling plumes of fog as he labored up what would normally have been considered a gentle slope. Each labored step made his throat burn from the cold and his legs ache. His feet were numb as he crested the hill and his destination came into view. It was a granite fortress with walls seven to ten meters high, and guard stations high on the wall, with searchlights and huge wooden towers in the corners. It was almost breathtaking even from this distance. The old castle walls of Krakow did not seem as impenetrable as these appeared to be, nor were they as ominous in appearance.

After rounding one more curve, they arrived at a massive set of wooden doors with a huge German Eagle above it. Outside this door, they waited for two hours before they could enter. While they waited, another trainload of prisoners had arrived and marched up to join them at the gate. There were nearly two thousand prisoners at the door when it opened. Staszek looked around, and saw an ocean of humanity broken down to its basic elements, trying to live moment-to-moment, yet expecting death at the same time.

Once inside, the prisoners were pushed into a large garage yard where they would be processed, but not today. At the far end stood German offices one level up from the yard. Next to them, two machine guns and their operators sat dutifully, waiting for a reason to get some target practice. Next to the guns stood a man with colorful patches on his shoulders and collar. He appeared to be the commandant, reviewing the new internees.

By the evening the two thousand were added to by another five hundred prisoners. All waited in the cold, and all were scared of what was up the stairwell at the far end of the yard that went up to another unseen level of buildings. Staszek examined the walls and was struck by the massive stonework. The sheer wall fronts made climbing the walls nearly impossible, and if that were tried, there was an electrified barbed wire fence on the top of the walls. *This camp is like no other this side of Hell,* Staszek thought, as he scanned the fortress. How close to the truth his intuition was, he did not fully comprehend.

The men stood in the courtyard for a full 24 hours before the processing started. Staszek was not processed until nearly the end of the second day. When he reached the table, he was asked, "Name, religion, place of birth, occupation, and classification."

"Stanislaw Niklewicz, Catholic, Zurawieniec Poland, Carpenter" was Staszek's answer. The prison scribe, with his head shaved smooth, had a large open ledger at the "N" section, and confirmed the name on the official registry. At the far right column was added, "Incorrigible offender, return not desired."

Staszek stared at the scribe, who had kept his head down throughout the encounter as he confirmed the information that was listed in the ledger. The left temple had a small red birthmark that looked a little like a Rose. It looked familiar but...

"You are number 115988," The scribe told Staszek, who now looked back at the gaunt figure working at his book. Staszek was about to move to the next station when he stopped and with quiet deliberation said, "The mark looks like a 'rose', or maybe a 'wart'."

The scribe froze momentarily and looked up and stared at

Staszek without expression for nearly 10 seconds, then stood up in a confrontational manner that put the guard next to him on alert, and said, "Don't forget that number or you'll lose more than your *pants!*"

Neither of the sentries responded visibly to the seemingly innocent comments. However, inside of Staszek a spark was rekindled this cold winter afternoon. A tear nearly came to his eye, as suddenly he did not feel so alone. As he made his way up the stairs he looked back and there were easily 30-40 lifeless bodies on the ground that had been stripped naked by those who shared their things. Under his breath he was repeating "115988, 115988, 115988." He glanced back at the table where the scribe was working with the next prisoner and then was blocked from view by the stairs. He wanted to turn and go back but did not dare.

His attention quickly turned to one of the Kapos, who was stinging the prisoners' backs and heads with his long willow stick as they went by. Another one taunted them with, "You came in through that door but you will only exit that way." He almost cackled with glee as he pointed to the two tall chimneystacks above them. From both of them there was smoke drifting into the sky, with an odor of burned flesh and hair; a smell no man would ever forget. Guard dogs stood at the top of the stairs on very short leashes and barked savagely, snapped, snarled, and jumped at the terrified men that had to walk past them. Occasionally a poor soul would get too close and in an instant a piece of his leg or thigh would be shredded and bloodied by the dog's fangs.

At the top of the stairs, Staszek entered through the main gate with anticipation of relief from the crowded and cramped quarters he had been experiencing in the confines of Radogoszcz, the prison train, and the processing area. He hoped to be in the open spaces of even this massive camp rather than the compressed feeling of the tight quarters and hundreds of people he had lived with for nearly five months. However as he cleared the gate he was overwhelmed by the mass of people roaming place to place in this compound. *My God there are 10,000 people here,* he thought as he used his skills to estimate the crowd. As he walked further into the camp he looked down between the rows of barracks, where he saw more men in striped suits wandering around. Then there was the next row, then another row, with again more men. Twenty-five barracks that would look like ants covering a sweet spot of honey, the camp was entirely packed. 15,000, 25,000, no 30,000 men, he estimated before he got to one of the three quarantine huts he would live in for the next ten days. He leaned over to one of the men next to him to share his estimates. "There have to be 30,000 men here!" Staszek said with some awe.

The man was just as overwhelmed and said, "Did you see the camp outside the wall as we came in? There had to be 20,000 men out there." He looked around and said, "The Kapo said that those huts there were the Russian Quarters. It looked like they could have another 10,000 people in them. I counted five chimneys on top of one of the huts." In a loud whisper he added, "The life of someone there must be a short one."

Then with complete surprise and confusion Staszek saw that there were children walking around the camp wearing tattered rags and grossly misfitted shoes. "There are kids here!" That surprising fact came from a veteran soldier of only 19 years himself. Then in front of one of the huts were women sitting and standing against the walls of their barracks. Staszek certainly knew that both women and children had been arrested but he just did not expect them here. All of these revelations and new surroundings had Staszek reeling from the mass of people in such a small area and suffering this large misery. His heart sank at the intensity of it all.

As they walked, the size of the camp and the crowding left them dumbfounded. "How?" or "Why?" crossed nearly everyone's lips or crossed their thoughts as they entered the quarantine hut. Once inside, their only thoughts were, *Oh Holy Mother of God, save us.* Or conversely, *God why have you abandoned me?*

Staszek was in front of a building that said "showers" and as he was about to enter, he looked at the mass of striped suits that offered little protection to the men wearing them from the oppressive cold. The aimless milling around was their effort to keep warm. He looked up at the roof, where chimneys posed like cannons that aimed their muzzles and charges at the sky. *Even the snow is gray and dirty here*, he thought, while a mental chill made him quiver for a moment after thinking about what was making the gray smoke inside the chimneys.

As Staszek entered he was told to strip naked, and a moment later he was pushed down onto a chair and had his head shaved down to the skin. Staszek squirmed as his head was shaved with a well-used razorblade that pulled most of his hair out rather than shaving them. The "barbers" were careless with their technique, and left cuts and holes in the skin of many of the prisoners that would surely fester in a day or two. No care was taken about open wounds or bruises; the razor cut everything that wasn't flat. Many of the men wanted to shave their own bodies and groins for fear of what could happen to them at the hand of the careless and unsanitary barber. Afterwards, they were rinsed with a stinging solution of some kind of insecticide/disinfectant before being moved into the showers where the water was either ice cold or scalding hot. What the prisoners did not know was that a third option was available for the Germans. Nozzles discreetly placed low on the walls could release poison gas and kill a hundred people within a couple of minutes. Today, ice water was sprayed on Staszek and the others. One of the men lamented, "The Germans want only bug-free men to die of exposure here." His comment earned him a beating from one of the Kapos nearby.

As they exited the shower, they were ordered to run out into the cold weather naked and to continue to the block of buildings that were numbered "16" with "17" and "18" beyond it. They were given clothing and the now familiar striped jacket. The prison clerk who issued the jacket asked Staszek, "Name?"

"Niklewicz, Stanislaw." As he spoke, one clerk was looking through another ledger and found "Political Prisoner, Poland, black dot, one bar." He collected the pieces of red cloth and a black "P" that corresponded to this information and handed it to the next clerk who asked, "Number?"

Staszek froze, and for a moment; he forgot the number. "NUMBER!" The clerk exclaimed a second time. The SS guard that was chatting with another guard turned his head towards Staszek when he heard the repetition of the question.

Staszek's eyes darted back and forth as he thought "1158...9, no 1159..." then it came, "115988." He blurted out and with no small satisfaction for remembering it. The clerk looked up from the table as he inked the number by hand onto one end of the cloth strip and placed a black ink dot below where the triangle would go, "You'd better be right, or you're dead." He mumbled under his breath. Staszek handed the strip, with the components placed in the required places, to a third man who, using a treadle sewing machine, produced the completed strip and attached it to the jacket pocket.

Staszek now had his number that was preceded by an upside down red triangle with a black dot below it, a horizontal bar above it and a "P" in the center. The red triangle meant he was a political prisoner, the dot meant that he was to be treated with severity, and the bar was that he was to be watched. It was not a good combination for someone who did not want attention drawn to himself.

He proceeded to the next area where he received his footwear, called "claquettes," which were made of roughly cut blocks of wood with a strip of canvas nailed over the top to form the upper part of the shoe. They were called claquettes, because of the noise they made when walking on the cobblestones of the camp. The most uncomfortable and least protective footwear were the claquettes and that is what Staszek got. Though Staszek's feet were nearly healed, the hard sole and uneven balance on the cobblestones outside caused him pain in his heels and brought back his limp as he passed through the hut to an isolation yard for the quarantined men.

From there, his group was taken outside for "appell" (rollcall) under huge spotlights. It was 5:00 PM and dark like tar. There they stood for *an additional 12 hours,* where still more men collapsed from the cold, fatigue, and hunger. After the 5:30 AM roll call, a hundred liter container was rolled out from the kitchen area and each of the remaining prisoners was given a cup of coffee and 1/10 kilo of black bread with lard on it. Finally they were taken back into their quarantine barracks that had no heat and no place to sleep except on the floor. The men slept head to foot across the floor for the rest of the day. After the long periods of standing, the floor was a welcomed change, especially by his feet. In this blockhouse, Staszek spent the next ten days before being cleared to join the rest of the camp in work details.

The details were both internal, consisting of cleaning, laundry, administration, and external details. External included grounds keeping, facility maintenance, wood gathering/cutting, disposal of ash from the Krematorium, and finally the quarry, where granite blocks were mined to be used for Nazi buildings throughout the Reich.

Because of Staszek's prisoner status and that of the others in his hut, they were guarded by some of the most vicious Kapos. One of their sadistic routines every morning was to hose down everyone with cold water for "hygiene" purposes. This action would kill a couple of men by exposure to the frigid weather while wearing soaking wet clothes. Typhus that was spread by lice was a major concern, and was dealt with early and often. Diarrhea, tuberculosis, and other diseases caused by being in poor sanitary conditions were the biggest killer of the prisoners who hadn't been shot while escaping or of "other" natural causes.

Food came irregularly, or sometimes not at all. When it did come, it usually consisted of a quarter liter of unsweetened tea, watery soups of potato peel and sour cabbage. Rarely, there would be a small square of meat, usually horse, that would find its way to a person's bowl. On the ninth day of quarantine, a prisoner was picked out by the Kapo to receive a special treat. One of the frailest men in the hut was brought to the front of the hut by the guards, with great fanfare.

The hut's main Kapo put his arms up as if a circus master and pronounced, "This man could not manage to die during these past nine days, so he has earned a special allotment of food." With that, the Kapo reached into the box and pulled out a jar of jam and, using a ladle, he scooped out a full serving from the jar and first took a mouthful for himself, then gave the rest to the sickly old man, who with relish gobbled down the sweet sticky portion of jam. After which, the Kapo said, "That is all that will be served today," and left, leaving them all watching the old man who did not smile or acknowledge the event. He just returned to his spot on the floor licking his lips. The Kapos left the rest of them hungry for the rest of the day. Staszek tried to get the old man to drink some water, to have fluid in his stomach but the old man refused and pushed Staszek away.

As the men settled back to their spaces on the floor, the old man groaned and cried out in pain as he grabbed his stomach. He rolled side to side and curled into a fetal position for nearly 45 minutes before he vomited blood and jam onto the floor. Within an hour, he was dead from the very sweet sugary food that ate into the walls of his malnourished stomach, causing it to hemorrhage. Staszek knew about that, and so did the Kapo.

Staszek had been scared many times over the past five years, but watching men being killed by beatings, disease, starvation, and sadistic methods was terrifying. There was no one to help him, and he felt powerless to help others. The almost constant pressure in his chest and the flushing of his face from the burning in his stomach had almost paralyzed him with fear. Being alone with what were actually 60,000 others placed him into the darkest abyss void of humanity. He felt like a trapped animal that had nothing to lose except his life, a life that meant little to those in the camp and apparently nothing to the rest of the world. Staszek was left with the ultimate question he could pose; what his life was worth to him. At that moment, he wasn't sure. An instant later, he knew that it was worth everything.

Author's notes: Chapter 19

Radogoszcz Prison was burned to keep prisoners out of the hands of the Russian Army. The Russians would have used them as conscripted soldiers to fight against the Germans. Some of the Germans that were captured in Łódź by the advancing Red Army traded information for their lives. The Volksdeutsche and former Gestapo informers switched loyalty to the Reds. Journals with the names and codenames of the prisoners and their deeds as well as background information from the Gestapo were given to the Russian Secret Service (N.K.V.D.) That organization was renamed and exists to this day as the Communist Secret Police or the K.G.B..

"KZ"= Konzentrationslager; Concentration Camp, sometimes known as "KL". Along with Auschwitz, Mauthausen-Gusen (Gusen being the other sub camp of Mauthausen) was the only other Category Three concentration camp. A camp that was a "One" had prisoners that could be re-educated and used for future service. A number "Two" was for the more serious sins committed against the Reich, and were mostly political prisoners. The "Three" meant it was to be an extermination camp. Prisoners here were guilty of the most serious sins, and were liable to endanger the state if released. The prisoners in the camp were not expected to live longer than six months. Though there were hundreds of labor camps, and more than twenty concentration camps that were also known as death camps, only Auschwitz and Mauthausen were formed *specifically* to murder people through work, disease, hunger, beatings and executions by bullet, poison, medical experimentation, and any form of brutality conceived by the guards and Kapos of the camp.

The average **daily** quota of deaths in Mauthausen was nearly four hundred from non-execution reasons. Executions would account for an additional forty-five deaths. The other labor camps had been formed to produce labor pools for fabricating war materials in occupied areas and cities. In those camps there was some incentive on the Germans part to have the workers survive for a longer period of time, as efficient workers were becoming scarce. However, those who could not produce their quotas were quickly eliminated. The old, very young, infirm, or politically undesirable met a quick end as they arrived to the camps. By May the number of killed would near fifteen hundred per day.

"Arbeit Macht Frei," or "Work will set you free," was a slogan touted by the Germans at the labor camps, a depraved slogan that was intended to give false hope to millions. This sign that was hung over the gates of several camps started in Auschwitz where it was placed by the camp commander Major Rudolf Hoss. He never intended it to be any part of a mockery of those coming into the camp, but rather a philosophical statement of his based on the writings of a German novelist in 1873. The book was about gamblers and con men who would find their way to virtue through labor.

The National Socialists (Nazi party) adopted the phrase in 1933. Prisoners would add the words, "durch den schonstein" (through the chimney) when the first part was stated.

Picture #6: Front wall, north of Main Gate

Picture #7: Roll call area: Main gate in the distance

Chapter 20
February 1ˢᵗ, 1945: Mauthausen KZ.

THE BARRACKS DOOR opened with a crash at 5:15 AM, and the German voice barked out orders that were mimicked by an eager dog on a short leash. On this last night of quarantine, roll call was completed by 7:24 AM. The morning was remarkable not for the light snowfall that had piled high enough to cover the men's feet, but the rapid roll call itself. Staszek could not stop shivering, even with two blankets over his head and shoulders. One was his while the other he had taken from the man who died next to him last night. The bitter cold had the ranks of men shaking and swaying, or marching in place, like stalks of wheat in a moderate breeze, moving somewhat randomly while they endured the process. The morning light had started to compete with the floodlights, mounted on several stations high above the barracks that brilliantly lit the entire area. The gray of the sky began to meet the gray of the gloomy world of the camp.

The only thing worse than the cold was the terror Staszek felt in the roll call area, with thousands of men around him yet he had the feeling of being singled out and watched. The paranoia was not totally unfounded. There were enough eyes scanning and observing that at any given time he was indeed being watched.

How I wish I were home, he lamented. *Will I ever see my family again?* The thought gripped his heart, and tears welled up in him. He fought the feeling. He could not let himself succumb to the helplessness that was overpowering him at this moment, made worse by the cold and the unknown that waited secretly before him.

This was the first time Staszek and the remaining men (about half of the original number had died) had been marched outside into the assembly area with all the other prisoners for the 5:00 AM roll call. He was afraid he would bite his tongue off if it got between his chattering teeth. The bitter cold knifed through him down to his bones. There was a little irony in that the beatings on his feet had crushed the nerves that conducted sensation from his skin, and the numbness moderated the icy feelings that he felt higher up his legs. The stinging cold was part of the Germans' greater plan, which involved the counting and recounting of the prisoners under these inhuman conditions as a way to eliminate the weak. This was a slow and deliberate procedure to identify all prisoners in the camp via the roll call that was performed once, and then checked again twice more with the expectation that the weakest would die during the process or panic and start to run, which earned them a bullet. Each day since the beginning of the New Year, nearly 1,500 new prisoners arrived in the camp. Keeping the census of prisoners at a steady level meant needing to kill the same number before the next arrivals were processed. Therefore, by necessity the days started early in the camp, and prisoners literally dropped dead.

Today's roll call was completed slightly early, as a parade appeared with a marching band followed by a cart pulled by prisoners. Work started promptly at 7:30 so the roll ended with enough time to view the parade and not interfere with the start of work. The cart passed in front of the ranks carrying a single man. An eerie sight as the gray clouds became slightly more luminescent and a small band of nine prisoners playing a song from a German comic opera on two clarinets, four violins, and three accordions added to the surreal atmosphere. Staszek looked around and saw that most of the prisoners had their heads down while others, like himself, were looking around trying to figure out what was happening.

The procession continued to a large stone wall where the cart was pulled to a halt, and the man, with his hands tied behind his back, was pushed out of the rickety cart, forcing him to fall from a one meter height to nearly flat on his face against the cobblestones. He moaned in pain from the impact that stunned him, and turned a couple of stones blood red. He tried to turn over without the use of his tied hands, but before he could move onto his side he was dragged to the granite wall and stood up with his back against it. He tried to stand, but his knees buckled and he fell onto them. He was again hoisted up by two of the Kapos, and this time his knees held stiff, barely. Then in a fluke of weather the clouds parted slightly and a warm beam of sunlight highlighted the man adding color to the gray and brown around him. It also made the blood on his face nearly sparkle and glow.

The commander of the inspection stood to the side, facing the assembled prisoners, and proclaimed through a loud speaker, "This man tried to escape, and failed like those before him and those with him last night. He has been tried for his crime and has been found guilty. We will now carry out the sentence." With that, the officer turned to his NCO, who in turned ordered five soldiers standing at attention in front of the prisoner, "Ready, aim–fire." At once, all five rifles fired and tore through the man's chest causing him to drop forward again onto his face. This time there was no pain. The sunlight, sensing the injustice also withdrew back into the clouds, darkening the mood to mimic the lack of conscience of the oppressors.

This execution place was called the Wall of Lamentations, or Wailing Wall. Here people were usually placed facing the stone and then shot. Since most of the men shot here cried in anguish as they were about to die because of who they were or what they believed in their hearts, the wall earned the label it was given. It was the rare man who could die with dignity under these horrors. But some did, even if their faces were badly bloodied. All the prisoners stood at attention and did not say a word at the execution, but some flinched. Most did not look at the event, and those who did were thankful that this wasn't their turn to die, while the others, in their fatigue or sadness, wished that it had been.

To Staszek, his immediate thought was, *those damn Germans, they are the same everywhere, and the more the brutality, the more they enjoy it.* Staszek's disgust at the behavior of the Germans towards other human beings came to a revelation: *they think they are the Master Race. They are more than delusional! They must be insane,* a thought he'd had before. Today he was certain that they were the latter.

The beatings by Commandant Pelzmann and Bloody Joe in Łódź were brutal and frequent, but continued for as long as they felt the need to get the information they wanted and to make a lesson for others to learn. At Mauthausen, all the information that was needed or expected had been gathered. There was no pretense to the Germans' action here. Death was frequent, and would come by many methods at most any time. The only limiting factor was their evil imagination.

The marching band and firing squad was just one more grotesque way the Germans did business. Staszek had looked at the execution and felt glad it wasn't him. For a brief moment he had stopped shivering as the cold was forgotten when the rifles came up to the shoulders of the SS guards, but he was angry and hateful of the carnival-like procession the Germans made of this event. His thoughts were intensified by the recurrent sense of frustration of not being able to do anything about the crimes committed here, nor to be able to fight back in any meaningful way. While in the forest or in Łódź, he felt he could do something, but here he felt helpless and terrified by the unbelievable wickedness in the camp. He had the urge to run, but did not know where he could go. He had no options. Like the others, he was hopelessly trapped. *This is what Jakob must have felt like in the Ghetto.* Staszek reminisced at seeing Jakob and waving the Scout hand sign at each other. He remembered looking at him through the peephole in that building wall. "Jakob must be dead. No one could have lived this long in these conditions." Staszek look around and could see what the Ghetto must have been like, and that it was his turn to be penned up like an animal.

Even while terror surged again through Staszek as he saw what was happening all around him, and he feared that he would be next. He fought to find calm and resolve within himself, but in this endeavor he was rarely successful. Focusing his contempt on the guards and the prison did distract him a bit. The senseless beatings and inhuman behavior had started to harden him further rather than break him. He reached for and pulled out of himself the courage and resourcefulness that served him well over the past years. As Staszek was flooded with all these thoughts and emotions, his will grew to a point that he was determined not to die silently in the night. If he had an ounce of strength left he told himself that he was going to make a difference, somehow. Time would be the determinate of what could or would be done. Until that came to pass, there were requirements for him to stay alive and he was determined to fulfill them. Keeping his thoughts focused on ways to survive seemed like a good idea. Finding allies would be better. He had to find both. Knowing that Wart was somewhere in the camp was a boost for his sanity. He decided that was his new goal: to find Wart. This mental exercise gave him a sense of strength and purpose, and it also distracted him. It was a monumental task to find a specific person in the camp of 60,000 but he needed to try.

While deep in his thoughts and coping with his fears, he was suddenly aware of a voice barking, "115988," and then a pause that snapped him back into the present.

"115988" was repeated. The sound of his number being called gripped his throat. He looked down at his pocket to double check if it was really his number. The first morning out of quarantine, and someone called him out of line. In a haze Staszek reflexively stepped forward and was promptly hit several times across his back by a rubber hose.

"Don't move until you're told to do so," the Kapo next to Staszek screamed. The stinging was breathtaking, but Staszek stood as rigid as he could and tried not to squirm.

"115010, 116023..." The foreman called twenty more numbers. "Step forward," came the order. The directors of the camp needed carpentry work, and Staszek first assignment came because of his statement on his registration, "Carpenter."

He was told to step out of line, and was placed together with the group of twenty-one men. There he was approached and asked by a prisoner who was foreman of carpentry, "Are you a carpenter?"

"Yes, I am," Staszek answered with a straight face.

"Where did you work?" the foreman asked.

"Opoczno." Staszek answered, truthfully and accurately.

"Mr. Wach's shop?" the foreman continued.

Staszek was unnerved by the comment. Would answering this question compromise Mr. Wach and the underground? "I was an apprentice in many places, I did not know who owned all the shops."

The foreman did not pursue the questions. He knew the answers, and appreciated him protecting his manager. "All right then, go over there."

With that, Staszek was ordered to the carpentry shop at the far side of the camp, to work on furniture meant for the SS offices. He did as he was told. Now he had to figure out how to be a real carpenter.

His woodworking skills were limited to what he learned at Mr. Wach's shop in Opoczno and what he knew from working at his father's store. He hoped it would be enough. All he knew right now was that this assignment was not the quarry that he'd heard about for the past ten days, so saying yes to being a carpenter was not a problem, and was said automatically. He knew from gossip in the hut that the quarry should be avoided at all cost.

Staszek was assigned to work with someone who appeared to know what he was doing. After several attempts to use basic finishing tools in the skillful ways that were commonly used by the carpenters, it was clear that his skills were not at a high skill level. Since no one was working fast, Staszek learned on the job and slyly watched others work to see how things were done. He was catching on quickly, and getting away with it. He worked a long day while being in constant fear of being found out, but he was inside a building rather than in the snow outside at the quarry. In late afternoon, the foreman came around to see the work Staszek was doing and picked up one of the sanded legs for a simple desk. "You sand the wood like it is an old stick. Mr. Wach would not have taught his apprentice this poor of a technique."

Staszek became apprehensive at the rebuke, and felt that he had been found to be a fraud. "Then I am sure that it wasn't in his shop where I learned sanding, or I would have learned to have done it the right way," Staszek tried to maneuver out of the lie.

The forearm stared at him, handed the piece back, and said, "If you were there, you might have been busy doing other things. I know that Mr. Wach was vigilant for his workers and channeled their skills in many places where they were most needed." He walked away as the shop Kapo started to drift by.

It seemed more than coincidence that the foreman used the Scout motto of 'Vigilant,' and the use of Mr. Wach as a safe house for the Scouts as they passed through an area. Or was it a trap? The terror came back to him as he weighed the possibilities.

At the end of his workday, Staszek left the workshop, and had managed to tuck a couple dozen sheets of paper that the furniture parts came wrapped in into his trousers. He planned to use the paper as layers of insulation inside his clothing for some warmth. In this barracks, there were about 200 Poles, but also a scattering of Czechs, a couple of Spaniards, and one Englishman. Finding a place to arrange the paper into his pants without being noticed was out of the question. He managed to slide them between his shirts while under his blanket. The paper wasn't much insulation, but was better than nothing.

The barracks had more order to it than the quarantine hut, in that it had a stove and a person whose job was to not let the fire die out or burn down the barracks. The fire extinguisher next to the stove was polished to a reflective level, something done to earn favors from the Kapo. That person was called the "Kalefaktor," and he also had the task to keep the toilets clean. There was a "Blockalteste," or Barracks Elder, who was in charge of keeping order among the prisoners, who reported to the "Lageralteste," or Camp Elder. Each barrack had a permanent Kapo who worked for the SS as an extension of their discipline. Not least of the positions was the "Kaffeeholer," the man who brought the so-called coffee to the barracks in the morning.

The bunks were stacked three high, with two to four men to a bunk that had some straw on them, but for the most part were bare wood. The bedstraw was often taken and used as insulation in the men's clothes, though the man would be beaten if caught. Food, such as it was, came to the barracks via a cart, and the men lined up with their bowls to get their rations and their predictable whippings from the Kapos while they waited outside for the morsels given to them. There was little to do other than talk after what food they got. They would complain about the cold, the food supply, who looked sick enough to die during the night, and they speculated when the war would end. More important was WHO would liberate them. The betting was that it would be the Russians. When the frustration of the lack of control of the environment became too great, the topic would always turn towards women. Whether it was a wife, mother, girlfriend or a one-time lust-driven night, stories and exploits helped pass time.

Staszek received his scoop of food and sat down on one of the steps to eat the turnip and sausage broth soup. It was mostly turnip water and the grease from the horsemeat sausage that was somewhere in the pot, but still added some taste to the broth. He consumed it within a minute of receiving it. Having the warm food inside so quickly decreased the chances of losing it to someone else while it was on the outside. As a Scout he often ate whatever food that could be gathered, whether it grew from the ground, walked or crawled over it, food was food. This soup was consumed without much analysis or thought about it. It was warm and that was all that he could think about.

As he sat, another prisoner sat down next to him, much closer than was needed to be on the step. Staszek was licking his bowl when a small nugget of meat was dropped into it. Staszek was startled by the gift and looked up to see the face of the prisoner who had been at the registration table when Staszek was processed into the camp. Though structurally young, the man was aged by the pale color of his skin and almost total loss of body fat. Staszek picked up the meat and looked at it then he looked at the sickly-looking man who was smiling at him. Staszek said, "You need this more than me, Wart," and handed it to him, though the smell was very seductive. Staszek looked around carefully, to make sure that no one heard him use the codename, "Wart". When he was satisfied that he wasn't overheard he turned his head back and said, "It is good to see a friend's face," as he smiled with pleasure for the first time in months.

The stick figure pushed the meat back and said, "I would have expected that honesty from a Scout, but I still want you to have it, Pants." Wart was truly pleased to see him, and added, "Welcome to Barracks Eight. It is not as bad as some of the others, but you'll grow to hate it nonetheless." A sardonic smile crossed his face with the greeting.

Staszek popped the meat into his mouth before Wart could change his mind and said, "I didn't think you would remember me."

Smiling, with a tear welling up in his red eye, Wart said, "For a person who had a codename as bad as mine, how could I forget? I did not know your name until that first day here, but I thought I recognized you. Your wise guy comment confirmed it. I just did not want both of us to be sent on the "Last March Patrol" if the guards figured out that we knew each other."

"Last March Patrol? What's that?" Staszek asked.

"Every week, the prisoners the Germans really want to work to death are marched deep into the woods to dig a huge pit for the bodies of mostly Russians that are killed in Barracks 20, or the "K" as it is known to us, usually working with no food at all. The Russians' bodies are carried out there throughout the week, and then buried all at once." Wart thought for a moment and added, "The catch is that the 200 workers who dig the hole are shot after they finish the job and are tossed in with the Russians. That's why it's the Last March Patrol," Wart described the horror in a matter of fact way, and muffled a cough with his fist. "I was selected to work registration because I can speak Russian and Czech. Most of those in Barracks K are Russian prisoners who go from registration to the grave in hours, if not minutes, after they are documented. I've heard rumors of 2,000 to 2,500 bodies buried at a time. I think it must be true. I never see them a second time. Four to six thousand new prisoners can come in each week, yet the population is staying about the same. I know that they are not walking out of here,"

Wart said grimly. He continued, "That's why it's called the 'K' Barracks; the "K" stands for Kugel (bullet)." As they sat and tried to comprehend that staggering number, a cloud of smoke drifted over them as the wind changed. The smell was unmistakable as the remains of those processed through the Krematorium ovens.

Staszek was no longer able to think too deeply about the atrocities that were becoming commonplace in his life. The smells made him change the subject, so he asked, "When did you get here? How did they catch you?"

Wart said, "The Gestapo swept the streets one day, just after I got into Opoczno, and before I knew it I was on the ground and bleeding from the beating they gave me. They had been waiting for my contacts and me, so they caught six of us that day. We were betrayed. I am the only one left from there. That's been over a year." He swallowed hard, coughed a shallow cough, and said, "I've been here for eight months, and I'm not doing too well." Wart's eyes started to well up with tears again. "How about you?" he asked Staszek.

Staszek gave a short version of his travels and problems, that he had become "Flame," and worked in the Underground until captured.

Staszek continued, "What can we do to get out of here? If we stay here, they will kill us for sure. I can't just wait for that to happen." Staszek's eyes started to dart side-to-side looking for spies who would be listening.

Wart leaned in closer to Staszek and whispered, "We will talk more about that soon. For now be vigilant, there is a Scout troop here in the camp. I'll keep you informed." The two stood and shook their left hands with the little fingers separated from the others, then walked away.

Returning to his bunk, Staszek had a little more energy and more confidence that he would live through this ordeal. Just then, he felt the sting of the willow branch penetrating down to his ribs and he let out a yelp that earned him two more quick stings. Apparently he did not bow to the Kapo when he got to his bunk. He squirmed in pain as the stung areas became warm. The sadistic Kapo smiled as he walked through the hut stinging anyone who was in the wrong place at the wrong time.

At the end of the first week in the furniture shop, a Kapo with his truncheon swinging up into his hand and down again walked slowly among the workers in the shop. He looked at their identification stripes by using his club as a long hard finger to poke at them. He grabbed them by the upper arm and squeezed hard to assess their muscle mass, much like a farmer checking to see if the fruit was ripe for picking. Another Kapo with a ledger book with numbers in it followed him. When he called out a specific number, the second would say "yes" or "no." The Kapo chose a series of numbers from men at one bench with the second man and fifth being suddenly pulled by their sleeves and clubbed once on the back of his neck when the "yes" was given. They were then pushed to the door where another four or five Kapos were waiting.

He had done the same thing to ten others in the shop of over a hundred workers. When he got to Staszek's bench, Staszek bent forward slightly to cover his stripe and to look frailer, as he worked on a corner of a table. He knew why the guards were coming for the men who stood a little farther away from death than the others. They were to become like Sisyphus with his eternal walk up the mountain, except these men were going to the quarry. Their walking would stop when their heart did. Staszek's efforts failed when the truncheon came down on his back, buckling his knees slightly and forcing him to twist with the pain. The Kapo grabbed his arm and called out "115988 dot." The other Kapo responded, "Yes," which caused Staszek to be beaten and whisked towards the door and pushed out of the building where he fell to the ground, tripping over the toe of his wooden shoe. He was lined up with a dozen others and was marched along a path that took them to the quarry. He felt the difference between the unheated building that at least had many warm bodies in it compared to the outside. It was not good. Since his fear and stress had greatly increased in the past several minutes and ironically he was generating ample heat at the moment. Breathlessly he scanned side to side, looking for a place to run, but it was in vain.

At first the group marched around some of the barracks, but eventually they headed out of the camp and down a cobblestone slope to what the Kapo called, "A visit to my friends, the Stairs of Death." The creepy laugh of the Kapo and the sight of the 186 stairs that were spoken of with the greatest of tribulations by the other prisoners soon appeared before Staszek. He would have felt his heart sink if he was not in the grip of shock and foreboding.

As he and the others walked towards the steps, their wooden shoes sounded like horse hooves clacking on the uneven stones. From the top he could see down the 200 meters to where the line of men formed five across in groups of a hundred, waiting to start their trek up the steps. It looked like Dantes' Inferno, only in snow with the Devil's trolls whipping and beating the damned as they tried to climb up to the sky.

Staszek and his group were squeezed together as they descended into the pit. They walked down the hillside of the steps, while men came up the steps, five abreast, carrying stones on frames that were strapped to their backs by strong webbing that crisscrossed the chest. Some men had to carry the stones on their shoulders or against their chests, using their hands to support the stones if they were not given a frame. These men without a frame were mostly Jews, as the Yellow Star of David on their shirts marked them. They were so close together that the head of the man on the lower step was nearly touching the stone or back of the man on the next higher step. They moved in time with the man in front of them, one step, pause, and then the next. The steps were icy and wobbled; each step being potentially the prisoners' last. All this was done in an orderly manner, forced by the whips, sticks, and bludgeons of the Kapos.

On the edge of the steps closest to the quarry was a sudden drop without a rail or room for error. The dirty snow that covered the ground was on top of ice that had frozen beneath it, making it even more slippery. Staszek had trouble going down the steps with his painful and very cold feet in the clumsy wooden shoes. His heart raced at the thought of having to carry a stone up the steps under these conditions. A prisoner next to him who looked as if he had made this trip many times saw the terror on Staszek's face and said, "Every stone and piece of rock or pebble down there comes with the price of one life." The words sank to Staszek's soul. The man continued, "Do not forget them, and do everything you can to avoid being one." Staszek looked towards him and just caught a glimpse of the man's eye before he turned back towards the path. No other words needed to be said.

At the bottom of the stairs Staszek was lined up and fitted with the wooden backpack. "I have more respect for horses now" he mumbled as two prisoners showed him how to put a 30 kg (66 lbs.) stone on his frame and lift it on to his back, alone. The weight was tremendous, and he felt like he would go down on his knees, but he recovered with the encouragement of a willow whip snapping on his shoulder, reinforcing the sense of being a beast of burden. He turned to look up the stairs he would soon climb. A ribbon of men inched their way up the stairs. He was among 1,500 men that made this trip four times in the morning. Each time his heart sank at the thought that he would be saddled like this for the rest of his life, a life that did not look like it would be long.

Before the midday meal, the sun burned through the clouds and added a glaring light off the snow, partially blinding many of those who were looking upwards. Staszek moved slowly to the base of the first step and stopped as he prepared to start his ascent. At that moment he was mesmerized in disbelief as the unimaginable happened about three-fourths of the way up the stairs. He watched and as if in slow motion, one of the men near the top of the stairs appeared to have slipped on the ice and lost his footing. As the man tried to recover his balance, he was straightened up by the weight on his back that in turn pulled him backwards and off his step. His suddenly waving and outstretched arms startled the men on either side and below him who in turn lost their balance. "Oh my God!" Staszek gasped as the men started to fall backwards like dominoes down the stairs, taking one row down after another. Like a human avalanche of men and stones they tumbled backwards with some men falling over the edge of the cliff to their deaths while others were crushed under the weight of the cascade of men and rocks. It was happening too quickly for most of them to scream, even if they had the strength to do so. Red color started to appear all over the steps and snow, as it was mixed in with the tumbling mass of men and debris. There was a torrent of screaming voices that came from men on the periphery, and resonating in the echoing chamber of the quarry as feet were crushed; shins, arms, and skulls were broken in the chaos of the disaster.

The men who were spared from the stones were met with the clubs and sticks of Kapos who were outraged at men making it to the top without a rock in their possession. Men near the top that had dropped their stones during the tragedy quickly picked up any stone near them to avoid the beating that was being served further up the stairs. Those who were still on their feet with their stones now had to maneuver up the stairs while staying away from the cliff and certain death from the sixty-meter fall. They also had to avoid getting too close to, or stepping up onto the hill where the guards would routinely shoot anyone trying to escape.

The guards and Kapos at the top looked up as the screaming and hollering cascaded over the stairs. Most of the guards started to laugh and point at the scene, while a couple of foreman instantly became angry because production would be greatly decreased this day. The men who did not fall were whipped with sticks to make them complete their journey up the "Stairs of Death" that literally earned their name today.

With little time to think about what he had just witnessed, Staszek made his way up the steps to deliver his stone as part of a next wave of human mules. He moved forward with his reflexes and senses at their highest settings, driven by unabated terror, while the sun continued to highlight the gore and revulsion on the 186 steps.

Carefully navigating around the stones, bodies, and smashed limbs heaped on the stairs, Staszek and the rest of the group of prisoners worked their way to the top of the steps where a cart on rails was filled, one stone at a time. That cart was then pulled the rest of the way to the top of the hill by fifty more men. Once he delivered his stone, Staszek was sent back down to retrieve the loose stones on the steps, a task both physically and emotionally painful. The bodies of the dead were being stacked on the edge of the stairs to be collected later; the wounded were carried up the hill and taken to the sick quarters. Those with the Yellow Star, whether dead or just wounded, were tossed over the cliff on the orders of the Kapos.

As Staszek helped to move the bodies to one side he came upon one corpse that was crushed and both legs were broken which made lifting and moving it difficult to grip. As he did so, he noticed that this man had leather shoes, as did some others on the stairs. Staszek estimated that they would fit him and, after scanning to see if there was a Kapo in whipping distance and finding none, he quickly untied the large shoes, and despite them being covered in blood, slipped them onto his feet. The blood made his hands sticky, so he wiped them on the prisoner's shirt, conscious of the deed; he apologized and thanked him at the same time.

Staszek's crouched posture amongst the hundreds of men who were moving in all directions on the steps, allowed him to return to work as he swung over to the next body to move it without breaking his rhythm or bringing attention to him. The difference in comfort in the leather shoes was great especially for his heels when compared to the wooden clogs, even the warmth, though slight, was something that would save his toes from the cold. One of Staszek's needs was for the time being, taken care of.

The immediate need of the camp bosses were the stones. They had to get the stones up the hill. The bodies could wait, but the work could not. The hospital, such as it was, had three to four men on each bed, often with mixed diseases, and often one or more already dead but not moved away. Broken bones, dysentery, yellow fever, typhus, cholera, and festering wounds were all under-cared for, due to the sheer numbers involved and complete lack of supplies. The doctors, nearly all of whom were prisoners themselves, could not keep up with the demand. Ironically men that would have died straight out if left in the elements, suffered a little longer under the valiant efforts of the medical staff. Upper body problems or broken bones were treated with aspirin while problems of the lower body were given suppositories, if there were any left. If an anesthetic was needed, the German male nurses, using one of the wooden shoes, would simply apply a sharp crack to the head of the patient to supply an effective dose of "anesthesia".

Healing was very slow or nonexistent in a body that was starving, as was the case for all in the camp. The very sick patients, or those too weak to work, were seen by Dr. Ramsuer who would give an injection of gasoline in their hearts. He saw and found no use for their existence to continue so it was terminated. That meant that if a prisoner needed more than three days in the infirmary, he was beyond help. The only way to avoid the hospital was to keep working or be a Jew. The Jews were denied medical care, so the hospital was not an option for them.

Staszek worked the stairs for nearly all the weeks during February and March. By the beginning of April, he weighed 55 kg (121 lbs.) as the food never made up for the calories used to do the work has cost him more than 18 kg (40 lbs.) beyond the 8 kg (17.5 lbs.) he lost in Radogoszcz. In the evenings, he would examine his boney, bruised body and examine the open wounds that were made by the straps from the backpack. Those deep grooves on his shoulders could not match the welts and scars made by the whips and sticks to his body delivered by the SS guards and Kapos. The backpack protected his back from the whips, but left his neck, head and legs as easy targets. Seven to eight trips up and down the stairs was expected of each prisoner per day. Each trip was like climbing through the gauntlet to Hell.

The first trip of the morning would have Staszek's legs feeling like lead, but it got worse with each cycle on the stairs. The only reprieve during the day was a fifty-minute break at noontime where a rest period was found in the ten-hour work cycle. This would have been eliminated if not for the fact that the SS guards wanted a break for themselves.

Their leftovers from the SS meal were given to the Kapos, while the prisoners were given a thin soupy gruel.

The only time where there was obvious life in the prisoners was at this break. This is when they were dismissed for the meal and they had to walk quickly, (to run was physically impossible) to the lines for their meal portions. Service depended on where you were in line when the whistle announced mealtime, which meant pushing and pulling in the line. It also meant that if you were on the stairs, there would be little left for you to eat. The stronger you were, the better chance you had to get what was served as food. If by chance you had a good relationship with a Kapo and they were serving a meal, it was worth fighting to get into his line, for he would scoop the food from the bottom for you.

Staszek learned a lot about the camp from other prisoners, some of who had been in the camp for nearly a year. No one had lived longer than that. Six months was the life expectancy of the average prisoner. Staszek learned that the man with the colorful patches was indeed the commandant of the camp, Captain Franz Ziereis. He was known as "Baby Face Ziereis" because of his soft features that maligned the cruelty and homicidal activities. Staszek heard that he was making extra money sending his prisoners to work for civilian contractors.

Interestingly it turned out that Manfred Bachmayer, (his deputy), and several others dealt with their former friends, now enemies, by sending them to work in the quarry like the other prisoners. One was a man called Bergen, who was a wealth of information to anyone who would listen. He once was an administrator for the camp, but fell into disfavor with someone of higher rank, who had him sentenced as a criminal. Bergen knew his days were numbered, and that getting his story out would be his revenge on those who placed him here. Staszek had an interested ear and remembered the stories Bergen told about the guards and their histories. Two of the more infamous were Trum and Niedermayer, who were known to be the most brutal of all of the guards, and were to be avoided at all cost. They competed for the most murders committed per day by a guard, and were truly disappointed if they failed to have the highest number.

While working the quarry stairs, Staszek learned that if he would look for stones that were large on one side but small on the other, that made them effectively lighter than the standard stone. Loading a stone onto his carrying frame with the big side towards the Kapos, who always stood away from the cliff where they could not see all sides of the stone helped with the deception. Those lighter trips were few and far between, but each helped prolong his life. However, if spotted carrying a stone that was too small, the guards would have a second stone added to the frame or would force him to carry it in his arms.

Bergen also told him that in the early days of the camp, Spanish prisoners, those who opposed the Fascist Dictator Franco, had to carry stones up to 50 kg (110 lbs.) in weight and would make fifteen trips up and down the stairs per day, something that was simply inconceivable. Many died within days of starting this punishment.

At the end of the workday, a barracks cook provided the evening meal. The term "cook" was used loosely, as the containers carrying the soup were delivered and the cook stirred the soup, and then served it with bread or crackers. After the meal, there was free time where the prisoners were allowed to roam and be social with the other prisoners. This was a time where Flame and Wart made contact with the Scout movement in the camp. Starting as a small group that reached nearly fifteen men, the Scouts picked up where they left off in the outside world, looking for ways to foil the Germans and stay alive.

The Scoutmaster was one of Staszek's instructors when he joined the Grey Ranks, Mieczyslaw Letowski. Letowski had organized a network of Scouts in key areas to help anticipate changes in the German activities, especially as they related to distribution of food, new prisoners, hospital activities, and especially to gather names of the officers, guards, and soldiers who were brutal in their behavior to the prisoners. He broke the network down to a barrack or two barracks for the hives, to avoid having the whole network vulnerable.

Today the plan for keeping track of the criminals in the camp, so they could be hunted down after the war was over. He said, "We cannot let them get away after the war is over without being punished. They must be held accountable." Letowski insisted on and championed the goals, as he was adamant that the Germans would soon lose the war. Several copies of the names were kept on waste paper so they could be discarded if necessary, but still have others to show the allies when the time was right. Staszek gave him his list of names, which included those from Radogoszcz, names and faces that he would not forget. Those of the guards in the quarry were named several times by other Scouts and reinforced. At the same time, there were a couple of names of guards who defied their orders and risked their lives to help prisoners through providing extra food, or having them sent to the hospital or assigned to menial tasks as they recovered from illness or injuries. That list was very short.

With Wart having access to limited administration files, and another Scout working in the hospital, they could identify any of those listed as being at the camp, or where they were transferred.

The Scout leader gave instructions for survival in the camp. "We will use codenames like we did in the Grey Ranks while talking about this organization, to protect us from being identified easily." The members looked around at each other and mentally tested themselves on the codenames they knew, and of those they would have to reveal theirs to. The leader continued, "The younger and stronger Scouts will be assigned to help older or sicker members avoid being taken advantage of during meals and work duties when they become weaker and more vulnerable. Something as basic as making sure the weaker person makes it through the food line and gets their portions, would help them survive. Those who are dying and cannot consume food any more would still go through the lines with assistance, and their food would be shared with others. A sacrifice of the highest kind, by the person who is dying." Everyone understood the reality and necessity of this plan and said nothing more. He continued, "We have about one hundred and forty Scouts in the different barracks. We are not many, but there is strength when we work together." It was this fraternal mindset that helped save the lives of many Scouts who would have succumbed to the ordeals if left alone and unprotected.

Another strategy was having a German-speaking Scout always close by, to help translate the orders of the German guards who became frustrated easily when the prisoners did not understand their orders, which often led to beatings or death of the hapless and confused victim.

Keeping strong convictions on nationalism, religion, camaraderie, and/or family was discussed and reinforced during meetings, to help with morale and keep the focus on survival. Being physically fit, morally straight, and faithful had been hallmarks of the Scouting movement, and lent itself to the crisis of courage in the prison camp.

A side benefit for the Scouts was their sense of unity and renewed optimism. Many men who had similar experiences from the first day of the war and had felt that they had battled alone, were now brought together after all these years with kindred spirits to be lifted from the depths of despair. One of the most basic ways this was done was through humor. Even in terrible situations, teenagers and young men will inevitably produce obscene and sexually orientated jokes, or derogatory nicknames for the guards and play practical jokes on most any occasion. Laughing at themselves, the Nazis, their henchmen, and Death itself, gave some mental balance to the prisoners. Fighting to stay alive required that a person grasp at every survival method they could think of. The Scouts found their strength to survive by working together, but this strength was not always a match for those who were determined to eliminate them from the face of the earth.

The struggle continued at many levels of involvement, but chances for survival for even the Scouts were grim.

Author's notes: Chapter 20

Mauthausen had the lowest rate of typhus, the disease carried by lice. It wasn't due to hygiene as much as that when typhus was found in a barracks, any or all of the prisoners, sick or fit, in that building would be killed. The barracks were designed for 200 prisoners, but by 1945 each held 500 men of all nationalities.

To put these numbers into prospective, if you have ever attended a professional football game in the United States, the typical seating capacity of their stadiums is approximately 58,000. Imagine all those seats representing the population of Mauthausen. Then imagine that multiplied by three to reflect the number of dead that came to be from that evil camp.

Picture #8: New prisoner processing yard

Picture #9: Bottom section of the 186 Stairs of
Death with men carrying rocks to the top.

Picture #10: 186 Stairs of Death from aerial view. Parachute jump is at the top right.

Chapter 21
April 12ᵗʰ, 1945: Mauthausen KZ.

STASZEK LOOKED AROUND carefully, and leaned down next to the ear of the new man, who had just picked up a 15 kg stone to carry. "Don't take that stone. Those sons of bitches will think you're lazy and give you a second one to carry." Staszek said in English with a soft slow voice. The American, who until today had worked in the camp by laying tile in one of the new krematoriums, looked up in some surprise. "Take that one." Staszek pointed to a larger stone next to the first choice.

The American paused for a moment.

"Take it," Staszek repeated with a little more intensity. Unsure, but going with the calm voice, the American took the larger one into his arms. As he did so, another new man to the quarry snatched the smaller one like it was a prize and almost grinned when he shuffled over to get a place near the front of the group, on the side away from the guards. Staszek said, "Wait a minute, we'll stand in the middle of the group." The American did not want to stand and hold his stone, but wanted to get moving so he could get rid of it sooner. The knowledgeable words in English made him wait until Staszek started to move and said, "Now we go."

The two placed themselves back several rows of five-man groups among the fifteen hundred prisoners who slowly started up the stairs. The mandatory shouting and swinging of the whips by the guards

377

started with the first step on the stairs. "Schell!" Burned the air. "SCHNELL! SCHNELL! (FASTER! FASTER!)" Echoed over the stairs. At the fiftieth step the whipping became more aggressive. The dogs sensed the manic energy from their handlers, and barked more and pulled at their leashes. A wide-eyed SS guard picked a random prisoner that somehow caught his attention and hounded him for several stairs until a guard higher up took over the task trying to force him to make a mistake. The other human mules sensed the danger as they moved quicker to get through the gauntlet and make it to the carts at the top of the stairs. Like yellow jacket bees around a piece of meat, the guards directed their attacks at a selected prisoner. At step 125 the prisoner made his mistake.

The rubber hose swung by one guard came down on his back, and that made him drop his stone down in front of him. The German guard yelled and beat the man and pointed to the small stone he was carrying and made him pick it up. The guard yelled at a Kapo, who took a larger stone that was stacked on the hillside and brought it over to the prisoner and dropped it on top of the first stone. The sudden added weight made the prisoner lean backwards and crumble to the ground. As he went down, the top stone slid back into his face causing him to drop both of them as he cried out in pain from the injury to his nose and mouth. This enraged the SS guard, who beat the prisoner while he was down protecting his face with his hands. The prisoner, desperate to avoid the blows, tried to get away by running. That earned him a bullet that knocked him sideways off the cliff and onto the jagged rocks at the bottom. For a brief moment, there was silence as he fell, and the shot's echo reverberated through the quarry. The only noise was that of the barking dogs. Then the guards started to look for their next victim.

The American looked stunned, turned to Staszek, and said, "Thanks." The prisoner who'd just been killed was the one who'd picked up the smaller stone that had been the American's first choice. The new man's effort to beat the system cost him his life. The American was in shock for most of the rest of the afternoon. As they stood for another load he asked, "What's your name? I'm Hank." He asked many questions of Staszek, and learned many tips that would help him stay alive in the quarry. As Staszek learned from those before him, he shared what he could with the newest slaves on the Stairs of Death. The American looked to Staszek as an interpreter for orders, so he kept close to him. More than once, knowing what to do when ordered to do it saved his life.

During the last week in March and the first week in April, changes were in the air. The weather was becoming milder, with rain soaking everything and everybody, but the work was unchanged, If anything, it had become more intense. Curiously, the camp laundry was no longer in operation after the 5th of April, and the prisoners were not only in rags, but filthy infection-carrying rags.

Staszek's new friend, Hank, was assigned to a different barracks, the one where Wart was assigned, but Hank would share time at lunch or after work talking with Staszek when the opportunity allowed. Staszek liked to practice his English, and the American, who did not speak German, would get information and tips about what the guards would say or do. Staszek had Wart and another fellow Scout in the barracks with the American keep an eye out for him. When Staszek functioned as an interpreter for the American to communicate with his barrack's Kapo, "Arnold," it usually earned him a swat from Arnold's stick for being a "nosey person." Arnold was a "Red," or political prisoner, Kapo. Unlike his "Green" counterpart Kapos, who were known criminals, Arnold did not hit Staszek hard, knowing that his work was easier when the American knew what was expected of him. Still he had to show the prisoner who was boss. Arnold was an opportunist, and would make things easy for himself, even if bending the rules was necessary. There were more and more Red Kapos taking over duties of the Greens, who were leaving the camp for some reason.

During this time the Scout group merged with a Polish Resistance group in the camp. Not unlike the French, Dutch, and Russians, they were trying to watch out for their own people any way they could. By being part of a larger group, the Scouts had more shared information, which gave them an advantage in learning about problems that were developing or gossip that needed filtering. It was clear that things were happening at a faster speed towards the end of April. Vigilance was indeed needed, since the reasons for the changes were unclear. While sitting in a tight circle on the ground, Wart told the group that many of the new prisoners were being sent immediately to "the showers." The showers, in this connotation, meant the gas chamber below the infirmary. Hundreds were being sent there each day.

Staszek and a dozen more in the group that worked in the quarry said that the guards were attacking the men on the stairs sooner and harder than before. Death was waiting on each step, at each station, and with each guard. There was no respite for the quarry workers. An ominous air hung over the group. The unknown worked its silent terror on each prisoner's mind slowly, insidiously.

Another group member added that the younger SS guards were being moved out of the camp and being replaced with older soldiers, some with visible injures. There were also guards coming from the Vienna Police Department as replacements.

Still another member said that the Kapo in his barracks said that he was offered a commission in the German Army if he wanted to leave the camp. "He decided to stay, since he didn't like to walk much anyway, and the Army did not sound like a good idea to him." Then the member added, "That pig is a disgusting murderous asshole, but he is not stupid." Those who knew the Kapo nodded slowly in agreement.

Wart coughed, and this time he produced greenish-brown and red sputum that fell onto his chest. Embarrassed at what he coughed up he tried to joke, "Damn I bet that will stain my shirt." The nervous laugh of his friends tried to cover their sadness at the meaning of the symptoms.

The Scout leader continued, "At this time, with the first sign of anything unusual happening, pass the information through the network." He added, "If any of the sons of bitches guards leave the camp, make sure that their names are in the journals. Those who have copies, check your list with those of the other scribes regularly as you add names to it." Staszek was one of the scribes who had a copy of the names and he was determined to make sure that his list would survive long enough to be placed in the hands of the Allies. At least six members also had lists, knowing that some of them might not stay alive long enough to share them so copies were passed to new Scouts as the demand was made. Staszek had his rolled up and hidden in one of the hems of his shirt. He nodded, and looked at one of the other contacts who nodded back when lists had to be compared.

April 27th started with the typical roll call and two repeats of the counting of the prisoners before going to the quarry. The prisoners were marched to the bottom of the steps but, unlike most days, prisoners were sorted at the foot of the stairs. Jews and non-Jews were grouped separately. Staszek looked around and noticed that there were many more guards on the stairs than usual. There were also more at the top at the edge of the cliff that was called the "parachutist drop". This highest point on the rim of the quarry was where the guards either pushed prisoners off to their deaths or had prisoners fight until one managed to push the other off. The victor often was thrown off the cliff by the guards afterwards, to watch him claw at the air like a parachutist climbing his shrouds.

Staszek and Hank's group were placed at the back of the Jewish prisoners. All the Jewish prisoners, as singled out by the Star of David sewn on their shirts, followed through with the routine of carrying their stones to the top. This time, when they deposited their burden in the cart they were herded to the edge of the cliff into five rows facing the edge. Each prisoner entered the lines behind the man before him until the line was packed tight from the edge of the cliff back to the cart. Everyone knew this was not a good thing, but did not know what the diabolical sadists had planned. Then it started.

The dogs were turned loose on the lined-up men who had their backs to the dogs. Some dogs were trained to bite at legs while others were trained to jump onto the back of a prisoner and bite their necks. The onslaught of dogs panicked everyone except the guards, who were much amused by the instant chaos of the event. Men immediately tried to get away from the dogs coming from behind and that pushed those in front towards and off the cliff's edge. The screams of the men who were suddenly airborne filled the air. Pushing and fighting while trying to get away from the dogs as well as the cliff made a scene of fast-boiling humanity that was instantly consumed by terror and conflict between two hopeless situations. In a matter of minutes three hundred men were bleeding to death or had been crushed to death on the rocks below.

Those left on the stairs, including Staszek and Hank, were caught in the avalanche of men and stones scattered when the dogs attacked. Staszek and Hank dropped their loads and started to climb quickly past the dogs and scrambling men up to the unloading area. As they approached the cart, more guards were above them whipping those who got there without their stones. Staszek yelled, "Pick up a rock!" Hank found one, as did Staszek, before they continued forwards toward the cart. Together they got to the rail cart to deposit their load but as Hank raised his stone he lost control of it and dropped it sideways, missing the cart but not the Kapo that it rolled into.

Staszek got his stone into the cart in time to see the enraged Kapo start to beat Hank. A SS guard turned around to join the beating, using the butt of his rifle. As he was about to strike Hank over the head with it, Staszek impulsively yelled, "Nein!"(NO!") and put out his hand to stop the blow that would have easily fractured Hank's skull. The guard turned at the outburst and snapped the rifle butt sideways hitting Staszek squarely in the mouth. The impact dropped him to his knees and then onto his side, as he covered his bloody face with his hands. His lips were severely cut and his front incisors and canines, both upper and lowers, were shattered. He was stunned, and tried to stand up but fell again from his disorientation after the blow. Other prisoners coming up the path without their stones made the two assailants turn on them, thus giving time for Hank to recover enough from his blows to see Staszek on the ground. Hank stood and helped Staszek to his feet, and they went up the hill, where many surviving prisoners stood or lay with the other injured. The guards in this area ordered them to head for the infirmary, adding inexplicably that this was "Jew Week to celebrate the Führer's birthday on the 20th." Without question, the walking wounded helped each other into the camp and to the infirmary for evaluation. Hank and a Scout helped Staszek get to the quasi-safety of the hospital.

The infirmary was already full of sick and dying prisoners, triaged according to their new injures, namely by bleeding, fractures, and consciousness. The bleeders were given rags to apply pressure to the areas. Broken bones were reduced by having a helper hold the person down while the doctor or skilled bystander pulled and set the bone the best they could. If it did not hold or was too unstable they would try once more. After that they had others to attend to. The unconscious could wait, because, "They do not know the difference anyway".

The infirmary was a huge and gloomy ward, with beds crammed with the soon to be dead, who moaned through their suffering until they were too exhausted to make a noise, the silence heralding the end of their misery. There were nearly eight hundred in the space designed for three hundred and fifty. Only one prisoner doctor was in the ward for the sick and dying, while the occasional SS physicians would come for special reasons, such as medical interest for experimentation. Then what was left waited for Dr. Ramsuer.

Staszek fit into the first group, with the massive amount of blood covering him. He was given a rag and a place on the floor to sit while applying pressure. Hank had to leave the building since he'd escaped serious injury and had to return to the quarry. The doctor came back to Staszek sometime later and examined his mouth where he found the fractured teeth to be totally destroyed. There was an SS dentist in the infirmary whose main purpose was to examine prisoner's teeth to determine if there was gold in them. When found, those teeth were extracted after the prisoner was shot while escaping. For quick and easy identification, the dentist usually placed an "X" on their sternum with an ink pen on those with gold teeth. The dentist was called over to examine Staszek.

The dentist casually took a probe and simply stuck it into the centers of the each broken tooth, with Staszek writhing in pain as the electric shock of metal on a bare nerve exploded in his face and head as each tooth was slowly explored. A piece of wood was pushed between his molars kept him from biting down on the dentist while a male nurse held his head firmly. The bright light used to illuminate the oral field was dim compared to the flashing lights of pain that Staszek saw from behind his eyes. The dentist completed the examination and stated simply, "All the incisors are destroyed and there is nothing else of interest there." Meaning he wasn't going to do anything else, and that there was no gold in Staszek's mouth. The dentist told the nurse to get some gauze and make a cylinder from it about six centimeters long, soak it in medical alcohol then pack it into the teeth to kill the exposed nerves and let any infection drain. When placed into his mouth and told to bite into it, the jolt of pain made Staszek lurch up against the restraint placed on him by the nurses. One of the male nurses reached for a claquette and struck Staszek squarely on the top of his head. That form of anesthetic mercifully knocked him out.

Looking at the unconscious figure being hoisted back up onto the table, the dentist paused and told the nurse, "Call Dr. Von Stutt down in the village. He's been asking about subjects to practice his implant techniques. He could practice on him." With that, the dentist casually wiped his hands on his apron and went to the next patient to see what he could find.

When Staszek came to consciousness, his face was swollen and throbbed intensely. Crusted blood was on his lips, cheeks, and down his neck and shirt. He was offered some water to rinse his mouth by one of the infirmary's prisoner aides. Staszek tried to rinse but the water spilled out of his mouth because he could not seal his fat irregular lips. What water came out was bloody with small clots. Staszek was kept in the infirmary overnight, where he shared a bed with a prisoner who'd had his thigh and knee crushed by a falling stone that same day. The moaning from the man kept Staszek awake for some time. In the middle of the night, in quiet moments between episodes of his own pain and that of his bed-mate, Staszek was sure that he could hear muffled screams and the sounds of pounding coming from below him. The screams lasted for several minutes, as did the pounding of many hands on the walls coming up from the floor before the moaning stopped. Staszek's fatigue lulled him into the sleep of an exhausted man. What he did not know was that there was an additional gas chamber that held 150 people, was actually built below the infirmary and the Germans were working it during the day and into the still of the night.

The next morning Staszek awoke when his bed was jostled. Apparently the man next to him had died during the night from a hemorrhage in the thigh, and was being removed. The dead count for the night numbered into the dozens.

After using the toilet and receiving soup that was salty and stung his lips, Staszek waited for the doctor. Shortly thereafter, the doctor, who was a prisoner himself, said, "Dr. Von Stutt will be here tomorrow to evaluate the extent of your injury. He is a local dentist who happens to be an expert on facial injuries and reconstruction. He has a special interest in prosthetic teeth. He will tell you what he can do. Until then you are to help the aides with the other patients." Staszek was surprised, but also devastated at the information. First that he might get a real dentist to look at him, but also that the odds were good that nothing would be done and he would either be worked or starved to death soon. Neither option was good, and both were a real possibility. He worked the remainder of the day, cleaning the beds of the bedbound patients and moving bodies of the dead down the stairs to the Krematorium for disposal. The words of the Kapo on the stairs when he arrived gripped him, as the prophecy seemed to be coming true. "...You will only leave through the chimney." The thought of the flames in the oven chilled him to the bone.

The exertion from two days before, as well as the lack of food, made him feel exhausted. His instinct was to run and hide while healing, but his feet ached and his legs were like rubber. He could not hide in the ocean of lost souls that were watched by hundreds of hateful eyes. He tried to think of a plan, but his face and head felt like they could not hold a cohesive thought. *"May God help me. Holy Mother of God, give me strength,"* had been a prayer that he had repeated in the past, and now was calling on it again to make it through the rest of the day and to give him peace.

After the afternoon roll call, Wart came into the infirmary on a stretcher. He was very pale and confused. The doctor looked at him and told Staszek to get him some water, and to make sure he drank it. He was placed on a bed and Staszek brought him a metal bowl with some water. While holding Wart's head up he said, "Wart, drink this." The words were slurred by his swollen lips, so he tried again and pressed the bowl to Wart's mouth. Slowly Wart started to swallow but he coughed weakly several times. After 30 minutes, Wart finished the bowl of water. Staszek returned to Wart's bed as often as he could to rehydrate him.

Just before the evening roll call, Staszek was called to the doctor's desk where a small man, about 45 years old and holding a black bag, was waiting. This was Dr. Von Stutt. Staszek looked at the compassionate-looking face and bowed slightly from the waist as a sign of respect.

Staszek was sat down in a chair while the dentist set out some instruments and positioned a light to see into the mouth. Without saying a word, he examined Staszek with obvious skill and care. He looked at the damage and said, in German, "The lips are lacerated, but will heal without problem. There are some indications that there are some fractures of the maxillary arch, but not the mandible." Looking and prodding with an instrument, he sighed, "The incisors and two of the canines are not salvageable." Staszek's heart sank even more. After a little more time, the dentist placed the instruments back into his bag and sat down next to Staszek. There was a long pause as he looked around to see if anyone was listening. Not seeing anyone, he explained, "This is a terrible injury. Did you get hit with a pipe or the butt of a rifle?"

"Rifle," Staszek slurred slightly, first in Polish then in German.

Slightly surprised, the dentist said, "Yes I can see that to be true," in German. Then in Polish he said, "If this was a different time and different place I think I could replace your teeth with some porcelain implants at my office here in Mauthausen. A group of us were working on the technique at the University in Vienna for some time now with excellent results. But with the way the war is going there isn't any hope to be able to do anything for you. You should leave the teeth as they are to allow any infection to drain out. I can pull the broken roots out, but that will be about all. Otherwise they'll become infected and the pain will be unbearable."

Staszek said, "Your Polish is very good."

The dentist bowed slightly to Staszek, and said, "My mother was

Polish, and I went to dental school in Warszawa before Vienna. It would be wise to keep that information to yourself."

Staszek nodded, and then with some relief but also some hesitancy, "I had an alcohol-soaked sponge placed on my teeth, I don't…"

The dentist said, "I brought some Novocain that I use on the SS officers when they come to see me. They won't miss it. That should allow us to do the work now."

Staszek agreed, not wanting to chance the infection, and knowing that he would not have a better opportunity for expert care than now.

The procedure took about an hour, but it was done expertly and thoroughly, down to some stitches that closed the biggest wound.

When he was done, the dentist said, "I wish I could have done more. You are a good candidate for the prosthetics."

Staszek tried to smile but the anesthetic was wearing off and the throbbing was returning. "Thank you," was all he could say.

The dentist, understanding the situation, closed his bag, turned and walked away. As he got to the door the prison doctor was returning. The dentist said, pointing to Staszek, "He is no use to me so he can return to work in a day." He left the building without looking back.

Staszek returned to his bed and sat down next to a new patient who was occupying the other side. The man was not moaning, just shivering. Staszek stared at the door and thought how strange that out of nowhere in this wasteland of evil there was a glow of humanity in a little man. The spontaneous thought, *God heard me*, warmed him, and he started to cry. So that no one would notice he turned, covered the shivering man, and walked back to Wart's bed. When the evening soup arrived, Staszek got his and sat down with it next to Wart. Thinking, *He now needs the food more than me*, Staszek slowly fed him a sip at a time and sat there the rest of the night giving him water whenever he became more aroused. Whatever solid food was at the bottom of the bowl Staszek crushed with his fingers and placed it into Wart's mouth to swallow. He was lucky; today there were four chunks of something in the bowl. By morning, Wart was looking around and recognized Flame and smiled. Together, they were able to get the morning portions that would make them live another day for service to the Germans.

After morning roll call, Staszek was released to his barracks, along with Wart, who went to his. Staszek arrived just as the new Kapos and the barracks Kapo were rousting the remainder of the sickly men out of the barracks to their jobs. The Kapo was the same one who made the frail man eat the jam that killed him a couple of months ago. He had a sadistic manner that would expose itself suddenly with no apparent provocation; then he would be unflustered at other times, making him an unknown quantity and therefore even more dangerous. When the barracks Kapo saw Staszek, he said, "You have been ordered to report to Barracks 20."

"Barracks 20? Why?" The terror had returned and the feeling of being powerless came to a crescendo. "That is the death hut. I was working in the quarry I can still do the work. Why 20?" Staszek pleaded his case through swollen lips and missing teeth.

The Kapo shrugged, "I don't know why, and I don't care. As far as I'm concerned, you are on this list, so what do you expect from me? Look at yourself. You won't be able to eat, and if you don't eat you can't work, and if you can't work you are no good to us. So now you can dig graves."

Staszek, in a moment of sheer desperation lashed out with a fist that landed on the Kapo's chin, which earned him a club to his back from the other, and a boot to his stomach from the first that sent him down onto his knees. Gently touching his chin and laughing at the lack of damage, the Kapo ordered "Get over to 20 for Last Patrol duty. Make yourself useful while you can." The Kapo called to the newer Kapo and ordered him "Escort this Polish tick from my ass to Hut 20. Make sure he makes it there or dies trying." That seemed to amuse the barracks Kapo, as he laughed at his own sick joke. He waved them towards the door, scratching his chin slightly.

In a daze, Staszek walked in an unsteady line, pulled by the arm. His balance made him drift from one side to another, almost numb from what was happening to him. His head was still thick from the swelling in his face and he had a pounding pain behind his face and from the bruise on the top of his shaved baldhead. Once he got to Hut 20 he was placed in line with about 200 other weak and dying men. His thoughts were of his mother and family. He started to apologize to them for not being stronger and fighting back at this dark time, but he was so frightened, tired, hungry and drained, he was becoming reconciled to this last job as a condemned man.

A shaved head, pasty white skin covered in sores, and a mouth that is swollen with black and blue lips; a condemned man, he mused. The barking dogs broke his chain of thought as they danced on their short leashes. Standing there, he did not exhibit a look of health in any sense of the word. So he was going to die today. If not, then probably tomorrow if he did not do something soon.

He stood at one end of a line while the roll was taken again. He was only a couple of rows from the back of the group, and could see an ocean of bald heads like his, their ears sticking out disproportionately to the size to their naked, dirty heads. Most of the heads were hung down and swaying slightly, lost in their trance-like state, holding visions of what death would be like. However, with the long wait Staszek's head began to clear. He started to look around and calculate how far he could get if he made a break for freedom. *"Maybe a hundred meters?"* He estimated the open area he would have to cover; then focused on the dogs. Guards with rifles stood at each end of every tenth row. Every third guard had a dog that looked hungry. The NCO walked behind his two corporals, who checked off names of each person in each row. Staszek looked up at the watchtower nearby. That guard seemed to be looking at him, just like the guards and the dogs on the side of the group were. *"Maybe ten meters if I was fast,"* he recalculated, more realistically. "Maybe if I hold still when the gate opens, they'll walk off without me." He knew that he was now becoming delusional or careless. He decided that it was the latter. He had to get serious. His only chance now would be once they were outside and into the forest. He knew forests, and he had to plan for that. His sense of immediate danger was coming up, and he no longer felt hopeless as his brain went into survival mode once more. He would die fighting in the forest and not go passively to his death. The vision of *the fox that would again beat the hounds in the forest* stirred in his memory.

He watched the soldiers go to each person to confirm their identification. Up through the rows, they worked carefully and methodically. The sergeant who seemed to be in charge was in a heavy Eastern Front overcoat, steel helmet, and his machine gun hung under his arm. He walked behind the other two showing a moderate limp. The helmet's shadow shielded part of his face allowing only his tense lips to be seen. It looked like he meant business and was keeping things in order. *Just a replacement soldier from Russia, here to free up the younger guards to fight for Hitler,* Staszek guessed. From a distance, he watched the soldier guards move through the lines to make sure they had who they thought they did on their list. *After all, when the Germans write down that you were shot while escaping, they should at least have the right body to go with the name.* Staszek's sarcasm and black humor started to blossom along with a feeling that was strangely melancholy, or more likely the case, he was in extreme shock at being in a hopeless position that guaranteed his death.

When his turn came he answered the questions about name and number that were checked off the list. When the roll-takers passed, Staszek relaxed a little and looked to the right where the two guards were turning a corner and going behind him to the next row. From his left side came a shrill voice yelling, "Are you Niklewicz?"

Startled, Staszek turned his head towards the sergeant and started to nod when the stock of the machine gun slammed up into his stomach doubling him over and knocking him sideways onto the ground. The sergeant came up to him and kicked him, taking his breath away. A moment later the stock of the gun came down on his ribs but not nearly with the same force as the first strike. From above him the voice yelled again, "Are you Niklewicz?"

From the ground Staszek nodded as he tried to get the words, "Ja, Ja" out at the same time he brought his knees up to protect his stomach and his arms went up to over his bare scalp in a fetal position. His right hand splashed into a mud puddle as he fell and mud went into his mouth and right ear. He did not know what he had done this time, or if this was just the Germans being German. In either case, he was helpless. All his energy that was building a moment ago was suddenly knocked out of him and he felt drained. His plans for possible escape in the forest had evaporated with this attack; he had no ability to fight back now- he was almost frozen in pain. On the ground he was trapped with no fight left; he was spent and his last piece of energy left him. This was the end. He was almost broken.

The soldier shook Staszek's shoulder violently and hit him once more with the butt of the gun. Once again the impact was firm, but not destructive. *How many more times? How much longer?* Staszek thought. He waited for another blow and hoped that it would end this misery now. But rage also entered his thoughts that rejuvenated him slightly, "I won't die here." He heard himself say. He decided that if he got up and ran, the guard in the tower would end this fight and he would at least die a man on his feet rather than on the ground like a bug. He started to roll over to fight or run; the time was now to die, and he would be the one who would decide how!

He started to press himself up off the dirt, when the soldier kneeled down on Staszek's back with most of his body weight, crushing him back into the mud and stopping him from moving away, effectively pinning him face down. Staszek using what strength he could draw from pushed up hard and started to move the sergeant when all of the soldier's weight finally ended the effort to move. From above, the voice ordered, "Corporal take over the patrol. I am taking this man in for questioning."

"Ja wohl," The corporal responded.

The sergeant steadied his weight on Staszek as he once more tried to push up onto his elbows. At his maximum effort he began to lift the body on top of him, the sergeant lowered his face closer to Staszek's head, and said in whispered Polish, "Stay down Stas, it's me Kurt." Stunned, Staszek froze for a couple of seconds when the words seemed to sink in, Kurt felt Staszek relax, and he stood and kicked at Staszek again and ordered, "Get up you pig's ass." Slowly Staszek got up on his hands and knees and finally onto his feet. Once up, he was shoved forward and almost fell but caught his footing. Behind him, the 200 men minus one were walking out the gate to the forest to dig their own grave.

When they were out of sight from the Hut 20 Patrol and the other guards, Kurt pulled Staszek in between a couple of the barracks. "Sorry I hit you so hard, but I had to make it look real." Then after looking closely at his childhood friend he added, "You look like shit."

Staszek, confused but overjoyed, smiled his toothless grin at his old friend as he spit some of the mud out of his mouth, and said in German, "It certainly seemed real to me. As for my looks, thank your friends." The words were spoken in a pointed tone of voice. Kurt did not say anything and Staszek for a moment was sorry that he did.

Looking side to side Kurt pushed his helmet higher on his head to expose his face and added, "Listen, we don't have much time. I saw your name on the infirmary roll call and needed to get you away from the quarry." He paused and looked around. "There will be many more dead there by tomorrow and getting you to my detail at Hut 20 was the only way to do it."

Staszek was speechless at the turn of events and what he was hearing from Kurt.

Kurt continued, "So I'll take you to the infirmary and tell them that I want you there until I can investigate a problem with your records and I will question you further. The administration office is flooded with Gestapo dossiers on the prisoners. Checking records is a common problem. They should leave you alone for a day or so. After that, you're on your own until the Americans come."

"Americans? What are you talking about?" Staszek asked in complete bewilderment.

"The war is almost over. The Americans are no more than a 100 km from here, but the Russians are only 70 km away. Who gets here first is anyone's guess," Kurt said, with complete candor. "All the regular soldiers will be moved out in the next couple of days; no later than the 3rd, with more Austrian Police and new Kapos replacing us to run the camp. Just hold out for two to three more days and I think that will be an end to all of this." Kurt waved his hand towards the rest of the camp while never taking his eyes off of Staszek.

Staszek was overwhelmed at the news and had more questions than Kurt could or would answer. "Listen Stas, there are Red Cross boxes of food meant for the French in the garage storage area. The French prisoners have already gotten one each and the rest are being stored for use by the SS. Get to them if you can."

Staszek was angry again, thinking that the Germans were stealing the Red Cross boxes from the starving prisoners. Even if they were for only the French, at least some prisoners were getting parcels.

Kurt stated, "There aren't enough vehicles or time to take all the parcels with us when we pull out tomorrow. I was ordered here just this week to clean up problem areas, loose ends, and organize the newer guards, but it looks like I'll be leaving with the rest in the morning." Kurt looked around to see if anyone could see them. "Be careful, and do not stay in the infirmary longer than a second day. There is a contingency order to kill as many prisoners as possible and the infirmary and groups of the sick are the easiest places to do it quickly. They will be stacking the dead for the Krematorium, because the graves cannot handle the dead that are being buried outside the fences. I'm sure that if Germany loses the war, the Kapos will try to exterminate any prisoner that can testify against any of the camp guards or they will try to disappear in the night."

"Where are you going?" Staszek asked, but knew that he would not get an answer.

"Who knows? I'm just a soldier, and they're trying to hold the army together. Berlin is being bombed, and the Russians have surrounded it, if they have not already overrun it." Kurt started to breathe a little faster, feeling that he was trapped like Staszek. "I don't know what will be left of Germany, the army, or me, for that matter."

Staszek looked at his troubled friend and said, "You'd better stay away from the Russians. Once you crossed the border into Poland, it will be hard to get away from there. I know that they are killing Germans and Poles in their Gulags; no one will be able to stop them and I won't be around to save your ass this time," Staszek boasted through his thick lips but with true concern for his friend.

Kurt snapped back, "Too bad. That face would certainly scare some of them off. Of course the old face would have scared them all away." Kurt looked at the battered face of his friend. Taking Staszek's chin in his fingers and turning his face side to side he added, "You do look better without teeth," Kurt laughed and a tear came to his eye, trying to hide his fear and pain through humor. His fatigue, through years of combat into Russia and the long, slow retreat, had drained him too. Staszek put his hand on Kurt's shoulder in mutual sadness and understanding as they anguished over their futures. These two old men of only twenty years of age were crying over their plight, and renewed friendship, brief as it was, in the middle of Hell.

"Stay out of trouble, and hide if you have to. The commandant, those lunatic SS and Kapos that work here will soon be gone. Hear me, you have to make it for only a few more days. They will try to save their skins; that only means they will be more ruthless." Kurt offered in final advice. "We'd better get inside and you'd better look scared."

Staszek said, "That won't be hard." After a couple of steps he whispered over his shoulder, "Someday we will laugh and drink to the good old times."

"Ja wohl," Kurt confirmed.

With nothing more needing to be said, and the chance that they would be overheard, they became silent. Staszek turned and headed to the infirmary ahead of the sergeant and his gun.

Once inside Kurt, told the doctor at the infirmary, "Prisoner 115988 is to be placed on hospital duty for two days while I investigate his records for crimes against the Reich." The prisoner doctor on duty did not understand, but knew better than to question a sergeant of the guards, and noted the orders in the logbook. Once the doctor acknowledged the order, the sergeant turned without saying a word and limped towards the back gate.

Looking at Staszek's face and again at the orders the doctor said,

"Since there is nothing wrong with your arms and legs, you are to help the orderlies move the dead out of the unit." With that, the doctor noted the new order in the log and dismissed Staszek with a nod of his head and finger pointed in the direction of the work detail.

In short order, Staszek was lifting corpses from the places they died in the infirmary and carrying them down the stairs to the Krematorium with other workers. There, the bodies would be reduced to the ash that represented all that remained of their earthly lives. Dozens of wrists or ankles that were no more than taut skin over bones were the handles he held on to for the rest of the day. Down the steep flight of stairs, he traversed to the space outside the closed doors to the oven room where people who were finally freed from their pain were stacked like so much wood. No one was allowed into the Krematorium room or the room next to it that looked like a shower. Both places stayed a mystery, as well as the symbol of total control to most, including Staszek.

When Staszek fell asleep upstairs that night, his nightmare swirled around his vision of his body being carried by one or two other prisoners and placed on the pile below the infirmary. They dragged him down the stairs while his brain protested that he was alive, but they could not hear him. He was frozen inside a motionless body and could not force words out of its mouth even though he was screaming. He jerked to a sitting position and looked around the dim room. The light from the searchlights outside gave the room an eerie glow and confirmed with equal sadness that he was still in Mauthausen. Several patients who heard his scream looked up at him; then turned back to their own nightmares and waited for the next person to shriek their innermost terror.

The next day was the 2nd of May, and the orders had changed. Staszek and another fifty men made the cycle in and out of the building for the entire second day. This time he was given a wheelbarrow that was filled by workers who carried buckets full of ash up the stairs from the lower floor of the building. Staszek noticed that the chimney was no longer producing the smoke and fine ash that it was notorious for. His wheelbarrow detail now rolled the ash of hundreds of bodies to a mound outside the fence. Making dozens of trips throughout the day tormented him as he stared at the ash and the chunks of teeth and bone that were mixed together in his wheelbarrow. *How many do I have here? Where were they from? What did they do to end this way?* The questions were endless, and without an answer.

The task was beyond understanding, and the only way for Staszek to continue was to focus on getting out of the camp and getting even with those who did these hideous things. He was getting his confidence and focus back to living; something that he would need soon.

When he was allowed to return to the barracks he went to number Seven where Wart was assigned. The wheelbarrow job continued into the night with another group of men. There was plenty for them to do.

Staszek became concerned about possibly working at this task on the third day, since he'd been warned by Kurt not to be there after two. It was clear that the doctor did not care about the old orders, but was concerned about getting the infirmary emptied. There seemed to be an unusual amount of overly sick prisoners becoming heart attack victims that day and evening, when the chief SS doctor was on duty with his syringe and gasoline. They were being pronounced dead after the doctor examined them behind the portable curtain. The evening of the 3rd, Staszek was sent back to his barracks, where there was no meal provided to any of the men. Since mid-April, whatever portions were normally served were cut in half; now they may or may not come at all. The weakest prisoners were dying a dozen at a time in every barracks, on work details, and in the roll call area. A person could not turn or move anywhere in the camp without coming across a fresh corpse.

A meeting was called of the Polish Resistance members to debrief each other on the progression of events in the camp. When the group huddled around several bunks, the information began to come quickly from all members. Staszek was one of thirty-three men who still had the strength to fight, if necessary. This number was down from over a hundred just the month before. The members were surprised to see him back since he had been assigned to the Last Patrol March. He answered their looks with, "God didn't want me, and the Devil was afraid of me." No one asked more and the matter was what it was; luck of the most unusual kind.

The leader said, "Since Commandant Ziereis disappeared last night, a replacement stooge has taken his place. Police Captain Kern has been walking around in circles, not knowing what to do. We are in danger from the new guards, and from chaos in the camp itself. We need everyone to be ready for action. We have heard that liberation is only a couple of days away, and if that is the case the Germans may do something even more despicable than they have already. There are thousands of people who are weak and desperate, who could still try to take over control of the camp, which could cause a guard to panic and open fire on everyone in the sights of his gun. Therefore, we have to be ready to fight to survive this hellhole a little longer." Mumbling and hand gestures were moving randomly as punctuation to several simultaneous discussions. The leader continued after saying "Quiet down. We have ten pistols with extra bullets, one rifle and one automatic machine pistol, which will be assigned to those available when the order is made to strike out at our jailers." He looked around and continued, "We may not have enough weapons, but we will have enough men to overpower the dwindling number of guards." The mumbling increased, with more heads nodding and giving positive support to the idea.

Then he inserted a shocking statement to these men, "We will be ultimately responsible to General Urioff, who will give the orders to take over our barracks," this immediately produced a rumble from the men when they heard that a Russian would be in charge of them. Before the discussion got out of hand the leader roared, "SILENCE!" Members immediately looked toward the door to see if any Kapos were coming in. "This is not open for debate. No matter what resentment we have towards the Soviets, at this time we are few in number, and the need to succeed is paramount. We WILL work as a team. We will also continue using codenames as we have for last couple of months for any specific orders to avoid anyone of us to be plucked from the group because of any leaks in the network."

A voice asked, "What other weapons do we have?"

Another voice, "How long do we need to hold out?"

Still another, "What about getting food? I heard that there are Red Cross parcels stored."

The leader acknowledged the nervousness in the questions and calmed them. "The person that can answer those questions better than me is General Urioff. General would you talk to the men?" From the back of the group, a man in his 40's dressed in the gray and blue striped jacket worked his way to the front of the group and looked the men over. Most were stunned to see a high-ranking Russian alive, let alone one in their hut.

The general started with, "If we have to choke the bastards with our bare hands we will do it. We will overpower those we can, and take their clubs and sticks. We will fight with anything we can get. Comrades, we have waited six long years to do this, and it is nearing that time." The men agreed with the statement with a rumble of, "Yes we will."

"Live a prisoner or die a free man."

"For Poland!"

The determination of the men grew.

Staszek held up his empty steel bowl and pulled a claquette from the foot of the man sitting on a bunk above and next to him then shook it in the air as he pronounced, "We can use even these to overpower the Kapos. Then we can take their weapons." He was painfully aware how the claquette had knocked him out several days ago. The man, who Staszek took the shoe from, jerked it back and replaced it on his foot. Several of the men took off their claquettes and shook them in the air, suddenly aware that they were in fact, armed.

The general continued, "We don't know when liberation will come, but we will be prepared. When the time is right, the orders will be spread. Until that time, keep your eyes and ears open, and let your Scout leader know what you find as soon as you can. Stay in groups, protect each other, and we will survive this challenge." The brief message resonated with the men and they became less agitated and more hopeful.

Shortly thereafter General Urioff and the Scout leader came by and shook the hand of each Pole in the barrack. The Poles used their codenames, as had been decided earlier. When they got to Flame he stood and shook his hand while giving his codename. Flame was identified by the Scout leader as one of the interpreters, and one of the members who had the list of names of the enemies of humanity, and that he was from Łódź. The general talked to Flame for a while, about what would be expected of him and the rest of the members. Flame was very uncomfortable to the point of wanting to defy the Russian leader, but he respected orders if not the man, so he would do what was needed. As they moved to the next man, Flame looked around and asked, "Where is Wart?"

One voice said, "He was sent over to the infirmary a little while ago."

Staszek stood up suddenly, "Why?"

The other prisoner said, "The Kapo ordered it because Wart has the lung sickness that makes his breathing difficult and that irritated the Kapo, so they sent him away."

Staszek told the group, "I was told that they will start eliminating the sick in the infirmary when liberation is near. I am going after Wart."

When he got to the infirmary Staszek told the nurse, "I have come for..." Staszek paused. He did not want to use the codename Wart but he did not know for sure his prisoner number. Then it came to him, "103,741- Karol Iwanczyk."

The male nurse, being alone and overwhelmed by the sheer number of beds and dying prisoners, pointed to a bed several rows in.

Staszek went to Wart and said, "Karol I am going to take you with me."

Wart coughed, and then coughed several more times before acknowledging his friend. He nodded and reached up, gesturing his need for assistance to get out of the bed. "Get me out of here," Wart begged. Without hesitation Flame pulled Wart's arm over his neck and shoulder to lift him up. As Flame struggled to get Wart on to his feet, something that was taking all the strength they both had, a hospital aide came over and helped him onto his feet. Once up and steady the aide whispered to Flame, "You must get him out of here and not return. Now it is time to 'Be Vigilant'."

Flame said to Wart, "You are coming with me. Do you think you can sleep here all day over here? We have things to do." Wart rolled his eyes at him and used his remaining strength to walk out of the infirmary. Flame took the message as the warning it was and nodded to the aide, then pressed on, "Let's go."

Wart took steps as he could, but his breathing was very labored. With Flame helping, he developed the energy to walk away from his deathbed. With effort, the two made it to Flame's barracks and his bunk. The Kapo came over, and in a loud voice bellowed as he saw the two figures head for the bunk, "Are you collecting corpses? He is not one of mine." Then he saw that it was Staszek, who was carrying him, and recognized him as the one that had punched him three days before and said, "And you, what are you doing here? They sent you out of the wire."

"And then they sent me back to do this work, so here I am," Flame snapped at the puzzled Kapo. "If you don't like it take it up with the sergeant of the guard who is in charge. I'm sure that he has nothing better to do than answer your questions."

The Kapo, knowing everyone was on edge, did not want to be conspicuous, so he said, "When he dies, you take him out of here. I don't like litter in my hut." He turned and walked to the next bunk and yelled at those who were there. One of the other Scouts saw Flame and Wart coming back and snuck into the Kapo's quarters and brought out some black bread and a can of milk. The can had French words on it. He opened it, poured the milk on the bread, and handed it to Wart.

Wart took the bread and sucked on it. The other Scout smiled and said, "The son-of-a-bitch Kapo has a dozen tins of things in his locker; he won't miss these." Flame nodded to him, and said, "There is more of that in the garage. We have to get some for all of us." The Scout agreed, and said that he'll talk to the Scouts in the administration office and see what they could do to help liberate the boxes.

As morning broke on the 4th, roll call was held, but most prisoners did not come to the assembly area. Most had huddled all night in groups of nationalities or work units, finding strength and security in numbers for the first time. They slept in shifts and started to break into the lockers that the Kapos controlled. The Kapos, for the most part, started to leave and hide among their remaining German handlers. Some regrouped with armed guards to retake key barracks or buildings, and regain their ill-gotten loot. General Urioff gave the order to break out the weapons, but rather than giving them to the Poles, he distributed them to his Russian troops in Barracks Twenty.

Most of the prisoners in Barracks Seven who could walk and had adequate strength, headed for the garage to find the Red Cross boxes. Others sought vengeance and began attacking Kapos and other guards who were isolated or in small groups. The sicker men stayed in the barracks near the stoves for warmth and the protection of larger numbers. Flame stayed with Wart in one of the corner bunks, away from the door. He was going to wait it out. Like Kurt said, he'd made it this long; he would have to survive a little longer.

"Flame, I hope we are not liberated by the Russians. I don't want to die a prisoner of another slave master. I did not live a year here to be turned over to the Russians." Wart stated with passion and fear in his wobbling voice.

Flame replied, "Me too, Wart. We have to hope for the Americans. It's our only way to see Poland free again." Seeing his friend's apprehension grow he said, "You and I will walk out those gates, and we'll get the biggest beef roast with more potatoes and butter than we have ever dreamed of." Wart smiled at the thought. Flame continued, "We'll make those sons of bitches serve US! Then they'll put us in their staff cars and drive us home after finding some great Polish Vodka and beautiful Polish women to keep us happy and singing songs all day and night."

Wart, leaning against the wall, smiled and said, "Singing songs for only part of the night if there are women with us." Both laughed at the innuendo. "Flame, what do you think, blondes or brunettes?"

Before Flame could answer there were shouts from the door where several Kapos burst through the door swinging their longer heavy clubs and sand-filled hoses, striking at anyone and everyone in reach. Leading them was the bastard who was the barracks Kapo, who carried a club and a bayonet that he used expertly. The groups on the floor and on the bunks for the most part were too weak to move and were easily broken with the impact of the weapons, as the Kapo wreak his anger on those around him.

The thirty or more mobile prisoners responded to the invasion with shouts of warning and rage. Instantly one of the Kapos was tripped and fell in a heap, which allowed him to be swarmed by a dozen boney men who fought like lions as they spent their pent-up fury in a hail of fists, elbows and claquettes. The two other Kapos advanced to the center of the group and crushed the backs and heads of many in a matter of seconds as they forded the sea of breathing skeletons, swinging their weapons and stepping on as many as they could, but to their surprise, the once-timid slaves of the barrack soon overwhelmed them. Their clubs were twisted away and quickly used on them.

In front was the bastard Kapo of the barracks, and he looked like a man possessed as he ignored the killing of his cohorts. He continued to wade through those who were in arm's reach. He killed or threw off the men trying but failing to overpower him with the immense strength he had in each arm. Like a windmill swinging side to side he slaughtered each man with ease.

Flame, who saw the advancing Kapo decimating the men in front of him with his bayonet, scanned the room for options and a weapon. Wart wrapped a blanket around his left arm to be used as a shield if the Kapo with the blade reached him. This Kapo who was the most vicious of all wheeled his blade and baton with deadly accuracy as he sliced and crushed men in front of him. With a mighty crack he collapsed a man who as he fell gave the Kapo a clear path to Wart and Flame.

Flame, being next to the looted locker that belonged to the Kapo, found himself quickly becoming the target in the Kapo's eyes. The bayonet and club cut a path straight for Wart and Flame with nothing between them. Screams and yells filled the building as the floor started to turn red. Desperately looking for anything that could be used as a weapon, Flame spotted the extinguisher next to the stove. Flame lunged towards the fire extinguisher and picked it up to use it just in time as a shield against the club and knife, deflecting a strike from each of the Kapo's hands. Flame was able to block the blow from the club with the canister but he was knocked backwards by the impact. The next swing of the blade went towards Wart, who had the blanket sliced off his arm in one stroke and was about to be clubbed by the other hand when Flame inverted the bottle and sprayed the chemical solution on the chest and face of the murderer. The liquid stung the Kapo's eyes, forcing his arms up and stopping him in his tracks. That was enough time for six more men who had initially moved away from the onslaught to return and jump on the Kapo. One of the men suddenly twisted the bayonet from the Kapo's hand and plunged it into his chest. Only a gasp and the sound of the bayonet's point hitting the floor hard through the Kapo's chest was needed to silence the barracks. Those who had been holding him down saw that he was finished. They melted to the floor, totally consumed from the effort that demanded nearly all their strength. One wide-eyed man looked up from the corpse of the Kapo to those around him and smiled in victory. The smiled lasted for only a moment or two before he closed his eyes and died next to his tormentor, no longer his victim.

Back in the corner Wart had watched Flame get up from the floor and rolling the cylinder away before he returned to the bunk next to Wart. Both were shaking and breathing hard. After what seemed like an hour, the exhausted prisoners who were uninjured started to attend to those who were still alive but wounded, while others moved the dead onto bunks.

The Kapos were carried outside and dumped between the buildings, and covered with blankets and debris to hide the bodies. For the rest of May 4th, the men in the barracks shared the food the Kapo had locked up. Others went around to other barracks to see what was happening there. Flame and another Scout went out to see what the guards and administrators were doing. Not surprisingly, they found the camp nearly empty of guards. No more than 500 were left, and they appeared to be taking extra defensive positions, but for the most part they ignored the prisoners. Though there were men in the gun towers, they did not seem to want to add to the carnage that Mauthausen personified. Many of the Russians with General Urioff had broken out of the camp and were looking for the guards and other murderers in an attempt to serve justice the Russian way, "The only good enemy is a dead one."

On the morning of the 5th, Flame and Wart were awakened by distant artillery fire that sounded like thunder. It was coming from the direction of Linz in the west. As they listened the barrage of explosions intensified. "They're coming!" Flame whispered to Wart.

Wart came up to sitting and listened intently. "Americans or Russians?" He asked.

"It is from the west, so they have to be Americans." Flame said, and the thought raised their spirits tremendously.

They left the barracks and walked slowly through the assembly area. In the distance, many sick and infirm were working their way towards the barbed wire fences to be the first to see their liberators. Some of them were literally crawling, hoping to make it to the fence. At the same time, local security guards from Vienna in the towers had begun to dismantle their guns.

Prisoners were becoming armed with weapons as they broke into lockers and buildings. Some of the younger and healthier Scouts brought tins of food that were liberated from the garage, to Flame, Wart and others. From one bag that was opened for them to take from, Flame took two tins of cigarettes and placed them into a backpack type sack that he'd made from a pair of pants. He started collecting tins, jars, and any valuables that he could liberate during his trip around the camp and buildings. Wart needed frequent rests and continued to weaken, to the point where he sat down every 10-20 steps, eventually stopping along the wall of one barracks and saying, "I need to rest here, near the gate. That way when they open the door I don't have to go too far."

Flame looked at his fading friend and said, "In no time we'll be free, and we'll get a place to live it up."

Wart smiled and said, "I can't wait." They sat on the ground for a couple of hours. They had no work to do, and no place to go. So they sat. "Blonde, or brunettes?" Wart asked again, his sunken eyes relaxed and peaceful.

"One of each the first day, and then maybe a redhead," Flame boasted. "How about you?"

Wart said, "I don't care as long as she is fat, soft and warm." They laughed and cried a little at the same time.

Just before 1:00 o'clock there was a rumbling sound outside the main gate. The prisoners who were now roaming freely in the area climbed to the top of the ramparts of the watchtower to make sure of what was out there. From over the wall they saw five tanks with WHITE stars on them. "AMERICANS!!" was the call. "AMERICANS ARE HERE!!!" The cheering and the crying started like a ripple from the top of the wall and spread to those on the ground below. A cry, and then cheers from weak, disease-laden lungs cascaded over the assembly area like a great wave pouring over a beach and embracing all who could hear or see. Flame and Wart got up and hugged each other. Flame rubbed Warts head as Wart did the same to Flame. Both were fully overwhelmed in joy.

Arms raised in triumph pumped up and down towards the sky. Prisoners embraced other prisoners while crying tears of thanks. Many others got down on their knees and prayed their thanks to God, while others, wrecked with pain, could do no more than sob in memory of those who could not see this day.

Then it became quiet again. No one had the keys to the gate, so its massive bulk was unmoved. For two more hours the tanks sat at the threshold of the camp, not willing to force the gates for fear of hurting those who would not move away from the gate and the stonewalls on either side. Everyone waited for the key.

While this was happening, from different corners of the assembly area there started a new sound, a sound of hissing, whistles, catcalls, and jeering. The sound of hate and defiance grew as groups of men pushed or dragged the Kapos who had stayed in the camp to the assembly area as the "new" prisoners of the camp. The survivors were purging the brutes from their hiding areas, and were unable to stem their hatred for these murderers. The bodies of those who were already dealt with, like those in Barracks Seven, were brought out for display. It was not long before the fear of the meek turned to the rage of the liberated, and each Kapo or guard who was hauled into the assembly area died by the fists, feet, claquettes, and stones that eventually turned the area into pools of red.

At three o'clock, the keys were found and the doors opened, allowing the tanks to roll in, stopping even more vengeance from being served. As the Americans entered, they prevented the killings of more of these criminals, or there surely would have been more than the sixty dead in the courtyard that afternoon.

Wart's breathing was very shallow and labored and made staying on his feet nearly impossible during this time. He held Flame's arm to hold himself up, and when the tanks entered the camp he said, "Help me to the gate, I want to touch an American tank."

Flame said, "Me too. Thank God it is a white star on them and not a red one." Wart nodded his agreement.

As the tanks rolled to a halt, a wave of humanity spilled onto them. The multitude of bodies each wanted to touch a tank or an American soldier that was with them. Wart and Flame worked their way to the tanks where Wart placed both hands onto the warm metal siding. He looked up to the commander sitting in the hatch, and smiled and waved to him as the warmth rushed through his body. The commander looked down at Wart's red watery eyes and broad smile, saluted him and Flame. Wart waved a frail acknowledgement to the commander then turned to Flame and said, "Let's go over there." As he gestured towards an empty area of the stonewall cut out beyond the gate. "I'm really tired."

Flame, with Wart's arm around his neck, helped his friend walk to a clear area against the wall and gently lowered him to the ground. As Wart touched the ground, he sat balanced for a brief time then lost his strength and leaned over onto Flame. Like melting wax the stiffness of Wart's body softened and he continued down as Flame lowered him onto his lap. Sitting on the ground with his legs out straight, Flame cradled Wart securely in his arms and rocked him gently. Flame just looked around at those celebrating with the GIs and to those like them on the ground who were just absorbing the significance of the moment. Flame could feel Wart's ribs through the ragged fabric of his jacket. The ribs labored with long pauses to move up and down for every breath.

A minute or two passed as Flame watched thousands of men standing or sitting all around him waiting for something to happen, though they were not sure of what that would be, and frankly it really did not matter. Flame felt tired but exhilarated, at realizing that he had lived to this moment and there was now hope for a future. It truly felt like he was being resurrected and coming to life once again.

Wart recovered slightly then turned his head to look up as he smiled gently at Flame. He said softly, "Sorry, but being a free man is hard work and I need a nap right now."

Flame's arms felt the muscle tension change in his friend and that caused a tear to well up then drop down onto Wart's face. Flame wiped away that drop and a second tear as he said in contrived joy, "Being free feels good doesn't it?"

Flame waited a long time as he stared down at the peaceful face, but Wart never answered him.

Author's Notes: Chapter 21

From January 1945 to May 5th 1945, 28,000 were killed in the main camp and its sub-camps. After the murder of 150,000 people, and now the liberation of more than 65,000 survivors, the hideous function of Mauthausen came to a close.

Mauthausen was liberated thanks to the reconnaissance party from TPD 41st Cavalry Squad from the 11th Armored Division of the American 3rd Army. Their arrival at the camp on May 5th stopped the outright slaughter of more prisoners in the camp by the remaining Germans. However, the sad state that the troops found the living prisoners was beyond belief. The spectacular visual horror of the sick and walking dead was unmatched by anything, except perhaps the repulsive, pungent smell of the death that blanketed this camp. The soldiers, who'd also shared in the liberation of Dachau and Buchenwald, found Mauthausen to be the worst of all the camps. The nearly unanimous description of the feeling that the prisoners who survived the camp shared was a sense of "Resurrection." The sensation of coming back from the dead when they were liberated was as accurate as it could have been.

On Liberation, the Communal Grave that was the task of the Last Patrol was filled to capacity with 10,000 bodies. An additional grave was dug in the middle of the SS's Football field for 5,000 more dead. On April 5th 1945, there were 98,973 prisoners in Mauthausen. On May 5th, there were approximately 60,000 survivors.

In the following days, approximately 3,000 more former prisoners died, as did Karol (Wart), some from the sheer joy of being free. By the 11th of May, even after steady relocation of former prisoners, Mauthausen still had nearly 17,000 survivors in the camp.

Picture #11: Typical Stone on wooden frame carrier. To the right is a syringe that was used to inject gasoline into the heart of prisoners that were no longer of use.

Chapter 22
May 6ᵗʰ, 1945: Mauthausen KZ, Austria

THE WARM LUMP in his stomach was a good sensation that made Staszek feel alive as he sat down on the tailgate of a parked truck outside the garage gate. The small portion of the thick and hearty soup was the third one he had had today. Yesterday after the liberation there was nearly a riot over the food and parcel boxes that were swarmed over by anyone who had the strength to get to the storage areas and kitchens. He got a parcel box and still had most of its content in a sack tied around his waist for safekeeping. Leaning back he looked at the chunks of the huge concrete German Eagle that was in pieces on the ground. It once stood above the gate and had been pulled down and smashed by the liberated prisoners within minutes of the gates being opened. Its pieces were thrown up against the outside wall as so much trash.

The core of these prisoners was the Antifascist Republican Spaniards that fought against the Fascist Dictator Francisco Franco. Franco, supported by Germany and Italy, disposed of his opponents by sending them to German Concentration Camps. The zeal to celebrate freedom that the Spaniards felt was some of the greatest of all the nationalities. Staszek walked among these ruins with relief as well as fatigue from the events of the last 48 hours.

Today there were enough American soldiers to control the camp but yesterday there weren't enough to stop the revenge on the remaining guards by the prisoners. Those U.S. soldiers that tried to stop the attacks did not do so with strong conviction after seeing the camp and the condition of the prisoners; they were in sympathy with the justice being done. Staszek milled around the areas where commotion was occurring to see who was involved. For the most part he did not have feelings one way or the other as to the outcome of most of the confrontations. The men he would want to see brought to justice were higher ranked and disappeared into the night days ago.

By the end of the second week of Liberation, more than three thousand more people died at Mauthausen because their health situation could not be reversed. Some left the camp before they were strong enough, and died in transport to displaced person camps, or by train back to their homelands. Mauthausen had to be emptied in order to clean up the filth and to preserve the records for history.

The displaced person camps in the area were quickly made from former military or factory housing and barracks, such as the Messerschmitt plant in Regensburg and the former German Army Base at Hohenfels. But the process was very slow due to the sheer number of souls involved.

The more than seventeen thousand prisoners who stayed in Mauthausen were slowly nurtured back to health with a wholesome gruel. As many prisoners found out at the price of their lives, large quantities of complex foods such as jams and meat would overwhelm the capabilities of their stomachs. When the stomach was suddenly overwhelmed with large quantities' of rich found, it would cause a painful death. Much like the sadistic death imposed by the Kapo back in February when he gleefully gave jam to the malnourished man to watch him die. The American soldiers did much to help save many more lives including donating their blood as mobile hospitals were brought in to do their merciful work. The Americans, as always, were unselfish in their willingness to help the survivors of disasters; with this one being one of the greatest most of them had seen.

Staszek had met with the remaining Scouts and decided to stay in the camp with those who did not wish to leave. All had their own reasons to wait in this place and to grow stronger, even though just days ago there was no doubt that they would have died here. Others, such as Polish, Russian, and Spanish Resistance groups had left the camp to continue to bring justice to those who had died in the camp, through the pursuit of the Germans who had escaped in the last days before liberation. These groups seized communication lines in efforts to locate the SS units that fled the camp, and in some cases, when they were found they engaged them in battle.

Informational records gathered in the camp as well as from recaptured camp administrators, guards, and the living prisoners, were collected and shared by both the Americans and the Russians, who sent thousands of pages of documents and microfilm back to Moscow for review and analysis. Those documents, along with documents captured in Poland, provided the Soviets with significant information about those who wanted to return home and those expatriates who did not. This information would have profound impact on those who ended up living behind the "Iron Curtain" that would appear in only several more years.

It was during this same period Staszek was singled out by Hank, to the Military Police. Hank vouched for Staszek as a dependable interpreter and friend to him. On that recommendation Staszek was eventually assigned to the U.S. Constabulary as an interpreter. When interviewed for the job, Staszek was able not only to help interpret, but also to give the names of many guards and other prison officials who committed crimes against humanity. His list matched and added names to several other lists that were given to the American intelligence corps. Over eight hundred names were eventually collected and positively identified as war criminals over the course of only one month. Those names included Bloody Joseph and Walter Pelzhausen, the commander of Radogoszcz prison, who was captured in Germany and brought to trial. Captain Franz Ziereis, the commander of Mauthausen, was shot while trying to avoid capture and gave an eight-hour confession on his deathbed as to the atrocities that occurred under his watch at the KZ.

During this time, Staszek was one of many who accompanied units of the US Constabulary on raids and missions against suspected German military criminals who were "wanted" individuals, and as such were tracked down and captured throughout Germany and Austria. The satisfaction of being part of these roundups gave closure to much of Staszek's bitterness.

The Americans used Staszek's service to assist in the task of interrogating captured Germans. The job paid him a modest salary but it also gave him commissary privileges. He was able to buy food, clothing to wear, and other items that he could trade for room and board in the Mauthausen area. His strength returned as did his energy, and he thrived in the exhilaration of being free again.

With his new freedom, and especially with the resources available to him, Staszek sought out and approached Dr. Von Stutt, the dentist, who gratefully worked out an arrangement to fix Staszek's teeth in exchange for basic supplies. The residents of Mauthausen were treated very badly for their tolerance of the camp near them. This left many of them suffering hunger and lack of other goods. Staszek took advantage of this situation by seeking his room and board in the doctor's home.

While living there, he received dental services from the doctor in exchange for helping to provide daily essentials for the doctor's home and family. At one point, Staszek borrowed a staff car from the Army's motor pool, and then bartered some old used boots for a full-grown sheep that he then bartered with the dentist for the final restoration of his front teeth. When questioned about the oily sheen on the leather seats in the car, Staszek said, "It's a lanolin leather preserver."

That was accepted as an answer, but he was instructed not to do it again, because the carpool mechanics said, "It smells like wet sheep in the car." Within a couple of months Staszek had a full set of teeth again, and began to pursue other niches to fill, flashing a broad smile like he had as a boy.

The end of 1945 found Staszek assigned as the interpreter and driver for Lt. Colonel Mroz, who worked with the U.S. Constabulary in Regensburg, Germany. Staszek, along with many others, was housed in the apartments that were the one-time quarters for German engineers who worked on the Messerschmitt planes. When he walked into the apartment that he was assigned to at the factory, Staszek walked over to the bed and touched the clean sheets and pressed on one of the three soft mattresses. He felt a lump in his throat from the sense of freedom and safety the room promised. He went to the window and unlocked and slowly pushed it open to look at the view that was not blocked by barbed wire or guard towers.

For most of 1946, Staszek shared quarters in the barracks at the Messerschmitt factory with two other men. All three were thrilled to find that it was a co-ed facility and new very close friends were quickly made and enjoyed. With a regular residence, Staszek was able to write to his mother and family who until September, of 1945 thought he had died in Mauthausen. The news in return was grim as the Soviets were as brutal in Łódź as were the Germans, once the celebration for the expulsion of the Germans ended and reality of their new masters set in. Only the reversal of roles for the Volksdeutsche from citizens in a Litzmannstadt, a German city, to targets of abuse by the Russians gave solace to the oppressed Poles in the Polish city of Łódź.

From his duty station in Regensburg, he accompanied the Colonel Mroz and other staff members to all parts of Germany, and also to France. These trips included meetings regarding the problems of displaced people in the German camps, and their resistance to being repatriated into the Soviets' hands. Staszek was asked his opinions on many of these matters and made his feelings clear that what waited for the liberated prisoners in Poland was a new and different kind of prison with new wardens from the east instead of the west. The Americans heard these comments but often they were muted by the term "Allied Country" when Russia was mentioned. Staszek on more than one occasion had to curb his words in order not to make it difficult for the Americans he was working for.

The actions against the Germans in Bavaria were coming to a close while at the same time the interactions with the Soviets were getting more difficult. Secrecy, deception, and withholding of information became more of a problem. Especially if there were Poles involved in operations. The time came when exchanging of information between the two occupying forces stopped or was selectively restricted by the Russians. Dealing with them during this time proved to Staszek that he did not wish to repatriate to Poland, and there was a strong probability that if he did he would be singled out as an undesirable refugee upon his return.

Staszek felt that he wanted to move to a whole new world and start a new life. He talked and dreamed of many places and he decided that the best place to move to was Australia, of that he was certain. Australia was a country that he'd read about, and since he wanted his new life to be one that was away from the ravages of Europe and the threat of imprisonment in Russia, Australia was as far as he could go. In November of 1946 Staszek was released from the services of the U.S. Army and was to be moved to Hohenfels Displaced Persons Camp to begin the petitioning of the Australian government for immigration status. Though Col. Mroz encouraged him to come to America, Staszek was set on going 'Down Under'. Staszek was grateful to the Colonel for his kindness and support, but he had made up his mind. Until he was there he would continue to survive. On his last official duty for the

U.S. Army, he was sent to Mauthausen with Colonel Mroz for a final debriefing, acquiring his separation papers from the constabulary, and their goodbyes.

On that day Staszek calmly walked through the open camp gates of Mauthausen with a sense of victory and satisfaction. He headed for the transport that would take him to a train for the ride back to Germany and to Hohenfels. The twenty-one year old war veteran climbed into the open back of a truck and sat down on the bench with several other men for the ride to the Linz train station. Like the rest of them he sat quietly, lost in many thoughts and visions among them the face of Wart and of so many others that would never know this moment. The truck turned the corner from the Class 3 fortress of pain and death as Staszek turned to look forwards to the road ahead- he never looked back.

When Staszek was released from his service and arrived in Hohenfels, he purchased an Opel automobile with money he saved and some he borrowed to start a small delivery business in the area. With the car, he was able to buy, sell, trade, and barter for essential items, such as clothing, blankets, canned foods, nylon stockings, chocolate, and vodka. He continued to function as an entrepreneur, rejoined the Scouting movement and took part in troop activities as an assistant Scoutmaster in Hohenfels. He rejoined the Scouts on one condition and that was that he would not go on overnight hikes. He reasoned that he had spent more than four years sleeping on the ground or on wooden bunks, and he swore to himself that he'd never do that again. This condition was understood and accepted by the other leaders. Scouting had helped to save his life and he wanted to share the experience with the boys who were coming of age while in the camp. Scouting rekindled that excitement he had as a boy, though the innocence and carefree joy that was part of the journey through Scouting was muted by painful thoughts that occurred mostly at night. Faces, names, and places would drift into his mind and those memories would jolt him awake as the abrupt and tragic end to them were relived over and over again. These nightmares would last for many years to come.

One of his new and happier ventures came to be when he met Adam Podstawny, an electrical engineer who had built a 16 mm movie projector and sound system. Using Staszek's car and connections with the Army, USO, and the YMCA program that gave him access to dozens of camps in Bavaria, he and Adam were able to rent full-length Hollywood movies and newsreel shorts to present in the camps. They traveled to camps, showing their movies in community centers, mess halls, outdoors, and other types of auditoriums. This became a lucrative venture.

At the same time, Staszek tried going back to school at the camp to get his Gymnasium equivalent certificate. He had signed up for a course given by Professor Wolny in Polish history. It was there that he met Alicia Miller, one of the other students, who later became the professor's fiancée. Because of Staszek's wheeling's and dealings, he only made half of the classes as he continued to work and do his own business. With not enough time to do everything that needed to be done, school became expendable and he dropped out. The movie business had the greatest allure to him, and he thought he could always go back to school when he was "old."

During one of the movie presentations in Hohenfels, his eyes fell on a beautiful blonde girl who was coming into the auditorium with Alicia, the fiancée of the professor. As Alicia and the blonde girl worked their way to the middle of the converted dining hall and found three seats together, Staszek could not take his eyes off the blonde. The young blonde girl was sparkling with excitement and energy. Her braids added a youthful charm that enthralled him. He fumbled as he laced the last loop of film onto the spool, entranced by the movements of the girl and her smile. Their eyes met for a brief moment, before she quickly turned away, embarrassed that he was staring at her. Alicia spoke into the girl's ear, as Alicia focused on Staszek.

"Look at me once more," Staszek mumbled under his breath, hoping that the blonde girl was interested enough in him to give him a second look. After a painful minute, the girl looked over her left shoulder, with a look that melted him to his core. His hands came off the projector and he just stood there transfixed looking at her.

"Hey Romeo, go introduce yourself, since you're useless to me here. Her name is Emilia, and she's Alicia's sister," Adam taunted him from behind, adding a slight nudge to press the point. "Getting going or you are going to tear the film. Go."

Without a second thought Staszek went around to the end of the row where the two young women were seated. He bumped into and pushed passed the knees of several people without once taking his eyes off of Emilia. Once he got there he reached for her hand, it felt soft and warm. While standing very straight and proper, he bent at the waist, brought his lips to the back of her hand and kissed it. As she withdrew her hand slightly, he said, "Hello, I am Stanislaw, but I want you to call me Staszek. May I sit with you?"

Emilia looked over at Alicia, her sister, for a moment and then to the back of her hand and finally up to the young man in front of her. Her smile broadened a little more as she raised her shoulders and giggled once.

Picture #12: Staszek and Colonel Mroz

Picture #13: Adam and Staszek with movie projector

Picture #14: Photo of Emilia and Staszek on the front of his car.

Epilogue
May 10ᵗʰ, 1972 Passport Control, Warzsawa International Airport.

"PLEASE COME WITH me," The passport officer ordered Stanislaw Niklewicz as he waited in front of the customs desk before entering Poland for the first time in thirty years. As he was escorted away from the checkpoint and towards an "officials only" door he called back to his daughter, Elizabeth, in a loud voice, "Wait for me here, get a soda."

The words made Elizabeth hold her breath since that was his prearranged code he had given her as they were getting off the plane just minutes ago. It was a strange conversation coming off the plane. Staszek had asked Elizabeth if she had some gum left, upon which she gave him the remaining pack of Dentyne. He also told her in a brief definitive statement that if he told her at any time to, "Wait for me here, get a soda." It signified that if he wasn't back in three hours she was to go to the American Embassy and report that he'd been taken away by the Polish Government. Elizabeth went to the waiting area, sat down, and focused on the closed door, her heart in her throat and completely stunned by the series of events that had occurred since they landed.

In a small room with no windows, but with pictures of the Polish and Soviet Presidents on the walls, Staszek sat at a small table alone for over one hour. At that point a uniformed Polish officer and another man came into the room and sat down across from Staszek. The officer

417

flipped through a file folder and examined Staszek's passport and the visa that he filled out several months earlier that allowed the visit to this restricted country to occur. He placed it on the table in front of him and stated, "Comrade Niklewicz, it has been a long time since you have been home. I am sure that your family here in Łódź has missed you." The sarcastic dry humor of the Passport official of the People's Republic of Poland did not impress Staszek, though how fast the official had retrieved the folder did. Apparently it had been prepared and brought to this entry point after his visa was granted.

"I am an American Citizen. What is the problem?" Staszek asked in a demanding tone, ignoring the officer's first question.

"Very well, we have many questions about you and why you did not return home after the People's victory against the German invaders." The officer barked without any more pretenses.

"That was a long time ago, and I have found a new life in America." Staszek answered definitively, with a slight wave of his hand and slow sideways motion of his head as part of his explanation, his eyes never leaving the inquisitor.

"Perhaps you can remember long enough to explain about the murder of a Soviet officer, Lt. Sukolov, in 1944, near the River Bug." The uniformed man leaned forward from behind his desk with his fingers interlaced and waited for the answer.

Staszek looked at the man with a questioning stare then looked up to the picture of the Polish President. He then reached into his pocket and retrieved the pack of gum, then unwrapped one stick and placed it into his mouth. The 15-20 seconds of stalling gave him time to think of a response. He shook his head and said, "I do not know anything about a Soviet officer being murdered. That was wartime. I do not remember such an event." Staszek paused for a moment, then continued, "I am an American Citizen and I can not help you with that matter."

The man in civilian clothes leaned back in his chair seeing that this was not going to be done quickly and lit a cigarette. He blew the smoke to the side of Staszek who felt a little queasy at the current situation and now the nasty smell from the smoke from the Russian cigarette did not help. "Mr. Niklewicz, or should I call you Mr. Pants or Mr. Flame, would that help you remember more?"

The smoke was no longer Staszek's main concern and his head cleared and became focused. His old senses heightened and he stared straight back at the man thinking, '*I did not break for the Germans, and I am not going to start now'.* After which he stated, "You obviously have the wrong person." He repeated, and then leaned back into the chair with his own fingers intertwined. The man crushed out his cigarette and flipped through the folder.

One hour later, the official door opened once more, and this time Elizabeth saw her father coming out of the room. She hurried over to him, and he put his arm around her shoulder as they continued to the exit. While they walked, Ellie took his dry hand into her moist one as she looked up at him but didn't know what to ask. Staszek said, without looking back, "I was not the person they were looking for, and they were not interested in detaining an American Citizen."

Ellie looked at him in bewilderment, but knew not to ask anything further. She glanced over her shoulder to see if they were being followed, as Staszek looked straight ahead assuming that they were.

Staszek walked towards the exit, all the while fully expecting to be arrested once he was outside, but it did not happen. They hailed a cab and as they climbed into the back seat, Staszek paused and glanced back at the doors of the airport. Standing in front of a window near the door was the man in civilian clothes from the passport office watching him. Their eyes met and for that brief moment, his actions and his decision to go to America were validated. He got into the cab and the man watched the car drive away into traffic. Staszek now had one more face etched into his memory that he would not forget as did the man at the door who looked back at him.

Author's notes: Epilogue

Jan Szymański survived the war in Mauthausen Concentration camp, as did Staszek. Jan had been shot during the mission at the church then brutally beaten by the Gestapo who had sent him to Mauthausen a month before Staszek was sent there. Due to the size of the camp and his job in the laundry and kitchen while Staszek was in hard labor, Jan and Staszek never knew of the other as being in the camp. Jan worked as a cook preparing German-type food for the SS, by virtue of what he saw in his restaurant's kitchen. Jan went back to Poland immediately after liberation to see his family. However, he was soon imprisoned there and was eventually sent to a Gulag in Russia where he was held without any charges ever being placed against him. He was released in 1954. The rest of the Niklewicz family survived the war in Łódź.

Today both Radogoszcz and Mauthausen prisons are open as war memorials so the new generations will never forget the price that was paid back then for their freedoms now. A price paid by millions of souls that they will never know but should forever thank.

In 1949 the Catholic Church and the Mangini family in Martinez, California sponsored Emilia and Staszek for relocation from the displaced persons camp. Five years after the war was over they were able to repay the immigration debt by working on a farm for a year in America. Almost ten years to the day of when the war started, Emilia and Staszek were finally free people in a free land.

Staszek died in 1990, after a career in the retail and wholesale industry. His legacy, along with Emilia, his wife is five children, seven grandchildren, and five great grandchildren. They moved to America because that was the country where Emilia wanted to live as a free person, of that she was certain and for that we are thankful.

Picture: #15: Staszek Niklewicz 1948
Powodzenia i pożegnanie.
(Good luck and farewell.)